What readers are saying about
The Least of These

Reading *The Least of These* is like walking in someone else's shoes only to find that the shoes were yours all along. This is a powerful book, and one that will (and should) haunt you for the rest of your life. I'm different because of this book. That's because it reminds me of who I am—desperately in need of God's love, mercy, and grace. It will do that for you, too. Read this book and then give it to everybody you know. After they wince, they will thank you. Then we can talk and maybe even learn to love each other.

Steve Brown
Broadcaster and author, KeyLife.org

I've spent fifty-five years in ministry, and I've always been drawn to books that do more than tell a great story—they reveal something true about life and about us. *The Least of These* is one of those rare books. It's a gripping, deeply personal account of a boy growing up in a home marked by cruelty and violence, yet pierced by moments of love and human connection.

But this isn't just his story—it's ours. It invites us to wrestle with life's hardest questions: Can we be honest about who we are if it means risking rejection from those we love? What does the grace of God look like when it meets our deepest wounds and fears? How do we respond to the urge to control—or to being controlled by—others?

Read this book not only to understand more, but to become more. It will stay with you—and it will make you a better person.

Dr. Joel Hunter
Pastor of Community Benefit, Action Church, Maitland, FL

This book is riveting, haunting, and engrossing. I didn't know Shari, but I get emotionally sad when I realize the loss that the world has suffered with her death. What an advocate! What a writer! I want more of her books!!

Faithe Stephens
Publisher, Henry Lyon Books

Very well written and a book you will not put down until finished. There is something for everyone to learn and take away from reading this book.

Anonymous

I'm so proud of my sister for writing *The Least of These*. Her words remind us that God's love knows no boundaries. It is a love that reaches, heals, and reminds us that no one is ever forgotten, no matter who they are or what they have gone through. A beautiful reflection of God's unconditional love and grace for us all.

Karen Lovell

An intense, emotional journey from someone who suffered immensely and still chose to love like Jesus. *The Least of These* is not afraid to address the darker aspects of life and shows how God's grace and love can redeem anything the darkness throws at you. A must-read for anyone, especially the LGBTQ+ community and others who are marginalized.

Adam Scott, health care provider

My husband John and I have known Shari Pacanowski and her husband Rick for over 40 years. They have such a strong relationship with our Lord. The way she put her heart and soul into everything she touched, whether it was her family, friends, or anything she did, her soul was so honest. You couldn't find a truer and more loving person. Shari put her family's and friends' feelings ahead of her own. I was honored to call her my dear friend.

Maria and John Kontros

The Least
of
These

The Least
of
These

FINDING FORGIVENESS, HEALING,
AND GOD'S REDEEMING LOVE

Shari Pacanowski

HIGHERLIFE PUBLISHING

Oviedo, FL

HigherLife Development Services, Inc.
2342 Westminster Terrace, Oviedo, FL 32765
(407) 563-4806, HigherLifePublishing.com

Copyright©2025 Shari Pacanowski

All rights reserved. No part of this publication may be reproduced, distributed or transmitted in any form or by any means, including photocopying, recording, or other electronic or mechanical methods, without the prior written permission of the publisher, except in the case of brief quotations embodied in critical reviews and certain other noncommercial uses permitted by copyright law. For permission requests, write to the publisher, addressed "Attention: Permissions Coordinator," at the address below.

G.I. Joe® is a registered trademark of Hasbro, Inc. SPAM® is a registered trademark of Hormel Foods, LLC. Coke® and Coca-Cola® are registered trademarks of The Coca-Cola Company. Facebook® and Instagram® are registered trademarks of Meta Platforms, Inc. YouTube® and Google® are registered trademarks of Google LLC. Amazon® is a registered trademark of Amazon Technologies, Inc.

Publisher's Note: This is a work of fiction. Names, characters, places, and incidents are a product of the author's imagination. Locales and public names are sometimes used for atmospheric purposes. Any resemblance to actual people, living or dead, or to businesses, companies, events, institutions, or locales is completely coincidental.

Cover Photo: Shari Pacanowski
Book Layout: Faithe Stephens

Ordering Information:
Quantity sales. Special discounts are available on quantity purchases by corporations, associations, and others. For details, contact the "Special Sales Department" at the address above.

Published 2026

Printed in the United States of America
30 29 28 27 26   1 2 3 4 5

ISBN: 978-1-964081-76-2 (paperback)
ISBN: 978-1-964081-77-9 (ebook)
LCCN: 1-15011582891

Contents

Dedication

To Stan, the brother I always wanted.
I am a better person because of your
love, wisdom, and vision of life.

Acknowledgments

To Ashley, my daughter, effectively known as "Girl," for her consistent encouragement and support to believe in myself, especially when I struggled and doubted my ability to write this story.

To my husband, Rick, my forever love, for his encouragement and tireless effort to get this book published for all the hurting who so desperately need God's love, mercy, and grace.

Content Warning

This novel contains material that might prove to be controversial to certain readers. While none of this is graphic, this book contains potentially triggering subject matter, including (in no particular order) substance abuse, grief, sexual assault, rape, alcohol consumption including underage, recreational drug use (smoking), strong language, homophobic violence and hate speech, the AIDS crisis, homophobia, emotional abuse, controlling parents, pedophilia, sexual predator, child abuse, domestic abuse, physical abuse, and religious abuse.

Prologue

"ONCE UPON A TIME ..." As a child, I loved stories that began in this fashion. Those words echoed in my mind and launched every storybook adventure I invented to escape whatever circumstance I'd been thrown into. Each sentence carried me to another time or place where things would be different. I would be different—someone else or something else—older, stronger, or even younger, but stronger still. It didn't take long to release those hopeful tales. Childhood was brief, and whimsical stories had little place in my space and time.

Time. All actions, ideas, observations, and events begin and end within it. Our body functions are time-based; the beat of a heart and the draw of a breath are measured by it. Each second brims with opportunity and can redirect an entire day. A single choice sets the path of the next moment. In those moments, we make the difference; our actions, reactions, interactions, and intentions propel outcomes. I spent much of childhood trying to slow moments to a halt, until I accepted I had no power to control or conquer them.

As I became a man, time and I jousted again. I learned to multitask and tried to compete with it, proud whenever I seemed to win. After all, I am Samson Izbicki, master of time management—or so I thought. Then, time after time, time proved the stronger opponent and put me in my place to fight another day.

Oh, the battles I waged with its riddle of characteristics. Time was short and long; right and wrong. It was good, bad, happy, sad. Hard then easy. It changed and stood still; down, up, on, off—sometimes all at once. Time was "ripe," full or part, a charm—and it didn't wait. I had too much and too little. I worked to keep it, save it, limit it, stall it. I tried to make it, share it, give it, take it, hunting for spare time to invest in playtime. Soon enough, time became money. I stretched it, squeezed it, froze it. I borrowed, bought, and spent it like scarce currency. As soon as I thought I held it, it flew. As an advertising executive I set it, planned it, scheduled it, and arrived promptly on it—or ahead of it. I reined it in, checked it, raced against it. I used it and killed it in the same day. I reveled in having time just long enough to lose it and find it again. I measured time by success, divided it, made up for it, and for a long season tried to beat it. In the meantime—each and every time—I grew wearier of it.

Near the end of my forty-year lifetime, I became painfully aware of how much I had wasted. With the future stolen, only past and present remained. I spent what was left, wishing for more, day and night, drifting backward until I was out of time. A wasting disease ravaged me. I grasped and battled for more hours, but the wage of my war was death. In the end I didn't stand its test—no one does.

I am now free from time. In this place where I linger, it matters little. I haven't yet decided whether I am relieved or mourning. It is strangely disconcerting—yet comforting—to feel the burden of time lifted. The control freak that I was—am—finds it hard to release its hold on me.

I thought I had all the time in the world to do, to be, to become whatever I dreamed in those childhood fabrications of distraction. On my final day, March 13, 1995, I took my last breath and passed from time into timelessness. Only then did I fully understand how brief our time in life truly is.

Preface
In the Beginning

My life, if measured by success, probably exceeded others' expectations. It did not exceed mine. From a young age I knew I was meant for more. I would be someone, do something, what had never been seen or accomplished before. I felt it deep in my core. Nothing could divert me from that destiny. It did not seem possible that I could be ordinary. I believed it so strongly that every obstacle disappointed me each time I hit opposition. It seemed unbelievable, because I knew this kind of life was not what was meant for me.

Even now, as I hear those words—my last words—echo, I cringe. That was it? My final words? My last hoorah? Surely I should have imparted a jewel of wisdom, declared something unforgettable, or at least offered a line that could change a life. After all, I majored in communications at a respectable college. I was praised for public speaking, regarded as a communication guru in small circles—well, really small circles. Friends would say I always knew the right thing to say at the right moment—whether you wanted to hear it or not. Having been silenced as a child, I thrived on being heard. I felt valued when my opinions and ideas were considered. I was not to be seen or heard.

Words. They are the most powerful tools we hold. They spoke time into existence and will mark its end. Once released, they can never be retrieved. Depending on timing, substance, delivery—or even silence—they can bring beginnings or endings, joy or pain, life or death, in an instant. Our thoughts and emotions take shape as words in the mind's eye, flashing by in response to people and events. Sometimes those events were so overwhelming they left me speechless, groping for what to say.

I often wrestled inwardly when I couldn't name what I felt. Poetry and song lyrics fascinated me because they captured emotions I couldn't. I loved words, except for the ones I wished I'd never heard—or the ones I regret having spoken in anger. Regret filled the space they left behind. I longed for more patience and a deeper vocabulary. I dreamed of fluency in Italian, French, and Spanish, but mastered only a handful of phrases—usually the sharp ones I hurled when someone cut me off on the highway.

More than anything, I wished I had learned to pause before speaking. Words came too quickly; they escaped before I could temper them. They gave me identity, voice, a sense of value—but also a blade I too often swung carelessly, leaving wounds I couldn't take back.

I also loved to hear myself speak—don't we all? I liked the sound of my own voice. It felt validating when people sat and listened, especially when they seemed to understand. I soared when I stood at a podium, teaching a proven sales concept, and felt accomplished when someone applied my advice and succeeded. Those who knew me would say I always had something to offer—whether they wanted to hear it or not.

I craved being the first to know, relishing the thrill of sharing new information: "Did you know?" I would beam, "Were you aware?" I would whisper, rushing forward in all my glory. I delighted in making people laugh and lived for the chance my words might encourage someone to be their best. Yet too often, in frustration, I wielded those same words like a sharp-edged sword.

Contrary to what listeners assumed when I was harsh or blunt, I believed I had their best interests at heart—most of the time. I lived for debate, for sparring, and if I couldn't win an argument, I went down fighting. I truly thought I was right, until I discovered how often I was wrong—more than I cared to admit.

Most of my friendships were with outgoing people who talked easily. I dismissed the quiet ones as shy or shallow, not realizing until too late that their silence often came from confidence, not lack of depth. They had mastered the art I ignored: listening. I, on the other hand, needed to speak, to fill space with advice and observations, to be heard. Only now do I see that the stillness of others carried more wisdom than all my words.

What others mistook for meddlesome advice was usually me trying to fix their lives. To me, the answers seemed obvious, and I believed if people let me run things, the world would be better. I was certain my words could solve any problem; how could I be wrong when everything felt so logical? Only later did I realize that much of my drive to direct others came from avoiding my own struggles. I never stopped to wonder if advice wasn't the answer—that maybe the real gift was listening. Not listening to respond, but truly listening. Yet I never offered that, not once to friends, family, or colleagues. Instead I filled the air with opinions, convinced they were needed. I pontificated, but I never said the one thing that mattered most: "Listen to that still, small voice inside yourself." I had silenced mine long ago, so why would I tell anyone else to honor theirs?

My famous last words were not what I had hoped. They offered no great wisdom or life-changing insight. I'm not sure I had ever spoken them as an adult, but as a child they surfaced often: "I made a big mistake this time, didn't I?" I asked, knowing I had.

CHAPTER 1

Genesis

I SLIPPED QUIETLY INTO life, stunned and overwhelmed. Frail and underweight, I was nothing like the strong, burly boy everyone expected. I hadn't chosen to come here, and as I grew, it became clear no one had chosen for me to arrive either. On November 17, 1955, as I lay exposed to the faces gathered around my birth, I had no way of knowing that time and nurturing would be scarce. If I'd understood as a newborn what I would later learn, I might have begged to remain in the quiet darkness I had left behind.

I was smacked on the hind end and named Samson A. Izbicki. My mother, Gertie, had given all six of my siblings saintly names, but for me she chose one that spoke of strength, as if she knew I would need it. That was the first in a long line of smacks meant for my own good, and the first of many labels I would carry. My life quickly became a pendulum of too much and too little—too much noise, confusion, criticism, and tears; too little time, love, laughter, and food. From my earliest days I was reaching for what I lacked, retreating from what overwhelmed, searching for balance that never seemed to exist.

I felt what was called love and care, though it mostly taught me compromise and sacrifice—words I didn't yet understand. What I felt most was pressure—the weight of arriving after two older, stronger brothers. Rob and Jude already knew how to endure, how to bend without breaking. If I could, I would have asked how they managed to survive each day, but they could never share what they had learned. Like them, I had to figure it out alone.

I soon discovered questions were not welcome in the Izbicki household. Children were not meant to be seen or heard, and so we weren't. We obeyed quickly, accepted what little we were given, and lived a kind of half life, careful not to trip over our father's temper. Holidays meant dressing in our best and lining up on the plastic-covered sofa, smiling for relatives who glanced at us with pity. Beneath the surface, we squirmed, desperate to touch the single gift glowing under the blue-lit tree. Only Rob, our oldest brother, sat still, never reaching. When money was tight, he gave up his present so the younger ones could have theirs. I remember the hollow look in his eyes, the silence of sacrifice already etched into him. We thought this was simply how families lived.

The most overused word in our house was *family*, though it rarely fit its meaning. To me it seemed more like property— house, car, money—all belonging to Auggie, my father. His favorite topic at meals was ownership. As surely as morning came, the Marine would slam a heavy hand against the chrome table, rattling china and teeth alike, then launch into a lecture while tossing back a juice glass of whiskey. To him, family was less about love than about control, less about connection than possession. As I grew older, I was stunned to discover other households didn't end their prayers with tirades like his.

What began with a slam nearly always ended with a crack. No one but Auggie—never the Easter Bunny, Santa, or even God— could take credit for what we had. If we dared believe in magic, it stayed buried in secret places of the heart. The crack of the strap was inevitable, sparked by a giggle, a word, a spill of milk—never striking the same target twice, but always striking someone. The sound itself became ritual, random yet expected, echoing through our small home and leaving us to retreat into our own private hiding places.

Tears always provoked more rage. At the first sob the Marine's leather strap appeared—thick, long, and merciless. He swung it with a vengeance on bare skin, shouting until he had no more to spend, always ending with, *"That was for your own good."* Year by year the outbursts grew quicker and harsher, his nightly glass of whiskey growing fuller, his control thinner. As our family grew, so did the violence, and each of us learned to retreat into the safety of our thoughts, building small shelters of imagination against his storms.

In time, my siblings and I formed a rough union, a child's version of a "special ops" unit, a system of signals to warn of his arrival and avoid his wrath. As our number reached seven, each of us had our role, sprinting through the house at the sound of his rattling truck, passing word like a baton in a desperate race. When three sisters joined the ranks, the balance shifted. To Auggie, daughters carried no value. His pride lay in the four sons who would extend the Izbicki name, heirs to his prize. He boasted of us as possessions, proof of his worth, while we perfected our strategies for survival.

Our early warning system, born of necessity, included everyone. Being a carrier of "the prize" earned no privilege; each of us listened for the rattle and groan of the Marine's old pickup as it pulled into the driveway. That sound sent shivers through us. In an instant the alarm would pass from room to room like a baton in a relay, and we scattered to our hiding places in the cramped two-story house, erasing signs of play before he stepped inside.

"Go!" Rob would whisper, scooping up our army men in his shirt, and I'd race through the hall to signal the others. By then my brothers and sisters were already moving, as if their ears were tuned to some invisible frequency. Each of us received the warning and slipped away, disappearing like leaves in a sudden gust, leaving behind no trace of our existence—no toy on the floor, no laugh hanging in the air—before our father's heavy boots crossed the threshold.

We would sit in silence, waiting to learn if our father's day had been productive or punishing. The slam of the kitchen's screen door told us instantly: The sharper the crack of wood on metal, the worse our night would be. If no sound came at all, uncertainty filled the house. Was he still among the rows of carefully ordered gardens, or pruning the evergreens at his small nursery? That place, stocked with shrubs and Christmas trees for anyone with cash and patience to endure him, was his pride and livelihood.

It was the only true trade he carried from boyhood, after leaving school in the sixth grade to labor on my grandfather Miroslaw's farm. Whenever his mother abandoned him for a new romance, he was sent there, dumped like baggage, learning discipline with calloused hands. By ten, he claimed mastery as landscaper, carpenter, and jack-of-all-trades. But whatever skills he gained were shadowed by anger, a fury that too often trailed him home, filling our house before collapsing upstairs in a whiskey-drenched stupor.

No sound from the screen door could also mean the day had been worse than usual and that he was in the garage with the bottle of whiskey he kept hidden there. When that happened, my sweaty-browed siblings and I, already tucked in corners of the house, knew we would not escape. What began in the garage never stayed there. Sooner or later it staggered inside—limping, swaying, crashing into walls—filling the house with a heaviness that shattered everything in its path.

At last he would collapse in a drunken stupor on the bed upstairs, the man himself reduced to a heap. Only then, with the soft click of the bedroom door, did we breathe again. That sound was our reprieve, our release from holding our breath. It also summoned a gentler presence: Mother, moving quietly from room to room, whispering comfort and pressing a kiss on each frightened forehead.

This evening ritual from our mother, Gertie, was our only connection to tenderness, offered by a woman who drifted through each day like a piece of wood on water. Bittersweet as it was, we clung to those brief moments of comfort, always scarce and always in demand. She was exhausted, overworked, and undersupplied, struggling to exist as much as we did. Like us, she escaped in her mind to places where laughter and compassion still lived. She, too, hid from the long arm of ownership. Raised in the shadows of the Great Depression, her own childhood had been stolen, every scrap of food or affection rationed.

Her lack of education left her vulnerable to those who valued possession more than partnership. She had been passed from her parents to a husband who saw her chiefly as a vessel to produce heirs to the Izbicki name. This role—wife, mother, caretaker—was all she allowed herself to be. To others she looked fortunate: married, fertile, dutiful, with a house full of children. She lived up to every expectation of a good Catholic wife, keeping order with relentless energy. Yet beneath that façade, her dreams remained buried, unspoken, perhaps even to herself. Silence became her inheritance, and by extension, ours.

From our vantage point, she was our refuge—hollow and threadbare, yet still a refuge. She was constant, bearing and feeding us as best she could, striving to meet the standards of her Italian Catholic heritage. She worked feverishly to prepare us for survival and to present the proper image beyond the four walls that confined us. We learned to accept this as love, and our Catholic schooling, bartered for like everything else, eagerly filled in the blanks.

For me, and for those born before and after, the lesson was clear: God, like His earthly wardens, seemed full of the same wrath we endured from the Marine. None of us were willing to be his sacrifice. We discovered instead that good grades and hard work earned a safer kind of approval. I was fortunate—academics came easily, and compliance felt like protection.

Social situations, however, were harder because of my appearance. I was tall for my age but carried myself awkwardly, my head thrust forward as if trying to see beyond my view. I tried to project strength, yet my lanky limbs betrayed me. I lacked coordination and looked clumsy at sports. Others didn't find me unattractive, but my deep-set dark eyes and unruly black hair made me stand out among my siblings. I shared few of the Polish Izbicki traits—except for a very prominent nose.

I worked to hide my stance and gait, but any slip drew criticism. I knew I was different, and my push to blend into "normal" created constant conflict. Girls, oddly, were drawn to it, which misled those who questioned my true nature. I prayed to God, Jesus, and Holy Mary, Mother of God, to make me like other boys—strong and manly like my brothers. I tried to change who I appeared to be and blamed myself when I failed. I frequented the confessional, pouring out my heart to fathers who listened and sent me to penance. It didn't take long for one of these "messengers of God" to exploit that trust, using my insecurities to groom me for his own iniquities.

CHAPTER 2

Sacrifice

IN CONTRAST TO MY other siblings, my brother Rob was olive-skinned and dark-featured like me, though his light gray eyes revealed the Izbicki line. As firstborn, he held a unique place: For nearly a year he alone had our mother's full attention while our father served in the Marines during the Korean War.

Mother, still young and naive, poured herself into her baby boy, eager to present him as a prize to her returning husband. Living with her parents gave her time to ease into married life, while our grandparents and relatives lavished Rob with attention, teaching my mother the basics of motherhood in the process. Rob, easy to care for, received their love freely.

Meanwhile, our father was overseas, waging war and collecting medals. Medals meant to prove valor brought him no peace. He dropped them from the side of the slow-moving boat carrying him from harm's way, watching them sink into enemy waters, wishing his tormented soul could follow.

For those at home, his return was staged as a hero's welcome. But the man who came back was damaged, carrying images of death—both enemies' and those he had sent to die. For Rob, the first year of life wrapped in love's security would prove to be the only one, for with our father's return, that fragile spell was forever broken.

As years passed, cheap whiskey became the hero's weapon against those memories, burning them down night after night.

For all the honor prepared at home, he struggled to reconcile battlefield horrors with small-town life.

The tender moment when our mother presented Rob to his father should have been a homecoming. Instead, it marked a turning point for us all. Peace was elusive to the Purple Heart hero. From that day forward he would rule our home as the controller of destinies, the king of his castle, the determiner of fates. The Marine, with a new commission, intended to carry it out with ruthless precision—beyond anything anyone could have foreseen.

Rob learned submission quickly, earning a small place in the Marine's fractured heart. But when our brother Jude arrived a year later, Rob learned the meaning of sacrifice. By the time our numbers grew to seven, he had accepted his role as leader, peacemaker, and defender. His humble spirit could not watch us suffer, so he often took the blows himself, confessing to crimes he hadn't committed just to shield us.

"It was me, sir. I wasn't thinking," he would blurt as we stood in a row, interrogated over offenses we often didn't understand.

We trembled, sweat streaking our faces. Again and again I fought to hold back tears—first of fear, then of shame—as Rob endured punishment in our place. We didn't even know what rule we'd broken, only that someone had to pay, and more often than not, it was him.

After the rages ended, Rob would comfort those left trembling, and we comforted him in return—the only repayment we knew for his sacrifice. Yet his efforts rarely satisfied the Marine's need to punish. Many times, Rob and I were beaten beyond comprehension until we stood shaking, urine running down our legs.

Rob sensed we had to be smarter than our father. He urged me to stay prepared, always one step ahead, never underestimating the Marine's moods. Though he struggled, on some level he knew education could be our escape from Griffin Avenue.

My brother Jude joined the ranks on a stormy September day, crying for attention from the start. Fair-haired and resembling our father, he was elevated quickly, becoming the Marine's protégé. Submission came easily to him, and the harder he worked, the more approval he gained. His natural physique and intelligence amplified his capabilities. There was nothing Jude couldn't do well. He excelled at school and sports, a true "man's man," and Auggie's pride. But as his body grew, so did his ego and greed, drawing him ever closer to our father.

The more Jude demanded respect from us, the more we resented him, and the more he tormented us by flaunting his position. His vain, power-hungry spirit thrived on our suffering. Often he let Rob or me take punishment meant for him. He would cozy up to us, then betray us to the Marine, racing to report our indiscretions and claim his reward. He neither sought nor offered comfort.

The one thing he could never claim was the love and respect our siblings freely gave Rob. No matter how he tried to pit us against each other, he could not win it. Instead, he manipulated his way into our trust, exploiting our hunger for affection. At times I loved him deeply, laughing and enjoying his company. Moments later, when he turned on me, I wished I could blast him into a million pieces. Jude's double nature gave him power to control and destroy the unsuspecting, and like the Marine, he showed no remorse.

CHAPTER 3

Fulfillment

AUGGIE'S WELL-OILED SYSTEM WAS tested when Anne, my oldest sister, arrived to strain an already fragile family budget. Falling in line behind me and our brothers, she was the first female in the ranks—an unwelcome addition in our father's eyes. Born on a warm February day, she lacked the equipment to strengthen the Marine's troops. Her blonde locks framed a face still marked from a forceps delivery, and her frail body rejected nourishment as if staging a hunger strike against the world she had entered. Our father marked her birth as he did the others—with a three-day bender. This time, however, he drank not in pride but to soothe his disappointment.

Mother battled feelings of failure for not producing another son. Her persistence in feeding Anne eventually paid off, and Anne grew strong enough to wedge herself into a world that barely acknowledged her. Each small victory was met with setbacks as she struggled in a male-dominated household. Her sweet nature soured into tantrums, desperate to be seen and heard. Over time she learned what she couldn't beat she must join, transforming into a tomboy who competed fiercely with us to prove her worth. But her gender offered no protection from the Marine's wrath. She stayed quiet and watchful in his presence until puberty, when her changing body gave him new ammunition to chip away at what little self-esteem she had left.

From dusk to dawn, Anne rescued her hand-me-down dolls from our endless schemes. They were constant hostages in our war games, pitted against battered twelve-inch G.I. Joes already scarred from years of battle at the hands of cousins before us. Rob, Jude, and I ritualistically tortured the dolls, tacking them to walls, demanding secrets, and when no answers came, pelting them with metal darts as missiles.

"Tell us where your troops are or you'll be sorry!" I'd shout at an enemy soldier.

"Take that—and that!" we cried, laughing as darts slammed into burlap-wrapped Barbies, our chosen prisoners of war.

Despite our teasing, Anne played beside us, happily shaping mud pies while we dug escape tunnels in Auggie's ever-present piles of soil and sand. Treading on that virgin earth was forbidden and punishable, yet we couldn't resist its call. To prove her toughness, Anne would taste her gritty creations, daring us to do the same.

"Come on, chicken, I dare you," she'd tease, but we always refused.

"You're gonna make yourself sick, and we'll be in trouble," Rob warned, but she never listened.

No sooner had our play begun than the warning of Auggie's truck sent us scattering. The grinding gears, like an old coffee mill, marked his approach—first to second, second to third, then down to first as he entered the driveway. In seconds we scrambled to hide every trace of fun and bolted for cover. Anne or Rob usually made room for me in their hiding spot, knowing I was rarely quick enough to reach mine.

Anne would wrap her arms around me, trembling with fear. I loved being held, though once the danger passed, we acted as if the other carried some disease. I admired her deeply. Growing up with rough-and-tumble brothers gave her a strong physique and an outgoing personality. She was a natural leader, dividing and conquering social groups that once shunned her. An above-average student with above-average social skills, she impressed her peers with toughness and confidence, never letting them glimpse her hidden doubts.

She used their confidence in her strength to lead even as she fought feelings of inadequacy. Amid the chaos, Anne and I grew close. Often I sought her comfort, though sometimes she lowered her wall and wept with me. She confessed her fear of disappointing her friends at school. They never saw the tears and anguish she carried, or knew how worthless, stupid, and dirty she sometimes felt—echoes of the Marine's cruel words. If her friends discovered this truth, she feared they would abandon her.

So Anne kept moving, working, studying, and playing hard, giving everything her all in the hope someone would recognize her true worth.

"Slow down. You're gonna kill yourself, and then where would I be?" I'd warn her.

"Sam, I have people to see, places to go, things to do! If I stopped now, I'm not sure I'd get back up," she'd reply with a wink.

That summer brought another sister to our weary ranks. Joan arrived with ringlets of hair, fair skin, and lips red as a storybook princess. Auggie was charmed, especially when she smiled at him moments after birth. Others knew it was only gas, but he saw it as a sign the gods favored him. Unlike the rest of us, Joan seemed almost happy to enter her new world. She even hesitated at the customary "for your own good" slap meant to spark her first breath.

Docile and thoughtful, she required little care—sleeping until fed and feeding until sleep, content in ways none of us had been.

During her wakeful moments, Joan sat quietly in her feeding chair, observing the chaos around her. She rarely cried or demanded attention. Somehow, she seemed to know the reactions our father craved, grinning from ear to ear whenever he entered. She played independently amid turmoil, while Anne eagerly cared for her as Mother struggled to manage the rest of us. My brothers and I adored her and silently pledged to protect her.

As she grew, Joan learned quickly what was expected and complied without resistance. That eagerness to serve taught us she could be taken advantage of. By the time she recognized the horror of our life, martyrdom had become her escape. We encouraged it, handing her our chores in exchange for extra playtime, and she bore the load without complaint. Jude found her pliable nature amusing and exploited it often. Even when his schemes proved selfish, she followed along, convinced his intentions were good and allowing herself to be dragged by the nose.

In November 1961 and again in August 1964, Auggie gained more reinforcements—my brother Pete and youngest sister, Emma. But their lives were different. Shielded by the five of us, they grew up largely untouched by the Marine's wrath. By then, our weary parents scarcely noticed two more children. Pete and Emma thrived, unaware of our earlier struggles, guided more by us siblings than by parents who were incapable of true care. Only later did they realize the love and protection they'd known had come from us.

Auggie and Gertie had finally completed their Catholic duty of bearing seven children, and birth control was no longer needed. The Marine, further seduced by alcohol's numbing grasp, ignored the toll those years had taken on Mother's appearance. For Gertie, the fading of his groping, whiskey-laced advances was a reprieve. At last, she could keep some small part of herself to herself.

CHAPTER 4

Faith

SURROUNDED BY A CACOPHONY of madness, days, weeks, and months dragged as if time had screeched to a halt. Each morning seemed to bring harsher circumstances than the last; each night ended with hungry bellies, broken spirits, and weary minds. Life on Griffin Avenue demanded creativity just to survive.

Mornings followed a strict routine. Sleepy-eyed children shuffled from bed, to toilet, to breakfast served cafeteria-style. We pulled on our worn Catholic school uniforms: plaid skirts and white blouses for the girls, navy pants and white shirts for the boys. At a glance we looked neat, but the threadbare knees and dingy collars revealed the truth. Even so, these clothes were better than anything our parents could provide.

"Stop right there in yur tracks!" Mother barked. Rob froze, and the rest of us followed.

"Smile. Let me see them teeth!" she snapped at me.

"Samson Izbicki, march back upstairs and brush!" I exaggerated each step as ordered.

"Robert Izbicki, tuck in that shirt! Girls, retie them laces."

Afraid of being left behind, I hurried down the stairs.

"Samson, slow down before ya break yur neck! Did you just roll yur eyes at me?"

After inspection, we grabbed our labeled lunch sacks.

"Outta my way, jerk," Jude muttered, shoving me against the wall.

"Hey! What was that for? Motherrr, Jude ..." I cried, only to meet her glare.

"Keep movin', Samson. Girls, quit chattering—you'll be late!" she ordered as we burst through the screen door.

If it was cold outside, we pulled on hand-me-downs or Salvation Army jackets that had seen better years long before we were born. Then came the five-block trek to Holy Blessed Virgin Mother of the Universe Catholic School. "Holy Hell," as the older kids called it, was a refuge for some of us and extra punishment for others.

Rob, the most determined of us, had decided from his very first day that this was not where he intended to spend eight hours. At six, he struggled to grasp what he had done so wrong that he deserved such punishment. He worried about those of us left behind at home. He begged for a pardon, pleaded for release, and when that failed, he bargained. If he made himself indispensable—cleaning rooms, washing dishes, helping with babies, fetching mail—surely Mother would reconsider.

But nothing changed. His efforts won no reprieve, and the school gates still swallowed him each morning. Soon he realized all the chores were in vain; he might as well save his energy for a better plan. Rob agonized over details, constantly scheming ways to escape the confines of school, but every attempt ended the same—trapped for another long day.

Each morning Gertie returned to her brood, relieved to have one less child to manage, only to find Rob standing at the kitchen screen door. His eyes brimmed with hope as he offered excuse after excuse, weaving stories in hopes she'd let him stay home. But each time she carted him back, placing him firmly in the sisters' charge. His last attempt ended when she betrayed him to the Marine, who gave him "reason" to obey with the leather strap.

Rob's lesson soon became ours as each of us reached school age. We discovered quickly that impressing the middle-aged, weary-from-sacrifice nuns demanded more than any of us had to give. Still, we tried, eager to please. Unlike Rob, I felt excited when my turn came. For me, "Holy Hell" was not at school—it was on Griffin Avenue.

Our parents rarely noticed our efforts at school until report cards came, but it didn't lessen our drive. We pressed on without help, managing our time carefully to preserve what little play we had before Auggie returned us to silence. We excelled, even as teachers seemed determined to discourage us. Doing well was expected, yet if we excelled too much, the nuns claimed we had spent more time studying than confessing—another no-win situation. To them, everything circled back to God, and their mission was to tame offenders of the Almighty with yardsticks and rulers, cracked across heads or hands for the smallest infraction.

We quickly learned that God, too, was easily offended. The mighty yardstick of penitence struck often and hard—for writing with the wrong hand, looking the wrong way, or speaking in the wrong tone. Giggling invited the worst wrath, proving to us that God had no sense of humor. He was a serious God, ready at any moment to strike with thunder and lightning for missing morning Mass, stepping out of line, or even needing the lavatory.

At Holy Blessed Virgin, it was clear God watched constantly, seeking out those who dared forget homework or chew bubble gum. He demanded quiet order, rigid discipline, and guilt without tolerance for weakness. This had to be true, for the nuns assured us that God made man in His own image. We believed it, because the Marine matched their description of Him—angry, exacting, and quick to punish. Their lessons only confirmed what we already feared: Faith in the unseen meant living under constant judgment.

At lunchtime, I forced myself to swallow the government-issued SPAM® and cheese sandwiches.

"There are starving children in China who would love to have that lunch, Samson," Sister Mary Alice barked, smacking the back of my head with a ruler.

I would have gladly given it to those children. I was a starving child too, but forcing down the tasteless food only worsened with the nuns' constant reminders that lunch was for nourishment and the contemplation of sins. Their stern warnings against idle talk crushed what little appetite remained. Idleness, they said, was the devil's workshop.

While they fussed with their stiff habits, I sat imagining a different tray. To my left, a boy opened a shiny new lunchbox; to my right, a girl pulled out bologna sandwiches and chocolate cupcakes. My eyes drifted between their blessings and the meager ration my mother had packed—a sad excuse for lunch, always the same, always a reminder of what we lacked.

School meals always began and ended with enough prayers to cover the sins of the morning and guard against the temptations of the afternoon. By the time the four o'clock bell rang, the air was heavy with the energy we'd been forced to bottle up all day. In the cold months, that left us less than an hour and a half to play; in warmer seasons, more than three. I lived for the warmth of spring and early fall.

Each afternoon, I met Rob at the side exit doors. It was his duty to shepherd us home. Rain or shine, sleet or snow, we trudged along the five blocks back to Griffin Avenue, releasing pent-up energy with shouts and leaps. On the way we plotted our childhood wars, directing tattered G.I. Joes® and dime-store army men to imagined fates. We dared each other to acts of rebellion—stealing crab apples from neighbors' trees, pelting giggling girls, or darting across to the forbidden side of the street. We never backed down from a dare, no matter how small or foolish.

Our favorite pastime was snowball battles with the younger, more vulnerable boys along the way home. I was the frailest of us, yet felt invincible when shielded by Rob, Jude, and Anne. Safe behind my human fortress, I hurled snowballs, though most missed their mark and occasionally struck my own brothers.

"Come on, try and get me!" I'd shout with borrowed courage, ducking as a snowball slipped short and smacked Jude instead.

"I didn't do it!" I'd insist as he charged after me. He always caught me, once shoving me face-first into a snowdrift.

"You want more of this, you little fag?" he screamed, pressing my head into the snow.

"Off him, you stupid jerk!" Rob snapped, yanking Jude back. That only fueled Jude's rage, and the two tumbled into a furious fight until Anne wedged herself between them, forcing them apart.

Suddenly she froze. "Do you hear that?" she whispered. We all stopped. The grinding gears of Auggie's truck carried down the street, slow and deliberate. None of us could tell if he was coming home or heading out again. Heart racing, we cut through a neighbor's yard, desperate to reach the house before he did. I prayed he was leaving, not returning.

We knew our snowball wars were crimes against our earthly father—if he ever found out—and sins against our heavenly Father, sure to be confessed at the next morning's Mass. But a dare was a dare. Rob and I never refused Jude's challenges, even knowing he would gladly betray us to the Marine. His tactics were no secret, yet we still risked it for the joy of playing together.

The nearer we came to Griffin Avenue, the more guarded we grew. Our senses sharpened like sentinels at a war camp, ready to change course if Auggie's truck was already in the driveway.

That was always a sign of trouble. An empty drive was our all-clear, and we'd burst through the screen door—often slamming it hard enough to wake a sibling. Snatching the single cookie allotted for a snack, we scattered to our shared rooms, dropping schoolbooks and changing into play clothes. If our uniforms weren't too soiled, they were carefully folded to wear again the next day, washed and pressed only on Fridays whether needed or not. Soon patched jeans or faded shorts and T-shirts replaced the day's attire, and we darted from window to window, scanning the drive to confirm safe passage.

"Slow down there! Where's da fire?" Mother called.

We adjusted our pace, grabbed our treasured troops, and raced to scale the wall that led to the nursery below.

In the winter, our battles shifted to the frozen lake at the wooded entrance beyond the nursery. With crude clamp-on blades turning our shoes into skates, we became world-renowned hockey players wielding invisible sticks and pucks. If the Marine caught us, our game ended quickly as he hurled the abandoned blades we'd tossed aside while running for cover. When the ice was too thin, we built forts and launched fierce ice-ball battles.

No weather was too harsh for us. Half frozen, we fought against the cold and against Mother's constant warnings.

"Don't stay out there too long or you'll catch yur death a pneumonia!" she'd yell as we dashed into the snow. We seriously wondered what in the world pneumonia was.

These cherished times always ended too soon, the prattle of Auggie's truck announcing his return. As it lumbered toward its mark, we gathered every trace of play and darted for cover, using trees as shields. We paused only long enough to gauge how much time remained before reaching safety. Any miscalculation meant arriving at the screen door too late and risking his glare—always a dangerous mistake.

We aimed to be in position before the first grind of the truck's gears. When homework awaited, we lay quietly on the painted bedroom floors, books open, feigning studiousness as he entered the room across the hall to shed his dirt-caked clothes. On the best days, he ignored us. On the worst, he prowled deliberately, intent on finding a target for his anger. He would slip into our rooms, grin curling at the corners of his mouth, like a cat ready to pounce on an unsuspecting mouse.

"Well now, what do we have here?" he sneered. "Which of ya li'l bastards needs a good whoopin'? Ya li'l pricks doin' homework? Why? Yur dumber than a box of rocks, ya li'l sons o …" His voice trailed off as he turned.

He taunted and demeaned us, insisting our efforts to better ourselves were useless and that we'd be lucky to become half the man he was. He boasted of the hardships he'd endured, trembling with rage as he spoke.

"You li'l piss ants will git a real education when yur ten," the Marine barked. "Auggie's school of hard knocks, that's right." Swatting the nearest child for emphasis, he stumbled away.

No one dared move, even to breathe. My mind spun in confusion. If our grades slipped, his fury only worsened. Fear rooted deep, joined by the gnawing hunger in our bellies, as we wondered what the "magical" age of ten would mean. I didn't dare imagine it—only knew it promised something terrible.

From the start, we were trained to believe every warning the Marine delivered. His threats were not idle—they were faith to us, truth without proof. Homework finished, drained from fear, we whispered crash-and-rescue games with our toy cars, trying to distract ourselves until the inevitable summons to dinner.

CHAPTER 5

Breaking Bread

"DINNER'S READY!" MOTHER SHOUTED from the kitchen. Her voice carried up the stairwells, slipped through walls, and even hummed through the heating ducts until it found our ears.

Always hungry, we ran from different directions, often colliding as we scrambled to the table.

Mealtime was a spectacle. Even as a child, I wondered who had invented the odd ritual of seating such mismatched people together and expecting harmony. Each dinner became so etched into our psyche that the very idea of "family dinner" would stir unease even into adulthood. With hands washed and stomachs eager, we slid into our assigned places—the youngest near Mother, who never seemed to eat from a plate herself. Rob drew the short straw, seated beside our father. The rest filled in the gaps. Our parents anchored the too-small table. Auggie was wedged against the ivy-covered wallpaper, while Mother claimed the open end for quick access to stove, sink, and refrigerator.

In constant motion, she stole bites from steaming skillets while piling our plates with overcooked vegetables, underdone starches, and meat that was never quite right. By the time nine mouths crowded in, it was "get while the gettin' was good." There was never quite enough to go around.

After a short pause for prayer, Auggie launched his tirade.

"Are ya kidding me? I PUT DIS FOOD ON DIS TABLE! I work my fingers to the bone, breakin' my back ta feed youse ungrateful piss ants! Ya better be prayin'. I keep doin' it—coz then where would ya be?" he barked.

We ate in silence, trying to wall off our minds as his cutting criticisms rained down on Mother's cooking. He cussed, complained, and cussed again, his ridicule growing sharper with every bite.

"Yur trying to kill me, ya worthless, brainless wop! Is it too much to ask for one meal dat don't taste like dog crap?" he raved, food spilling from his mouth.

Mother rarely answered. Only when the weight of her duties grew unbearable would she forget herself and speak.

"I am doing the best I can, Auggie," she whispered.

On these occasions the Marine was relentless in putting her back in her place. Her defiance always cost us, unleashing his pent-up fury. Time seemed to slow as his hands reached beneath the table, flipping it and all it held into the air before crashing down on us. Mother bolted from her chair, casting us a quick, apologetic glance. She crouched, arms raised to shield her face from the onslaught.

Mismatched cups, plates, and silverware spun through the air before striking at dangerous speeds. We braced ourselves, pushing back in our chairs as far as possible. The heavy table-turned-missile caught arms and chins of those leaning forward for a bite or sip. The eruption sent the youngest into sobs and the babies into shrill wails that pierced our ears.

Fear thickened the room, smothering us. The Marine stormed forward, stomping over shards and broken plates to reach his target—our mother. We stared at her frozen, expressionless face as she trembled with fear and anger, carrying the weight of all of us wide-eyed around her. With each shove and shake, she seemed to shrink smaller and smaller.

When at last he was spent, he turned on us, barking the only warning he ever gave.

"Run, ya li'l bastards!" And run we did, survival instincts on high alert, for we knew when that warning came, even he feared himself.

With every ounce of energy we bolted in all directions, tripping over glass, sliding on food-slick floors, desperate for escape. The slowest or nearest usually took a few licks as we wrestled our way to freedom.

Shaking in closets, under beds, or huddled in basement corners, we'd listen for the slam of the screen door, his retreat to the garage for hidden comfort—unless, of course, he chose to hunt us down and extend his tirade.

As he washed down his fury with alcohol, the Marine shook with disbelief at the depth of his own anger. Fear gripped him, but his children—scattering in all directions—never knew his warning sprang from a place so dark he feared what might happen if Pandora's Box opened completely.

His exit always left Mother kneeling on the floor, cleaning spilled food and what was left of her dignity. After regaining her wits, she ordered bedtime. Lights went out one by one, another day ending with empty stomachs and broken spirits. Later, Auggie stumbled into bed, breath sour with whiskey and unfiltered cigarettes, stripping away what little remained of her dignity.

Dinnertime wasn't the only meal marked by outbursts. I learned quickly that breakfast was not a time to dawdle, even on Sundays with nowhere to be. One Sunday stands out. We had all, except Father, gone to Mass the night before so Rob and Jude could spend the next day at our cousin Jill's. They were being picked up at ten. That gave me, at five years old and uninvited, a chance to sleep in. I rose a little after nine, sulking upstairs, wishing I were older so I could join them.

At nine thirty, Mother called me down to say goodbye and eat breakfast she had prepared. Father sat at the table, chewing the last piece of toast.

"We're out of bread and eggs," Mother said as I reached the table. "Wait a few minutes and I'll make you oatmeal."

I frowned. It wasn't that I disliked hot cereal, but I would have chosen toast. With no bread, I sat quietly while the oatmeal cooked. Soon she set the steaming bowl in front of me, dropping in an ice cube so I wouldn't burn my mouth.

"See that! Yur coddlin' the little wimp again. He can blow on his food like every other human bein'!" the Marine barked, coffee dripping from his lips. "Oh, that's right—he ain't no normal human bein'," he spat.

They argued as Mother calmly defended herself. My appetite vanished, nerves twisting in my stomach. The Marine's voice grew louder before he left for his cigarettes. Lighting up, he buried himself in the newspaper.

I stared at my bowl, unsure if I wanted it. Finally, I tasted a spoonful. It was cooler than expected, almost too cold, and I hated the flavor. I swirled the spoon a few times, spilling some over the rim just as my father turned the page—then all hell broke loose.

Mother returned to find the Marine forcing my face into the bowl of cereal. I fought to lift my head, but the harder I struggled, the harder he pressed. My body shuddered from lack of oxygen. Mother's scream finally made him release me. Choking and coughing, nose and mouth full of mush, I slumped in my chair. He laughed hysterically as she rushed to wipe my face. After several nose blows and hacking coughs, my lungs cleared.

"That'll teach the li'l rotten, spoiled freak ta eat his food 'stead a playin' in it," he sneered, still laughing as he left through the screen door.

Mother was shaken. She wondered how long he would have continued if she hadn't intervened. She told me to wash up and promised she'd get bread as soon as possible. She also vowed never again to let the weekend arrive with a short supply.

I stood staring in the mirror at all five years of myself. The image looked strange—cereal smeared everywhere, even dripping from my nose. I might have laughed if it had been a joke, but tears warmed my cheeks and humiliation pushed out any humor. Moving from the mirror, I wished I could disappear into nothingness.

I sat on the closet floor, hiding and missing my brothers. I remember wondering why I wasn't older and stronger like them. Why was I the only one cursed with "poop-brown, dago-wop eyes," as the Marine called them, always harsher in tone? I wished for Jude's blue or green eyes, and yellow hair Father seemed to favor.

I fiddled with a few army men but longed for Rob's portable radio, dead from worn batteries. Leaning back against the wall, I began listing the cruel names Father had hurled at me. Too many to recall, most were words I wasn't allowed to say, let alone think.

"Shit-brown eyes, you little bastard, wimpy queer faggot, stupid, dumb, idiot, freak," I whispered, humming them to the tune of "Twinkle, Twinkle, Little Star". Tears streamed as I sang the final words: "How I wonder what you are…."

CHAPTER 6

Values

BY THE TIME THE five of us were in school together, we had become a force—competing as fiercely in class as on the driveway basketball court. The nuns compared us constantly, admonishing the ones behind to "be more like" the proficient siblings, and warning the well-behaved not to turn out like the undisciplined. Mother Superior reminded us often that any infraction would be reported straight to our father, whom she unfortunately knew.

There were endless meetings in her office as Auggie bartered landscaping for tuition. The sisters looked down on us, preferring paying families. Though Auggie never entered the chapel, he refused to appear unable to afford private school. His motives for sending us to what we called "Holy Hell" weren't about class size, discipline, or academic advantage. He didn't care if we were schooled in Catholicism either. His reasons were rooted solely in the festering bigotry beneath his surface, like a sore that never healed.

The Marine was a proud card-carrying member of the "superior race." At any moment he'd climb onto his soapbox, boasting allegiance to a white supremacist group, flag, and symbol he'd never actually been near. Misinformed, undereducated, and overzealous, he backed any party that seemed to support his views.

He was a connoisseur of racist remarks—ones I'd never heard elsewhere, even into adulthood. He shared them freely, without conscience or shame. His children would not be educated beside Jews or coloreds. He had a slur ready for every race, creed, gender, orientation, or religion—except white Polish Catholics, though even they weren't safe from his scorn. He would have proudly worn the white-sheeted uniform of the devil himself had he been invited.

His venom wasn't reserved for minorities alone. He held firm contempt for women, the overweight, the handicapped, even the rich who paid his inflated landscaping bills. Daily he pushed his doctrine on us, and for years we absorbed it. With little access to outside ideas in our mostly white parish community, we were sponges. Repeating his values brought us his praise, so we treated them like gospel.

That was, until Jude was overheard giving a new student from a wealthy biracial family a tongue-lashing behind Sister Mary Margaret's back. She grabbed him by the ear, dragging him so fast he could barely keep his feet, and called Auggie to the office immediately.

Of course Jude's punishment was shared by all of us—insurance against anyone following his lead. After the Marine's tirade, I sat sobbing, wrestling with contradictions. I never knew whether to expect praise for copying him or punishment for the same act.

Looking back, it was probably fortunate we feared using his doctrine at school or church. Though the thoughts pulsed through me, fear of chastisement left room to observe those he condemned. There weren't many chances, but sometimes I crossed paths with an overweight girl or a boy from a mixed family. Playing beside them or simply watching, I questioned Auggie's conclusions.

What's so wrong with this one? Or that one? They're just like me.

But like a switch flipped from afar, my thoughts snapped back—I was supposed to hate them, vehemently, because Auggie did. And he never lied. If he spoke it, it was gospel.

CHAPTER 7

Communion

EACH MORNING AT SCHOOL we split into our classes and filed into the old Gothic chapel for Mass. Hands folded, hearts anxious, we dipped into holy water, crossed ourselves, genuflected, and took our seats—kneeling and rising in unison. Remnants of holy water lingered on my fingers, and I imagined warmth spiraling up my arms. I sat quietly, searching my soul for hidden sins to confess, not out of fear but with a penitent spirit. I wanted to be pleasing in God's eyes.

I loved Mass, the chapel's ornate features, and its sorrowful idols. The Latin from Father O'Brien flowed melodically. His robe brushed past me as he swung incense, its fragrance filling the air with mystical fog. Candlesticks and chalice gleamed with power, as I hadn't yet grasped the symbolic nature of the ritual.

I watched the altar boys with envy, longing for their status. Emotion welled as children's voices rose in hymns, echoing through the arches and mingling with the pipe organ's thunder. I often peeked through prayer-closed eyes to catch every movement of the drama. When the priest finally gave the sign of the cross, dismissing us in peace, I hesitated, staring as if waiting for an encore.

I waited impatiently for my First Holy Communion and all it entailed. After finishing catechism classes, I stood with anticipation for my turn at the perfunctory confession that preceded Communion. At last, today was the day. My palms sweated, my knees shook, and I silently rehearsed the procedures I'd memorized a hundred times. I didn't want to appear a novice. I believed if I performed this step of faith flawlessly, Father O'Brien would see something extraordinary in me and choose me as an altar boy. Like a star awaiting discovery, I entered the confessional.

When Father O'Brien pulled back the curtain, I froze. Tears slid down my burning cheeks. My tongue betrayed me—only jumbled blurbs escaped as I tried to voice my sins. Nothing came. What was I here to do?

The priest mistook my silence for deep penitence and leaned closer for a glimpse.

"Samson?" he said, smiling, then gently prompted me with the words to begin.

"Fa-Father, forgive me, I have …" I stammered, mumbling to follow his lead. My voice dropped to a whisper as I confessed sins I thought too terrible to forgive. I braced for harsh reprimand, but instead he granted absolution, instructing only one Hail Mary and one Our Father.

"Samson, I'll keep my eye on you. There may be a priest in the Izbicki family yet," he said, blessing me. "You may have what it takes to be one someday." Relief swept through me.

I wiped my eyes on my cuffs and left the confessional, unburdened. Kneeling at the nearest pew, I prayed, vowing never again to pinch my sister, lie to my father, or skip bedtime prayers—the "terrible" sins I'd confessed. Then I joined my classmates filing from the chapel, feeling light, white, and clean as new snow, even if the moment hadn't gone quite as I imagined.

First Holy Communion was a day to behold—special suits for boys, veiled dresses for girls, and parties rivaling birthdays. Relatives traveled from miles away to celebrate the new inductees, and it was no different for the Izbickis. Pinching aunts and hair-tousling uncles arrived with gifts and praise, and I felt exalted above my siblings. After the customary lineup on the sofa, we were finally set free.

We joined cousins already deep in games, the air alive with laughter and conversation. I couldn't remember a day of such freedom. "Whoopee!" I shouted, not caring who heard.

Tables draped in lace held dishes of homemade treats. Buckets of ice overflowed with orange and grape sodas—enough for each child to have their own. On a smaller table sat the most beautiful white cake we had ever seen. Even my father seemed at ease, surrounded by men laughing at his exaggerated stories. They roared at his punch lines, toasted him as glasses were refilled, and leaned in for the next tale.

The women traded recipes, refilled dishes, and smacked hands reaching for more. On his way to the kitchen, Auggie spun my smiling mother playfully as Sinatra's voice floated from the radio. I sighed, wishing the day would never end. For once, all was right with the world, and the heavens smiled down with sunshine.

Guests left one by one, sated by food and drink, while Rob and I lingered on the porch steps, soaking up the last attention from departing aunts and uncles. Father O'Brien accepted a ride with the final visitors, apologizing in his deep, throaty voice for too much Irish whiskey, and thanked Mother for her hospitality.

When the last car pulled away, we sat reliving the day. Rob recalled his own First Communion. Instead of a party, he and our cousin Jill had been taken to a fancy dinner by their godfather.

"Today was so cool, wasn't it, Rob?" I asked, full of satisfaction. "Really cool," Rob replied quickly. "I wish it was mine again. You should have seen that restaurant, Sam. The food was sooo yummy. I can still almost taste it." His eyes stared off, fixed on the memory.

It had been his first time in a restaurant, and even now he could almost taste the food and picture the room as if he were still there.

I nudged Rob from his thoughts, and he caught the warning in my eyes. Then he too heard the commotion inside. Arm in arm, we raced to the dining room window just as the leftover cake—the centerpiece of the day—smashed into Mother as the Marine flipped the table.

"What did ya open yur big fat dago mouth and say to that pig?" he roared, hoisting the table. "How many times I gotta tell ya to keep yur ugly mug shut?" His voice carried down the street.

"I'm sorry, Auggie! I thought ya wouldn't mind if she knew!" Mother stammered as the cake splattered across her new dress, bought just for the occasion.

We didn't stay to watch more. We ran toward the front of the house, where our siblings were chasing lightning bugs. At our signal, they fell in behind us. But escape routes closed fast—the front or back entrances left us exposed in full view of our parents.

Frozen in panic, I looked to Rob for an answer. He stood still, deep in thought, then broke the suspense with a choice—he opened the front door.

"Run upstairs, fast!" Rob said, pointing to the side steps. He stood between us and the Marine's view as I bolted up, collapsing across the landing to peer through the railing. I shook uncontrollably, feeling too terrified for Rob to hide with the others.

As if he had eyes in the back of his head, the Marine turned on Rob. Mistaking his stand as a challenge, he staggered forward, slurring threats and swinging at air. Rob's eyes met Mother's cake-smeared glance, silently pleading for help. All he saw was a sad apology for what she knew would follow.

Her voice rose from begging to screams as the Marine struck again and again, dragging Rob from his mental escape back into torment. The leather strap seared his flesh red and numb until he curled in the fetal position, shielding his head and face.

Tears streamed down my cheeks, rage swelling so fierce I nearly screamed. Inside my mind I shouted at him to stop, begging God to strike my father down with lightning—anything to end it.

Rob drifted in and out to far-off places. Mother's frantic voice finally pulled the Marine from his frenzy. Red-faced, sweating, and dazed, he looked around at the destruction as if for explanation, then stormed out the back screen door, slamming it behind him.

Rob lay still until Mother pressed a cool rag to his welted skin. She turned to clean the mess of cake and shattered dishes while Rob, silently crying, limped to bed. Those of us who had escaped gathered around him, offering quiet comfort to our defender. I crawled in beside him, shell-shocked by the day's sudden collapse, wishing I'd been brave enough to stand as he had.

"I'm sorry," I whispered again and again, as though it might make amends.

That night, hidden beneath sheets, I opened my composition notebook. I loved the scent of paper, the scratch of pencils, the rows of books in libraries. Writing became the only way to release pain that grew heavier each day. I didn't want to forget; I wanted to set it free. I wrote stories constantly in my head and longed for someone—anyone—to know mine. Maybe if they read every detail, it would all stop.

But I knew better. If anyone found my notebook, as had happened before, it would only make things worse. If Mother read it, she'd dismiss it as imagination. If the Marine read it, he'd give me more to write.

For about a year I'd been recording things only I could understand, so if my notebook was found, no one else could read it. To be sure, I signed each page with my middle name, Aaron. It felt like being a spy—someone different than plain old Sam. I created a code, like the decoder rings we had, so only Aaron and I knew its meaning. I tracked pain by marking lines for each day, never dating them. I didn't need to. I just wanted to see what I felt. After recording, I tucked the notebook back on the shelf. Even on the worst days, I made my marks. It gave me something to look forward to.

Then I slipped into bed, sheets pulled over my head, and cried quietly. My most special day had been ruined, and Rob had suffered for all of us. It should have been me. I felt stupid, cowardly, hating myself. Under the sheets I pinched my arms again and again, trying to take his pain. For days afterward, people asked about the bruises covering me. I lied, saying I didn't know where they came from.

That same year was Joan's first in school. She dawdled behind us as we urged her to hurry, but she was thrilled to go, proud of her new status. At the kindergarten entrance she acted so grown up, eager to begin. Within hours the nuns noticed her compliant, helpful spirit. Relaxed, they turned to children needing stricter discipline. Their opinion of her grew with each passing day, and by midterm she was singled out for special privileges given only to students with humble, sacrificial hearts. Joan shone like a light in darkness compared to the rest of us.

"Hey guys, guess what Sister Mary Agnes said today?" Joan called as she ran toward us after school. "She said I'm gonna be an egg-cellent nun when I grow up," she bragged with a whine in her tone.

I wasn't sure how to feel. As much as I admired priests, nuns scared the life out of me. I studied her, picturing her in the black-and-white habit, stern-faced like the sisters—it didn't quite fit. Yet I could see her surrendering to church service, because when

I thought about it, the perky chameleon always became whatever anyone needed her to be.

CHAPTER 8

Expectations

For almost a year after my First Communion, life at the house on Griffin Avenue grew eerily pleasant. Auggie's business boomed even through autumn, and to all of us watching cautiously, he seemed happy for the first time in years. His tirades quieted, his drinking tapered, and he acted as if he'd been granted a new lease on life. Much to our amazement, he offered to play catch with us when he had extra time, showing us how to fast-pitch without scolding our mistakes. He rarely criticized at dinner, sometimes teased the girls, or toyed with the youngest. He began asking about our schoolwork and listened with surprising patience. Don't get me wrong—we still endured horrendous punishment when he lost his temper, but not as often, and even his name-calling seemed in a less vicious tone.

The family became more of a unit, gathering Sunday nights to watch the Ed Sullivan Show. Auggie jeered at Ed's guests as if they had walked into our living room, pointing at the screen and barking critical slurs while we laughed. Yet he was so intrigued he always let it run despite his disgust. He chuckled at the comedians, sometimes grabbed Mother and danced in circles when musicians played the latest hits. And though it aired on a school night, he often granted us a bedtime extension, which always brought cheers.

Auggie made new purchases for the house, upgrading bathrooms and appliances. He converted the back porch into a bedroom, bath, and office for himself. Mother loved her refreshed kitchen with rich cherry cabinets, but the most cherished change came with wall-to-wall carpeting that covered the old painted floors. Auggie's transformation may have been a false sense of security, but we all relished it like parched refugees at an oasis. The calm lasted into early spring as he landed job after job, word of mouth carrying his reputation.

Mother, energized by this new freedom, grew closer to her sisters, inviting them more often. That meant plenty of cousin playtime. With Auggie's schedule booked through spring, Gertie and her pack enjoyed a long, comfortable winter of rare peace.

Rob, though relieved, stayed cautious. He knew better than to trust this calm. Always on guard, he waited for the other shoe to drop, ready to sound the alarm if disaster struck.

"Don't get too comfortable; you can't trust him and you know it," Rob whispered at bedtime.

His instincts, honed to perfection, proved right sooner than later. In the weeks leading to his March birthday he was filled with anxiety, worse than ever before. Distracted at school, fidgety and unable to concentrate, he grew impatient and agitated at home—which was unlike him. Each day brought him closer to the one we all dreaded.

He would be the first to reach the mystical age of ten, and he feared its implications. We sat speculating on what might come. To our surprise, his tenth birthday passed without incident. In fact, it was his best ever—he finally received the BB gun he'd long begged for. He basked in the attention and loved the celebration.

At day's end we remained puzzled by our father's earlier threats about turning ten. But as spring thawed, we would painfully learn what he meant.

Despite autumn's mild start, the winter was fierce. Arctic blasts brought heavy snow, more than in recent years, wreaking havoc on Auggie's schedule. By March he had to postpone all outdoor remodeling jobs. Construction in the area ground to a halt, and laid-off workers snapped up the few indoor repairs available. With limited options, he sold mostly firewood, struggling to keep up with the flood of orders. But the income was far less than his other jobs.

Financially, the year had been profitable, yet his savings dwindled. It wasn't enough to cover expenses until spring without belt-tightening. Fuel costs rose, and each day he checked the oil tank, hoping it wouldn't run dry. With eight mouths to feed and clothe, pressure mounted. His drinking increased, and so did his outbursts. Even minor incidents set him off, and to us it was clear he was crumbling under the weight.

March came in like a lion but went out like a lamb. Before cabin fever could boil over, the soil softened under melting snow and spring rains. Nurseries began calling in locals as migrant workers parked pickups and trailers near farms, hoping for daily work. Growers favored seasonal labor for its low cost and paid locals a bit more, all under the table. They needed hands to uproot and pot trees before they grew too large, so they hired whoever was willing.

Auggie was well known for his steady work and his ability to ball trees with little root damage. Growers sought him out and paid better than most. All winter his large, callused hands had cut burlap and coarse rope to prepare for the busy season. As expected, the calls came—and with them, the winds of change.

"Robert, git down here, ya worthless piece a cow shit!" the Marine bellowed.

Rob's mind raced. It was the first day of spring break, and he had lingered a few minutes under warm blankets, planning the day ahead. We were all waiting for the old truck to leave, taking Father with it. Excited, we'd decided to play in the basement with

Rob's new bag of plastic cowboys and Indians—a late birthday gift from his godparents.

But when Mother called him down, her expression told me something was wrong. Instead of explaining, she sent him to the garage where our father waited, instructing the rest of us to eat breakfast.

Rob was still in his pajamas, so he ran upstairs, changed into shorts and a T-shirt, pulled on his jacket, and hesitantly made his way to the garage. Dying of curiosity, I slipped out the door and hid outside, hoping to learn what was going on.

Rob searched his mind but couldn't recall leaving anything out of place. He knew he hadn't disturbed anything when he'd cut through the garage the day before to avoid a run-in with the Marine. Entering cautiously, he stood a safe distance as Auggie loaded burlap and rope into the truck.

The Marine ignored him at first. Rob fidgeted uneasily until, at last, Auggie turned, grinning from ear to ear. Relief flickered—but only for a moment.

"Hahaha! There ya are," he laughed. "Git yur rear end back in the house and put on some old clothes and shoes."

Rob, confused, hesitated. The Marine's voice snapped again, harsher this time.

"Git going! We don't have all day, ya li'l bastard! And make sure ya eat a good breakfast, cuz yur gonna need it!" he yelled, hurling a roll of rope at him.

Dumbfounded by the Marine's demands, Rob ran from the garage, nearly knocking me over. He grabbed my pajama top and yanked me inside.

"Are you crazy, Sam? If he'd seen you, he'd have killed us both!" he whispered harshly.

After changing again, Rob entered the kitchen where Mother was packing two lunches—one in Father's black metal box, the other in a paper sack Rob prayed wasn't his. Between bites of egg and toast, he asked quietly, "Why did I have to change into old clothes?" His questions went unanswered.

"Quit talkin' and eat," she said softly.

"It's the first day of spring break," he tried again, but she didn't respond.

When he finished, he carried his plate to the sink and stood waiting. At last she handed him the paper sack and began explaining, trying to make it sound like an adventure. Rob received it as if she'd told him someone had died.

"It's time ya know what bein' a man is all about, Robert. He's gonna teach ya his trade. Yur gonna love bein' outdoors, helpin' him with the job. Behave yursel' and mind yer father. You'll be a man jus' like him today," she said.

But Rob didn't feel like much of a man—and he didn't look like one to me.

Rob frowned. Nothing seemed worse than spending the day with our father learning his trade, whatever that meant. He was both disappointed and frightened. Mother rambled on, reminding him he was now ten years old—grown enough to help out. Her words echoed the Marine's grin when he had warned us we'd learn from his school of hard knocks at that age.

Rob trudged toward the screen door, still not fully comprehending. By day's end, he would wonder no more. We scattered as the Marine stormed inside and into his office, nearly knocking Rob over. Summoned by name, Rob stood before his father's desk, hands in pockets, head low.

The Marine sat with furrowed brows, glaring at his firstborn's small frame and timid posture. In a vengeful tone he laid out what would take place and what was expected. Rob listened silently as questions were hurled like darts.

"Do ya think life's 'bout playin'? Hell no it ain't!" he barked. "Life's 'bout hard work an' sacurfice. High time ya put away yur toys an' pick up a shovel wit' me. Maybe dis'll put some muscle on dat pitiful body! You li'l bastards took advantage a me long enough—now ya earn yur keep.

"Is it possible fer ya ta stop lookin' so pitiful? It's embarrassin'! It's yur job ta help me work ta buy food an' stuff fer youse ungrateful pieces a rat crap! I don't have all day, so move it!" he shouted, ending his tirade.

The Marine paced the small office, pontificating about his own childhood and how he had already earned his keep by Rob's age. He fired questions, but Rob knew better than to answer. Leaving the room, the Marine brushed past him, smacked the back of his head with his hat, and stormed out, cursing all the way to the truck.

With a heavy heart and lunch in hand, Rob took his place beside our father on the torn seat of the truck. As it backed slowly from the driveway, he caught sight of us peeking from behind pulled shades, checking if it was safe to leave our rooms. I was devastated. My day was ruined, and I had no idea what to expect. All I knew was that Rob—my protector and closest friend—was gone to points unknown, and I was terrified.

That night Aaron recorded more than the usual tally of incidents. H lllll, N llllll, J lllllllllllllllllll, M llll.

CHAPTER 9

School of Hard Knocks

THE DIRT ROAD LEADING to the back fields of the nursery farm was littered with rows of makeshift motor homes and rusted-out cars and pickups. Auggie nearly ran over a small boy in clothes too small and dirty. He swore at the boy, yelling slang-filled curses, then swerved as if to hit the jalopy parked behind him. Rob braced himself so he wouldn't be thrown forward and saw one of the men raise a middle finger as they passed. Enraged, Auggie cussed again and downshifted, grinding the gears.

The fields they passed held row upon row of dogwoods, hemlocks, oaks, and elms, with shrubs stretching in the distance. About a mile past the campers, he pulled the truck into a cleared area beside the trees. Barking at Rob to stay put, he walked over to a man standing next to a white truck marked "Strong-Arms Nurseries." Rob watched Auggie's mood transform. He smiled and laughed with the man, pointing back toward the truck. The man gestured to something in the fields before climbing into his vehicle and driving away.

Auggie returned, climbed back in, and steered down a cutaway path deeper into the rows.

Rob had never seen so many trees in his life. He watched row after row disappear behind them until they stopped at the far end of a field. The Marine barked, "Get them tools unloaded pronto!"

From where he sat, Rob saw groups of men, women, and children his age crossing the soggy spring earth toward trees marked for removal. As he grabbed the door handle, the Marine caught his arm.

"We can and will outwork these job-stealin', worthless spicks!" he spewed, pointing with hatred.

Rob wasn't sure why, but he instantly felt he should be angry at people he hadn't even met. Putting on his meanest face, he followed the Marine as they began to work.

With no instruction, Rob was clueless. He fumbled, trying not to look inept. Their assigned plot was five acres crowded with overgrown dogwoods and hemlocks, thick with weeds, some taller than Rob's waist. Tagged trees stood just under Auggie's six feet.

After fetching water, tools, and burlap, Rob's job was to clear weeds around each tree, then kneel and slide burlap beneath the ball of earth and roots Auggie freed with his spade. Four or five thrusts loosened the soil, and the root ball was wrapped and tied. Within minutes they moved to the next tree.

By lunchtime they had unearthed thirty-five trees—fifteen short of Auggie's expectations.

Disoriented and dizzy from the sheer magnitude of the work, Rob fought to swallow the packed lunch Mother had sent. Waves of nausea passed through him as he tried to focus. Several times the Marine swatted him on the back of the head, insisting he hurry.

The noontime heat rose, burning off the fog that lingered between the trees. Swarms of gnats, flies, and mosquitoes, dormant through the spring melt, came alive. They rose in visible clouds, clinging to flesh and hair, drawn by sweat. Rob swatted and slapped at his exposed skin, irritated by their persistence as the Marine chided him.

"Quit bein' such a li'l sissy," the Marine said. "Ya better git used to them, coz they're only part a the fun out here." The word fun *confused Rob.*

Angered by the jeers, Rob turned to hide the tears rushing his eyes. He forced himself toward the afternoon's labor, unwilling to risk further punishment should the Marine catch his emotions.

The afternoon heat proved harsher than the morning. The sun scorched plant and flesh without mercy. By mid-afternoon, migrant workers packed their dirty tools and children into trucks, leaving in search of the day's pay. Rob assumed Auggie would follow, but instead he pushed faster and harder, cursing the others' weakness for quitting when daylight remained.

When the count of unearthed trees reached seventy and the sun dipped westward, the Marine finally loaded the truck, satisfied with their accomplishments. Rob leaned against the passenger door, passing out from dehydration and exhaustion. He faintly heard the Marine's complaints about female drivers as he sank into nothingness.

Jarred awake by the sputtering chokes of the truck shutting down, Rob fought to keep his eyelids open. Alone in the cluttered cab, he shivered as he pulled himself out, nearly collapsing onto the blacktop. From the left of the truck, he saw Auggie guzzling from a brown paper-wrapped bottle, liquid dripping down his chin and chest. Their eyes met, but neither spoke. Rob forced himself to put one foot in front of the other, masking his pain and exhaustion.

The truck's return sent us all fleeing, but I watched from behind the upstairs blinds as he staggered halfway up the walk. He tripped on a raised slab of cement, and Mother rushed to catch him, breaking his fall. I couldn't believe what I was seeing. What had happened to Rob? He looked terrible. I wanted to run down, but fear of my father drove me back into hiding.

Rob opened his mouth, but no words came. He now understood what Auggie's school of hard knocks was all about as he shuddered in Mother's arms.

Gertie was mortified. The sight of him—covered in dirt and sweat, sunburned, scratched, and welted—shocked her to her knees. Tear-filled eyes empty, Rob gasped as he collapsed into her arms. She gathered strength and carried him like a limp infant through the house to the upstairs bathroom. She laid him gently on the floor, started a bath, then stripped him down to his once-white, earth-filled briefs.

I stood in the doorway with tears in my eyes, desperate to do something to help.

Mother poured liquid bubbles into the bath, turned her back, and urged him in. Rob slid his briefs over bruised, bleeding knees and stepped into the water, twitching as the warmth stung his open flesh. Bubbles camouflaging him from view, Mother knelt and softly washed away dirt and silent tears.

Gertie fought back her own tears, hiding the disgust she felt for Auggie as she ran the washrag over Rob's knees. After drying him, she applied aloe to his sunburn, ointment to his scratches, and nearly gasped at the blisters forming on his palms. No sooner had she finished than Rob turned to vomit fragments of lunch. She anchored him upright as he heaved until only bile burned his throat.

"What happened to Rob?" I asked sheepishly. "Did he fall or somethin'? Why's he bleedin' so much? Rob, you okay?" My questions went unanswered.

Why won't anyone tell me what happened? I thought. Mother put Rob to bed and went downstairs in silence. I ran to Anne, who peeked from behind her door, and we sat guessing what had gone on.

Hours later, Rob drifted in and out of sleep. In dreams, muffled voices argued below—"coddled," then endless nonsense and curses, then "please," followed by a loud crash that pulled him upward.

He heard feet running, something falling with a thud. He drifted again, then crying children stirred him fully awake. He sat up, disoriented, unsure how he'd gotten there or what time it was. Three sets of eyes stared from the corner, and he searched their expressions for explanation.

Jude spoke first. "What did you do to make him so mad, Rob?" he whispered.

Puzzled, Rob listened, then understood all too clearly what had happened while he slept.

"Mother is ba-leeding!" I whispered, shivering at the same time.

Rob rose from bed, limbs screaming with pain and fatigue, and crept downstairs, listening at each step. The disruption in the kitchen had ended with the slam of the door, and we followed cautiously, trying not to make a sound. At the kitchen doorway, we saw Mother bent over, straining to right the table. She faltered under its weight until Rob carefully stepped between food and broken glass to help. Surprised by our presence, she turned quickly, rushing to cover her swollen right eye.

Rob froze, overwhelmed by her appearance. Tiny splatters of blood dotted her face like chicken pox. Shaking, he forced his anger down deep. Mother forced a smile, insisting she'd fallen over the plates, but he knew the shiner came from the Marine's hand—likely from defending him.

Bathed in guilt, he set aside his own misery and helped put the kitchen back in order. As she sat with a frozen piece of meat on her eye, we watched him pace from screen door to table and back. A deep loathing grew within him; rage pressed against his small frame, but he knew size made confrontation impossible. Seeing our unrest, Mother distracted him by offering toast and hot chocolate. Being the little boy he still was, and weak from losing every meal, Rob soon ate gratefully. Afterward, she called bedtime orders, and we filed upstairs behind him. H llll, N llllllll, J llllllll, M ll.

Later that night, as we were all tucked into bed, Gertie sat quietly nursing her wounds, kneeling beside the bed, praying he would never return from the garage.

Against her silent protests, Auggie demanded Rob continue working with him every day that week.

Rob stayed ill and exhausted the first three days, but by the fourth his strength improved and he better managed the jobs. He paced himself, sneaking breaks when the Marine's back was turned. To endure, he made up games in his head—cutting through a jungle, on a safari hunting wildlife among the bushes. He pictured his lunch as a condemned man's last meal. He imagined his aching limbs as a soldier's wounds in battle. To block out the Marine's constant complaints, he created elaborate escape plans from an imagined prison camp. What he refused to imagine were the things he missed at home, where the rest of us played.

When he arrived home those next days, Rob carried an air of pride, acting as if we were the ones missing out. Jude, unaware of what Rob endured, grew envious. Rob flexed his new biceps, rubbing it in just enough to sting, then reminded Jude he'd soon be ten himself. Jude anxiously counted the months, while Rob—though jealous that we were still free of work—feared for what awaited us.

That Friday, heavy rain made the fields inaccessible, and Auggie gave Rob the day off. Rob was thrilled until he realized our father might stay home too. That thought dimmed his relief; life was always restricted under his watch. But to our surprise, we heard the pickup leave at its usual time. We tumbled in our beds with excitement, giddy at the freedom ahead.

The day unfolded as we had hoped—light, playful, our father's shadow gone. That night, Rob lay in bed, whispering the most fervent prayers of his life. At morning Mass he would beg God to send oceans of rain, to grant him mercy with every storm.

Over the next two years, Jude—and eventually I—joined Rob in the fields, working beside the Marine on days God didn't grant us rain. Every school break except Sundays was spent in his school of hard knocks. Our prayers grew more creative. Along with rain, we pleaded for the one thing most begged to avoid: sickness. For us, illness was the only other acceptable excuse to escape the fields, so we prayed with fervor to be spared by being sick.

CHAPTER 10

Rejoice

THE SUMMER AND FALL flew by, and before I knew it, Christmas had arrived. It was still dark outside when I crept down the stairs, careful not to make a sound. I found the cluster of plugs hidden beneath the tree limbs and slid them into the wall outlet. With a spark, the tree lit up. Big blue bulbs glistened and twinkled as I tilted my head side to side, closing one eye, then the other, squinting so the lights smeared like magic across the branches.

I waited for my brothers and sisters to wake, hoping to sneak a glimpse at what had been left under the tree. Spunky, our mutt, gnawed playfully at my fingers as I fought the urge to touch the six or so packages nestled among ribbons and fluffy white cotton snow. From where I sat, I couldn't read the tags, and impatience grew. But tradition held: No one touched a gift until its giver was present. Even if the others woke, we'd still have to wait for our father.

Pete was the only one who still believed in Santa. The rest of us had long since given up, as Auggie had claimed that role years before. I remembered the magic I once felt and was saddened I couldn't summon it anymore. I had loved that jolly old man and felt betrayed when I learned he wasn't real. Father recently mocked me, saying only sissies believed in Santa, and that I was the biggest sissy he'd ever known—so I might as well keep believing if I wanted. The memory stung, and I shrugged, trying to shake it off.

I sat staring at the presents, trying to guess their contents by shape. I whispered guesses into the air, then slid onto the floor, straining to read the tags. The stairs were still empty, so I knelt and spied Joan's name on the gift nearest me. Moving quickly, I checked each one—Pete, Jude, Anne, Joan, and even one for Rob. I was thrilled for him. Last year he'd received nothing so Pete could have his gift.

I could see no more, as those I'd read were stacked on top of the others. Moving them risked leaving evidence of my snooping. Startled, I jumped back as Spunky's tail struck me. For a second I thought I'd been caught. My heart pounded as I climbed back onto the couch, aching to know whether my father had kept his word or not.

For weeks leading up to Christmas, the Marine had tormented me. He invented endless reasons why I would be the only one waking up to no present on Christmas morning, growing more creative with each jab.

"Queers don't git presents," he sneered. "You'll git what ya deserve—and that's nuthin.'"

At the time, his words cut deeper than they threatened. I couldn't believe he'd actually do it, but that morning I wasn't so sure. As the sun rose behind a cloudy winter sky, I drifted asleep against the sofa arm, dreaming of Christmases past.

Startled awake by my brother, I opened my eyes to see Rob looking down at me.

"Come on, Sam," he whispered, unplugging the tree and pulling me upstairs to the room we shared with Jude, who was just waking with a yawn.

"If he caught you, we'd all a got it good," he whispered angrily.

I knew he was right and stood with my head low. We heard rustling in the hall and the bathroom door's latch click. We dove onto our beds, feigning sleep. Mother stuck her head in and told us we could go downstairs. No one had to tell us twice.

We hurried down the stairs as Gertie switched on the tree lights.

"Nobody better be touchin' them presents! Ya do and I'll set fire to 'em!" the Marine shouted down.

Pete squirmed inches from the tree while the rest of us lined up on the sofa, waiting for our father's entrance. Auggie descended slowly, and the yearly ritual began.

"Has any a ya been good enough ta git a present from me?" he asked. "I don't think so." We sat nervously as he picked one up, pretending to open it.

Finally, he relented and motioned for us to join him.

"Come here and see fur yourselves then. I ain't lyin'," he said as we left the sofa for a closer look.

We knew the drill and played along. One by one, everyone searched for their package and tore at ribbons and paper, revealing their gifts. My brothers and sisters laughed and giggled at the contents. I moved to see the gifts left and searched for my name. Picking up a rectangular box, I checked for a tag.

The Marine lunged forward and snatched it from my hand. "Does that have yur name on it, ya li'l prick?" he asked, spitting as he spoke.

"No, sir," I replied shyly.

He grinned, holding the package closer to inspect.

"I told ya, ya little weasel. See? I was right. Ain't nuthin' under that tree for ya!" he said, tormenting me.

I strained to glimpse what my brothers and sisters had received. Nervous, angry, and heartbroken, I refused to let him see me cry. He had really done it. I couldn't believe it. I was stunned.

Rob and Jude looked over red and blue plaid shirts. The girls held up the matching sweaters they had asked for. Rob seemed especially surprised to have a gift.

Gertie was busy helping Pete set up his fire truck and hadn't noticed the conflict until she caught my face. She remembered the night before, when she had found Auggie rummaging through the gifts she had neatly placed under the tree. She could have sworn he pocketed something as she entered the room. Fearing confrontation, she'd said nothing, even imagining maybe he was sneaking a gift for her. Now she knew exactly what his intentions had been.

The Marine stood holding the last gift under the tree. I looked at it, almost afraid. He searched it over, settled his eyes on a blank spot, and pretended to read a tag that wasn't there. Toying with me, he extended it as if to hand it over, then snatched it back.

"Look, everyone!" he announced in a high-pitched mockery. "I was wrong; Santa did come to our house, and look what he left!" He waved the package over his head.

Everyone turned, anxious to see what Santa had brought.

"It's for Sammie," he said, laughing so hard he could barely speak.

Then he read the fictitious tag aloud: "To Sammie, my favorite little queer!" he yelled, nearly doubled over with laughter.

My face flushed crimson. Tears stung my eyes. I wanted to rush him, scream at him. Inside I was already screaming. I wished I were a big man so I could kill him. But instead, I shrank— smaller and smaller, until I was no more than a speck of dirt.

Embarrassed for me and unsure what to do, the others stared sympathetically. Gertie brushed Auggie aside and urged me to open the gift. I didn't want it. I didn't want anything. I just wanted to run far away. But she pressed it into my hands, pulling at the wrapping until finally I relented and opened it. Forcing a smile, I excused myself and walked slowly to the bathroom.

In the bathroom, I sat motionless on the commode, tears streaming down my flushed cheeks. I was devastated, humiliated, thoughts colliding one after another.

After several minutes I muttered, *All that for a brown shirt. I hate brown. They know how much I hate brown.*

I had wished for so many things—army men, the same plaid shirt Rob and Jude received—anything but this. More than anything, I wanted this day to be different, to be someone else, anywhere but here.

Fearing the Marine might come after me, I wiped my face and slipped back to the tree just as Mother turned on the radio. I sat watching the others and softly hummed with the choir's hymn:

"Rejoice, rejoice, Emmanuel ... Israel ..." the radio blared.

Echoing over it, the Marine ranted as he poured his first drink of the day. "Rejoice! You worthless idiots better rejoice, 'cause next year you ain't gettin' nothin'!"

We placed our gifts neatly back under the tree for relatives to see later and gathered at the kitchen table. Gertie prepared the first meal of what would prove to be a very challenging Christmas Day.

Aaron recorded H 11111, N lllllllllll, M lll.

CHAPTER 11

Day of All Days

I STOOD IN FRONT of the shelves at the Five and Dime, torn between two transistor radios. Though I was an above-average reader for my age, a few of the package words confounded me. Still, I was determined to make the perfect choice. I had waited for this moment for what seemed like forever, vibrating with anticipation the entire fifteen-minute ride to the store.

For months, I had hoarded every dime, nickel, and penny I could find, earn, or con out of siblings, Mother, or anyone I came across. My mission: Six dollars and ninety-nine cents for the radio and batteries. I was willing to do almost anything for it. I had endlessly begged Rob to let me use his radio, and more often than not he relented. His was gray and ran on four small batteries.

I was sick of the same old station Mother played while cooking. Occasionally, she'd turn the dial, and for a minute or two I'd hear songs I'd never known before—and I wanted more. Sometimes she stopped completely, a strange look in her eyes when the Righteous Brothers sang "You've Lost That Lovin' Feelin'." She loved Sonny and Cher's "I Got You Babe," dancing and singing along. I was okay with those, but I craved more Beatles, Turtles, Dave Clark Five, and Herman's Hermits. I memorized every word of the Beatles' "Help!"—like it opened a window into my thoughts. But the song that echoed most in our house was Dave Clark Five's "Catch Us If You Can," the anthem for our early warning system. I even secretly liked the station Auggie played in the old truck. Sometimes I wondered if music was the only thing we shared.

Music was balm to my battered soul. It dissolved the tension, restored me, gave me strength for another day. I longed for it constantly. Rob used his radio for the same escape, but sharing wasn't enough. I needed my own. Music wasn't just desire—it was survival. I hungered for it more than food, more than air. And today, I would have it.

I lifted one box from the shelf and then the other. Just touching the radios gave me a thrill. I scanned the aisles, half hoping for an announcement over the store's speakers to mark my purchase.

Rob rounded the corner, arms full of batteries he had saved for. "Did you decide which one you want, bud? We have to go soon," he said with a smile. He understood what this moment meant.

I inhaled deeply, took the dark gray one from the shelf, and held it up like it was treasure. Then I grew wings and flew to the checkout counter. Bursting with pride, I placed the radio and a pack of batteries on the counter. The gum-chewing checkout girl seemed far more interested in Rob than in me and my radio—but I couldn't have cared less.

She popped a bubble and said, "That'll be six dollars and ninety-six cents."

Surprised it was three cents less than I expected, I poured out the change from my pockets, scattering it across the counter. I pocketed the extra three cents and the two army men mixed in with the coins while she impatiently rechecked my count and bagged the radio.

"That's a lot of coins," she said, looking at me like I was an idiot. "How old are you? First radio or somethin'?"

"I'm nine," I said, puffing my chest. "Isn't that radio cool?" She only rolled her eyes and handed me the bag.

This was the day of all days. I skipped from the store and used my last three cents in the gumball machine. On the sidewalk, Rob helped me insert the batteries, and I tuned in my very first music from my own radio. Blowing bubbles, I spun the dial from station to station, certain I was in heaven. I couldn't remember a more perfect day—until Mother came out, made me spit my gum into her hand, and scolded me about my teeth. Even that couldn't ruin it. On the car ride home, she reprimanded me for playing the radio too loud, but I could hardly wait to find a quiet spot in the house where I could be alone with it.

From that day forward I spent every spare moment with my music. I wrote down the names of bands and songs, keeping a list of favorites in a notebook hidden in my dresser. I belted out lyrics when no one was around, which wasn't often. I even chose music over the family's Sunday night television ritual, unless the guests were groups I wanted to see.

One Sunday evening, I was stretched across Rob's bed with the radio pressed to my ear, turned down so low I had to strain to hear. Lost in the music, I barely noticed the rest of the family in the living room. I felt so comfortable—until the Marine grew irritated with something on the show. On his way back from re-filling his whiskey glass, he spotted me.

"What are ya doin', queer bait?" he barked. "Give me that thing, ya stupid little fag; you deserve nuthin'!"

As he reached for my radio, I instinctively pulled it tight against my chest and rolled face down, using my body weight to shield it. The Beatles still sang as we fought. He yanked at my arms while I clawed and scratched, teeth bared like a dog in a tug of war. The Marine reached under me, flipped me into the air, and slammed me back on the bed. I kicked wildly, but he finally tore away my lifeline, holding it like a prize.

I stared through tears as he grinned with evil delight. Slowly, deliberately, he twisted and crushed it. The volume wheel snapped off, and for a split second I thought I heard the Beatles scream for help—as I was doing inside. With every snap and grind, another piece of my heart broke. Time seemed to halt as shattered pieces hung in the air like suspended notes—melodies and harmonies drifting beyond my reach. The Beatles, Dave Clark Five, and the Righteous Brothers seemed to claw for the antenna, struggling to catch the wavelengths of my hopes and dreams. I stretched out my hands, desperate to rescue them, but watched helplessly as the music collapsed, obliterated under his army boots.

Misshapen gray shards scattered across the floor, batteries rolling away as if fleeing the wreckage. The wrist strap dangled from his belt buckle as he reached for the leather strap—and with it, a storm of rage rose from the depths of my heart and soul.

Impulsively, I jumped to my feet and swung at him, crying out in protest—only to be knocked back where I had started. He ripped off his leather belt and beat me senseless as the radio's wristband fell to the floor. After the first few blows from the buckle, I lost all inhibition. I screamed, kicked, clawed, and tried to roll off the bed. He struck again and again. I howled in pain, fell to the floor, and he kicked me in the stomach, sending me onto the broken radio pieces. As he bent to grab me, I rolled under the bed, pressing against the wall, gasping for air. He was going to kill me. I didn't care—part of me wanted him to. But even more, I wanted to hurt him back.

It took only a moment for him to lift the bed off its frame and hurl it across the room. He yanked me up by the waistband of my jeans and flung me onto the dining room floor. I landed hard, breathless, certain it was my last breath. I glared up at his furious red face, daring him. He hauled me nose to nose by the front of my shirt, squeezing my throat until I dangled like a puppet. Then, with a final slam to the floor so violent I thought I'd crash through to the basement below, he let go.

Cursing, he stormed out the kitchen door.

This was a defining moment—a day of all days. For the first time, I retaliated. My bravery didn't come from courage but from a deep chasm finally broken, and like my radio, the damage was irreversible.

I sat motionless on the floor, wracked with pain and unable to process what had just happened. Mother stood in the living room, mouth agape, frozen in place. The others had run when they heard the Marine explode. I would have too, if it hadn't been me. Rob came down the stairs and sat beside me; even he didn't know what to do or say. He had never fought back during one of the Marine's rages. I shook uncontrollably as he slipped his arm around me in silent support.

"Samson, what has gotten into ya? I think you should go ta yur room," Mother said almost quizzically.

She had witnessed everything and hadn't tried to stop the Marine. She would have let him kill me—or maybe not, but that's how it felt. Bruised, bleeding, and battered, I sat there abandoned. No rescue. No comfort. I felt like an outsider, an orphan. No mother, no father.

The pain cut deeper than anything the Marine had ever said or done. It had Mother written all over it, and I knew I would never see her the same way again. Tears rolled from my swollen eyes, and I brushed them away angrily. No, I thought. She was just like him—and I didn't care anymore. They would regret this.

I was so broken I wondered if I could even make it upstairs. I thought I might just die there on the dining room floor. Then Rob lifted me to my feet. It felt like floating on the wings of eagles as he half carried me to bed. He curled up beside me, placed his radio in my hands, and held me. He understood. If he could have, he would have taken it all on himself.

"You can have my radio, Sam," Rob whispered. "I was planning on getting a new one anyway."

"BEDTIME!" Gertie yelled up the stairs. Rob obeyed, said good night, and left my side.

In the bedroom, Jude muttered a few nasty remarks, but I didn't respond. I shut down, pulled the plug on my emotions, turned on my side, and curled into a ball. I wanted to cry, but nothing came. The hurt was buried deep in my chest. Clutching the radio with a death grip, I rocked back and forth, trying to push the pain and anger down until it shrank to nothing. Finally numb, I drifted to sleep. H lllll, N lllllllllllllllllllllll, J llll, M lllll.

I was almost ten, soon to join the Marine's troops. Over the next months, my life became a nightmare I could never have imagined, and music was the only salve that soothed the wounds inside me that grew each day.

CHAPTER 12

It's All in Your Head

MY INDUCTION INTO THE working world made Rob's and Jude's look like a walk in the park. For weeks beforehand, I was consumed with the nearing date. Withdrawn and anxious, my imagination produced the worst scenarios possible. It didn't help that Jude tormented me at every chance.

"You're worthless, man. Why don't you just stay home with the girls and bake cookies?" he mocked, swaying his hips like a fashion model. "You'll last five minutes, then we'll carry you out in a wheelbarrow! First snake you see, you'll keel over!" He laughed, punched me in the back, and walked away.

He carried on for weeks, using everything from bees to bears to frighten me. When I didn't respond, he used my lack of strength against me, hitting, tripping, or pummeling me whenever Rob wasn't around. He taunted that the Marine would beat me every second of every day—as if he didn't already at every opportunity.

One afternoon after school, Jude and Rob went fisticuffs over it.

"Jude! Cut the crap! Leave him alone! He has enough to worry about!" Rob shouted, landing a hard punch to Jude's arm.

The two wrestled to the ground, though Jude usually won these skirmishes. Rob made a quick move when Jude rolled to get up, jumped on his back, and held him face-down in the grass. He drove his elbow into the small of Jude's back, pinning him. I piled on to help.

"Say it, Jude, or I'll hold you here all day!" Rob ordered.

"Sorry!" Jude screamed, desperate for relief from the pressure Rob applied.

Rob gave me a quick nod, and I bolted as he leapt off Jude and followed. Jude caught us just as we yanked the screen door open. He barreled through, knocking us both down.

Gertie saw us fall and grabbed Jude by the collar as he charged inside. For a moment we thought we'd won—until Jude spun his sob story, painting Rob and me as the culprits. Covered in grass from head to toe, he played the victim perfectly.

No matter how much we protested, Mother accepted his version. Rob and I were sent to our rooms while Jude stood grinning, triumphant. Betrayed again—by both Jude and Mother.

As if dealing with Jude wasn't enough, the Marine was relentless with his jibes about attendance in his school of hard knocks. He reveled in my misery, always finding new ways to rattle my cage. He didn't need to be inventive—I suffered anxiety attacks just at the sight of him. I was obstinate, refusing to show a reaction no matter how far he pushed. Inside, though, my blood boiled. I knew I was making it harder on myself, but I would not give him the slightest satisfaction, even if it meant broken bones.

The day before I was to start working in the fields, Rob insisted I walk with him through the backyard behind the garage. We stopped near the pigeon coop, Rob nervously wringing his hands.

"You gotta understand some things before tomorrow. It's not gonna be easy, Sam," he said gently. "It's hard work. I hate it. You're gonna despise it. I wish there was something I could do so you wouldn't have to go, but there's no way to stop this."

"What do you guys do out there all day? Where do you go? Will there be snakes like Jude said? Is *he* with you all day? What's it like?" I fired a million questions.

Rob explained as best he could. I was panic-stricken. Tears rolled down my cheeks, and by the time he finished, I wanted to run away.

"Let's go, Rob. Let's run away! We could be so far gone before tomorrow no one would ever find us!" I begged.

"Where to? Where would we sleep and get food? How would we get away?" Rob asked. "He'd find us and kill us anyway, Sam."

He was right, but I still wanted to be far away. His reassurances didn't work.

That night I prayed harder than ever. Where was God? Why wasn't He listening? I stayed awake most of the night. By sunrise, fear turned to indignation and then resolve. "Fine!" I thought. "If I have to do this, everyone will be sorry. If I go down, everyone goes with me. He will not see me sweat!"

Well, maybe not everyone, I decided, as I marched behind Rob and Jude. Passing my sister's room, I felt a twinge of disappointment. It was spring break, and instead of sleeping in and playing, I was going to "become a man."

After breakfast, my brothers went to load the pickup with the day's equipment. I was summoned to the Marine's office and stood, as Rob and Jude had before me, in front of his desk. He followed his daily script: a few "you bastards," multiple "faggots," and several death threats, droning on with his interrogation. I didn't really hear a word. I had gone so deep inside my mind that focusing was impossible. He ended with more threats and then slapped me so hard my vision went black for a moment.

It was a tight squeeze on the front seat beside my brothers and Auggie. As we pulled out of the driveway, I closed my eyes and listened to the radio that sputtered with more static than music. Jude rattled on to our father, while Rob tried not to crush me against the door. Just as I thought I'd lose my breakfast from the Marine's erratic driving, a woman pulled out in front of us.

He slammed the brakes, throwing us into the dash. Cursing furiously, he rolled down the window and shouted at her—and then at nearly every car and truck for miles. Out of the corner of his eye, he caught my attempts to hold back vomit.

"You puke in this truck, you worthless little bastard, and you'll be licking it up!"

I pressed back into the torn seat, careful to avoid the spring sticking through. Closing my eyes, I held my breath as visions of licking the filthy truck floor filled my head.

We made a sharp left onto a dirt road so riddled with potholes our heads bounced off the ceiling and each other. Along the way, scores of trucks and campers lined the road, people clustered around them even this early in the morning. The path wound for miles through thick woods before opening onto a vast field that seemed endless. Everywhere I looked there were trees, bushes, and shrubs—but no houses. Men worked alongside children, some younger than me.

The truck lurched to a stop. The Marine barked orders. Rob reached past me for the handle, and the door swung open so fast I spilled out onto the ground. Rob and Jude moved quickly, but as I scrambled up, the Marine grabbed me and slammed me against the truck.

"You listen here, you worthless faggot! You get in my way or on my nerves today, I'll bury you in this field—ya hear me?" he bellowed into my ear.

I couldn't hear anything for a minute except ringing—and then it began. My brothers moved like lightning, unloading wheelbarrows, shovels, spades, and burlap.

They tossed rope down to me, but it slipped through my hands and hit the dirt. Jude shot me a dirty look as Rob jumped off the truck and landed beside me.

"Sam, just get moving. Do what we're doing. Help however I tell you. You can't just stand there. Move!" Rob whispered, scooping up the rope and pushing me forward.

And move I did. I had no idea what I was doing, but I copied Rob step for step. Out of the corner of my eye, I caught Jude sticking out his tongue and making faces, but I ignored him. I just kept moving.

After about an hour, I hit my breaking point—physically and mentally. My limbs felt detached, moving on their own as I struggled to put one foot in front of the other. I kept repeating, "Don't think! Just move!"

From the start it was clear I couldn't handle the work. Each of us was given a tree, our job to clear the weeds around the trunk. They stood taller than me, thick and stubborn, pushing back no matter how I shoved or stomped. I copied my brothers, using arms, legs, even my weight, but nothing worked. My arms lacked reach, my legs failed, and my body wasn't heavy enough to bend even small stalks. What took them minutes cost me twice the time.

Mosquitoes, gnats, and bees rose in clouds, swarming my sweat-soaked skin. Slapping at them for relief only drew the Marine's rage. He screamed at the delay, so I grabbed the very stalks that tormented me. When the first bee stung, then the second, I bolted toward mud for cover. That infuriated him. He dropped his spade, knocked me face-first into the muck, and when the third sting hit, ripped off his belt and lashed me with the buckle until I lost count.

I lay sprawled in the dirt, soaked in urine, but at least the bee stings were numb. He had found my weakness. Each time I failed at tasks my brothers managed, he piled on harsher work and sharper ridicule. With every blow, punishment, and insult, whatever hope I clung to was crushed.

At lunch I gagged with each bite, unable to swallow. The Marine came up behind me, shoving the sandwich into my mouth, forcing it down. I choked, collapsed to the ground, and vomited it all back up. Spitting on me, he kicked my side, and I prayed someone in the field would step in. Rob tried once or twice, but burdened with his own wounds, he knew distraction meant disaster for all of us.

By day's end, Rob half carried me out of the field and into the truck. I was stunned I'd survived. My skin itched with welts from stings and bites, my arms and legs burned with dirt-packed scratches, and every movement scraped against sunburn. Sitting was agony on my bruised backside.

At the house, Mother looked me over while stirring dinner. Without emotion she ordered us to the tub. Gone was the tender care she'd given Rob after his first day. There would be none for me.

Rob rushed to fill the bath while Jude tried to shove past. Rob pulled me through the door, slammed it, and locked it. He stripped off my clothes, and I slid into the tub. The warm water turned brown in seconds.

"We have to hurry, Sam. Wash quick before he gets back from the garage," Rob urged. "I know it hurts, but you have to get clean."

I dragged the rag over my arms and legs, biting back cries as the soap seared. Dunking my head into the water to rinse my hair made the sunburn sting even worse, and tears welled. When I climbed out, Rob's eyes glistened—he knew exactly what I felt, and he hated being powerless.

He slipped into the filthy water next. We left the worst of it for Jude. Being last in the tub was always miserable, but for once it wasn't me—and I smiled inside.

I eased into bed, aching everywhere, when Anne came in with her arms full of supplies: aloe for my burns, mercurochrome for cuts, and cool rags for bruises.

"Here, Sam, let me put this on you," she said softly. "You poor thing, I'm so sorry."

She blew on my cuts to ease the sting as she dabbed the red liquid. Humming softly, she spread aloe over my arms and face. Tears slid down my cheeks at the first hint of kindness, and I felt both ashamed and grateful. She held me close, brushing my hair back. As I pulled the sheet over myself, the fresh strap marks on my back and thighs showed.

"Wanna know a trick I use to make the whippin's hurt less?" she asked. I nodded. "Look," she whispered, lifting her shirt to show double waistbands. "Wear a couple pairs of underwear. It helps."

That was genius. From then on, I planned to wear as many as I could fit. She was the smartest nine-year-old I knew.

"Rob told me you did great today. He said you worked hard and were strong. I'm proud of you, Sam," she whispered.

Her words carried me into sleep. When the dinner call came, I had no strength to move. I hadn't kept down a bite of lunch, and waves of nausea killed any thought of food.

Apparently, my absence at the table wasn't noticed, because the next thing I remembered was my brothers climbing into bed. Gertie came in, said goodnight, and bent over me. "You need ta toughen up, li'l man. Tomorrow's comin' quickly," she whispered. I turned away as she tried to kiss my forehead.

By week's end, the Marine's barrage of abuse had broken my spirit. He went out of his way to use me as an example—as if he needed one. Days slid into weeks, and I couldn't take it much longer. I had to get creative. I tried everything to escape the fields, inventing stories and faking illnesses I'd read about or heard on the news. I pressed a hot wash rag from the radiator to my forehead to feign fever. I coughed, gagged, even forced myself to vomit—but never won reprieve.

I sat at the window in the cold months or turned the box fan on high, praying to catch pneumonia. I stood near sick classmates, even considered throwing myself down the stairs. When I succeeded, I reveled in the rare reprieve, lying in bed lost in daydreams. But I grew dangerously preoccupied with sickness and death. Guilt always followed, driving me to confession, begging for relief from a God who seemed busy elsewhere.

By midsummer, I resigned myself to my plight. Instead of seeking escape at home, I found it in the fields. Knowing I'd be beaten anyway, I turned belligerent—entertainment for my brothers as we worked. Channeling anger and frustration, I mocked the Marine behind his back, threw mud balls, and coaxed the others to defy him. Their laughter fueled me. Comedy became my shield, giving me courage to face whatever came. My brothers thought I'd lost my mind, but my antics lightened the days—except when punishment dampened them. I grew incorrigible, defying the Marine more, which only brought harsher consequences. Standing my ground without reaction enraged him further.

One sweltering June day, we were hauled into the fields to unearth arborvitae and rhododendrons for one of Auggie's landscaping jobs. I kept instigating trouble until the Marine was beyond limits. At lunch, he granted a rare reprieve, giving us minutes to run through the fields. I overdid it, overheated, doubled over with stomach pain, and collapsed. Assuming another stunt, he jerked me to my feet, nearly pulling my arm from its socket. This time I cried out. He ordered me into the back of the truck.

My task was to shift each shrub from the tailgate to the front as they were loaded. Though not full grown, they were deceptively heavy. When I lifted the second one, it slipped, crashing to the ground and snapping the burlap around its roots.

The Marine saw the ball destroyed and flew into a fury. In one leap he was on the truck, yanking me up like a rag doll. Face red with rage, he hurled me into the muddy field. I landed hard on my back, the air crushed from my lungs. Pain shot through my head and spine as I rolled onto my side, gasping. My brothers bolted in fear until the Marine threatened them, forcing them back to work while I lay stunned in the mud.

Nearly half an hour later, a white-labeled truck pulled into the field. As the Marine walked over to it, Rob called out, urging me up. I sat slowly, wiped my face with my sleeve, and staggered toward the truck, still dazed. By the time I reached them, Rob and Jude were finishing the last of the rhododendrons.

"Just act like you're helping, Sam," Rob whispered.

Jude frowned, clearly resentful. To him, Rob's compassion for me was treachery, but he kept silent and threw himself into his work.

The Marine returned to the truck bed and told us we'd have to come back later for more, so we headed home. As we finished unloading the shrubs, I vomited all over myself and the driveway. Mother, hanging clothes nearby, assumed I had a stomach virus and sent me to bed, worried which of us would get it next. Infuriated by my absence, the Marine gunned the engine, tires squealing as they left to finish the job.

Alone in my room, I reeled with nausea and whimpered from the pounding headache I'd tried to hide. Later, I heard the call for dinner. Though I felt slightly better, I couldn't eat.

This time, my empty seat at the table was noticed. From below, his voice thundered: "Where in hell is that snot-nosed bastard?"

I froze, trembling head to toe, bracing for him to storm upstairs. I felt I couldn't endure another round.

"You go ahead and eat, Auggie," Mother said quickly. "I know you're starving. I'll go check where he is."

As she entered my room, I closed my eyes and pretended to sleep. She went back downstairs, and the house grew quiet until the Marine began his nightly dissertation after prayer. I slid out of bed and pressed my ear to the floor vent, relieved to hear only minor chatter. When the screen door slammed, signaling his exit to the garage, I relaxed.

After dark, I crept to the kitchen, stomach growling, hoping for a snack. Mother sat at the table making a list and turned as I entered.

"Can I have a snack? I'm hungry now," I asked flatly.

"The time ta eat was at dinner. Ya wanna sleep through it, that's yur fault," she scolded, turning back to her list.

Crushed and starving, I trudged upstairs. In the bathroom mirror, I saw myself—still filthy from the fields, blood in my hair from where I'd fallen, a bruise under my cheekbone. How could she not see the blood, the dirt, the bruises? Then I realized: She did see. She just didn't care.

The pain welled up again, deeper than anything the Marine had inflicted. She didn't ask, and I didn't tell. That had to be the reason. *She wouldn't simply ignore me … would she?*

I marched back downstairs, ready to confront her. She was still at the table.

"I got hurt today," I said, waiting for a reaction. Nothing came. I stepped closer so she could see me.

"You'll live. Are ya bleedin' to death or somethin', Samson?" she asked sarcastically.

"Actually, I am," I said, pointing to my head and leaning forward to show the blood in my hair.

She squinted, then stood, fetched a rag from the sink, and wiped at the mess.

"You're filthy. Ya shoulda bathed when the others did. You've got a cut here."

"I was sick when they were takin' baths, remember?" I winced as she rubbed the wound.

"He threw me from the back of the truck," I blurted—then instantly regretted it. Her hand cracked across my face.

"Quit makin' up stories! Don't you ever accuse your father of somethin' like that! He works hard ta put food in your mouth, and words like that shouldn't come outta it!" She was screaming louder than I'd ever heard.

"You need ta buck up and do what's asked of ya! He works hard at his occupation. You and your brothers will take over his business someday. Quit whinin' and do as you're told and stuff won't happen!"

Her voice dropped, sharp and final. "It's all in your head, Samson. Them stories is all in your head."

I couldn't believe my ears. She knew exactly what the Marine was capable of. She had stood by and watched him do worse than throw me from a truck. She'd felt his wrath herself, yet had the nerve to call me a liar, to disregard my pain. Worse still, she said I'd someday take over Auggie's business.

I may have been only ten, but I knew I never would. I was going to be someone, and that wasn't "all in my head." Forced into his work now, yes, but I would escape. Someday I'd move far away, work for a big company, wear suits, and drive a red sports car.

Frustrated, angry, filthy, and hungry, I went back to bed as waves of desolation washed over me.

The truth was, much of what happened that day—and so many others—would remain "all in my head." My efforts to convince her otherwise were futile. She denied everything with an unwavering certainty that left no room for truth.

Years later, grown and hoping for even the smallest validation, I tried again to tell her about the Marine. She brushed it aside, accused me of bitterness, and ended the conversation the same way every time: "It's all in your head, Sam."

CHAPTER 13

Pipe Dreams

MY BROTHERS AND I anticipated the relief of fall's northern breezes and the swirl of colored leaves. Winter break from the school of hard knocks was always highly anticipated by those forced to attend. My imagination ran wild as the reprieve from the fields neared. Of course, there was never real hope the abuse would end, but it felt more manageable in the house on Griffin Avenue than in both places.

It was hard to imagine this house had once been Auggie and Gertie's dream home. What about it caught their eyes or called them here? What part of the plain, boxy layout made them move in with hopes and dreams—and then fill the rooms with more of the Marine's troops? Even as children, nine of us overcrowded the space, bargaining not to be the gender that lost more room as they kept adding occupants.

We all envied Rob when he moved to the small room downstairs, once a porch that had been closed in. I'd sit on his bed and dream of a space of my own.

The only things I saw and felt were the shadowed corners of rooms heavy with sadness. Mismatched, ordinary objects seemed ready for retirement long before they were carted into this house. Sounds of frustration, pain, and fear filled the air, and there was barely space to breathe my own oxygen instead of what a sibling had just released. We were so close it felt like we shared thoughts.

We never questioned when we passed a sibling half hidden beneath a bed or sitting cross-legged in a damp, mildew-smelling basement corner. We were professionals at seeking even the smallest spot to call our own, though peace lasted only minutes before someone found us. Quiet, uninterrupted places were impossible, so we became proficient at shutting out voices, sounds, and people altogether.

The rooms were either frigid in winter or torrid in summer. In winter, we layered clothes; in summer we fought over the box fan, begging for relief from the stagnant heat. At night I stripped to my underwear, sweat soaking the sheets, itching from insect bites, praying for a breeze. In winter, drafts poured from poorly insulated windows. I'd curl into a ball, covers over my head, conserving warmth. Barefoot, I'd sprint to the bathroom, cringing as my feet hit the cold linoleum.

Before sleep I often envisioned a place of my own—a larger house with a spacious bedroom, plump blankets for winter, window air conditioners for summer. Snacks would be at my fingertips. The dream expanded to other states far from Griffin Avenue. I pictured myself with a high-paying job, wearing suits in a well-furnished office like those on TV. I fantasized about speeding down highways in my red sports car, traveling the world, surrounding myself with things I'd never had.

At first, these dreams were empty of people because I craved space. Over time, they filled with those I longed for. Too often, though, I imagined steering that red car off a cliff—dying, then rising as someone else. Sadly, I'd wake in the same room, the same house, with the same Marine and mother. I'd reassure myself that someday, through hell or high water, life would be different, and I'd rock myself to sleep.

Despite all the horrendous events in the fields, I had grown to love the outdoors. Clouds against the blue sky, random sunbeams, brilliant sunrises, and looming sunsets casting shadows across the fields were breathtaking. The trees, offering their colorful leaves to the winds, filled me with sadness and wonder. I imagined how cold and alone they must feel, standing naked and unprotected against winter's elements. My deficiencies were many, but not when it came to imagination. I used it to escape, even if drifting away for a moment carried a high price. On a particularly hard day, I did just that. My mind wandered with the fall leaves in a breeze, and sure enough, pain and disappointment quickly replaced wonder.

My name is Billy and I live in a nice home with three bathrooms. I am ten years old and have my own bedroom with a big bed. Airplanes hang from my ceiling. I have three tall windows, a private bathroom with sailboats on the walls, and a bathtub with big feet where I can disappear beneath the clear water. My room has baskets filled with trucks and cars, but my favorite things are the bookshelves like the library's. They're filled with books I can read whenever I want. In the corner stands a radio I can play as loud as I like. Sometimes I just lie on my bed, look at the stars painted on my ceiling, and listen to music.

My mom and dad's room is next door so they can hear me if I have a nightmare. When I do, they let me crawl into bed with them. I also have a dog named Max who sleeps with me. My dad puts us to bed at night, reads stories, and tucks me in, even when he's tired. He wears dark blue suits, white shirts, and striped ties to his important job. His hands are always clean. He takes me for ice cream and movies with popcorn. He's building a swimming pool in our backyard so we can swim every day. In California it never snows—it's always sunny and warm, and there are no bugs. My dad loves to fly kites with me.

My mom is very pretty and wears ribbons in her hair to match her dresses. She smiles a lot, cooks hamburgers and fries, and always makes cake for dessert. She hugs, kisses, and dances with me and my dad. I have a little brother and sister, but Mom and Dad love me best because I'm the oldest. Mom bakes cookies, lets me sit with her on the porch swing, sings to me, plays pretty music all day, and planted flowers with me in our yard.

I go to school sometimes and get good grades because it's easy. My teacher, Ms. P, is nice and decorated our room like a jungle. She loves me, gives me candy from her treasure chest, and surprises us. I have many friends in my class, and we have fun making things to hang on the walls. I love going home after school because my family is always waiting in the driveway.

My dad once took only me on vacation to the beach. It isn't far—I can see it from my bedroom window, just past the mountains. He drives a fancy red car with a removable roof. He told me he loves me so much he'll buy me a red sports car when I turn sixteen. When I grow up, I want to be just like him.

"Samson, ya lazy queer, git it in gear. Are ya deaf or somethin'?" the Marine barked as he kicked me in the side of the head, sending blood gushing from my nose. "Ya better stop that nose or I'll leave ya here in this field to bleed to death."

I rolled, jumped to my feet, and stood with hands cupped in blood.

When the Marine moved a few rows ahead, Rob grabbed a rag from the truck and held my head back to slow the flow. As it eased, I whispered to him about the daydream I'd just had.

"Sam, those aren't daydreams. Those are pipe dreams—'cause none of that's ever gonna happen. Now hurry up and git movin' before he sees us talkin,'" Rob said as we went back to work.

CHAPTER 14

Answered Prayer

WHILE MOST CHILDREN OUR age filled free time with extra-curricular activities—little league, school sports, or swimming at community pools—Rob, Jude, and I worked. Not only in the fields but also as laborers on Auggie's landscaping and remodeling jobs. We spent the hottest days pulling weeds, sifting soil for rocks, and hauling every kind of tool and plant imaginable. We mixed cement with hoes, held boards in place, and dug holes for flowers at some of the most beautiful homes in the area. We'd dream that, one day, we would live like "the other half," as Auggie described them. We watched mournfully as children played and swam in the pools we landscaped around. Sometimes customers showed compassion and brought us treats or drinks, but more often they simply watched from windows, inspecting our work.

We preferred private homes because the Marine's temper was checked by residents' watchful eyes. There, the three of us could work without his endless taunting and criticism that came with fieldwork. Still, I discovered quickly that this environment didn't excuse slowing down or grant any special privileges. One day I slacked off more than usual and paid dearly as soon as we reached the driveway on Griffin Avenue. It took the Marine less than a minute to exit the truck, pull off his belt, and reach the passenger side door. As we stepped out, all three of us were beaten into the house. It wasn't uncommon for everyone to be punished for one person's mistake. Once he started swinging, he didn't care who was on the receiving end. These post-job punishments grew more frequent as the weather grew hotter and his patience thinner. More often than not, despite longing for play, we silently wished for longer hours of sunshine to keep us at work, knowing full well what leaving the job site meant for us.

On a cloudy Saturday in late October, we arrived at a wealthy family's home to begin building a retention wall along their driveway. Our job was to haul rocks and mix the mortar to hold them in place. The skies threatened rain, just as we had prayed, and after hours of lugging back-breaking pieces of flagstone it began to sprinkle. The Marine, frustrated that we couldn't finish, told us to clean up and load the truck before the skies opened. While we followed orders, he went to the door to inform his clients we would return the next day. Rob, Jude, and I were elated, whispering ideas for how we'd spend the rest of the day. Our prayers had been answered, and we felt light on our feet.

Looking forward to the afternoon's freedom, we moved quickly. Just as we finished loading the truck and climbed in, the homeowner came running through the rain and handed each of us an ice-cold bottle of Coke®. Smiling, he praised our hard work. We thanked him and immediately opened the bottles, savoring every drop. We usually only got this special treat on Fridays, and lately there hadn't been enough money even for that. Auggie smiled and thanked the man, but as soon as we reached the end of the driveway, he screeched the truck to a halt and began reaming us out for accepting the forbidden treat.

"You li'l bastards made me look bad back there when ya took them Cokes, so ya can consider that yur Friday Coke coz ya won't be gittin' one then. Ya all will pay for that," he screamed, spitting on Jude as he spoke.

Spirits dampened, we sat back quietly, holding the now-empty bottles. Passing one large home after another, we made our way, the Marine scolding us and cussing at other drivers. He pulled the pickup into the lot of a small tavern he occasionally frequented. We looked around at each other, unsure whether to be excited or frightened by this diversion. He rarely stopped anywhere with us in tow.

He rolled the windows halfway up and leaned toward us with a smirk. Grabbing and twisting my arm, he shouted loud enough for anyone nearby to hear. "If ya dirty li'l bastards move from this truck for *any* reason whatsa ever, ther'll be hell ta pay, ya hear me? It's a damn good thing you ungrateful shits took them Cokes coz now ya won't be thirsty and you'll have somethin' ta piss in while I go in and handle some business," he barked sarcastically.

Slamming the door, he went inside the bar, leaving us staring wide-eyed after him.

The three of us sat side by side in the truck, unmoving for a long while. It became clear he wasn't returning anytime soon. We shifted around, stuck our hands out the window to catch raindrops, and complained about wanting to leave. As the rain stopped, the hot afternoon sun peeked from behind the clouds, heating the asphalt. Humidity rose, and we began to sweat. Fearing the Marine's return, we argued about whether to open the windows further but decided against it, not wanting another reprimand.

Hours passed, and each of our once-empty Coke bottles became full, filling the truck with an acrid urine smell. We grew thirsty, hungry, and miserable from the heat and stench. Sweat soaked our dirty T-shirts. We tried to amuse ourselves by playing games and counting cars by color or make. We tried anything our minds could conjure, but the situation grew grimmer by the hour.

People entering and leaving the tavern gave us little notice. Just as we decided to crack the doors for air, the Marine appeared in the doorway, waving to those still inside. Inebriated, he stumbled across the lot, tripping over potholes. Swaying and nearly falling, he relieved himself at the back of the truck. Then he noticed the cracked doors. Angrily, he yanked the passenger side open. The full bottles and the stench hit him immediately, and he ordered us out.

"Are youse sonsobinches-ches stupid or sonthin'?" he slurred. "What kinda stupid ashfole wouldn't empty his own piss out in a parkin' lot?"

Frightened and puzzled, we stood there wondering how we were supposed to empty the bottles when he'd warned us not to open the doors. We dumped them behind the truck as the Marine fumbled for his belt. Still confused, we froze. He clumsily struck at us again and again, hollering profanities each time he missed.

A few minutes later another truck pulled into the lot. The driver parked beside Auggie's and sat watching behind reflective sunglasses. The Marine gave a few more licks with the belt, then bored of us, turned his anger toward the man.

"What chu lookin' at? Ya got somethin' ta say? Comemon out here and say it ta my face, ya sonsafinches!" he yelled, swaying.

The man didn't respond, just moved toward his own door. Tired, hungry, thirsty, and stinging from the belt, we climbed back into the truck. We each prayed this ordeal was over. Our hopes dissolved as Auggie sang all the way home with the radio blaring. He could carry many things, but not a tune.

By mid-November, we had spent many rainy afternoons in the tavern's parking lot in the insufferable heat, waiting for the Marine. Thankfully, our prayers were answered again when the seasons changed and granted us mercy. The days grew shorter and jobs thinned out. We were finally released to enjoy some semblance of a normal life.

We began anticipating the holidays and all they brought. Each of us made private lists of the things we hoped for and the gifts we wished we could somehow give. We returned to battles with army men and G.I. Joes. But things were different now. As we played the games we had loved before turning ten, something was missing. Something inside each of us—or perhaps in the toys—was gone. And no matter how hard we tried, we knew we'd never get it back again.

CHAPTER 15

Serendipity

ONCE IN A BLUE moon, good things occurred without explanation. Unexpected moments of pure wonder—when weakness became strength, divisions became unity, and adventure outweighed fear. When hills turned into mountains and dirt became the weapon of choice in battles of boys forced to be men, raindrops became healing waterfalls in the imagination of the captive. These rare flashes of joy helped make our days bearable. They are the memories stashed away, resurfacing years later as golden nuggets reminding us that life still holds good, no matter what we grow to believe. Few and far between, when they came, we seized them.

My brothers and I worked to exhaustion most days, but on one hot spring break day, serendipity rode in on a warm breeze and we weren't about to let it pass unnoticed. We were farther back in the fields of trees and shrubs than ever before. No roads or farm buildings were visible—only nature stretched for miles in all directions. I spun in circles, soaking in the beauty and freedom, imagining we were the only people left on earth. Just us— the four of us—though I muttered that even that was one too many for my liking.

Luck struck when the spade the Marine was using split in half. The spare one was loose as well. He cussed, ranted, and threw the spade into the trees. It had been a productive day, and though he hated to waste it, he had no choice but to leave us there and drive into town for a replacement. Before leaving, he delivered his customary lecture, laced with threats and degrading scenarios, and ordered us to haul the dug-up shrubs and trees to the end of the dirt road by the time he returned. Then he drove off, leaving us with some water, a dolly, and the dust kicked up by the truck's rear tires.

Jude began ordering us around, but Rob reasoned that if we finished the job quickly, we'd still have plenty of time for fun. Motivated, we hustled, loading shrubs and trees onto the dolly. Most were so heavy it took all three of us to position them. Moving them was another matter. We threw our whole bodies onto the back handle to lift the front end off the ground, then pushed with everything we had to get the wheels rolling.

Just as we finished, a storm cloud rolled in. As rain sprinkled down, we danced, letting dirt and sweat wash away. I lobbed a dirt ball at Jude and a war erupted. Minutes later dirt balls became mud balls, and we ran behind trees to launch volleys before retreating for more ammunition. The cooler breeze and sheer fun revived us.

Exhausted from battle, we loaded each other onto the dolly, pushing one another down the paths. Arms wide, we laughed and squealed as the breeze dried us. On a downhill slope, two of us boarded at once while Rob pushed, running hard to build speed. The dolly flew, lifting him off the ground so he shared the ride. We played until we nearly wet ourselves—until the rumble of the truck returned us to reality.

There were other times when we were gifted with the Marine's absence and played hide-and-seek in the orchards. Trees heavy with fruit supplied ammo for food fights—painful when they connected, but the sting was worth the fun of landing a hit.

One of my best memories came when we discovered a cornfield at the end of a tree-lined path. It was early summer, and we ran through the rows pretending to be explorers lost in a jungle searching for treasure. To our amazement, treasure is exactly what we found. At the edge of the field lay a patch of ripe strawberries.

We stood there, a starving band of adventurers, staring as if they were the last food on earth. The risk of punishment weighed heavily, but we agreed without words—they were worth it. We split up like a recon unit, scouting for danger. Finding none, we devoured the sweetest strawberries we had ever tasted, juice running down our chins and staining our shirts. To our relief, the Marine never noticed.

I searched for years to find strawberries as sweet as those, but nothing ever came close.

There were also days when we sat in the hot summer sun, covered in mosquito bites, sunburn, and bee stings, desperate for an ounce of hope. These moments came without reprieve from his presence—scattered through time like small blessings with huge impact.

Sometimes we'd open our lunch sacks to find that Mother had dug past the inch-thick oil in the government peanut butter jar to make sandwiches, instead of the detestable SPAM we usually ate. Other times, when she had a few extra coins in her purse, a true prize waited beneath the sandwich—a chocolate-iced cupcake. Nothing brought more thanks to God or sighs of relief. We'd nibble slowly, stretching the pleasure as long as we could.

On days like these, I dared to think maybe there was hope. Yet my young mind often concluded I didn't deserve more—that I was so despicable a human being that I should be thankful for whatever little I received.

CHAPTER 16

Obedience

I WAS SO EXCITED I was literally trembling. My knees felt like jelly and I felt a little lightheaded. I took extra time in the bathroom making sure not a hair was out of place. I smiled at myself in the mirror and then put on the most serious look I could because this was going to be a very serious day. I went over again and again the procedures I had been taught. Rob and Jude added the dos and don'ts the night before. I just knew I was going to be the best ever, even if I was a little older than most. I had waited so long and I admit I was jealous of Rob and Jude when they were old enough before me. I'd watch them during Mass, studying all they did and then critiquing them all the way home. Today was my first day on the job as an altar boy and I went into the church feeling ten feet tall.

Of course, I don't remember much of it. It was a foggy, incense-filled drama come true. Father Bernard, newer to our parish, patted me on the head and said I had done an excellent job. I had grown to really like him in the seven months since he joined the parish. All the kids loved his joking, friendly manner. I made it a habit to check which father was taking confessions and always waited for his line. His warm, reassuring voice and attentive questions made me feel that what I said and felt mattered. He made being an altar boy special. Sometimes, after the last Mass, he treated those he thought had done an exceptional job to ice cream from the ice cream man. I was picked every time for some reason, and I bragged to Rob and Jude. We would run out of the church as soon as we heard the jingle from the old carnival van.

Only one other boy besides me was usually invited, so I felt even more special when, for several weeks, I was the only one asked. Cones in hand, we walked to a nearby bench and sat giggling, trying to keep up with our fast-melting treats. Father Bernard showed me how to lick an ice cream cone quickly so it wouldn't drip—running his tongue one way, then back the other, and finally cramming the whole thing in his mouth with the cone sticking out as he tried to talk. We laughed until we were covered in melted drips. When he dropped me home, shirt and tie splattered, Gertie never complained. She whisked me upstairs to change, scrubbing the stains while giggling about the "holy" ice cream, probably dreaming I'd be a priest one day.

In the beginning of seventh grade at "Holy Hell," I spent more time than ever with Father Bernard. The Marine mocked my "new friend," but never stopped me unless work was involved. Father Bernard taught me chess, and we wrestled in the yard playing our own version of flag football. He explained priesthood in ways I could understand, and I began to wonder if I was being called. He encouraged me to volunteer at church and school events, always showing up to support me. When he heard I was struggling in a subject, he tutored me after school. My grades soared, and it felt like the only time I was truly happy was when I was with Father Bernard.

During the final semester of seventh grade, he sent Jude to pull me out of class. Jude, a school hall monitor, came rushing into Sister Mary Alice's class, chest puffed out and sash across him with pride. He thought I was in trouble and teased me all the way to the church where Father Bernard was waiting. He thanked Jude and sent him on his way. I was puzzled why he wasn't meeting me in his office as usual. He hurried me through the church, past the altar, and into the sacristy. Afraid I had done something wrong putting away the communion supplies after last Sunday's Mass, I blurted an apology just in case. He didn't respond.

We entered the sacristy and he closed and locked the door. It was a windowless room holding all the service supplies, with a sink in the back corner. *Why are we in here?* I thought.

As I watched, he removed the cincture from his waist and handed it to me to fold on the table. A million thoughts ran through my mind. The room felt warm, and I began to sweat. He pointed to the wall and softly told me to switch off the light. I walked slowly to the switch as he lit a candle.

"It's going to be okay, Samson," he said as I flipped the switch. "You trust me, don't you? You have nothing to fear. Good, young man, now come over here beside me."

I swallowed hard when he told me to take off my shirt. I couldn't imagine why, but I obeyed. Then he told me to remove my uniform pants, and that's when I felt something was wrong— but I obeyed again. My heart pounded so loudly I was sure he could hear it. Then he instructed me to lower my briefs. I stood frozen, staring at him through the candlelight, shaking from head to toe.

I didn't know what to say or do. I loved Father Bernard. He was the closest thing to a loving father and friend I had ever known. I trusted him, yet I wondered why I would need to take off my underwear. Did he think I was hiding something? I hadn't stolen anything from the church. Still, I pulled them off. He could see I wasn't hiding anything. He looked at me from head to toe and mumbled prayers.

After several minutes, he removed his cassock. We stood there naked. I thought maybe this was some ritual before taking on more duties as an altar boy. For a moment I was angry at Rob and Jude. Why hadn't they told me about this? What if I did something wrong? How was I supposed to know what to do? I searched for any reason to be standing naked with the priest.

When he had nothing more to remove, he began to touch me. I was confused, disgusted, excited, scared, and embarrassed as my body betrayed me. It responded to his touch. I felt wonderful and horrible at once. I tried to back away and fell to the floor. It hurt—no, it didn't. This can't be right. It can't be wrong—he was a priest. I won't do this. I have to. This is terrible. All I could think of was Father Bernard and me eating ice cream and laughing. Just when I thought it must be over, it began again.

In the end, he apologized. He cried and said he couldn't help himself. Then he became angry. He told me I had seduced him all along. I didn't even know what *seduced* meant. He accused me of being sneaky, of making him want me. I couldn't believe what I was hearing. After what felt like forever, he ordered me to wash up at the sink and put my clothes back on.

I obeyed, still trembling. He dressed in silence. When he switched on the light, he stared into my eyes for what felt like forever and sighed.

"We have a wonderful time together, don't we, Samson?" he asked, touching my face. "If you tell anyone, they'll make me leave the parish. I won't be able to help you or spend time with you. They'll take away your altar boy privileges. Imagine what your parents, your father, and your brothers would think. You'd be ridiculed for being attracted to other boys and men." He blessed me.

"But I'm not …" I lied as my voice trailed off.

I had no idea how he knew about the feelings I had for other boys. I had never spoken them out loud. If he knew, then my heavenly Father knew—and that was another matter altogether. Who else knew?

He ordered me to tell no one, and I obeyed.

CHAPTER 17

Rules of Engagement

SEVENTH AND EIGHTH GRADE were a disaster waiting to happen. Between Father Bernard and the chaos of working with the Marine, life was unraveling. Then Rob graduated from "Holy Hell" and moved on to public school. I was a mess, and nothing seemed to improve. One by one, everything I tried fell apart.

When I entered seventh grade, Jude was a star on the football team. Rob had been the star in his final two years at "Holy Hell." They forged a path difficult for anyone to follow, and I was far from normal. On the Marine's orders, I worked hard and tried out. The coach must have pitied me, because I made the team. Once again, two of Auggie's pride were playing, and the team won almost every game—no thanks to me.

There on the sidelines, a few feet from Father Bernard, stood the Marine, barking orders, inebriated and foul-mouthed. We tried to pretend we didn't know him, but everyone else did. Our coach despised him and had him removed several times. He cursed, flicked cigarettes onto the field, and threatened other parents in the bleachers. His attendance could have been meaningful—he never showed up for anything else—but the embarrassment outweighed any benefit. He stripped away what little enjoyment there was in playing.

I rarely got called from the bench, but when I did, I ran in with all the pride and gusto I could muster. I studied the rules, knew the plays, and imagined myself as strong and coordinated as my brothers. But the dream was short-lived. As soon as the ball was snapped, I'd find myself under hundreds of pounds of sweaty, angry players—and off the field I'd go, humiliated.

At the end of the season, bruised and battered but not defeated, I actually started a game. Two or three plays in, I was hit by an unusually large player. I landed hard and could barely breathe. I tried to get up, but pain shot through my shoulder, neck, and head. The Marine hollered at me to "get my sorry self up." I rolled over and crawled to my feet. The coach let me stay in, but with each play I was hit again and again.

I pushed through. We were winning, and I desperately wanted to be part of it. By the final horn, I couldn't move my arm, shoulder, or neck without excruciating pain. In the locker room I fumbled one-handed while everyone else celebrated. Then I walked home alone. The Marine had gone off to celebrate elsewhere, and Jude was with friends.

Gertie asked what was wrong when I came in. I mumbled something about getting hurt and went to lie down. The pain worsened with every breath. I no longer let anyone see me cry, so I lay flat, holding my arm, sweating. Later that evening, the Marine staggered into my room.

"Quit yur whining, ya li'l sissy. Yur sisters cun play better ball than you," he said, leaning, nearly falling face-first on top of me.

He swung at me but missed, then staggered from bed to dresser to doorframe, feeling his way out like a blind man.

I fought hard to keep from crying and winced with pain. I spent the night awake. Aaron recorded H, N, and nineteen marks. By morning, delirious from lack of sleep and pain, I could barely move. Jude made fun of me and punched my bad arm, sending me out of my mind.

"You touch him one more time, Jude, and I'm gonna kick yur butt!" Rob said, shoving Jude against the wall and holding him there.

The commotion brought Mother to the door.

"What's goin' on in here? Samson, what's wrong wit ya?" she asked, actually looking concerned. "Looks like a bad sprain, but since ya can't move it, I guess we should head over and have it looked at."

A few hours later, we sat in front of the doctor. It was obvious my mother didn't concur.

"No, it can't be. I think it's just a sprain in his shoulder," she insisted, giving her own diagnosis.

"Sorry, Gertie, but his collar bone is fractured. He should've been looked at right after the game. I can't believe the coach let him keep playing. This kind of injury is extremely painful. I bet you didn't sleep all night, Sam," he said, showing her the X-ray.

I felt slightly high from the pain pills and vindicated as we pulled in the driveway with my arm in a sling. Everyone ran out to see me, the injured soldier, asking questions and offering help. The Marine watched with a smile, mouthing "wimp" as I went into the house. I smiled inside because my injury excused me from working with him for the next eight weeks, should the weather hold. It was almost worth the pain.

When I recovered, I thought I'd try basketball. Rob, Jude, Anne, and Joan often played heated games in the driveway after school. I watched, memorized the rules, and was ready. The girls laughed but accepted me when Rob and Jude wouldn't take me on their team.

"You can have Rob too!" Jude shouted. "I can beat you all blindfolded and with one hand behind my back! Specially that wimp right there!" he added, pointing at me.

"Dream on!" Anne said, dribbling the ball.

His taunting spurred my sisters to push harder, and soon we were on our way to winning. The more infuriated Jude became, the harder we pressed, and in the end—with a wink from Rob—I nailed the final shot. As the ball swooshed through the net we roared with excitement, and to show what a killjoy he was, Jude knocked me down. Rob pulled him off and held him in a headlock until he conceded.

A few weeks later, Jude invited some football buddies for a "friendly" pick-up game. This was much more aggressive. I gave it my all as the Marine stood watching from the garage, sucking down whiskey and occasionally yelling orders.

"Block him, Sam. Are ya blind or somethin'?" he yelled from the garage.

So I reached to block the pass. My elbow came down hard on Jude's nose and blood spurted everywhere. I smirked, enjoying the moment. Usually, I was the one suffering injuries. The Marine flew from the garage wielding an open penknife. He grabbed the ball, stabbed it, and walked back inside.

We all stood there stunned and embarrassed. Our friends left one by one, giving lame excuses for their departures. So much for our "friendly" pick-up game. And so much for basketball— we no longer had a ball to play even with each other.

I played football in eighth grade too, but I never left the bench. Jude, the star the year before, had moved on to public school. Rob came to watch when he could, but he had new friends and high school games. He didn't miss much—our team lost every game.

I tried a few other sports—tennis, golf—and finally gave up. It wasn't that I wanted to play; I just thought I had to. I loved watching others play, but I thought trying would somehow make me like the other guys. It's not like I had a choice anyway. The Marine constantly demanded I try out for teams.

In the winter of my seventh-grade year, I was old enough to join the other "men" in the family on hunting trips. Guns were the Marine's first love, and hunting was in his blood. We fished on occasion, but hunting was the true winter ritual. Auggie packed up everything we'd need to survive if the world ended and we were stranded in the mountains. The four of us rode off imagining ourselves as mountain men. I, of course, was Daniel Boone, and we sang the words to the theme song like a mantra. We loved this new show and couldn't wait for each episode.

We arrived late at night at my grandmother's farm. Rob and Jude, already seasoned from two years of hunting, went right to sleep. I slept little, excited for morning. I had completed a hunter safety course and knew the rules. The Marine's laws of hunting were already embedded into my mind—and my hide—when he saw me holding my gun wrong. I was ready.

The first day all I managed was a possible case of frostbite. We were in the woods by five a.m. I was so tired from not sleeping and the below-zero temperatures that I fought nodding off. Rob and the Marine proudly got bucks with beautiful racks. I nearly threw up as they gutted and posed them for photos. The second day Rob and the Marine worked their way through the woods, trying to drive deer in our direction. Jude proudly displayed his buck that evening while I fought to stay awake.

On the third day, the three of them worked at driving a buck my way, and at daybreak, one came into my sights. It was so beautiful the way the sunlight hit it. It seemed to be looking at me and saying, *"Please don't shoot me."* I hesitated and couldn't pull the trigger. I inhaled, moved the sight off the deer, and fired, hoping beyond hope I hadn't hit it. The shot spooked the deer and he darted off past Auggie.

The Marine came up the slope so fast I didn't have time to lower the rifle. He grabbed my gun, pointed it at my head, and stared through the sights.

"He was in yur sights, ya miserable sissy," he shouted. "I oughta shoot ya right here and now! Ya think we're out here freezin' our asses off fur nothin'?"

I couldn't move or breathe. I believed he would shoot me right there in the woods on my grandmother's farm. He pressed the rifle against my skull, holding it there for what felt like an eternity. *Pull the trigger,* I thought. *Put me out of my misery.* He finally lowered the gun and shoved me down a snow bank, spewing obscenities as he walked away.

Needless to say, I never did get a deer. I was forced year after year to go on these torturous trips but never again would a buck or doe enter my sights.

I also considered wrestling and boxing but then looked in the mirror and quickly dismissed the thought. This body, this shell I hid in, was not built for either. The Marine loved boxing. He screamed racial slurs at Muhammad Ali and was elated when Ali lost his title for refusing the draft. He called him a wimp for not fighting for his country. I loved Ali, mostly because Auggie hated him.

The Marine had the build of a boxer and the biggest, strongest hands I had ever seen. I liked to watch matches and even did a class report on Gentleman Jim Corbett, the famous heavyweight champion, in Sister Mary Grump's class. No kidding—that was her name.

I kept searching for a sport that suited me. Baseball was out because Auggie thought it was for sissies. He probably hated it more because it fell in warm weather months—when we all worked.

So I abandoned sports and searched out hobbies. I tried airplane model building. I liked it somewhat, but the Marine took too much delight in critiquing and smashing my planes—especially if they turned out as nice as his. He'd fly his at the park with pride while mine were reduced to pieces.

Pretty much everything else was also for sissies, according to him. So I went back to my old failsafe love and threw myself into music.

The world around me seemed to be going as crazy as I was inside, with racial riots and anti-war sit-ins. Hippie and religious communes popped up across the country. It seemed the nation was splintered into hundreds of rebellious conflicts and the people would not be silenced. Love, liberation, and more love dominated televisions, newspapers, and radios. Women burned their bras and Gertie acted appalled, lecturing the girls often, though I sometimes wondered if secretly she was rooting it on.

Almost without me noticing, a love and sex revolution spread across the land, melting animosity like butter on hot bread. We were all brothers and sisters now, and everyone was either seeking out or becoming gurus in search of spiritual enlightenment—while holdouts like the Marine stood ready to "take them all out," as he often proclaimed while watching the news. I identified with every faction pushing at the seams, demanding freedom and justice for all. I felt they were somehow fighting my fight, releasing my turmoil in the war waged inside me. The rules were changing, and it couldn't happen too quickly.

Despite all the upheaval around me, in my own corner of the world, my junior high years were spent trying to please two men: the Marine and Father Bernard. I knew of only one sure way to do that—by being of service to them. And I knew all too well the rules of engagement, and the painful penalties that came if I dared not follow them.

CHAPTER 18

Education

IN THE MIDDLE OF one of the hottest days of the year, in the middle of a field of trees, Auggie decided it was time for a lesson about the birds and the bees. He was plastered, we were hot, exhausted, and not in the mood for any of his ramblings. The whole "educational moment" involved two birds mating.

"So youse see how it is done now?" he said. "And thas how the seeds is planet."

"And in case ya don't know, they NEV-ERR plants the seed in a bird who is da same sex as demself! So don' fagit dat, faggot!" the Marine added, staring me in the eye.

I caught his drift, even if his delivery was obnoxious and wrong in so many ways. Rob and I rolled our eyes as he stumbled into the hole he'd dug earlier.

Thankfully, that ridiculous display was the extent of it. I worked the rest of the afternoon with an upset stomach. It always happened when anything reminded me of Father Bernard. I thought I had buried those memories deep enough that they wouldn't be so easily resurrected. It wouldn't be so bad if I didn't feel transparent, as though everyone could see right through me and watch them replay in my mind.

Most of what I heard about sex, before Father Bernard and after, was from listening to my friends. Of course, there were the obligatory health discussions describing the reproductive organs and their functions, but never a real conversation about hormones or the experience itself. Since I was one of the few with firsthand experience, I'd sit back and just listen when the guys shared. Every so often I'd be busted when I corrected one of their comments. They'd immediately jump to attention, demanding how I knew.

"What? You didn't know that? I thought everyone knew that," I'd reply.

"Of course I knew that—I was just checking to see if you were listening!" they'd shoot back, looking confused and embarrassed. Who knew where they got their information, but there was plenty of it, and they were eager to share.

Even though times were changing and people were more open about sex, the idea of it being taboo was still ingrained in our psyche. I could tell just by the way my friends, who had all attended "Holy Hell" too, put on a brave front whenever the subject came up. I, however, had spent a reasonable amount of time researching what I could. The only thing I found in the school library was that it was a sin—period. I was confident that none of the new information out there changed that. For a sin as important as sex, why had none of it been explained in all my years of Catholic schooling?

I wanted to know just how bad of a sin it was considered and was shocked. Sex fell into the category of at least four mortal sins. Upset by my discovery, I feverishly searched the library for everything on the Catechism of the Catholic Church and mortal sins. I worried then not only for me but for Father Bernard. I also read that anyone who remained silent, did nothing to prevent someone else from sinning, took part in it, or enjoyed it was also a mortal sinner. I had to look up the meaning of *mutual* when I read about consent, but I wasn't sure whether I fell into that category or not. I did agree to meet Father Bernard after the first session, but I wasn't sure if it was obedience—or fear of losing him.

My experiences with Father Bernard gave me more of an education than anyone my age would have wanted. Deep down I knew something was wrong, but I never thought these acts were sending us both to hell without hope, as the church said. I concluded it was such a bad sin the church wasn't even allowed to speak of it. Maybe that silence was its own sin. By the time I got to the section about abstinence—which I also had to look up—I knew it was far too late. And by the end of my reading, I wondered if it would even do me any good to keep going to confession. I was certain I was headed for hell, and I was painfully aware of what hell meant.

The incidents with Father Bernard happened a few times that semester. Then, as abruptly as they began, they ended. One day I came to school and heard he had been transferred to another parish without explanation. I was devastated and relieved at the same time. For months after, I'd forget and expect him to come around a corner. When Jude, the monitor, entered my classes, my stomach still churned, but now for someone else.

I missed him terribly and felt abandoned. He had been more of a father to me than my own. The incidents confused and amazed me; I loved-hated them and him. I was left with a battlefield of feelings and memories so loud and real I sometimes thought I'd lose my mind. All I had wanted was to please him. Yet I carried a monstrous load of guilt because he always said it was me who had made him want me. I never knew what I'd done. All I wanted was for it to stop so our times could go back to ice cream, chess, and homework. I didn't realize until much later that I was grieving—not just the loss of him, but the possible loss of my faith, and the tragic loss of my soul, which I was convinced was headed to hell in a handbasket.

I also wondered who else could see through my facade. If Father Bernard knew I wasn't attracted to girls like most boys, then who else could? It had felt natural until I was told it was wrong. When I was younger, I never questioned why I felt the way I did. I recognized beauty when I saw it. Some girls were pretty, but I thought a few guys were too. I loved my brothers, sisters, and mother. I loved my father also, though I'd never admit it. I knew there were different kinds of love.

Before the incidents with Father Bernard, I wasn't out of touch—I saw couples together, but felt little about it. Watching happy couples, I only hoped I'd find someone to love too. Afterward, I convinced myself I was called to be a priest. Reading about mortal sins, I wondered if priests chose that life as penance, if maybe all were like Father Bernard. I loved the church and God and had considered priesthood before. Since I had similar leanings, maybe that was my path. Perhaps I could work my way out of hell if I stayed strong and didn't act as he had.

Not wanting to mislead any more priests, I stopped going to confession, which left me grieving my time with the fathers, the church, and God. After Father Bernard left, I developed crushes on the boys in school. By the time I left "Holy Hell" and entered public school, all I wanted was to be normal. So I forced myself to act like a normal guy and began dating girls.

It wasn't until the summer after I graduated that I had my first experience with a girl. Rob and his friends had rented a place at the beach and invited me down. A couple of girls we met joined us, and we spent the weekend drunk on the beach, dancing in the moonlight half naked and free. The last night I hooked up with one of the girls. What an education that was for both of us. She could tell it was my first time. She was confused by how I approached everything, but compassionate, showing me the ropes. I was relieved to have it over with. Afterwards, to impress the guys, I ran down the beach with her bra on my head laughing. They were impressed—I became "Sam the Man" from that day forward. We sat around smoking joints and bragging about my conquest as if I had struck gold. I did anything to cover up my true feelings. I just wanted to be one of the guys. I just wanted to be *with* one of the guys. I sat and drank, sunglasses hiding my eyes, watching the men, covered in suntan oil, walk the beach.

It was my first time with a girl, and it wouldn't be my last. Testing myself, pushing closer to "normal," I was sure. Each time was a lesson in how badly I wanted to be anyone other than myself. Sadly, I didn't realize I was searching for answers to questions that couldn't be answered.

CHAPTER 19

Vulnerable

Transferring from private school to the public high school was more than a culture shock. I couldn't wait for this moment, but when it arrived, I wasn't sure what to think. I felt like I'd walked into a movie halfway through. It wasn't the logistics. It wasn't the academics either—I was further ahead than my classmates. It was the amount of freedom and responsibility that left me unsure. I had always been told how to act, where to go, what to wear, and how to do things. Now there was this overwhelming freedom of choice. I felt vulnerable on all fronts. Everything from choosing my own classes to being allowed to express myself was new.

The rules and regulations were plain and clear—a trained monkey could master them. It was all the gray area that messed with me. Choosing what to wear alone was enough to knock my socks off. Everyone else seemed to have found their own style that worked for them. Social cliques separated themselves by attire alone. The preps wore collared shirts, the jocks wore T-shirts, the cool kids wore jeans and cut-offs, and you could identify any of them a mile away. What used to take me a minute in the morning now threw me into a quandary of choices that undermined what little confidence I had left. And this was coming from someone with only a few outfits to begin with.

I started out imitating my brothers—how they acted, what they wore, who they were—but it never felt right to me. Probably because it wasn't. I shifted between wanting to be brave enough to step out there and just be me or staying hidden behind my human fortresses, Rob and Jude, accepting their success as my own. If I continued to camouflage myself, I feared exposure sooner or later. I wasn't up for more humiliation. But if I took a chance and swung at just being me—whoever that was—I faced rejection. I wasn't up for that either. The whole issue exhausted me. I wanted teachers and fellow students to notice me, but I wasn't sure what I wanted them to see.

Rob and Jude transferred schools before I did. They seemed to fit in without even trying, or at least that's how it appeared. One morning before school, Rob came to my room.

"If you aren't ready to book in a few, I'm gonna have to catch you on the flip side, man," Rob said, glancing at his hair in the mirror.

"Can't make my mind up what to wear," I muttered, changing my shirt for the third time.

"Don't be such a spaz! That shirt is cool! Gotta split!" he said, heading down the steps.

It was so easy for him. He couldn't care less how he looked half the time. I couldn't understand where his confidence came from. I was a constant prisoner of my own insecurities. I finally chose the shirt he said was cool, and Jude and I caught up with him just as he was starting his car.

"Shotgun!" I shouted, jumping into the front seat of his cherry Mach I.

"I called dibs, you zit-faced queer," Jude said, tugging at the door.

I leaned forward to let him climb in behind me, but he wouldn't budge.

"Get in, Jude, or I'm outta here!" Rob barked.

Still, Jude stood there waiting for me to move. Rob let the car drift forward.

"Psych!" Rob yelled just as Jude reached for the back seat. He shifted gears, burning rubber halfway up the street.

I saw Jude in the rearview, waving his arms and screaming. We just kept going, laughing so hard my stomach cramped.

"That's what the rat fink gets!" Rob said, sliding a Three Dog Night tape into the eight-track. Music blasted—"Mama Told Me (Not to Come)"—with the windows down, and my worries melted away.

At a stoplight, a guy in a blue Camaro revved beside us. Rob pulled on his shades, floored it, and left him in the dust. The Camaro tried to catch up but couldn't, and we laughed as we saw him pulled over by the cops in the rearview.

"Where'd you get that hickey?" I asked, spotting the bruise on Rob's neck as we parked at school.

"For me to know and you to find out," he said as we split up for homeroom.

Man, I wished I was as cool as him. I watched him put his arm around a blonde waiting for him.

"Hmm … that's where he got it," I thought, heading to class wishing I had someone waiting for me.

After a few weeks of narrowly escaping the lunchroom and locker room freshman initiations, I felt like I was working too hard. For what, other than approval, I wasn't sure. Blending in and hiding behind my brothers gave me a pass from being stuffed into lockers or having my food messed with. Nobody wanted trouble with their younger brother. I had a few run-ins with the jocks and wedgies in the gym locker room, but aside from name-calling I was mostly unscathed—or so I thought. Even when I felt safe, I felt fake.

I wondered if everyone else was putting on the same act during the daily dramas that played out. I didn't like the friends I was making. We had nothing in common, and I wasn't happy. I'd spent so many years wrapped in required packaging to be presentable and acceptable that I was suffocating. Every now and then the real me slipped past my guard and I'd blurt something spontaneous. People would stare like I had two heads. I'd quickly pull the veil back over myself and submit to the fear.

I hated being a teenager. I felt like an old soul surrounded by children. If I stayed this dramatic with myself, I'd combust—or at least that's how it felt. Thoughts bounced around in my head like a ping pong ball, and I wondered what it would take to just quit. Quit thinking, quit the act, quit the whole miserable experience, and dare to be myself. *How much worse could it be?*

Unbeknownst to me, it was easier than I thought. Why I tortured myself I'll never know, but it all boiled down to not giving a flying fart what anyone thought. Who cares what they say? Who cares what they think? I had to face this like I faced the Marine. If I was going to hurt anyway, if I was going to be miserable anyway, then it was time to just stand. Stand up for myself? Maybe not that far. But I could stand my ground, take a chance, and just enjoy myself.

"Take a chance! I dare you!" I said out loud in front of the mirror as I checked the random outfit I chose.

I made a deal with myself not to overthink what I wore. No second-guessing. I was applying my new rules to everything—school, life, and whatever else came my way. I was putting myself out there with all my vulnerabilities. I was steel.

What's the worst thing that could happen? I thought as I walked into school.

From that day forward, things shifted. I was ready to pay the price for whatever came. I was free to choose.

It went better than I thought. The few friends I'd made early on, when I was my former copycat self, didn't blink when I drifted toward others in my classes. Mostly new friends who snuck behind the seventh wing to smoke. I didn't smoke before, but it made me look tough—and I needed to look tough to be brave. All the cool kids into music smoked, and I took to it like a fish to water. Hanging out with them felt natural.

Most were in advanced classes like me and bored with the immature social groups. Truth be told, we were bored with everything. After a few months, there were six of us who hung out regularly between classes and during study halls. When boredom won, we'd skip out, head to the park to get high, then sneak back into school, bloodshot eyes and all. Not a soul seemed to notice.

After school one afternoon I met Rob for a ride home and he saw what kind of shape I was in.

"Sam, you stoned?" he asked, smiling ear to ear as I nodded yes.

He bent over laughing. I thought he was making fun of me.

"Little Sam is gettin' high! I can't believe it, man. Don't you bogart me!"

"What, ya never saw anyone high before?" I replied, trying to joke back.

I was taking a big chance at being honest with him. I was afraid he'd judge me, reject me, or think I was worthless. But what if he didn't? Maybe he'd be disappointed, but we had history. Maybe he wouldn't hate me.

He walked over to my side of the car and pulled out a plastic bag of weed and papers, dangling them in front of my face. Life seemed so much easier when I opened myself up to possibility.

"Far out, man," I said, jumping to grab it. He pulled it away and swatted at me playfully.

I spotted Jude coming toward us and tried to warn Rob to hide the bag. I forced my eyes open wider and stood straighter, trying not to appear as wasted as I was. I was paranoid he'd fink us out to the Marine.

"Jude!" Rob yelled, waving him over. "Ya aren't gonna believe it! Come here!"

What was he doing? He's leaving me wide open! Jude will beat the crap out of me or worse, I thought angrily. *He'll rat me out to the Marine.*

Rob held the bag up to Jude and then pointed to me like it was mine. I was busted. Then Jude burst out laughing and grabbed the bag. I was two for two today. I hadn't seen those odds in a long time.

"Little brother tokes on doobies?" he teased, grabbing shotgun before I could.

"You guys both smoke?" I asked, still not believing it.

"Man, what do you think?" Jude mocked.

I watched him roll a joint and light it.

"Here, ya want a hit? It's your choice," he said, handing it toward me.

I wasn't passing it up for all the tea in China.

"Psych!" he said, pulling it back. We all laughed hysterically.

Relieved to be me—even if only temporarily with Jude—I sat back and closed my eyes as Sly and the Family Stone sang "Thank You (Falettinme Be Mice Elf Agin)."

CHAPTER 20

Choice

I SPENT MUCH OF my first year in high school either high, drunk, or both. High on whatever I could get my hands on. I became a connoisseur of ways to get high, though after a frightening acid trip where the leaves seemed to dance around me, I stuck with pot. In the late '60s and early '70s, weed and booze were cheap, and the laws lenient. If you were caught, it usually meant a slap on the wrist or being carted home to your parents.

Getting high was practically a rite of passage in those days. If it felt good, we were on it like flies on fruit. Hippies claimed hallucinogens expanded your mind, but I figured my life had been enough of a trip already. Sit-ins, protests, brotherly love—it was all about love, and no one needed it more than me.

Everyone smoked, wore cut-offs and tie-dye, and let their hair grow long, despite the Marine's protests. Braless girls with flowers in their hair proclaimed themselves flower children. The more bohemian the look, the better. Embroidered bellbottoms, muscle shirts, and flip-flops became the dress code, even in cold weather. It was "groovy" to sleep under the stars or join protests, even when no one knew what was being protested. The grooviest thing was simply being different, and I fit right in—I was already as different as it got.

My friends were mostly girls. I had more in common with them than they realized, though they seemed more interested in me than I wanted. I had a few short-lived relationships, but they always ended in friendship. I'd then immerse myself in music and getting high—it was my escape. There was nothing like drowning myself in Joan Baez, Creedence Clearwater Revival, Joe Cocker, Santana, Blood, Sweat & Tears, Crosby, Stills, Nash & Young, and The Who. I wanted to go to Woodstock so badly, but I was too young, and we'd never have gotten away with it.

I found a part-time job at a music store, and I was in heaven. Somehow, I even managed to buy my first car with what was left from my paycheck after I bought the latest albums. Between working there and with the Marine on weekends, breaks, and holidays, I was constantly on the move.

The older and stronger we grew, the more grueling the work with Auggie became. The Marine's age and condition worsened, and he made sure we picked up the slack. We spent every weekend the weather allowed working with him. He pushed us past our physical and mental limits. His abuse grew more ruthless with each passing day. He now saw us as adult opponents, so fists replaced the belt. He went for gut or kidney punches, and he'd kick us while we were down. When he did use the belt, he lashed like we were mules. It took every ounce of restraint not to kill him—or myself—to end the misery. I was no longer Samson. I was "fag" or "queer," all the time.

"Look at the li'l fag breaking a sweat. Move it, queer!" he'd chant as he walked circles around me while I worked.

Years of listening to the Marine left us searching high and low for peace of mind. And if Rob and I didn't have enough to deal with, we worried about the war. Peace signs were everywhere, but there was no peace to be found.

Young people held demonstrations all across the United States demanding an end to Vietnam. I hoped it would end before Rob had to sign up for the draft, but it didn't. We got high the day he did. When they instituted the lottery, we held our breath as numbers were drawn. The fear was indescribable. Only later did we realize we could have applied for college deferments—which probably would have driven the Marine over the edge. He was so into the war he wanted all three of us to volunteer as he had. I was surprised he didn't coerce us into enlistment at gunpoint. Each time Rob's, Jude's, or our friends' numbers weren't called, we celebrated. The fear never fully left until they called an end to it the year I graduated and instituted Selective Service.

By the time there were four Izbickis in high school, we were a force to be reckoned with. We were kids let loose in a candy store, rebelling against the strict, stifled rules of earlier years—after my initial adjustment, of course. It wasn't a flawless transition. Each of us, at one time or another, made fools of ourselves by standing to answer a teacher's question. The whole class would fall out laughing as we retreated to our seats. Auggie loathed the school because we were now the minority. He hurled racial slurs, but they fell on deaf ears.

I hadn't discovered anything in school or out that grabbed my attention. I was searching for that one vocation that would speak to me and point the way to my future. I was an above-average student pulling average grades in gifted classes. I lacked the stamina to study most days. The turmoil at home drained just about everything I had.

In tenth grade I chose a business education class and joined Future Business Leaders of America (FBLA). Designed for students interested in marketing and management, it was supposed to give me the skills needed to succeed in business. I figured, what did I have to lose?

It turned out to be my saving grace. Mr. Lebitowitz was an incredibly gifted teacher. He challenged me to dig deeper and showed me there was more to the world than I imagined. Mr. L— or Manny, once we became friends—had a unique way of turning my weaknesses into strengths. I think he saw some of himself in me. Students often chose his class thinking it would be an easy A but quickly realized it was harder than they expected.

Rumors spread that Manny was gay, but I didn't see it in him. He didn't fit the stereotype in my head, which I realized looked a lot like priests. I was surprised when he confirmed the rumors. His encouragement pushed me to put more effort into my studies, and it showed. I began excelling academically and fed off the competition. I soaked in the affirmations from teachers and peers—just a little went a long way. I was determined to leave an impression and basked in their accolades when I succeeded.

I had found my niche, and FBLA honed my skills. I had a new mission in life. I still had wars to fight inside, but now I finally felt I could win some battles.

The newfound confidence I gained felt good inside and out. I won first place in an advertising competition—fierce and intense—and my friends, who wanted it as much as I did, seemed genuinely happy for me. That, to me, is what true friendship is. The connections I made by taking this one chance, by choosing this one class, changed everything. Some of my best friends in life came from FBLA, not only because of shared interests and goals but because they became the family I needed while my own was failing with no end in sight.

In my senior year I became state president and Student of the Year. Local newspapers published stories about me, and friends and relatives called with congratulations. I was livid when my parents tried to take credit. I had worked hard and was proud, but unless it was in print the people I wanted to be proud of me never showed interest. It was obvious to anyone with eyes that it was Auggie's recognition I was working for, but I never succeeded. I often wondered what I might have achieved if I had even a fraction of the support, guidance, and encouragement throughout childhood that I later received from friends and advisors.

By the time I graduated with honors, I had chosen a college. Manny had become both a close friend and advisor. He had integrity, and unlike Father Bernard, expected nothing in return. His humor and energy were refreshing. He reminded me that love and commitment were real, and that friendship was a gift that kept on giving. Often I felt I owed him for saving my life in high school, but I knew he wasn't one to collect on that debt.

I could see light at the end of my long dark tunnel. I finally knew what direction I was heading educationally. I knew what I was and what I wanted to be. I knew the *what*, but it would take years of struggling—emotionally, physically, and mentally—before I ever figured out the *who*. My new success and accomplishments were one thing, but the internal turmoil was still very much alive. I knew what I had to do, but I couldn't reconcile that with what I had been taught and what I truly believed deep inside. So, with all my newfound knowledge and every ounce of courage I could muster, I waltzed into Anne's room and spilled my guts. She was sitting there alone, studying. I shut the door and blurted the words I had never spoken out loud in quite the way I was about to.

"I'm going to be a priest. I'm going away to college for communication and advertising, and then to seminary," I said with confidence.

"Okay?" she answered, her eyes full of questions.

"I'm pretty sure that I am gay, Anne, so I have no choice. I have to be a priest now, otherwise ..." I said, my confidence faltering as the words came out.

She looked at me, smiled, and gave me the most important advice I had yet to hear.

"Why would you want to be a priest? Just be yourself, Sam. I know you have strong religious convictions. I know you love God and the church. But being gay isn't a reason to be a priest.

I'm sure there are some who are. Just be yourself, go to school, figure it out step by step, one day at a time. Make sure your reasons are right if you still choose to serve God in that capacity. But for God's, yours, and everyone else's sake, don't do it just to keep from acting on your sexuality. That will never work."

If anyone should have known, I should have known that no words were more truthful than the ones she just spoke. My experiences with Father Bernard alone should have brought me to this conclusion, but guilt and shame still clouded my view. She didn't know about him and me, and I had already spilled enough to her that day. This would take more thought and prayer.

I missed being fully active in the church. It affected my relationships all around. I missed confession and communion. Even though I still attended, Mass left me feeling empty. I still felt a longing to be a priest every now and then. But was I using it to hide from myself if I went forward and committed myself to the church and God? How else was I supposed to deal with what had been drilled into me as sin?

I felt naked standing there, having told her I was gay. What astonished me most was her love and acceptance of me no matter who or what I was. We talked for a while, but I don't remember much else. I had already heard the words I had needed for a very, very long time.

"Just be yourself, Sam," she whispered as I left. I had never seen that as a possibility. It wasn't a choice. I didn't choose to be who I am. I didn't choose to be gay. Who in their right mind would? I couldn't imagine anyone. I sighed and realized, for the first time ever, that it was my only choice.

CHAPTER 21

Knitting at Stop Lights

THE CONDITIONS ON GRIFFIN Avenue had a way of motivating all of us one way or another. We each found our own forms of escape. None did it quite as well as Anne. She gave new meaning to the word *escape*. No one could ever find her in the same place at the same time if their life depended on it. She wasn't afraid of anything—except the Marine—or at least she never let anyone see her fear. She endeavored to try anything once and usually mastered it. No one matched her energy level as she multitasked her way through and past every obstacle. If someone told her she couldn't do something, she'd do it just to prove them wrong—and do it better than anyone else.

Of my three sisters, Anne was the Marine's target. He was relentless in his pursuit to make her miserable. If they were found in the same place at the same time, a guaranteed knock-down, drag-out altercation followed. The Marine didn't restrain himself physically with Anne, and no matter how much his beatings hurt, she toughed them out. It was the verbal abuse that echoed in her heart, mind, and spirit. He was a master of word wars, landing debilitating blows at the precise moment, stealing the victory from her every time. Then he pummeled her further with his final fatal words. She fought back, trying not to give him the satisfaction as she grew older, but he stole it every time. The Marine was well trained at profiling his enemy.

If she dressed up or down, it didn't matter—he always had some kind of smart remark. She made it a point to leave early for school to try and avoid him. In warmer weather, we all wore cut-offs, and on a warmer than usual May morning, Anne and the Marine crossed paths.

Anne wore her long hair pulled up in a clip that left golden wisps around her face and neck. Oversized sunglasses were propped on her head. She was smiling while tugging at her green gym shorts to see if they were long enough for school. Rules meant they had to reach her fingertips with her arm extended at her side. The strap of her tank top dangled over her bare shoulder as she tried to put on the shirt she planned to wear over it. She balanced her bag of books at the same time. Coming from her room, she ran right into the Marine.

"Well, my oh my!" he sneered. "Whatave we got here? Gertie, GERTIE! A bloody whore's in da hallway!"

Gertie came running from the bathroom and stood staring at the floor like a child about to be disciplined.

"Not surprised, a WHORE, dresses like a bloody whore!" he added, blocking Anne's exit.

"I've got a game today," she said, trying to move past him.

"Where in da samhill do ya think yur goin', ya li'l two-bit hussy!"

Knocked off balance as he slammed her against the doorframe, she winced and clenched her teeth.

"Not so fast, ya street whore!" he shouted, spitting as he spoke. "I cun tell ya right now them guys yur tryin' ta snare in yur black wida web are gonna be throwin' der money at ya today! Speakin' a money, where is my rent fur dis month? I should charge ya more fur livin' here coz yur prob'ly makin' a fortune as a street whore!"

This was a fresh pain comment for her and it hit hard. The new policy of her paying him rent because she turned eighteen before graduating was only a couple of months old. It still stung like the first day it was instituted.

"I'm not tryin' to do anything but go to school!" she said with venom. "Can you move, PLEASE, so I won't be late?" She tried to push past him.

"Dis ears my hallway and my floor. I don' move fur ANY dirty slut!" he spewed as he shoved her into the wall.

I witnessed his assault as I rounded the corner from my room and froze. I took small, quiet steps back to where I had come from. I hid behind my door listening, fighting off the overwhelming guilt that flooded me. I wanted to help her, divert him, do anything to stop him. But I couldn't move. I knew what moving would mean. I was furious at myself, Mother, and the Marine. I closed my eyes and pictured myself pulling a trigger and blowing us all away. I couldn't stand it.

"Anne, go ta yur room and change clothes, right now!" This was Gertie's big attempt at intervention, but her words fell on deaf ears.

Anne struggled against his weight but he wouldn't budge, continuing his insults as he shoved her again and again.

"Git da hell outta here, ya filthy tramp!" he barked and turned his attention to Gertie, who was cowering against the wall.

Anne slipped past him, down the stairs, and slammed the screen door as she left. I panicked. Anne was my ride to school that day and everyone else had already gone. I stayed hidden, afraid to move. The Marine went after Mother next. I heard him slap her and jumped as if it were me. She gasped and began crying. I stood behind that door, a coward unable to move and help the ones I loved. Through a crack, I watched in the hall mirror as the Marine pushed her down onto their bed. Holding her head back by the hair, he tore at her and his own clothing.

I closed my eyes tightly and thrust my fingers deep into my ears. I could still hear her cries and his tormenting words and wished I could just disappear. Tears poured down my cheeks as I trembled in shame. I didn't move until the slam of the downstairs door shook the floor beneath me. Then came the familiar rumble of the pickup starting and the screech of its tires as it exited the driveway.

My parents' door was now closed. I didn't know what to say to her or what to do. I stood outside, listening to her sobs, and wept. Finally, I snuck out of the house I hated so much and ran, shoving the whole incident from my thoughts the entire way to school. I was late, but late was better than never.

When I ran into her at lunch, Anne was excited despite all the morning madness with the Marine. She had worked three years on her after-graduation plans. She had managed to stay busy every waking moment of high school, and nothing was going to stop her now. We ate at the same table outside and she shared all her ideas. I was so proud of her and wished I had her strength and courage.

She was popular throughout the school and everyone seemed to know her from something she was involved in. *Involved* is an understatement. She was the senior homecoming queen, on the prom and senior banquet committees, and on just about every other committee I could think of. At one time or another, she had been student council vice president, a volunteer in the guidance office, and a member of the biracial committee. She sang in chorus and joined the chess, yearbook, ecology, and road rally clubs. She was a varsity basketball, hockey, and lacrosse player. She played speedball, softball, and dove competitively—and she still managed to keep an A-B grade point average. Our sister Joan happily followed her every move, competing frantically until she found herself pregnant and quickly married off to her high school sweetheart.

Anne did all of it to keep moving up and out, to stay as far away from the house and the Marine as possible. All of it to somehow show everyone that she was good, strong, and worthy of real love and adoration. With each trophy and award she hauled back came hopes that this would be the time Auggie would see who she really was—that he would love her and be proud. She worked so hard to be perfect for him.

She moved at the speed of light, sound, and practically knitted at stoplights. I wondered if she just couldn't stop—because stopping meant facing it all, and that would have been too much to bear. For Anne, it was simply easier to keep moving.

CHAPTER 22

Challenge

AFTER WORKING A LONG, hard summer with the Marine, Rob and I were at the end of our ropes. The long hours in the heat and his incessant abuse were more than we could take. It was one thing to be subject to him when we were younger, but we were now as tall as him, if not taller, and Rob and Jude were just about as strong. Humiliation and physical abuse were harder to swallow when we knew we could almost take him. Knowing Jude, he probably would jump in and support the Marine.

We were the only teenagers I knew relieved when school started again. It was Rob's senior year, and I had mixed feelings about it. I had enormous respect for him and wanted his freedom as well as my own from Auggie, but the idea of him being gone from the school scared me. We weren't as close as before. We ran with different groups of friends, had little extra time, and didn't share much in common other than where we lived and what we dealt with. We were teenagers, and we had our own issues to work out. Raging anger and hormones didn't make for good company, and we spent time searching for ways to relieve both.

School was a challenge for him but he worked hard and made decent grades. He planned to go on to college. He knew it was the only way to get away from the Marine and the nursery business. He was popular but didn't play school sports past tenth grade. He had his nose broken during a play in one of the high school football games. It wasn't the physical pain he had suffered from the game that ended it for him—it was the humiliation from Auggie's presence that was the final straw. That fall, instead of football, Rob and Jude set up a weight bench in the garage and began lifting weights every chance they could. Rob invited friends to lift too and the garage became a regular sweat and testosterone fest. I tried it out for myself when they weren't around and quickly found out it wasn't for me. Jude's nasty competitiveness ruined it for everybody soon enough. It didn't much matter to Rob, because between school, working with Auggie, and working at a local department store as often as he could, he had little time. It wasn't long before Jude was left lifting weights all by his lonesome.

In May when Rob graduated, Anne and I were the only ones there to root him on. Our parents didn't attend any of our graduations except for Jude's. Rob, Anne, and I went to all the graduation parties we were invited to, mostly out of curiosity and for the free food and beer. It was hard watching the way other families celebrated their sons' and daughters' accomplishments. We'd leave wasted, with full stomachs and heavy hearts. Rob celebrated until he realized he would have to do some time in community college before finally leaving Auggie's grasp. It was his dream to attend Penn State, but his grades were just under what he needed to be accepted to the main campus. I had to admit I wasn't ready for him to go, so I was secretly relieved.

Auggie was far from celebrating anything. School was worthless and those of us who attended were the same. He voiced this opinion so many times over the years, I could repeat his words verbatim. He fought consistently with Rob about college and told him he was wasting his time. The year that I graduated and was accepted to attend a smaller private college, he graduated from community college and was accepted to PSU. So we were both finally leaving Griffin Avenue, the Marine, and hopefully all that went with it behind us. I knew it was easier said than done, though. Rob spent his last summer under the Marine's thumb. He and a few friends took on jobs at the shore and rented an apartment there for the summer. I attempted to leave with him but the Marine put his foot down and refused to budge.

"Ya leave with 'im and don't come back ear ever," he shouted as he pushed me against yet another wall.

I don't know why I didn't just go. I guess I wasn't ready to leave everything behind. Despite all of the misery, this was the only place I knew. I didn't want to completely abandon Anne either, and that's what it felt like I would be doing. She still had another year under the Marine's rule without Rob and me. I wanted at least the summer with her.

The summer after Rob's graduation was one to remember, both in the fields with the Marine and off on our haphazard jaunts to escape him. Anne, Jude, and I drove down to Rob's place at the shore as often as we could slip away. We'd all get together and go to concerts and party on the beach. Their place was a dump, but who cared? He and his friends filled the bathtub with ice and a beer keg, and the kitchen table was covered with bottles of every kind of booze. Rob worked the summer at the shore waiting tables. He'd bring back steaks and food from the restaurant at night and we'd eat like kings and then party like animals. Then we'd sit on the beach wasted and watch the sun rise. I could tell he felt like he had let us down by not working with us in the fields, but he couldn't take any more and none of us could blame him. When summer came to an end, he had one last blow-out party and headed back, excited that he was finally leaving for Penn State. As soon as he got back he began packing his things. He couldn't leave a moment too soon. We saw his car sitting in the driveway when we pulled in from a longer than usual day working for the Marine. I wasn't thinking and jumped out of the truck and ran toward the house.

"Where da hell do ya think yur goin', ya sonsabishen queer?" the Marine yelled as I reached for the door.

Rob heard the commotion and reluctantly headed toward it. I moved quickly, ignoring his jeers, and helped unload the truck. Rob's appearance on the porch diverted the Marine.

"Well, well, if it isn't da college boy! Thinks he can run out on ever'body now! Ain't dat true?" the Marine said, approaching him.

"Hey! How's it goin'?" Rob replied, trying to lighten him up.

"How's it goin', he asst? Hum … well, ya can see fur ya self, life went on without ya, didn't it?" he said, walking into the garage.

"Cumin here, college boy!"

Rob smiled at us and headed in, expecting some sort of nasty altercation.

"So's I took a job that needs done quick, ya know what I mean?" Auggie asked, lifting the whiskey bottle. "Too big a job fur them two out there ta do on theirs own. Da job's gonna git done one way or 'nother, so if ya don't wanta kill them ya better help out!"

Rob was furious. He had one week before classes started and wanted to arrive early to figure out the school.

"So I don't have a choice, RIGHT?" Rob said loudly.

"Sup ta you, ya too-good-fur-nuttin' bastard! Sup to youse!" the Marine said with a nasty grin.

Rob stood a minute, trying to defuse his anger. He couldn't leave us with a job too big for us. He knew I was leaving soon as well and had things to get done, including repairs on my car. More than that, he knew if he didn't help, the Marine might kill us. Rob and I were both leaving him, so the Marine had nothing to lose. He was drinking more every day and it didn't take much to set him off.

"Fine, I'll do it," Rob said, walking back into the house.

The next morning before sunrise, Rob and I pulled out behind Auggie and Jude and followed them to the landscaping job. The Marine was relentless, and it quickly became clear he planned to use this jobsite to punish us for leaving him. The owner of the property was out of town, leaving us alone with his fury. By lunchtime, if Rob hadn't come, someone might have been dead—and I wasn't sure it would have been one of us.

All day I worked plotting the Marine's death. Every stone I moved and every tool I lifted became a possible weapon. I loathed him, but I refused to let him win. I had survived this long, and he wasn't going to push me so far that I spent the rest of my life in prison—though I was close.

At the end of the day, the Marine went on a tangent, hollering and throwing tools because I wasn't moving fast enough. Rob stepped up, putting himself between us, and the Marine flipped out. Rob stood firm in the hot sun, daring him to make a move. For the first time, we saw the Marine back down. He turned, walked to the truck without a word, and gulped from a paper-bagged bottle until we finished.

At the house we unloaded tools, covered in dirt and sweat, leaving a trail across the kitchen floor. We didn't get far. The Marine, drunk and swaying, stood aiming his .357 Magnum at us.

"Which one of youse bastards think ya kin take me on?" he said, waving the gun.

Gertie rushed in from the dining room, saw what was happening, then bolted out just as fast.

The Marine stumbled, pressing the gun into Jude's temple, swaying back and forth.

"How 'bout you, Judas? Ya think ya kin take me?" he slurred.

"No, sir!" Jude shouted, as bravely as he could.

The Marine turned the gun on Rob.

"Ya no-good-fur-nuttin' college boy, thinks he's smarteran me, wants ta take me on!" he sneered, words garbled.

Rob didn't move or speak. His face reddened as if he might grab the gun and kill the Marine. He was about to turn the gun on me when a voice called from behind.

"Auggie? Auggie Izbicki?" a man asked.

We all turned to see a policeman looking through the screen door. I froze, wondering if this was real.

"Auggie, sir, will you please step outside with us?" the officer said sternly. "Ma'am, could you make a pot of coffee for us?"

"Whatta hell ya want wit me?" the Marine smirked. "Dis here's private propaty and I'm a veter'n!"

We watched in disbelief as he walked out waving his gun, slobbering drunk.

We ran to the dining room windows. It was hard to hear, but we saw him hand over the gun, which they quickly unloaded. They led him toward the cruiser oddly parked in our driveway. My mind reeled. I was ecstatic, vindicated. Maybe he'd finally get what he deserved. The officers seemed to be calming him more than arresting him.

"Who called them?" Jude whispered.

For a moment no one answered.

"Who the heck cares? I hope he gets what he deserves!" I said, craning to see past Pete.

We watched as Mother carried coffee outside. When she returned, she joined us at the window, fear in her eyes. It was going way too easy for my liking. I expected the Marine to explode, to fight them like he fought everyone. I wanted them to cuff him, rough him up, haul him off, and lose the key.

We caught bits of conversation over the next hour, but in the end the officers simply kept his gun and told him he'd never get it back. They warned that if they were called again, they'd take the rest and drag him to jail. Auggie nodded, and they drove off, leaving him half sober in the driveway.

We scattered to hideouts, watching from bedroom windows, waiting for him to come raging inside. They might have taken one gun, but he had plenty more. I even thought about running out the door and never looking back.

Instead, we watched as the Marine shuffled to the garage and reappeared with whiskey. He sat in the driveway all evening, drinking, only moving to relieve himself behind the rhododendron. We whispered, wondering who had called the police.

Mother swore it wasn't her. I searched the faces of Emma, Pete, then Joan for a flicker of guilt, but saw nothing.

Just before dark, Anne came in the front door. She'd been babysitting across the street. We rarely used that door unless we were avoiding Auggie, so it struck me as odd she hadn't reacted when the police were in our driveway. She couldn't have missed it. Joan and Pete spilled the story, and Anne acted shocked, eager for details. Rob called as she walked past, and she poked her head in.

"Were you the one who called the man?" he asked quietly.

"How would I know what was going on? I wasn't even here," she said with concern. No one ever admitted to making the call.

Later that evening, the Marine dragged every gun he owned into the driveway, stumbling, dropping some, then smashing each against the pavement until they were useless.

"Come an' take 'em now, you commies, pinkos—who needs guns? I kin kill youse all with my bare hands!" he bellowed for the neighbors to hear.

A few days later Rob packed his car. As he said his goodbyes, Auggie emerged from the garage.

"Good luck and good riddance!" he said, shoving a twenty into Rob's hand before walking away.

Rob stared at the bill as if it were foreign, pocketed it, and got in his car. With everything he owned, a map, and a prayer, he pulled out from the driveway. He'd never been to Penn State, but knew any challenge there had to be better than what he was leaving behind on Griffin Avenue.

CHAPTER 23

Asylum

ABOUT A MONTH BEFORE graduation, I stopped at the mailbox before coming into the house. I leafed through the stack and found three official letters addressed to me. Scanning the return addresses, I saw they were from colleges I had applied to. Afraid to open them, I looked at the house, then back at the envelopes. I stuffed the rest of the mail back into the box, got in my car, and drove to the park. This was too important to face inside.

The park had become my refuge over the last years. It was the place to hang out—guys cruised for girls and pot, girls followed suit, and my friends and I skipped classes to get high in the woods. But most often I spent my time there alone under my tree.

I researched trees and found them mentioned in religion, science, philosophy, and theology. I felt a deep connection from as young as I could remember. It was as if we were kindred spirits. So many things owed their existence to trees—medicine, food, furniture, paper, even fuel. I felt I owed my existence to mine.

For me, my tree represented shelter and companionship. It absorbed all I shared—enough tears to last through a drought. Each leaf seemed etched with sorrow, and when autumn winds carried them away, it made room for new ones each spring. I often wondered how many others had found refuge beneath its branches.

But if I were to be honest, I believe my love for trees came from my grandfather when I was very young. We were visiting his farm in the middle of winter. He and I stood at the highest point on his land. As I surveyed the land below us, I noticed only the pine trees still held on to their leaves.

"Grandpa, why are pine trees the only ones with leaves right now?" I asked, studying his weathered face.

"Well, Samson, that's a good question. I heard tell a long time ago a story from a Cherokee Indian about a sparrow too injured to fly south for the winter. His family went without him, and he searched for a place to live so he could survive. He asked each tree if he could stay under its branches, but they all said no—except the pine. Even though it had no leaves, only needles and fewer branches, it invited him to stay. The Creator of the Universe saw that the pine gave what it had, which wasn't much, while all the other trees refused. So He made all the trees lose their leaves in the winter—except the pine," he answered with a smile.

I loved that moment in time with him, and the story sounded credible enough for me. I shared it with anyone I crossed paths with that year. As I grew, so did its embellishment. I began identifying with trees almost immediately, and though I loved them all, I was partial to oaks. As I grew old enough to work alongside the Marine, trees became my refuge. I hid among them and played in their rows when he wasn't around. Though I passionately hated working in the fields, I felt sorrow uprooting them and loading them onto trucks, yet also joy and renewal when we transplanted them into yards where children played—giving them new homes to live out their years.

On days when I felt down and out, I sought asylum beneath my tree's branches. It stood alone in a field, just as I felt I had in life. My oak witnessed the rivers of tears that poured from me. It was there whenever I needed to think, rest, dream, pray, or rant. More than a tree, it was the friend I needed to quietly be there and listen. Miracles happened there. Internal transformations occurred there. All my important decisions were worked out beneath it. It sheltered me from sun and rain and, in the winter, when it shed its leaves like tears of sorrow, we both stood together subject to the elements.

A lone hawk lived in that tree, and he and I had an unspoken agreement. We shared the tree so long as neither interrupted the other's space. The hawk would be gone for weeks on end, and just when I thought I couldn't take life anymore, he'd return—soaring high above—and I would feel hope again.

I pulled up and parked on a hill near my tree. I grabbed the bag with my stash of pot, cigarettes, and soda—always stocked for moments like this. I checked my pocket for the letters and walked slowly toward the tree. Just as I set my things on the ground, the hawk landed on the branches above me. The freshly mowed field glowed in the afternoon sun that slipped in and out from behind a cloud. A cool breeze blew through my hair. I wanted to savor this moment. I wanted to breathe in the possibilities. I lit a joint and circled my tree, taking in the view three sixty. Relaxed, I was ready for the news. One way or another, I was finally going to get away from Griffin Avenue and the Marine, and I wanted to hold this moment forever.

"You want to see them too, don't you?" I asked my tree.

Slowly, I opened the first letter. Reading quickly, I found the part inviting me to become a student. I was accepted. Anxious, I opened the next. It dampened my spirits—it was full for the semester I applied for, so it was a no. I had saved the best for last. It was from the school I really wanted. I shoved the two opened letters into my pockets and stood holding the final envelope. Looking up at the sun, I closed my eyes and prayed.

"God, please don't punish me for all that I am and all that I have done," I whispered while my tree listened. Its leaves rustled in the wind, begging me to proceed.

I reasoned with myself, smoked more, paced awhile. Everything would be fine. I could still leave; I had been accepted to the first college, even if it wasn't the one I wanted most. Slowly, I opened one end of the last letter to peek inside. I caught a word or two but couldn't see much.

"Get a grip; just open it!" I said out loud as my tree waited and listened. The anticipation was killing me. I tore open the seal and read the words like I had never read any before: *We are happy to inform you that you have been accepted for the fall semester….*

I fell to my knees crying and thanked God. I had been granted educational, emotional, physical, and mental asylum. I was leaving—going to a school I just knew would be my safe haven. Away from Griffin Avenue, away from the Marine and his constant barrage of pain. I was finally going to be free.

I ran circles around my tree, yelling and hollering. I read the letter again and wrapped my arms as far around the trunk as I could reach, hugging it like nothing else in my life.

"Wow! Two out of three ain't bad," I shouted as I ran to my car. I looked back at my tree as if waiting for it to follow.

"I'll miss you, old friend. But don't worry—I'll be back before I leave!"

CHAPTER 24

The Devil You Know

THE DAY HAD FINALLY arrived. I stood in front of the house, staring at it as if it would be the last time I laid eyes on it. I expected a full range of emotions, but melancholy wasn't one of them. It felt ridiculous that I hesitated to climb into my fully loaded car and drive away.

Graduation had been eight weeks earlier, a huge relief as I walked across the platform to hear my name called. Rob's and Anne's were the only familiar faces in the audience besides Manny's. They yelled encouragement, then insisted on taking me to dinner. After dessert, Anne and Manny left, while Rob and I slid over to the bar for a celebratory beer.

"To Samson—finally free of this place!" Rob toasted, mugs clinking. "It feels so good to be leaving. I can't wait for August. You ready to blow this pop stand?"

"You know it. I just have to survive the summer first," I said.

The bar was slow, so we went hopping, looking for others celebrating too. We knew nearly everyone in town and partied until plastered, crashing with Rob's friends for the night. We rolled back onto Griffin Avenue hungover and in no mood for Auggie.

"Glad he's not here. I'm heading back to the shore before he gets back, Sam. You coming down this week?" Rob asked as I opened the door.

"For sure—just me and Anne, I think. Can't wait!" I shouted, dancing around the driveway as he pulled away, radio blasting.

Before Rob hit the first stop sign I was already planning and packing. I wore myself out with the details. The next day we were back in the fields.

The Marine made my last couple weeks unbearable. Pete's tenth birthday had come and gone three years earlier and he still hadn't attended Auggie's school of hard knocks. The rules for Pete were looser, and that was fine by me. I didn't want him there at all, but with Rob's departure, the Marine pulled out all the stops to get work done by anyone other than himself. At this point, his full-time job of being a drunk consumed everything.

Pete joined Jude and me in the fields and that was that. Though he resembled Auggie and Jude physically, he acted nothing like them. He was diplomatic and could talk the Marine down better than anyone I'd seen. Too young to remember Auggie before he was a full-blown drunk, Pete expected nothing more of him than what he was and adjusted accordingly. It didn't hurt that he loved being outdoors. He was a natural in the fields and even seemed to enjoy the work, if that was possible.

He kept his head down when the Marine's temper flared and acted oblivious to the abuse of me or anyone else. From his viewpoint, this was all he had ever known—it was simply the way it always was. I put every effort into being invisible during Pete's hours of "instruction," but sooner or later the Marine caught up with me. His new form of humiliation included hurling rocks at me like he did the crows in the field. Restraining myself grew harder by the day, and I had to keep reminding myself I was leaving soon, never to work another day under his rule.

Pete and Emma were close, and it eased my mind knowing they had each other when I left. Well, at least Emma had Pete. She wasn't what most would call dependable. Their lives were so different from mine and my older siblings, and that felt good. Hard to believe that within a year or so they'd be the only children left on Griffin Avenue. Auggie would always be Auggie, but their time with him and Mother in that too-small house would be different. They didn't seem to hate it like we did. They didn't seem to clash with Auggie as much either. Our protection over the years showed, and I was grateful for that. Emma's bigger struggles were with Gertie, but Mother was too worn out to care.

Standing there looking at the house, I chastised myself for any sentiment. Why should I feel anything but sheer elation as I prepared to leave? Glancing up at the bedroom window, I sighed, remembering how it was our only view of the driveway and the world outside. Birds landed in the bushes we'd planted when I was in fifth grade; now they towered taller than the porch. I looked down the driveway, remembering how long it seemed when I was small, how huge the house once appeared.

Leaning against my car, I admitted to myself—I was going to be alone now. I had grown used to a house crowded with people and problems, conditioned to tight spaces and hiding places. How could I feel even for a second what I was feeling now?

Mother stepped onto the porch, searching for me.

"Whatcha doin' out there, Samson? Don't leave yet. Come in here a minute first," she said, pretending to tidy the porch. I'd caught her often stealing glances at me, thinking she was sly. She was a terrible actress and worse liar, though she fancied herself good at both.

She slipped inside, and through the bay window I saw her reflection—watching me watch her. I finally went in as she asked. As I stepped onto the porch, her shadow scurried away. Once inside, I thundered upstairs, stomping like thirty schoolkids. Auggie was passed out from an all-night bender. I figured I'd aggravate him one last time.

I wandered room to room, recalling moments with my brothers and sisters. Then I ran back down, just as noisy. I flopped on the couch, stared at the blank TV screen, turned it on, then off, then on again—finally cranking the volume and leaving it loud. In the dining room, I poked through the china cabinet. Its contents screamed of holidays I wanted no part of, so I moved on quickly.

I sat on Rob's old bed, thinking how much I already missed him.

Then I walked into the kitchen—and stopped. Mother stood proudly holding a confetti-covered cake. The words scrawled across it were nearly unreadable. She must have worked so hard, but still botched them, so she read them aloud for me.

"Says, 'Good luck, Samson!'" she whispered, nearly dropping the cake. "Surprise!"

I was so shocked I didn't know how to respond. There had been many surprises in this house, none of them good. I opened my mouth but nothing came out. Tears stung my eyes, then I saw Emma and Pete behind her holding homemade cards, and I melted. They hugged me, and we had cake and lemonade, laughing in the kitchen that had held so much pain.

An hour later I was ready to go. I let the screen door—our old warning system—slam behind me. Walking through the trees, I stopped at the mound of fresh soil always waiting to be hauled.

"I will die before I work dirt again! I'm getting a gardener, that's a fact!" I said aloud, pointing at it. Oh, how I hated dirt.

As I headed back, Mother came out, hugged me, and kissed my forehead, just like she had sometimes before bed when we were small. It felt so good, and I needed it so badly. We had shared so many bad years, and I was sure the damage was beyond repair. Maybe it still was.

"I love you, Sam," she said, her voice trembling. "I know it's been hard, but you'll do okay." Then she went back inside.

It was so unexpected. I fought tears at her understanding—and at the anger that had built for so long. I knew she loved me. I also knew she had too much and too many to divide herself between. Still, it didn't erase the betrayal, the abandonment. But her words were a first step, and I was going to take what I could get.

I walked to my car, head down, hesitant. I was afraid to move on. What if I failed? What would I do? I wished for the anger that once pushed me through the fields and school. Just a spark of it would get me moving, enough to leave this cursed place.

It's the devil you don't know you fear, Sam, I told myself. *This was the devil you knew, and you knew how to handle it. That's all that's wrong with you.*

I was about to get in the car when an old, familiar voice bellowed from the porch. There he was—the devil I did know—shirtless, clutching his glass of whiskey.

"Whatsa matta, Momma's boy? Too scared ta leave? Big world out der. Careful it don't swallow ya whole. Now git the hell outta here so I kin sleep, ya ungrateful piss ant!" he roared for all to hear.

That was it. I didn't think. I didn't hesitate.

"I love you too, you nasty drunk!" I shouted as I slid into the car.

That was all the motivation I needed. I pulled out, tires burning. At the stop sign, I threw on my shades, popped in a tape, and floored it.

"Sam, you survived that nasty piece-of-crap devil. You'll slay the one you don't know too! You can do ANYTHING!" I yelled as I merged into traffic, heading into the world alone.

‎• CHAPTER 25 •

Control

THOSE LAST YEARS ON Griffin Avenue were brutal. Until Rob and I graduated, all nine of us still lived under one roof. With almost-grown adults crammed into every corner, chaos was constant. The bathroom line never ended, and only Rob's room ever offered space, for less than two or three people at a time. We tripped over each other daily, which gave us every reason to stay away from the house.

While Rob attended community college and I finished high school, Jude was also in community college, claiming he'd someday run Auggie's nursery and landscaping business—turning it into a huge success. As much as I distrusted him, I believed he might actually do it. But I never thought he was doing it for the Marine. Jude never did anything unless it benefited himself.

Not long after Rob and I moved away to school and Anne graduated, she left for California. Soon after, Joan made a quick exit too. She had dated the same boy through high school and married him in a small private ceremony. She became the fifth to leave Griffin Avenue, chasing dreams with an ill-prepared husband.

The Marine, of course, had his usual rants. He never saw the point of college for men and even less for women. But Joan's marriage fit his narrow definition of what women should be doing. By then, he was drinking from dawn to dusk. The nursery business collapsed under his inability to finish jobs, so he finally threw in the towel and took a job with a local company.

Emma was ten when I left, already a heartbreaker and spinning out of control. We had spoiled her rotten, and leaving her behind was hard. She loved my record player, sitting for hours with music as her comfort, just as it had been for many of us. Rob and I took her to concerts to help her escape, while Gertie was too worn down to care. So Emma ran wild. By junior high she was in full rebellion, caught spray-painting school buildings and chased by security while screaming obscenities. On the way home from the police station, she jumped out of the car at a stop sign, flipped Gertie off, and disappeared to get high with friends.

Pete kept to himself. He hung out with his buddies and was so quiet at home that no one noticed him. I often wondered if any of us would ever really know who he was.

Once Rob and I left, the inmates seemed to run the asylum. Thankfully, I wasn't around to watch it unravel. I had believed leaving would be easy—that I'd drive off into the sunset and life would fall into place. Instead, I was restless, nervous, out of sorts.

Standing in my dorm room, I unpacked my few belongings. The room looked much like the ones I'd known, except now there were only two beds instead of four. I reminded myself I'd have just one roommate, not two brothers pressed in beside me. I filled my small bookshelf with the records and books I'd rescued from the warped cardboard box I'd jammed into my car. Reaching deep inside, I searched for what else I had carried with me.

At the bottom of the box, leaning against the side, were my composition notebooks. I had filled two over the years, and just last night Aaron added a fresh entry to a third—my final one as a resident of Griffin Avenue. My roommate hadn't arrived yet, so I sat against the wall and flipped through the pages of my life.

Entry after entry told the same story. "H" for how many times the Marine hit me. "N" for the names he called me. "J" for Jude's torment. "S" for school offenses. "M" for Mother's cruelty. The notebooks overflowed with pain. I couldn't recall every incident, but I felt each one as my fingers slid across the marks. Part of me thought I should throw them away, erase the record of misery. But another part knew I could never forget, no matter how hard I tried.

I was still numb from the drive and starving, so I grabbed a bag of peanuts from the groceries I'd packed. My mind wandered to who my roommate might be. I prayed he wouldn't take one look at me and bolt. Ridiculous, I told myself—I had filled out a preference form when I applied, and the admissions counselor assured me they matched roommates with shared interests. Still, I couldn't shake the worry. I wasn't sure if I'd been honest on that form or if I'd tried too hard to look "better" than I was.

I gathered up the trash from unpacking, bracing myself for whatever was next. Just then, the door opened, and a good-looking guy stepped in.

"Hey, I'm Auggie. Are you John?" he asked with a smile.

"No, I'm Sam."

"Oh, my roommate's John. Must be the wrong room!" he said, backing out. "Figures," he added, noticing the number above the doorframe. "I'm on the wrong floor. How dumb am I?"

"I got lost at first too, so that makes two of us!" I replied, relieved. "Catch you later!"

A rush of relief drained from me. I didn't need a guy that good looking as a roommate, and I sure didn't want another Auggie in my life. I grabbed my trash and headed for the bins.

Passing the dorm showers, I slowed near the resident advisor's (RA's) room. That room was my dream. If I had no other mission, it was to earn that spot next year. I had never had a room of my own, and I'd do just about anything for one. I planned to watch, learn, and qualify.

The RA's name was Sam too, and the coincidence broke the ice instantly. We clicked right away, talking about music, classes, and dorm life. My foot was in the door. As I walked past, he waved.

"Hey man! How's it goin'? Can you stop in on your way back?"

I nodded, grateful for the connection.

Outside it was warm and the skies were bluer than blue. That evening I was meeting up with a friend, also settling into her dorm, for dinner and it couldn't come soon enough. I was surprised by my inability to fully enjoy my first day on my own and wanted a taste of home. She was just what I needed. I wished we were in the same dorm, but there were no co-ed dorms. I emptied my trash and stopped in the advisor's room.

"Hey, your roommate's here. Do you guys want to come to a party tonight off campus? A few friends are gettin' together. You can ride with me," Sam the RA said.

"I must've missed 'im when he came in. I'll ask and get back to ya," I replied, hurrying to my room. On the way, I rehearsed introductions, then laughed at myself. When I walked in, he was on the floor unpacking albums.

"Beatles fan?" he asked.

"To be sure!" I answered.

We introduced ourselves and he plugged in his stereo. With music blasting, we became fast friends. He was Dan, from New York, and rattled on more information than necessary, but I liked him. The music was the key—and the stereo was frosting on the cake. I pulled out my albums, and it felt like we had known each other forever.

Sam stopped by to see if we were going to the party. We both agreed to meet him outside later. I can't deny it—I was nervous. I had gotten pretty good at being myself in high school, but this was a whole new ball game.

Our room filled quickly with other guys from the building, and before I knew it, we were all laughing and drinking beer someone had brought.

I met up with Becky for dinner and she was jealous of my afternoon dorm party. She and her friend Trish ended up in the same dorm but on different floors and were trying to get their roommates to switch. We ate quickly and ran through our schedules for the next day. We kept getting turned around on campus but finally figured it out by dark.

"I'm going with Sam, the resident advisor, and some guys from the dorm to a party tonight and I'm freaking out. I don't know anyone. Want to come?" I asked, hoping she'd say yes.

"Naw, we've got too much to do and I don't want to be worthless tomorrow," she frowned. "How did that happen? You book a party first night in? Enjoy, and don't forget to meet me in the cafeteria for lunch. I wanna hear all about it!"

We hugged and I left feeling better. At least my first day wasn't as bad as hers. I headed back to my dorm, still anxious about what the night would bring. Turns out I worried for no reason. Ten minutes after we arrived we were drinking and smoking pot. This was a place I was going to rule for sure.

That night in bed I replayed nearly every conversation from the day. *Did I sound cool? Was that stupid to say? What do they think of me? Was I funny? Did I go too far with that joke? Did I wear the right thing? Do they think I'm … ? Do I have to control every word that comes out of my mouth?* The questions wouldn't stop. I was paranoid. I remembered how I'd acted all night—loud, over-confident, wild. I was disappointed in myself. I wasn't being me. I was being what I thought they wanted. Here I was again, slipping back into old patterns. Would I never learn? Why did I always hide behind masks in new situations? Frustrated, I couldn't sleep. I left my snoring roommate and went outside for a smoke. What was it going to take? I couldn't go back to molding myself into someone everyone liked. Yet that's what I did. For the first few weeks, I was whoever I thought people wanted, and it drained me. I was always on. Always acting. Always disappointed.

Then, sometime after those first weeks, something shifted. I remember standing under a tree that felt like a decent stand-in for my oak back home, watching students rush to class. I studied their faces and attitudes. I liked watching people, imagining what it might be like to live their lives. Did they ever watch me and wonder the same? Probably not. If they did, they wouldn't discover much. From a glance they might think I was outgoing and fun, the life of the party.

I wanted people to see the real me, no matter the cost. I was tired of acting, tired of meeting new people behind a mask. The truth was, no one was holding me back but me. If I was going to step fully into this new life, I had to be honest—with myself and with everyone I met. That meant leaving behind the shallow, fake version of me I had used for survival. Still, the ghost of that false self followed me into every new relationship. But I was done pretending. On that warm afternoon, with the breeze wrapping around me, I decided it was time to let go and leave the act where it belonged—behind me.

I had fought too hard to get this far. Yet I felt sealed inside an impenetrable bubble, able to see out but convinced anyone looking in saw only their own reflection. Inside me were archives of secrets, stacked like stone walls, keeping me separate from everyone I wanted to be close to. I couldn't keep living that way. Those secrets had too much power, holding me at a distance from life and from love.

I knew I had to make a choice, right then and there, to open those vaults and risk being known. If I didn't, I'd waste this new chance at freedom. My need to control every word, every look, every move, had gotten so out of hand that I now needed to control my own need for control. The irony wasn't lost on me—but maybe, just maybe, it was the first real step toward freedom.

I looked up at the unusually clear blue sky, closed my eyes, and drew a deep breath, forcing out everything I had been holding in. *This is it,* I thought. *If I want people to know me—and for me to know myself—I have to shed this suffocating bubble that's kept me from fully living.* I took a step forward, half expecting to see the broken shell lying behind me on the grass.

"I am in control here and now," I whispered, stepping again.

I didn't care who heard. Speaking aloud had always been my way of pushing through fear, and I was ready to use it once more. *I rule here!* I told myself. For the first time in my life, no one dictated my every move. My professors would set expectations, but even those I could choose to meet—or not.

I wouldn't let fear, or the ghosts of Griffin Avenue, keep me captive any longer. I started walking, then running, words spilling out of me like ticker tape. With every stride, I felt freer. With every breath, lighter. My todays and tomorrows would rise or fall by my own initiative.

When I finally slowed, my chest heaving, I was smiling so wide it felt like my face might split. I collapsed under a tree, gazing at my new horizon. For once, I wasn't trapped inside a bubble of secrets and shame. I was out in the open, exposed, but alive. The power coursing through me was exhilarating.

For the first time, I began to believe that maybe—just maybe—I could live as myself, not as the person I had pretended to be for so long.

I wrestled with the old Sam as he twisted and clawed to deflate my newfound courage. His advances were fearful and negative, but this time unsuccessful. I was more determined than ever to live differently. I knew battles lay ahead and that I'd often be my own worst enemy, but today I drew a line, redistributing the power between us.

I thought about my alter egos. From now on, Billy's dreams would be fulfilled so he could rest. Aaron would stop recording only anguish and failure. The new Sam—*Sam the Man*—would be king of this kingdom. I might need allies from time to time, but I would stand on my own two feet, wherever that path led.

I looked down, then walked—no, ran—to my next class, realizing I was nearly late. The professor's syllabus had warned: Late arrivals meant ridicule and lost points. I burst in on time, breathless but relieved, and dropped into a seat.

Well, okay, I thought, flipping open my notebook. *Maybe not completely self-governing—but close.*

After all, I had chosen to follow the rules, to enroll in this class, to show up in this lecture hall. Who was I fooling? Still, it was *my* choice, and for the first time that was enough. I was in control, at least for the moment, and that was a start.

CHAPTER 26

Coexistence

THE FIRST SEMESTER BORED me out of my mind academically. I was organized and had the program down, but it felt like thirteenth grade. I searched the clubs and fraternities and hand-picked the ones that offered relief from the monotony. I put little effort into studying and more into establishing a name for myself.

My dorm room filled at night with men like me, looking for stimulation beyond the norm. We wanted something new, different, and intellectually challenging—so we challenged each other. Rules were simple: An open mind, complete honesty, and debate without judgment. Disagreement was allowed, but we had to leave agreeing to disagree.

Subjects changed nightly—war, sex, race, sports, religion, philosophy. Books were a favorite, so we devoured whatever we could find. Some of us stretched the "open mind" policy to include substances that promoted it, and often we moved outside to get high. Warm beer hid in closets, though not all of us drank. Smoking was permitted but discouraged indoors. Campus policy said no drugs or alcohol, but no one enforced it.

Peaceful coexistence was the only standard that mattered to the resident advisor—and I was all for that.

I found my niche, though it turned into more than I'd bargained for. Still, I can't say I didn't enjoy the benefits. In that charged environment I not only grew academically but also as a person. My new friends, mostly guys, surprised me with how open and reflective they were. I'd never been in the middle of men who talked like that. Women and men needed the same things but expressed them so differently, and I fit in both spaces, offering perspectives from either side. A few of those friendships became close, and I was stunned by how love and care could feel almost as painful as loneliness. But at least I wasn't alone anymore.

By the end of my first semester, I joined a committee studying campus housing needs. We reorganized the entire resident government system. My high school experience with student government had prepared me for leadership, and the respect I received from students and administrators filled me with pride. "Sam the Man" had found his place—not by accident, but because I had pushed myself to show I was capable.

By spring I had achieved my goal: resident advisor. The RA in my building moved out after New Year's, leaving the position open, and the dorm unanimously recommended me. It was more than validation; the stipend would help cover expenses, and my own room felt like a luxury I had never known.

When the dorms closed for the holidays, I drove back to Griffin Avenue, eager to see Rob, Anne, and Emma, news spilling inside me like a shaken soda bottle. Phone calls never matched being in the same room. As I pulled into the driveway, Emma came running, leaping onto the hood of my car. I scooped her up, marveling at how much she'd grown in such a short time. But then again—hadn't we both?

"Who is that strange man in the driveway?" Rob yelled.

I had let my hair grow to my shoulders and added a beard and mustache—the change was hard to ignore. After catching up with everyone, I slipped off to the park and sat beneath my tree, talking to it as if it needed to be updated too. The holidays loomed, stirring memories I'd rather forget, but I resolved to endure them and then return to my own space.

That night, Anne, Rob, and I went out, drank, and danced until the bar closed. We tumbled into our beds around three in the morning, grateful to have missed an evening with Auggie. We hadn't crossed paths with him yet, but Thanksgiving was tomorrow, and I knew we couldn't avoid him forever.

I woke to the smell of onions and celery sizzling in butter. That aroma was the only good thing about Thanksgiving in our house. The turkey never turned out quite right, but I still looked forward to eating it. My nostalgia evaporated when I walked into the kitchen.

"So, it's the *projigal* son returned!" Auggie sneered, food dribbling from his mouth.

"Prodigal," I corrected. "And if you're referring to the story, you're missing something. The father ran to embrace his son and celebrate his return. The past was the past." I sat at the table, bracing myself.

"*Projigal, smogigal*—same difference ta me. You been gone long 'nuff ta forgit dis is my house?" he barked, his eyes daring me to push further.

I knew nothing good could come of challenging him, but I didn't care anymore. Maybe I shouldn't have poked the dragon.

"How have you been, Auggie?" I asked, trying to lighten his mood.

"I been workin', that's how. Company's tryin' to kill us all over there!"

"Company?" I blurted without thinking.

He had taken a job at a local plant when Rob, Jude, and I left. He couldn't handle the landscaping alone. Nights suited him—he could function just enough as a drunk. I'd bet he drank the shift away while leaving most of his work undone. He still took the occasional landscaping job, but he was a washed-up drunk now.

"Ya forgit I was abandoned by ya all. Youse ungrateful punks!" he snapped.

Rob, Jude, and Anne walked in just in time for his rant. Jude sat beside him, trying to joke, but nothing calmed him. Mother wrestled with the turkey, struggling to get it into the roaster. I lifted it for her and Rob, Anne, and I grabbed coffee and slipped out the screen door. None of us were about to choke down breakfast while the Marine acted out.

The rest of the day went the same. We'd come inside long enough to warm up, then duck back out before his tirades wore us down. Dinner started and ended like every other Thanksgiving—with the Marine ranting, raving, and poisoning the table.

By nightfall I'd had enough. I headed to bed early, planning my escape for the next day. I wasn't staying there one more minute than I had to.

Rob and I spent the next morning at a friend's place and didn't get back until dark. I wanted nothing more than to head to school, but my dorm wouldn't open for two more days. As soon as we parked, we heard the screaming from inside. I froze, wishing I'd followed my gut and kept driving. Rob bolted for the house, and like a fool, I followed.

Leftover turkey, stuffing, and mashed potatoes were splattered across the kitchen like a prison food fight. The table was overturned. Mother had locked herself in the new bathroom off the kitchen. The Marine had Anne in a chokehold, while Jude stood back holding Emma. Pete was trying to talk the Marine down, and Joan sobbed like a child. My instinct was to run, but my legs wouldn't move.

"What the hell is going on here?" Rob shouted.

He regretted it instantly. The Marine dropped Anne and lunged, a drunken bull charging the matador.

"Go ahead! You wanna beat the crap outta me, then do it!" Rob roared, refusing to budge.

The Marine swung, lost his balance, and crashed to the food-slick floor. For a moment he lay still. Then he sat up, clutching his stomach, laughing like a madman.

"Das so funny even I gotta laugh!" he bellowed between gasps, his laughter louder than all of us combined.

No one laughed with him. The Marine crawled across the floor, clutching his bottle, and staggered out the screen door toward the garage. The rest of us just stood there, staring at the wreckage. It might have been funny in another house, but here it was just pathetic—another scene I longed to escape. We cleaned up his mess while Mother finally emerged from the bathroom, her clothes crusted with food, her face blotchy from crying. She couldn't meet our eyes as she slipped upstairs. I searched myself for sympathy or compassion, but all I felt was numbness.

"Who even lives like this and does nothing?" I muttered before I could stop myself.

"She does! We all did! Some of us still do!" Anne shot back, exasperated. "I can't wait to graduate and get out of here! Ya think it was bad before? He tried to rape her in front of Emma last week—on the living room couch! She doesn't even fight anymore. He's straight out of hell, I swear. One of these days, I'm gonna kill him!"

She collapsed against me, sobbing. I held her, choking back my own rage and tears. My chest ached knowing she was left to face him alone now.

"I'm so sorry, Anne," I whispered. "I didn't know. I've been so busy at school, and our calls have been so short."

"You didn't let me down," she said, wiping her face. "It's him. I just can't take much more."

"Home sweet home," Rob muttered bitterly. Then, turning to me, he added, "Why don't you come up to Penn State on weekends? Crash at my place."

"You can visit me too," I said quickly. "I'll sneak you into my dorm. Who's gonna rat me out? Not if they wanna stay there."

The next two days were nearly unbearable. When it came time to leave, Rob and I honked at each other as we split off at the red light on the edge of town, heading in opposite directions—away from Griffin Avenue, away from him.

I arrived back at the dorm to find my friends moving my belongings into my new room. They had cold beer and an awkward cake to celebrate my new digs. I was overwhelmed by their support. They had no idea what I'd endured over the holidays, and I wanted it to stay that way—for now. I needed to leave it all behind. This was my space. My place. For the first time in my life.

I wish they could all see me now! I thought as I joined the party.

"To Sam the Man! Our new rogue RA! How did we ever exist without you?" Dan, my old roommate, toasted.

CHAPTER 27

Inside and Out

IN MY OWN LITTLE world there is no pain. I never have to sacrifice anything. I don't need to be anyone but myself. I do what I want, go where I please. The problems only start when people enter. It's simple—me surrounded by music, sunshine, happiness—until I ruin it all by feeling alone.

"I can't win," I whispered. I shouldn't have gone back there. It drained me, followed me, haunted this new existence. Just when I thought I'd moved beyond it, here I was again, wallowing. How does all this pain survive every battle I've fought with it? How does it take me over again?

I sat at my desk with a mountain of projects—class assignments, dorm responsibilities, honor society tasks. I'd buried myself in work, yet all I could think was how much of a fraud I felt like. I spun in my chair and scanned my new room. Posters of bands lined the walls, alongside recognition awards and a few photos of family and friends. My bulletin board was cluttered with announcements and schedules. In the middle of my desk sat a brand-new electric typewriter. I had everything I needed to tackle the work in front of me—yet I couldn't shake the heaviness.

I went to the shelf and pulled down my composition notebooks. The newest one was filling with Aaron's poems now. No more tally marks to keep score—just words capturing my depression. I couldn't figure out why recording it this way felt better, but there it was in my hands anyway.

I picked up a pen but paused, rereading the entry I'd written the night I returned from Griffin Ave. I longed for a place I could truly call home—inside and out. I wasn't at home in my own skin. This shell God provided felt foreign, and I was sure He'd grown weary of my constant whining. It seemed He had far more pressing concerns than listening to me cry again. *It's okay,* I thought. How could I be honest with Him when I couldn't even be honest with myself? If I were Him, I'd be tired of me too. I was tired of me. Aaron's poem captured it better than I ever could.

Tell Me How

Tell me how I can knock down all my walls
The barriers of shame
The stones of fear
The pyramid of self-inflicted loneliness
That has dungeoned me into
A private hole of anguish

How can I explain things to You
That evade self understanding
Things that grasp me with hands of steel
Often near crushing me
Yet exist with such secrecy from my soul
That transferring them to Yours is out of my reach

How can I admit to You
That I refuse to admit to myself
How can I go about relating things to You
When I have yet to figure out how

How I'm going to find the guts
After I figure out how

By Aaron

My eyes filled with tears. It didn't get much clearer than that. How stupid was I? Man, I'm a fool. When am I gonna get anything right? When was I going to stay away from there—away from him and her? I needed to shut down my pity party. I put the books away and walked out into the rain. Imagine that—it was raining inside and out.

I had about an hour before my dorm welcomed a new resident. He was coming from Colorado and had car trouble on the way. Classes had already started, but being a freshman, he could catch up easily. I went back to my room to finish a few things before giving him the grand tour and laying out the rules. A few guys in the building had the flu, so I checked in on them too. After sending one to the infirmary, I was finally ready to work.

"Hi, are you Sam?" Zach asked sheepishly, startling me from my thoughts.

"Yep, that's me. And you're Zach?"

I needed a second to rein in my reaction. He was about five-foot-ten with sandy brown hair, a baby face, and haunting brown eyes.

"I'll show you your room. The grand tour's on the house this time. Usually I charge five bucks!" I joked, trying to lighten him up.

"Oh. man, I hadn't planned on that … oh, you're joking?" he asked nervously.

"Look, man, relax. It's cool around here. Nothing to be anxious about. I'm not a warden. We'll get you settled and into classes in no time. This place is easy to figure out, and since it's my job to make sure you're comfortable, you've got my attention. I was nervous at first too—everyone is. But we have fun here. It's not all rules and regs. Tonight a bunch of guys are hanging out in the lobby—you should come." I tried to reassure him.

"You don't say much, do you?" I asked as we opened the door to his room.

"You've got the place to yourself this semester," I added quickly. "Your roommate dropped out last week, and they probably won't assign another now that classes are underway. If you want one later, let me know."

He just stood there staring at the bare walls. The room had no window—everyone wanted one. He set down his suitcase and book bag without a word.

"You okay, man? Room alright?" I asked, confused.

"Oh, I'm okay. The … the room is okay too," Zach stuttered, shifting his weight.

I felt a pang of guilt. Open mouth, insert foot. Why couldn't I just let him be? Why did I always push?

"Sorry," I said quickly. "I didn't realize. There was nothing about that in the info they gave me, and—"

"It's okay," he interrupted softly. "It only happens when I'm really ne-nervous."

"Alright. Well, unpack and stop by my room when you're ready for the tour," I told him, retreating to my own space.

Fifteen minutes later Zach was at my door, ready to go. We toured the building, talking and laughing the whole way. His humor was sharp, and I hadn't realized how much I needed to laugh. Over pizza in the cafeteria, he imitated a swaggering jock so perfectly I nearly choked from laughing. By the time I had to run to class, it felt like we were already old friends.

"Don't forget—we meet tonight downstairs. You'll get to meet the rest of the guys," I called as I headed to marketing principles.

That evening, the debates began as usual. Zach slipped in about five minutes into a heated exchange on religion. His face flushed pink as he sat across from me. Since my return, the debates had taken on a sharper edge. I wondered if the others, like me, had brought back a piece of what they left behind.

"Man, you don't go around cramming beliefs down people's throats!" one guy shouted. "I'm sick of being told I'm going to hell for this or that!"

"Cool down," I said, trying to sound calm and steady.

"Why are people like that? Why are they always judging?" another chimed in.

"Isn't there something in the Bible about not judging others— an eye for an eye or something?"

I struggled to keep track of who was shouting what.

"Yeah, isn't there somethin' 'bout that? I got enough on my shoulders already. The world's pressin' me down. I can't do anything right. Then I go home and the first thing out of my step-dad's mouth is I'm gettin' fat and goin' to hell!" one of the guys yelled. "Then he's sittin' there makin' black jokes about some guy on TV. Why people gotta judge, man? It's bogus!"

"Don't judge unless you want to be judged," Zach said suddenly, his voice steady and clear. I froze, staring at him. "It's in the Bible somewhere. Means if you live in a glass house, don't throw stones. And you—" he pointed toward the guy, "—you said you can't do anything right. That's self-judgment. And those other people judging you? They're just control freaks. They want someone to condemn so they can feel better about themselves."

I sat back, stunned. *Who was this guy?* I almost said it out loud.

"Yeah, that's it!" another friend nodded. "But what do ya mean by judging yourself? Lost me there."

Zach leaned forward, calmer now, the stutter gone. "When you keep beatin' yourself up for every little thing, you're just doin' their job for 'em. You're lettin' their garbage live inside you. That's what self-righteous people count on—that you'll believe their lies. But you don't have to."

I was impressed, amused, and intrigued. Zach seemed wise beyond his years. Then shame and fear crept in. I felt like he could see straight through me, so I tried to change the subject—but it was like *I* was the one stuttering. This wasn't going to end well. Fear crawled up my neck like a snake. I felt like I was watching myself from the outside.

What about this? What about that? they asked. Zach had an answer for everything, creative and thoughtful. I wondered how anyone but a priest or nun could know so much.

"My dad's nothing but a drunk. He's got a lotta nerve judging me," another guy said.

I started sweating. Not the drunk dad thing. Not here, not now. I fought to keep my emotions locked down.

"So what does it say about being gay?" someone called from the back.

There it was. I stopped breathing, bent to tie my shoe, anything to hide my face. What if I blushed? Did I look nervous? Was my fear giving me away? Who had asked that?

"Says not to judge anyone," Zach replied, calm as ever. "Period. No exclusions, far as I know."

It wasn't often that I was speechless, but I was then. Zach saw things so simply. His eyes glistened, cheeks flushed as the room heated, yet he spoke with warmth and conviction. I needed to hear him say there were no exclusions. I almost felt like I should be taking notes.

"Man, did you see the campus is starting spring concerts?" someone asked, and the subject shifted.

After midnight the crowd thinned. I was drained, the adrenaline from the debates long gone. I had barely dropped onto my bed when there was a knock.

"Thanks for the welcome today. I needed someone like you on this side of the trip. This place already feels like home," Zach said, then disappeared down the hall.

"No problem. That's what I'm here for. Glad it feels like home," I called after him. I almost added that I needed him on *my* trip too, but he was gone.

"Home? I wouldn't know home if it hit me between the eyes," I muttered as I climbed into bed and killed the light.

One day I would find home. For now, maybe this was the closest thing. I closed my eyes and, for the first time in a long while, prayed—thanking God for Zach and begging Him to help me find home, inside and out.

CHAPTER 28

Responsibility

"HOLD UP A MINUTE," I mumbled. "You know I need caffeine and nicotine on Mondays! Slow down ... you went out with who and where?"

"Sam, I went to dinner Saturday night in the hotel restaurant, and word is you're a shoe-in for the White House internship!" Mariana repeated, eyes wide.

"You're kidding! That would be incredible. Did this come from someone who actually knows what they're talking about?"

"Yes. Would I say it if I didn't?" she shot back, punching my arm playfully.

Mar and I met at a conference and clicked within minutes. Though we lived states apart, we kept in close contact. She once confessed a crush on me after a Harrisburg event. I was flattered, but I wasn't ready to talk about relationships. That part of myself was locked away. Most girls accepted that I was focused on my career, but I still battled with the question of why they were drawn to me.

I dreaded the emotional confrontations—especially when rejection led to tears. Their pain cut me deeply, and I felt responsible. Having never felt that kind of passion myself, I had nothing to compare it to. It left me frustrated with both them and myself. Still, I was grateful Mar and I stayed friends. Otherwise, we would have missed out on a genuinely rich, mutually supportive relationship.

Mar and I parted at the airport, and I found a quiet seat with plenty of space to relax before my flight. I reflected on how awesome the conference had been. As vice president, all my expenses were covered, and I loved working the crowd as usual. The thought of a White House internship thrilled me—getting paid was just a bonus. I boarded the plane floating on cloud nine and buried myself in paperwork to tune out the usual flight commotion. The drive back to campus gave me time to recharge. I had come a long way in a short period of time. Nothing could stop me now.

I grabbed my mail before heading to my room. At the bottom of the stack was an official-looking envelope. I took the stairs two at a time and tore it open.

"FAR OUT!" I yelled, not caring who heard me. "THIS IS THE REAL DEAL! OUT-A-SIGHT!"

Guys came running from every direction.

"What's happenin', man?" Dan asked as I slid down against the wall, letter in hand.

"You can say you knew me when! I'm going to Washington for the summer—White House intern right here!"

"No way, you serious?" Zach asked.

"Says it right here in black and white!" I said, waving the letter.

"Man, that's cool—you gotta be psyched!" someone else added.

"Partyyyyyyy!" I shouted. "But first, I gotta call my family," I said, grabbing the payphone receiver.

No one picked up the phone on Griffin Avenue, so I called Rob. Halfway through his congratulations, I ran out of quarters and the call cut off. It was fine—I'd at least told someone.

For the next few days, I walked on air as preparations kicked in—background checks, interviews, and the all-important wardrobe decisions. I had shaved my beard after the holidays but kept the mustache. Between conferences and events, I'd built up a decent set of business clothes, but I wanted to stand out among the thirty-five interns chosen. Time was short, and I pushed hard to get everything done.

I had honor society fraternity business to close out, RA protocols to finalize, and final exams looming. Dorm issues still landed on my desk daily, and I needed to prep for the fall semester so I wouldn't be behind after the summer. On top of it all, I had to hit the mall for the perfect suits and shoes.

I stayed low under the radar, dodging anyone who might pile on extra responsibilities. My schedule was carved down to the minute, and there was no room left for one more sliver of anything.

Just when I thought I had it under control, the flu swept through campus and hit my dorm hard. It was the worst I'd ever seen. I posted a quarantine notice on the front doors, scrubbed the floor outside my room, and fumed when no one admitted to the mess. I thought I was living with adults, not kids leaving their waste for someone else. Finals loomed, and every room reeked of vomit and cough syrup. No one was spared. A few guys close enough to home left for medical care. Every class I dragged myself to was half empty, and those who remained coughed and sneezed until professors told us to leave. I had never been so sick, but I kept moving, determined to finish. Somehow, I breezed through finals. When the dorm finally revived, my only concern was whether my red nose would heal before I arrived at the White House.

I also planned to attend Anne's graduation before leaving. Dreading Griffin Avenue, I arranged to stay at Rob's friend's place, then return to campus right after we celebrated. It worked out. After the ceremony, we took her to lunch. Her car was jammed full, her good-byes to Auggie and Gertie already behind her. She wasn't going back. California was about as far as she could get. She looked better than I'd ever seen and determined to make a life of her own. First, though, she wanted to spend a day or two on campus with me before heading west.

The ride back to campus felt nothing like my last trip, and I was relieved not to be dragging those old feelings with me. I kept Anne in my rearview mirror the whole way. How crazy that she was days from driving to California with no real plan, yet I worried about losing her on this short trip.

Within minutes of our arrival the dorm turned into a multi-floor party. Everyone wanted to show her a great time. A couple hours later we crashed in my room. I locked the door in case of a random visit, though I knew administration had its hands full with the frat houses.

We had a great few days. She was headed to LA, planning to stay with a friend until she found a job and place of her own. If not, she'd settle for a cheap hotel. She wasn't worried. She wasn't scared. She was free. She just wanted to cross the California border and dance in the highway if she had to.

We cried as she pulled away, but I had a good feeling about her. She was responsible, capable, intelligent. I laughed and waved as she raised her arm out the window at the stop sign and yelled, *"California or bust!"*

About a week later she called from a gas station payphone. She'd made it. I was secretly relieved. I had so much to do before I left, and that call gave me one less thing to worry about.

The Watergate scandal dominated the news, and I worried it might cancel the intern program. It never did. I was floating so high I barely needed a plane to carry me. Striding through the airport in my new suit, I felt debonair and diplomatic. Years later, seeing the press photos, I realized I must have been high on cough syrup when I bought it—and even higher when I wore it. Still, at the time, I was proud no one else had the same one.

I was assigned to the president's office, with responsibilities covering the youth spectrum. I traveled to several states to speak to youth organizations about the executive branch. Most importantly, I helped draft correspondence, briefs, reports, and speech outlines. It was a remarkable time in history to do that work. In August, I helped draft communications during the transfer of power when Nixon resigned and Ford became president. For a moment, I even wondered if politics might be my path instead of the priesthood, still tucked in the corners of my mind.

By summer's end, I was enamored with Washington, the people I met, and the friendships I made. The experience humbled and energized me, and the resume boost didn't hurt. On my last day, I roamed the offices for a souvenir. On the edge of a desk sat a White House cup and saucer. I already had photos, but this was perfect. Holding my breath, I slipped it gently into my flight bag and grinned all the way to the airport.

As I boarded, I imagined the Secret Service yanking me off in handcuffs, my reputation destroyed as the "intern-turned-convict." I even rehearsed my protest to the press: "I am not a crook!" I'd cry, just like Nixon.

"I have no idea who put these things in my bag!" I'd insist, pointing at everyone else.

I laughed at my own joke—thankfully only to myself.

CHAPTER 29

Education

IT WAS IMPOSSIBLE TO top the summer I had just lived. Everything else felt eclipsed by it. I threw myself into my sophomore semester, trying to ride its energy. Overcommitted, as usual, that's how I survived. I shifted from sciences to arts and leaned into my RA job.

Counseling residents came with the territory. I was fine advising on classes, but unprepared when they showed up with personal issues. Every new resident carried a story and, for reasons unknown, decided I was safe to tell it to. Apparently, I had one of those faces. Their trust honored me—and terrified me. Most problems needed a professional. I offered referrals, but no one took them.

Everyone needs someone to talk to. I knew that better than most. If you find one true friend, you're lucky; more than one is a jackpot. Some of the new "green" guys lacked any filter and blurted out whatever weighed on them. It didn't take long before they learned the hard way—words were repeated by others who judged, mocked, or dismissed their pain.

Worse was when they spilled it all after partying. The next day, regret would hit hard. Inhibitions gone, secrets out, the cruelest hangover was realizing how exposed you'd made yourself.

I'd also learned that, more often than not, people hurt each other further through *competitive comfort*. Nothing stings worse than hearing, *"That's nothing, I ..."* or *"You think that's bad?"* —as if misery were a contest where the sickest, poorest, or most damaged wins. Most people, I was convinced, had no clue what sympathy or empathy were, so compassion was too much to ask. Speaking advice into someone's life instead of listening only piled on more wounds.

Most days I wanted to wear a sign: *Notice to all citizens of the dorm residence: DO NO FURTHER HARM PLEASE!* Instead, I pinned it to my bulletin board. It sparked plenty of discussion, though often I wished I'd added: *The only acceptable excuse for misunderstanding this sign is an abnormally low IQ!*

Here's where I struggled: My tolerance for stupidity was low and for selective stupidity, even lower. Instead of a family tree, some people seemed to be products of a family wreath. Sadly, many of them appeared to cross my path daily.

Alongside my new classes, I devoured books and articles that stretched my views. I even dug into multiple Bible translations and a concordance, partly to keep up with Zach, whose knowledge intrigued me. His insights piqued my curiosity, and I was getting a real education as my questions deepened.

The debates now ran four nights a week and began attracting co-ed students who'd heard about them. Topics grew edgier, touching on the relentless news cycle surrounding the gay rights movement—a subject impossible to avoid. I longed to participate more personally without spilling my own struggles. I wanted my input to go beyond vague guesses, to spark deeper thinking with history, facts, and honest questions.

Moderating every night felt too constraining, so now everyone had to take a turn. For me, it wasn't just about keeping order—it was about finding ways to actually help, not harm.

My course choices reflected my new mission while also keeping the door open if I pursued Divinity. I was still torn. I loved advertising and business, politics lingered as an option, and then there was the old failsafe—priesthood. A politician, a businessman, and a priest walk into a bar—it felt like the start of a bad joke. Most people I knew had chosen their path; not me. By the end of my psychology lectures, I'd diagnosed myself with several mental illnesses. It was a relief, though, to learn I had one less. Being gay was no longer considered a disorder by the American Psychiatric Association since it failed to meet the criteria. Even so, I was a walking, talking Petri dish ready for analysis. I could have told anyone who asked—but no one did.

Along with my classes and books, I consumed every newspaper and TV news report I could find. Though biased, West Coast and New York outlets leaned more open-minded, so I subscribed to whatever I could get delivered. Even if it arrived days late, old information was better than none.

I couldn't believe what was happening across the United States. For the first time, I felt like I was growing the courage to face, confront, and share some of my feelings as a gay man—though not openly, not yet. Still, I drank in all the information. It didn't take long before I formed strong opinions about the travesties unfolding on both sides of the debate.

The news pages were full of turmoil. Conservatives and gay men and women were locked in battle. Conservatives demanded stricter laws while the gay community demanded the freedoms those laws should already guarantee. People on both sides were dying for their causes. I admired their bravery. Strangely, I understood where both viewpoints came from. I knew I needed to take a stand, yet I was frozen emotionally and spiritually. To me it was simply a civil rights issue. Both sides, fueled by fear, belief, judgment, and ignorance, only grew stronger. How anyone got away with discrimination in jobs, housing, law—even murder and abuse—was beyond me. More people came out every day, yet still they were a minority. This battle, I knew, would rage for years. Neither side seemed likely to back down—and I couldn't see why they would.

I felt double-minded. The more I learned, the more furious I became at the conservatives' cruel tactics. Beating, jailing, even killing men and women simply for who they loved was appalling. How could anyone do such things in the name of God? And conversion camps? Don't get me started. Where was the love and compassion in any of it? No wonder people turned away from God when they probably needed Him most. If anyone could have prayed the gay away, it would have been Father Bernard and me.

I also understood where conservatives drew their religious fervor. They believed they were acting morally. But they seemed to have forgotten who Jesus was, what He said, and who He spoke to. They lived in glass houses, hurling boulders at hurting, struggling people who were already beating themselves up.

I was also furious at the gay movement as a whole. I was embarrassed by the negative stereotypes splashed across television and newspapers. I didn't want to know what went on in straight men's bedrooms, so why flaunt what went on in theirs? If they wanted to be taken seriously, couldn't they show some respect for themselves and the cause? No wonder conservatives were fired up by those ridiculous displays and outrageous portrayals of gay men. The images in the press were insensitive, obnoxious, and inappropriate for children—or for adults with no exposure.

The fight against discrimination was necessary. New laws were desperately needed. But had they considered that their actions only fortified the opposition's fears? They were fighting for their lives, yes, but I was angry that a few reckless voices might ruin it for others and add fuel to the fire.

I was a heart divided, but leaning further away from religious conservatives who justified violence against some of the most innocent people on earth. The whole subject exhausted me. I threw up my hands, lit a smoke, and went to bed. The battle would wait for another day.

The holidays were on their way again and I forced them out of my mind. If I pushed myself to exhaustion, maybe I'd fall asleep without thinking. It worked until the hall phone rang and rang.

"Why doesn't someone pick that up?" I muttered—then yelled when someone finally answered.

"SAM! PHONE! BETTER HURRY!"

I bolted down the hall as Paul McCartney's "Band on the Run" skipped on my stereo. Fitting.

"This is Sam," I said, feeling foolish.

At first, I couldn't understand the voice on the other end. Then I realized it was Anne.

"Slow down! I can't understand you!" I begged.

And then I did. Sobs, screams, whimpers—and finally the words: She had been raped at knifepoint, in her apartment, by a man she couldn't identify.

"I'm so sorry. So, so sorry," I kept saying. "Did you call the police? Anyone else? Do you have friends who can be with you?"

"Call the police? And be dragged through it all again, blamed for it? No. I don't want anyone else to know. If Auggie finds out, he'll say I deserved it!" she cried harder.

"I'm sorry, hon. You didn't deserve this! No one deserves this!" I said, though I knew she was right. Rape was too often seen as the woman's fault, and the Marine would have considered it his "I told you so" victory.

"Of course no one deserves this—so why do I feel like I did? Why do I feel so dirty and guilty? I can hear him now: 'Blonde whores deserve getting raped!'" she sobbed.

Between outbursts, I learned she was with a friend, packing up everything and moving back east. Her freedom adventure out west had turned into a nightmare lesson in cruelty. She planned to finish the semester, then leave during the holidays. I wished I could fly out, drive back with her—she didn't seem strong enough to do it alone. She promised to call and update me as she traveled. I hung up with a heavy heart.

"Why did this have to happen to her? Hasn't she been through enough?" I muttered down the hall.

I was thrown for a loop. The mention of Auggie ripped open everything I had tried to repress. He had done Anne so wrong. Would she ever recover? She had seemed to be doing so well, finally free of it all. Yet it was as if the cloud followed her wherever she went.

I didn't know much about the aftereffects of rape. I only knew how I had suffered after Father Bernard. Even as a child, I remembered the feelings of violation—of having something stolen from me I couldn't name. The guilt, shame, and embarrassment. Feeling dirty, disgusting, and utterly alone. My innocent trust in people was gone, my view of myself mutilated. I could only believe Anne was suffering as I had, and my heart shattered at the thought.

I fought Aaron as I reached for my composition book. "NO!" I told myself. I would not give depression permission to flood me this time. I was not going to fall apart—not now. If I wanted a breakdown, it would have to make an appointment. There was nothing I could do right now to help Anne, change the past, or influence the future. What I could do was get through finals and cram everything I could about violence and its effects. I would be prepared when I got back to Griffin Avenue to help her however possible.

I would find a way to gather information while also keeping up with my debate research. What was one more thing?

Man, I didn't know what I was in for. The more information I found, the more surfaced. It felt like swimming in the ocean without a lifejacket. Violence toward women alone had its own battles, with sides just as divided as every other issue of the day. Everything I read bled together like ink on wet paper, then split apart in directions I hadn't even imagined. Just when I thought I had learned all there was on physical and mental abuse, the gay community, and religion, new perspectives rose from the ashes. I felt like I was thinking in parables while reading them. The saboteur in my head stirred mayhem in my thoughts, leaving me torn in every direction. But I refused to let the chaos slow me down.

I couldn't have drawn a firm conclusion on any issue—especially those surfacing in the debates—even if someone paid me. Still, I would continue to educate myself on every side so I might educate others in turn. Maybe then, maybe someday, lines could be crossed. If not by others, hopefully by me.

CHAPTER 30

Defying Logic

I HAD ONCE AGAIN arranged to stay with friends over the holidays, but the plans fell through. When I turned onto Griffin Avenue, the old familiar dread came over me. I parked behind Rob's car and noticed Anne's next to the garage. Shouting echoed as I reached for the screen door. For a moment I just stood there. My gut told me to get back in my car and flee. I had another invitation to stay with Becky in New Jersey, but I felt like a coward and was tired of running.

I couldn't go inside. I couldn't face another dysfunctional blowout. I got back in my car and dropped my head to the steering wheel. "Why can't You just take me now? Right here?" I prayed out loud. "Are You there? I know I'm supposed to believe there are reasons for everything. But it's getting harder. I am so tired of it all. It just defies logic." Tears slid down my cheeks.

I was a frozen coward. I knew they needed me. Sooner or later these incidents were going to escalate to a point of no return. Someone was going to be hurt physically beyond repair. The emotional damage had passed that point long ago.

I opened the car door and lit a smoke, needing courage to walk in. Slowly I headed for the front door, wanting a vantage point. From the side window I saw Rob and Jude in each other's face. I couldn't see the Marine, but his obscenities shook the walls. Anne, nearest the window, spotted me spying. She wiped her eyes, signaling me not to come inside, pointing toward my car. I shook my head no, inhaled deeply, then took the steps two at a time and pushed the door open.

"WELL, WELL! THE QUEER-AS-A-THREE-DOLLAR-BILL HAS ARRIVED!" the Marine shouted, swaying and nearly falling.

"Do you never tire of all this?" I muttered.

The others had likely scattered when chaos erupted. Faces behind glass hung on the walls, silent witnesses to endless abuse. If walls could speak, this room would chill you. I swore the house groaned under the weight of it all as the wind howled outside.

I tuned in to the fight—it surpassed all logic.

"You seriously accuse him of that? I oughta lay you out right here!" Jude snapped.

"Go ahead! Give me your best shot! We'll see who's standing! You had to be deaf, dumb, and blind as a kid if you say he didn't do those things! You were right there, you idiot!" Rob fired back.

This was obviously about Auggie. Jude was defending him—what else was new.

"Here we are again. Do we never tire of this? It makes no sense, Jude. You know that, don't you?" I pressed, knowing I was asking for it.

For a minute you could have heard a pin drop, then all hell broke loose again. We yelled over each other, trying to be heard while the Marine sat laughing in his chair beside his blue-lit Christmas tree. Mother came out of hiding to try and break it up, but it was useless. The air felt charged with every past fight that had ever taken place in that room, and we were feeding on it. In the end Jude stormed out.

Rob, Anne, and I drove around looking for somewhere open on Christmas Eve to have a drink. Auggie was huddled in the garage still drinking, while the rest of the family crept from their hiding places, trying to salvage some shred of Christmas. We ended up at a friend's house and decided the whole argument wasn't even worth talking about. Instead we spent the night in a real Christmas celebration—love, food, family, fellowship. It was a breath of fresh air.

The rest of the holiday carried on as it began, and the drive back to campus was full of the usual thoughts and feelings. The only consolation was time spent with Anne, Rob, Emma—and my tree. I nearly froze sitting beneath it, grieving another ruined holiday. But it was always there, offering comfort and shelter. Hard as it may be for others to grasp, I felt it absorbed my grief so I could find peace, however brief.

I arrived back at campus a few hours before the New Year's Eve party I had planned. A few guys had taken over the event but bailed last minute—aggravating but not surprising. I grabbed a couple cases of beer and some munchies, then still had an hour to kill before people showed.

I wandered the campus and ended up outside the chapel. I'd never gone in, fearing it was sinful to attend anything but a Catholic church. Pulling open the ornate wooden doors, I found a simple space—no kneelers, gothic arches, saints, or stations of the cross. It was non-denominational, lit by candles flickering against stained glass. I slipped into the back pew and whispered a prayer for the New Year. Gratitude quickly turned to interrogation, filled with anger, resentment, and hostility. I didn't realize I was crying until someone behind me handed me a tissue. Embarrassed, I wiped my face and turned to see a man.

"Sorry to intrude," he said. "I won't bother you. I just wanted to help."

"Why? Do I look like I need help?" I snapped, knowing I did.

"Yes. You appear broken, and that's the best way to be in here. It's the hardhearted who miss this place's purpose. I'm Pastor Gray," he said, extending a hand.

This was why I preferred my tree—no interruptions, intrusions, or humiliation. I didn't want to shake his hand.

"It's okay. I'll leave you to your thoughts and prayers," he said, pulling his hand back.

"Ah … um … sorry. I don't mean to be disrespectful. I'm just not used to priests stopping to chat and hand out tissues," I explained.

"No problem. No disrespect felt. You're Catholic, I assume, from your reference to priests," he replied.

"Yes. Born and bred—and I've got the marks to prove it," I said, half smiling at my poor joke.

"We all have and leave marks. None of us is innocent. Confusion comes when we hold God responsible for man's marks," he said softly.

"Sorry, bad joke. I hadn't thought of it that way before, though I've thought plenty."

"We all have. We need somewhere to put blame. We need someone to pay. God is big—He can handle our anger and frustration. What grieves Him is when we stop asking questions. Questions prove we accept His reality."

"I don't know about that. Sometimes I wonder. Most times I feel I'm just talking to the ceiling. Straight to hell—do not pass go, do not collect two hundred dollars," I mumbled.

"Doubt is normal, especially when times are hard and situations defy explanation," he said quietly.

"I guess I don't doubt. I believe God is there. But He feels busy elsewhere most of the time, and I have a hard time understanding. More often than not, I just don't get Him," I whispered.

"That's no surprise to Him. We all have those times when we feel alone. He will never leave or forsake us, but He can be very quiet. I've grown thankful for unanswered prayers," he said, walking away.

I was even more bewildered. Thankful for unanswered prayers? It made no sense. I began to think I wasn't the only one with issues in this room.

"That doesn't make sense. Logically, if a person prays and God is always listening, why wouldn't He answer? You want me to believe He just sits there and ignores it on purpose, for fun?" I called out, louder now as he was several pews ahead.

"No, not for fun. Tell me—has this been the first time you've prayed? Think of the sum of your prayers over a lifetime. Wasn't it usually in times of crisis, when you were asking frantically for answers? When you have some time, look back on those prayers. I'd bet you'll realize, as I have, that not all of them panning out was a blessing. If you're looking for logic, let me ask you this— does faith have anything to do with logic?" he asked, smiling.

"Nothing makes sense to me lately. Honestly, not much ever has."

"I don't pretend to know what you're going through, but I believe we're given what we need to survive and even succeed. The struggles we face shape us for what lies ahead—for ourselves or for those we love. Each day comes with new grace to handle it. Many times I thought my prayers went unanswered, but His silence was an answer. He gave me strength to endure. That's God's promise. I'm old now, and while I don't like most of what I endured or want to repeat it, I can see the plan. God has a plan for each of us," the pastor said, sitting beside me. "Maybe I can't help you understand, but I can pray for you."

"A plan? Really? You mean I'm supposed to be stronger because of all this? It's eating me alive! His plan is for me to live on the edge, wishing I were dead, but terrified of offending Him? That being who I am—who He made me—offends Him? And ending it all would offend Him too? So His plan is that I exist only to offend? How can you sit there so certain? None of it makes sense!" I blurted, standing to leave.

"Son, I didn't mean to confuse you more," he said gently. "I'm saying He promises to be there. His ways aren't ours. Deep down you already know the answers, and I'll pray you see what He's showing you." His voice echoed as I pushed open the chapel doors.

"I'm not your son!" I shouted, storming back toward the dorms.

Plan? His plan is that I suffer all this? That I live dangling by a shoestring? My anger boiled over into pure confusion. Why couldn't anything ever be simple? Why couldn't something, anything, make sense?

How many times have I begged for answers, for direction? This is Your plan? I thought, glaring at the sky.

The evening was warm, the clear heavens scattered with stars. Half a block from the chapel, I stood frozen, screaming inside at God. Without warning, rain poured down. Lightning cracked, thunder followed, and wind whipped through the street. I ran.

"Perfect! Just what I needed—another thing that defies explanation," I muttered as I reached the dorm. The storm outside mirrored the one inside me.

In a few short hours the new year would arrive. My only plan was to be so high by then I wouldn't even notice.

CHAPTER 31

Crossing Lines

WHAT A YEAR IT was, my senior year. Other than summers with Rob, Anne, and friends at the shore, attending concerts, and suffering through the holidays, I lived buried under all the commitments I had accepted. Being on the list of "Who's Who" and president or vice president of several societies, associations, councils, and committees had its perks. It kept me so busy I had no time to think about my feelings.

I pushed myself past my limits but was still officially bored, so I finally did something I loved—I took the producers of the college radio programs up on their offer to become a disc jockey. If I had no other place to be on earth, I'd have been complete just sitting there spinning vinyl and sending tunes across the airwaves. Nothing cleared my mind like England Dan and John Ford Coley, the Eagles, Steve Miller Band, and Seals and Crofts. James Taylor, the Beatles, and Paul McCartney were essentials. Fleetwood Mac, Ray Charles, with a little Mozart and Beethoven mixed in, were added bonuses.

Spinning Earth, Wind & Fire, The Who, and an occasional Jimi Hendrix or The Doors was all I needed to survive, along with countless other jazz and rock bands. And when I actually had time to think, I gravitated to Gilbert O'Sullivan's "Alone Again, Naturally" or The Doors' "Break On Through (to the Other Side)"—songs that carried deep meaning for me and always sent Aaron to writing in his notebooks.

I loved movies, too, and often reviewed them on the program. Everyone raved about *Rocky*, *Taxi Driver*, and *Jaws*. We were all flipped out by *Star Wars* and *Close Encounters* as the world searched for meaning—even if far-fetched. But nothing compared to the calming, peaceful effect music had on me.

When I wasn't juggling all those commitments, I split my time between communication and mass media courses and anything ending in "-ology." I studied just about every theory-heavy subject available. I still made time for the dorm debates, now trimmed to two nights a week. Becky was involved in almost everything I did on campus, debates included. Zach was always there, and the crowd had grown into a sharp, informed group. I loved few things more than a good debate. The topics were impressive and often wide open, leading to incredible discussions.

Lately, though, some subjects struck nerves, and entire evenings spun around a single thought. Tonight was my turn to moderate, and I had butterflies knowing the latest news was sure to dominate—and it wasn't what I wanted to dive into. I was running late, and my tardiness clearly wasn't appreciated. The tension in the air told me a hornet's nest had already been stirred. Becky grabbed me as I walked in and whispered a warning, but it was too late.

"What in the world would give you the idea—umm … Sam, man am I glad to see you!" Zach said, my entrance breaking his thought.

"What's happenin'?" I asked as we exchanged high fives.

Before he could answer, I scanned the room and froze. A girl was crying, several guys stood red-faced, and someone I'd never seen before was climbing onto a table, trying to dominate the crowd. Whispers and finger-pointing filled the room, and unease knotted in my stomach.

"Let's see what Sam has to say about all this. There are rules for those who've never attended. If you can't stand the heat, get out of the kitchen, man!" a girl snapped, though her name escaped me.

"Let's see what I have to say about what? Looks like a war zone in here!" I said, bracing for the answers.

"News is they just elected the first openly gay man to public office in California. Some here take personal issue; others are just plain obnoxious. When it turns into name-calling, nerves are hit. Way I see it, everyone needs to quit spazzin' out," Zach explained.

Every muscle in my neck tensed. I rolled my head, but it felt like a boulder sat on top. I was in no mood for immature drop-ins, and I hoped we could move the subject along.

"First, could everyone please introduce themselves before speaking? Any objection to changing topics since this one's provoking animosity? Or can we agree to disagree and not fight about it?" I asked, sliding into a chair and cracking a beer.

Everyone spoke at once.

"WHOOOAAA!" I shouted. "This is not helping!"

"Listen! If you want to speak, you need to be recognized by Sam!" Zach barked, and the crowd finally quieted.

"Look, step forward one by one, raise a finger, and I'll give you a chance to speak," I said, leaning my chair back against the wall.

"You in the white shirt—why are you crying?" I asked.

She walked slowly to the front, wringing her hands. "I'm not cryin'! My eyes are watering from the abnormal amount of aftershave and testosterone in this room! Man!!!" she said, and everyone burst out laughing.

"Everyone might remember that and go easy on the stuff, or we'll need to hand out face masks!" I added, laughing.

"My name is Sandy—with a *y*. As you can see, I'm unusually sensitive to aftershave. Probably because I have little exposure to it—I'm a lesbian," she said confidently. "What's the matter? Never seen a lesbian before? Come on, admit it!" she teased.

"Thanks, Sandy with a *y*," I replied. "You wanna give me your take on tonight?"

"Be happy to, Sam. Seems the whole subject of being gay upsets a lot of people here. And if it doesn't, they've got a strange way of showing it," she said, eyeing the crowd.

"Okay, so you all heard about the first openly gay man elected to the San Francisco Board of Supervisors? Here's the obvious question—what does being gay have to do with his job and title?" I asked, trying not to show how disturbed I was inside. Hands shot up all around the room.

"Here's how we'll proceed tonight," I said. "Instead of me recognizing everyone, walk up front where Sandy is, speak your piece, then let the next person. We're adults—we should be able to do this in order." Heads nodded in agreement.

"It has everything to do with it! We don't need people like them in authority influencing the population. Before long there'll be street queens running for president, queers teaching our kids, preaching in churches, working in nurseries—and that's not right!" the first participant spat.

Sandy stepped back up. "Do you know the wounds those names create? You wonder why people are messed up? Maybe it's better we have people in office who *don't* share your attitude. They're already teaching in your nurseries, preaching in churches—you just don't know it because they're scared of you. We don't care what you do in your bedroom, so why should you care about ours?"

Another man stepped up. "Faggots are an abomination to God!" he said, storming toward the door.

My blood boiled. I'd had enough of hatred to last a lifetime.

"Check Proverbs 6!" Zach called after him. "It also says pride, lying, murder, and causing discord are abominations. Everyone lies, everyone's proud sometimes—yet you're not shouting that, are you? I challenge you to stay and maybe learn something. If you bring religion in, it's a whole new discussion. A debate means different points of view. We can discuss without name-calling. Anyone who disagrees can leave. We're here to broaden understanding, not make judgments."

"Nah … thanks, man. I can't see anything to understand here," he said, leaving the building.

"I can see his point though!" John from the third floor spoke up. "I was raised in a Christian church. I was taught it's a sin—that God hates it."

Sandy stepped forward again.

"We have something in common, John. I was raised in a Christian church too, by straight parents. I went to public school; most of my friends were straight. But as far back as five I knew I felt different from other girls. By sixteen, I carried shame—not from God, but from people. I was terrified I'd be sent to a conversion camp. Do you know what they do to kids there?

"I sat in pews beside liars, thieves, gluttons, adulterers—all acceptable. Meanwhile, folks in my small town suspected I was gay. Rumors spread, fingers pointed. I'm no biblical scholar, but that reeks of hypocrisy. If churches were only for the perfect, the pews would be empty.

"I reached a point where I still believed in God but couldn't stay in a religion preaching enough hell and damnation to last lifetimes. Even my own brother called me names and walked away. Thankfully, most of my family loved me, but the rejection cut deep.

"Those of you who haven't seen anything else think it's your job to judge me. I'm not asking for acceptance of my lifestyle—I can't accept many of yours. We just want to be loved and accepted for who we are, not condemned for who we love."

Sandy stepped aside.

You could have heard a pin drop until Joe from the first floor stepped forward. "You can't believe—no one can—that you're just made this way. The Bible says God hates homos. Sure, people sin, but that doesn't mean we want gays teaching our kids or harassing us at work. It's disgusting. It's not natural.

"I was raised Catholic. It's just not right. I've seen the stuff on TV—child molesters, deviants, drag queens parading half naked, shoving it down everyone's throat. If you don't want us caring what happens in your bedrooms, why put it on the five o'clock news where kids see it? It's against the law in lots of states. Maybe we should let prisoners run wild too. God made the rules—one man, one woman. We're supposed to multiply. How's that supposed to happen?"

I was about to explode. How Sandy stood there listening without body-slamming him I'll never know. She didn't flinch. She just looked at him, calm, almost compassionate.

"May I respond to him?" she asked gently.

I nodded.

"Joe, you're not perfect, so slide over and make room for one more hypocrite. I'm not naive—I know there are gay child molesters. But do you really believe there are no heterosexual ones? Most gay people I know spend their lives compared to deviants or criminals. Why do you think we're afraid to tell anyone?

"Do you think we *want* to be gay? Or that the five o'clock news is an accurate picture of us all? Here's a clue: There are already gay teachers, doctors, pastors, and priests. They hide because they're terrified of losing what they've worked for. You take a few TV examples and claim that's who we are. Is it fair to say all straight people are the same? Please.

"If you're calling it sin, then what about lying, gluttony, gambling, envy, pride? Why is being gay somehow worse? People can choose not to gossip or hate, but we're condemned for existing. Is coveting worse than stealing? Criticism worse than gossip? Hate less than impatience?

"At least gay people are being honest about who they are. We stand in front of laws, ridicule, and hate, and still claim our rights and our truth.

"I respect that you have your own convictions. Why do they have to be mine? The word *sin* has been misused and weaponized for whatever someone wants. I understand it to mean acting in a way that harms your own good. For me, being anything other than who I am would be the real sin.

"I've felt this way as long as I can remember. I was made this way. We're all struggling with something. I accept others' struggles, but the courtesy isn't extended to me. Instead, we point fingers. Why twist a small phrase in the Bible to make yourself look better? No one is perfect—so why so much hate? For me, it's about love.

"And bringing the law into this? Ridiculous. The law already promises freedom and equality, yet it's still legal to discriminate. People can be fired, arrested in nightclubs, even murdered for who they love. This is supposed to be a free country. And don't get me started on the idiotic laws still on the books that make no sense at all!"

The room was slowly emptying. I could see Zach itching to jump in. I sat frozen, afraid of losing control and blowing up.

"If you all don't mind, I'd like to interject a few things," Zach said frankly, unable to sit by.

Sandy and Joe stepped aside.

"This issue will exist as long as there's *religion* in the world—as long as Christians and others keep interpreting texts through their own assumptions and viewpoints. Every sect thinks they have the one true answer. My nana had a unique way of seeing life. If she were here, she'd ask why we keep judging and comparing ourselves. She'd remind us everyone has something to bear in life—even Jesus carried His own cross and cried out for His Father to take it from Him. What kept Him there wasn't force—it was His heart and His love for us.

"She would say He loved each of us equally—no one more or less. She'd warn that when we judge, we step into dangerous territory, because we are not God. She believed both sides of this argument are guilty of that. Every time I even thought about criticizing someone, she'd remind me to make sure I had no faults first. If I claimed to be better than anyone else, she'd ask me to prove it.

"What I learned is simple: People will disappoint you. They will hurt and deceive you. Everyone has issues that make them act miserably, shaping the way they treat others. Each of us has different sides, and every day we choose whether to cross lines or not. We're always searching for justifications for our beliefs and actions, always working to prove ourselves right. Aren't we?" Zach shared.

"Sorry, man, no offense to your nana, but what do *you* have to say? You always seem to know more than the rest of us!" someone yelled from the back.

"Okay, I believe every one of us is unconditionally loved by God. Love is the most important of all gifts—we are nothing without it. Since you brought up religion, I'll go there. First Corinthians basically says I can speak God's Word and reveal all insights, but I am still nothing without love. I can have unwavering faith and even die a martyr, but without love I am nowhere.

"We should love each other deeply because it covers a multitude of things. No matter what I say, do, or believe, I am nothing without love. I don't know everything, but I know no one is perfect. We're all unique—our fingerprints prove we are one of a kind, like God's final mark on His creation. To me, that means we're not to judge others, because we are all different. Sure, there's a list of sins in Scripture, but judging one another is just as bad as any of them," Zach said firmly as he stepped aside.

"I'm Carla. Since this seems to have shifted into religion, why do you think people twist up what seems like basic Christianity? Wasn't it always about love from the beginning?"

"Hi, Carla. I agree. Maybe you could share what you mean by 'basics' so everyone here has a clear picture of what you're saying?" Zach asked.

"Okay. Basics. Christians believe God created us and the universe out of love. Christianity is about love and relationships. To me there's nothing more sacrificial than giving Your own Son for undeserving, ungrateful people. Nothing more humbling than allowing angry mobs to condemn, spit on, stab, and nail Him to a cross, all so we wouldn't have to. Could we bear watching our son do the same? Would we have the courage to do it ourselves for others? It would be like a family member taking a bullet so we could live. That's amazing love! All of this so we may be forgiven and spend eternity with Him. And what does He ask? To love one another as He loved us. That's why I say—why is this more complicated than basic Christianity when it's always been about love?" Carla said.

"Thanks, Carla. Sadly, different tribes, denominations, or non-denominationals add little twists, and that's where judgment creeps in. Some get stuck in the Old Testament, where people lived under the law—God's laws—and believe rules are still required for grace. Historically, covenants were agreements sealed with blood sacrifices. But in the New Testament, Jesus was the final sacrifice, freeing us from the law. We are forever under God's grace. Grace is a gift—something we can't earn and don't deserve. It frees us to be who we are, owing nothing in return. Now, to put that in terms closer to our situation here at school …" Zach said, clearing his throat.

"I get all that, but how does this apply now? That was thousands of years ago. You mean it's true for us freaks today? Like here?" Kris from the first floor asked, wide-eyed.

"That's far out, man!" I cracked up—Kris's mind was always blown, usually with a little help.

"Alright, here's another way to look at it," Zach said. "Most of us didn't get a full ride. We're here on loans, grants, side jobs, maybe credit cards. We'll be paying this education off for years. Some of us are juggling rent, insurance, utilities too.

"What happened on that cross two thousand years ago was like the ultimate debt payoff—past, present, and future. Everything already covered. Instead of 'amount due,' the statement reads: 'Paid in full—by His goodness.' Why? Because He loves every one of us exactly as we are.

"He didn't say the deal only covers this group or that one. It's anyone who believes. And nothing can separate us from God—unless we turn our backs. Sadly, that happens when people dump Him because some idiot tries to speak for Him. But God? He's still cool with us. Isn't that a kicker?

"Humans muddy the waters with laws and rules about what this free gift should mean and how a recipient should act. They insist we fit *their* interpretation of 'acceptable' to participate, and in the end it becomes a twisted grab-bag version of grace. We pile on new rules and self-righteous ideas until the freedom in the message collapses like a house of cards and gets buried under the mess.

"Those we try to share it with either wear themselves out trying to measure up or run far away, convinced they never will. We also stop trusting. Do you trust something that sounds too good to be true? Usually not—because it usually is. When someone gives us a gift that feels too much, we push it back, thinking: *I can't accept this. I'll never repay it.* So when we hear about grace, we trip over the same problem. *Nothing's free.*

"How could God really love us just the way we are? We can't grasp how big He is. If change is needed, He's the one who does it—not us, not those around us. Sometimes it takes a lifetime; sometimes it never looks like change at all. But He can use us right where we are and loves us anyway. And His advice is simple: Love each other in the same way.

"What? You're all looking at me like I'm stoned, man? I'm saying everything was wiped out two thousand years ago—our judgments, hypocrisy, lying, all of it. Nothing we do can change that. Even when we give up on Him, He doesn't give up on us. He may not be thrilled with everything we do, but He still loves us.

"And I don't see Him as the 'Man' hiding behind every obstacle waiting to nail us with a ticket when we mess up. He's not sitting around saying, 'You're busted—here's your punishment.' Life already has its own consequences, and that's plenty. This universe He created is woven together like dominoes or a house of cards—every action has a reaction. Don't study for midterms? That has consequences. Pay attention and study? Different outcome. It's just how life works.

"You mentioned hypocrisy. I think we all—Christians and non-Christians—feel better ranking sins one to ten so we can look down on someone 'worse' and feel better about ourselves. That's human nature. But the truth is, we all have far to go. We want to sprint ahead, but half the time we're just spinning our wheels in the mud because we forget about love.

"We roll God up in a neat little designer tube, screw the lid on, and think we've figured Him out. How could that ever work? We don't stop to realize how enormous He really is. Christians especially think they aren't judging when they're just filtering everything through their tribal perspective of what's 'right.' And that's probably why they end up being judged themselves—by everyone, including the gay community—and honestly, for good reason." Zach stepped back as Sandy moved forward again.

"Define grace again, man!" someone called from the back.

"Grace? It's free. Unmerited. You did nothing to deserve it, didn't work for it, and it comes with no strings. God's favor—a gift done for you," Zach answered.

"Okay, I get that. But how does it apply to being gay? And why does the Bible sound so negative about it?" Sandy asked.

Zach stayed calm, his presence steadying the room. He always seemed like an old soul, weighing his words until they cut straight through the noise.

"Which part of *EV-ER-Y-ONE* in my description didn't you get?" Zach teased with a grin. Then, serious again: "Look, the Bible went through many interpreters, languages, scholars, and writers. All men, given the era. We can't know everything, but here's my take: He's God. He makes the rules. He sees from beginning to end.

"What if the warnings we read were God's way of trying to steer *all of us*—gay and straight, conservative and liberal—away from pain, discrimination, and judgment? What if they were less about condemning people and more about showing there was a way to avoid the conflict that history has proven would come?

"All I can really go on is the New Testament—the final covenant. And in it, Jesus never said a word against being gay. What He *did* say, over and over, was to love everyone unconditionally. We don't need validation to love.

"Sure, neither side has followed the 'manufacturer's recommendations' all that well. But He still loves both equally. That's the point. And honestly, I'm just beginning to learn this myself."

Sandy stepped forward again.

"I think it's more about how we live each day—how we treat others and the world around us. Tolerate and respect people and their beliefs. Live a good life, be kind, and seek wisdom. If more people made it their mission to love, what an example that would be!" Sandy said, grinning ear to ear.

"My name is Mary. Man, I don't get it! There's right and wrong, that's it! You can't agree with all this gay or lesbian stuff and still call yourself a Christian. What a great example of a Christian you are. Talk about doing damage for others!"

Zach exhaled and stepped forward. "I agree with you, Sandy. We're free to believe as we choose, and you and I probably share more common ground than not. We should have coffee sometime.

"And Mary, I don't agree or disagree with anyone here. I don't want to be a good example of a Christian—or any example at all. I don't want people looking at me to justify themselves. No, I don't know everything. Yes, I've got issues. And no, I'm not gay. But your judgment of me—and of who you think a Christian should be—tells me you listen to those who need approval. I hear, 'Look, God! Look at me! I'm better than this one or that one.'

"You mentioned damage, so here's my take: We all cause it because we are damaged. We crave love, praise, approval. Conditioned from birth to compare and compete, we grow arrogant and think we're better than others. We believe goodness is rewarded, so it stops being natural—it becomes performance. We're always looking sideways instead of up.

"I'd love to have coffee with you too, Mary, if you'd like."

He spoke with such love I had tears in my eyes. Mary, need-less to say, sat back down.

"Man, how come I never heard any of this before?" Joe said angrily.

"I don't know, Joe. I'll answer more questions if you want," Zach replied, as heads nodded.

"Why do people—not just in the gay community—look at all Christians as the same when we're just as diverse? Some don't realize their actions and words cause pain. People compete only when they think they can reach the finish line. They compare themselves to those who seem better—like the teacher's pet or the straight-A student. They freak out, don't want to work that hard, and decide they'll never measure up. Then they run from God.

"If Christians didn't try so hard to be something they're not, everyone would want to be like them. Lines would form outside churches, people waiting days for a ticket in. Could it be both sides fuel the battle with pain, anger, and misunderstanding? Maybe a few bad apples spoil the whole bunch. Outspoken ones get the press, while those hiding or just trying to survive latch onto what they see and hear and take it as gospel.

"Maybe when we're busy judging others, we don't have to face ourselves. Instead of fighting the good fight side by side, we fight each other. And the damage we cause in a split second—with one word or thought—creates a stumbling block so big generations can't climb past it. We put unrealistic expectations on each oth-er. Life is a process, and all of us are under construction." Zach looked around at the faces staring back at him.

I tried to find a reason to end it all. The tug of war in my heart and head tormented me. I wanted silence yet longed to hear more. I had questions but couldn't form them, opinions but no nerve to share. Sandy and Joe were still engaged but didn't comment. The room thinned, though enough people remained to keep it going.

"So, am I right to think you're saying both sides are wrong and right at the same time?" a girl asked, shifting in her chair.

"Yes and no. It's not for me, you, or any of us to decide. We forget why we were created—love. I agree with you, Sandy: It began with love and ends with love. And when we forget that, things only get worse. It's about returning again and again to the lessons of love, even when we don't understand—even when they look or act different than we do," Zach said.

"I have so many questions about love, compassion, and mercy for you, Joe. They say it takes seven compliments to undo one criticism. Words are often why people walk away from God. We don't have all the answers. We are not God. To me, it's about love and about holding a mustard seed of faith and letting God do the rest." Zach spoke so softly it was nearly a whisper.

Joe shrugged, sat with arms crossed, then after a few seconds of silence got back up and stepped forward.

"Okay, Zach, maybe I don't have answers for all your questions. Maybe I shouldn't judge gay people, but where's the line between right and wrong? God was angry at plenty in the Bible— He destroyed cities and turned folks into stone," Joe said, sounding slightly arrogant.

"Oh, none of us need reminding of God's wrath. But you know what set Him off most? When hypocrites twisted His Word and name to manipulate others. Jesus was a man too—don't you think He understands what it's like down here? He hung out like we are now, with guys like us.

"Noah was a drunk. David had an affair and killed a man. Rahab was a prostitute. Samson was a long-haired hippie freak. The Samaritan woman was divorced more than once. God chose an unwed mother to give birth to Jesus. Isaiah preached naked. And the list goes on. None of us is too much of a freak to be loved and used by God. Why can't we follow that example?

"How would you feel if science proved Sandy was born as she is? God already knows—we don't need all this extra information to love one another. And you're right, Sandy: If churches were for people without issues, the pews would be empty. We all—even the scholars—know just enough to be dangerous."

Zach had found his voice, and his words left nothing to the imagination. He made people think. From that day forward, I never heard him struggle to speak again. Sandy rose and moved forward.

"So you're saying you agree with me then, Zach? Or are you just open-minded?" she asked playfully.

"I love your sense of humor, Sandy—we need more of that. But I'm not an advocate for or against homosexuality. I'm an advocate for being real, against judging, and for equal rights. I'm for dialogue, discussion, and loving without condition. I admire your resilience. Every time we talk about this, we grow. I'm for loving a person even if you disagree with them. I want that same acceptance. I'm for listening with the two ears God gave us and shutting the one mouth we have—especially if our words cause pain."

He hugged Sandy, tried to high-five Joe, who refused. Zach sighed and walked out.

"Where the heck did that come from?" someone said. "That's why I'm an atheist—too much BS!"

"Sounds like he defends the faggots and loves them," another said as he left.

"Man, that was the most awesome thing I ever heard," a girl whispered.

Sandy extended her hand to Joe, hoping for a ceasefire. He looked at her with disgust and walked away. Her eyes filled with tears, but she brushed them aside. She'd faced far worse—it was obvious.

"Sorry. I sometimes wonder if these things should keep going," I said, walking up to her.

"Of course they should. The answer is agreeing to disagree. Every time we create dialogue—even an argument—the subject is brought to the surface again. The only solution is discussion, education, and, as Zach said, love. I'd do this every day if I could. Talking keeps it out there and relevant. Until it's handled with respect—until both sides stop the madness of murder, abuse, and bullying, and choose love—nothing will change. Don't apologize for Joe. It's his loss. I am awesome!" she said, winking.

"Yes, you are awesome—Sandy with a *y*! Thanks. You're right in more ways than one," I replied, gathering my things.

"Man, you didn't say a thing, Sam. You queer or something?" Dave from the second floor asked, throwing an arm across my shoulder.

I felt the urge to strike him—to elbow, kick, and drop him to his knees. But I heard Zach's words about love, stopped, and looked him in the eye.

"What if I am, Dave? What if I am?" I said. His arm dropped, and I walked toward my room.

So much to take in for one evening. My struggle between the spiritual and physical was being forced to the surface.

What if both sides stopped, erased their cement lines, and laid down weapons of hatred and judgment? What then? What if we truly loved one another and treated each other as we wished to be treated? Is that too hard to imagine? Judging by the reactions of some who left, we had far to go. But what if … "Imagine all the people," I thought—and I wasn't even listening to the Beatles.

CHAPTER 32

Closet Containment

I WAS RESTLESS. EVENINGS like tonight were happening more often, emotions accelerating with intensity. It felt like society had no more room to store its frustrations—not only about the gay and straight community, but so much more. Change was pressing at the seams, and they weren't holding. The pressure in me, and across the country, was at a melting point, heightened by news of hate crimes on both sides. Standing on the sidelines was harder; conviction grew daily. I searched through my collection for a book on this very issue when Zach stopped at my door.

"Hey, man, sorry I just walked out without thanking Sandy. If I'd stayed one more minute, I would've let loose!" he said, sitting on the edge of my bed.

"You mean that wasn't loose? Don't worry—she didn't expect a thank you," I joked, half serious.

"I knew you'd say that. I didn't mean to go on like that, but the words just came out. They were ready to crucify everyone—except me. I guess that's something," he said.

"Relax, Zach." I opened the closet doors. "I understood where everyone was coming from. You were right—it's a battle that will rage until we find a way to accept one another. But it's hard not to feel hurt when people call me names. I've heard this crap my whole life."

I froze in my tracks and slowly looked Zach in the eye. He was slow to respond, reluctant even.

"Sounds like the voice of experience to me. Am I right, Sam? It's cool. I'm good at keeping things to myself—despite tonight's rant," Zach almost whispered.

"Wow, that just fell out of my mouth, didn't it?" I said, unsure what to do.

A strange sense of freedom washed over me. Only Anne knew I was gay. I was pretty sure I'd told Becky one drunken night, but I never confirmed it the next day. I acted the same, waiting for her to bring it up.

I turned back to the closet and reached for a book at the bottom of a tall stack. I thought I could slide it out while holding the pile above, but the whole thing came tumbling down, hitting my head and feet. Zach jumped to help, but we needed more hands to stop the avalanche.

"Yes it did, man, yes it did," Zach said, trying to help.

"Looks like I need a new containment strategy. I guess I've had more than one closet overflowing. Maybe it's time to go through what I've stored for decades and decide what to keep and what to toss. Some things have been hidden a long time. Not everything is better in the light of day," I mumbled, stacking books by my desk.

"Sam, you don't need to feel uncomfortable with me. I'm cool with you. We're friends. I already knew anyway," he said, placing a hand on my shoulder.

"You did? I thought I hid it pretty well!"

"Sam, you don't think it's obvious? You've only gone out with a few girls since I've known you. You've got more girl friends than the rest of us, and I can see your pain when the subject comes up."

"Seriously? I repressed it so long I thought I was invisible. Has anyone else figured it out?"

"Yes, in fact just about everyone in this dorm has wondered at least once. But they're cool with you, Sam. You're an inspiration. We're not asking for details—it's alright for you to be you. I'm not judging if that's what you feared. Even with everything I said tonight, I was only making a point," he said, walking to the door.

"I think you just need to be real. You might be surprised by the reactions. Honesty goes a long way. You already know how some folks feel and what they'll say—you've probably said it to yourself for years. What's the worst that can happen? Do you really think telling the truth will ignite some cataclysmic chain of events? I doubt it. More likely, you'll live in the open and face the same fears you already imagined," he said, leaning against the doorframe."

"How are you so wise? Did you know I wanted to be a priest? I took all the prep courses, thinking maybe celibacy would stop this train wreck I felt headed for," I said, almost in tears.

"A priest? That's cool, but I don't think that's a safeguard. Don't they have enough to deal with? Ha! Okay, you be a priest and I'll be a sidewalk prophet! I'm here because I want to grow and help people. We could reach everyone with silly love songs. Seriously though, the world's not ready for our blue-jean wearin', rock-and-roll playin', people-lovin' selves yet. I want to be so many things, go so many places, try so much—who knows," he said, grinning ear to ear.

"Maybe I'm not the only one keeping things locked in closets," I laughed. "The picture of you doing that cracks me up—though it kind of makes sense. You're like no one I've ever met. Why am I picturing Woodstock as our kind of gathering?"

"You got it! Minus mood enhancers, with a different kind of free love, and a lot less mud! Otherwise, we'd be wide open to judgment, don't you think? Not to shift back, but I like getting to know people before I run off at the mouth like tonight. I hate being judged for what I think and feel. You don't know how bad it feels when people judge me first and ask questions later," he said, grinning.

"Me? No! I can't imagine!" I laughed. "And when the day comes you break out on your own, I better be your first call. I'd die to see it!"

"You bet. We'd have a huge invite list for that one!" he said, getting up.

"Thanks, man. Really. And thanks for the laugh." I raised my hand to his. His presence alone made me stronger. His humor could give a dishrag hysterical qualities.

"Least I can do. If you ever need me, want to talk, feel free," he said, walking down the hall.

I sat on the edge of my bed, feeling lighter, less pressure on my neck, a little more free. Dropping back, I stared at the ceiling. *Man, if You can hear me—maybe You don't want to right now— but thank You for Zach. He's really something.*

I couldn't fall asleep. My mind kept spinning in ways it never had. So many repressed things were shoved down so deep I no longer felt their pain. I had stifled the worst, compartmentalizing them like files in a cabinet. Behind each closed drawer were incidents, and the harder to access, the more critical they were. Aaron had documented them with crude markings, but my soul kept account by levels of pain.

Each memory brought a flood of anxiety, and if a person could combust from within, I was close. I wondered what to do with it all. The symbolism of "coming out of the closet" hit home. I had so many skeletons crammed inside it was overcrowded. Maybe that's why I blurted it out to Zach. I wondered what might trigger the next unplanned spilling of secrets—even as I knew "unplanned" meant I wouldn't know.

A new fear rose: being unable to control the venting, secrets falling out at random times and places. It felt like a tube of toothpaste that refused to seal again. I couldn't let emotions run rampant, yet I had no idea what to do. There was no more room for debate; I had to decide where I stood.

After a fitful night and a morning of skipped classes, I met Becky for lunch at a local café. After ordering, I got straight to the point. I couldn't risk small talk letting it slip. I needed control back.

"I am gay," I said, as if divulging a century-old secret from the archives. "If you have an issue with this, I need to know now."

"Wow, breaking news! Sam Izbicki is gay—film at eleven!" she said with furrowed brows and a crooked grin. "What were you expecting? A gasping tantrum? Disbelief, disgust? Wait— I'm feeling faint! Or do I run out crying? No kidding, man!"

"Well, the least you could've done was show a little sympathy for me, man!" I said.

"Sympathy? You want sympathy? Umm … let me think … noooo! That sympathy goes to me and every other girl who swoons in your presence," she said as I smiled.

"Pa-lease, Becky, we both know you couldn't swoon if you tried. I don't think you even have the capacity for drama."

"You told me this at least twenty times a couple months ago at that party—you were so drunk. I didn't bring it back up because I'm such a wonderful, caring friend. Well, truth be told, I just didn't want to hear your drama again!" she said, half choking on her lemon water.

"Oh, really? My drama? I am the least dramatic person you've ever known," I said in a British accent, raising my pinky as I sipped.

"Okay, what is this? You outing yourself now, or is this news just for pathetic me?"

"Indeed I am. In fact, I'm planning an extensive outing tour—dates, guides, the works! This is my retirement tour, since I'll be coming out one way or another until I retire!"

"It's about time. I was ready to start a calendar pool, betting how much longer you'd last. It's been excruciating watching you over the years. Honestly, I feel free just watching you today!" she said as we laughed.

"I'm scared out of my wits and sick to my stomach just thinking about it. But I'm done. It's finished. I'm scheduling who hears what, when, and just doing it. I can't store it anymore. I can't keep shoving things into a space already full," I declared.

Over the next several weeks I came out to almost everyone I knew. Some were supportive; others made it clear I was disgusting. The easiest were those who came out to me at the same time. None were surprised, and I felt sad I'd spent so many years hiding, thinking I'd done a great job when I was an open book to friends and colleagues. In the end, I realized the ones I lost weren't true friends anyway. I quickly found out who my good friends were.

In November I spent my birthday with Becky and a few new friends, as word traveled quickly in the gay community. For the first time in my life, I felt like me. I was mostly happy and even playing at a relationship with a guy from New York City. I spent a few weekends with him, frequenting gay establishments, until I realized it wasn't for me. Less than a month later, Harvey Milk was assassinated. My heart broke at the news. He was dedicated and hardworking, and if I'd been in California, I would have gone to the massive vigil. It was senseless violence.

For many, it sparked activism. But I wasn't sure yet where I stood. I was still getting used to my own skin, not feeling solid enough to step forward. I had ideas of what the gay community's face should look like, but I didn't know where I fit in. A few essential doors remained unopened, and graduation was near. Job offers were already on my desk.

As the holidays came, I dreaded making declarations. Deep down I knew I wouldn't find the courage to come out to family, and I was right. We spent the whole time reliving the same old agony, defeat replayed without detour. I started my last semester melancholy and moody.

As graduation approached, I accepted a dream job with a sales and advertising firm and was excited about my prospects. Becky landed a position in the same area, so we went house hunting together and found a great unit to rent. We'd be roommates, and our first new acquisition was going to be a dog.

I graduated with honors, with only Rob and Anne in the audience. Then Becky and I packed up and headed to Boston to start fresh. We fought for the largest bedroom—I won. The small house had two bedrooms and baths, giving us each a suite. After several nights on the floor in sleeping bags, we went shopping for beds and a sofa. On the way home, we stopped at the shelter and spent hours choosing a dog. We both fell for a beautiful Sheltie.

We tossed all our favorite names into a bowl, swirled them around, and agreed the first pulled would be his name. Becky drew Max. She soon thought we'd made a mistake. Each day when I came home from work, I found him curled up at the bottom of my closet. He dug through my things, pushing around dirty clothes and shoes, half in and half out, sprawled across my stuff. He looked uncomfortable but still chose to stay there. Some days he was so lazy I had to coax him out. And sometimes, when I'd had a hard day, I crawled in beside him and cuddled.

"We should have called him Sam!" she declared one evening when she found Max and I together in the bottom of my closet.

"Why? We wouldn't know who you were calling!" I responded, not getting her inference.

"He takes after his daddy. He chooses to be half in and half out of the closet, no matter how uncomfortable it is!" she said, laughing at her own joke.

CHAPTER 33

Rivals and Archrivals

THE TRAFFIC WAS BUMPER to bumper. I had to slam on the brakes several times because I kept daydreaming. It was hot with the windows down, and I wasn't sure I had enough gas to make it to the next exit. I chastised myself for not filling the rental before getting back on the highway.

I needed to invest in a new car but hadn't had time to sort through models. I wanted my next vehicle to be special—something that made a statement about who I was and where I was going. I car shopped in my head as each one passed. When traffic stalled, I scanned the lanes for something that caught my eye, but most were dull and plain.

I caught a glimpse of a red car about ten cars ahead, but every time I tried to move up, another vehicle cut in, competing for space. Memories of my brothers and me playing travel games on the way to work sites flooded back, until the bad memories spoiled the moment.

Frustration grew as impatient drivers pushed ahead. I laid on the horn several times when I was nearly forced off the road trying to avoid an accident.

It was times like these I wished I had a brown bomber so I could ram cars out of the way. The guy behind me rode my rear and I wanted to hit the brakes and teach him a lesson. Then it dawned on me—I should calm down. I was thinking a little crazier than normal.

A quick illegal pass on the right and back into the left lane put me next to the red car I was so set on seeing—and it was a huge disappointment. Horns honked at my maneuvers, but their driving was no match for mine. The guy beside me shot a nasty look, and while he did, I pulled out in front of him like I was on a racing team.

My exit came fast. As traffic opened, I floored it, crossed right, and flew down the ramp. I was disappointed I hadn't seen a car I liked, but I was honing my driving skills for when I did. I knew I'd find the right one sooner or later, and when I did, I'd know it without even getting inside. It would call my name. Billy's dream of a red sports car wasn't far off, but the rest of his dreams would take longer.

The past two years since graduation had been incredible. I was promoted to sales manager after a few months, and business was booming. I loved the responsibility and was motivated by future opportunities. I ate, drank, and slept sales.

I saved my vacation for this summer and was excited to spend some of it with Rob. I hadn't seen him except at holidays since moving to Boston. Last year I begged out of Thanksgiving and Christmas on Griffin Avenue, using work as an excuse when really I was tucked away in a Maine cabin with a guy I'd met. It was a holiday romance; by New Year's we no longer spoke. I missed seeing Rob and Anne and planned to stop and see her, too, before heading home.

Rob moved to Pittsburgh after graduation and worked in sales, too. He left school engaged to a girl I didn't care for, but since then they had broken it off and moved on. A few months ago, he called to say he'd met the girl of his dreams and couldn't wait for us to meet. She was divorced with two children he was crazy about. Our schedules lined up, so we planned a vacation on the Jersey shore this summer.

A couple of weeks later, I felt the familiar guilt-trip urge to call Mother early one Saturday. I wasn't sure why I kept calling—obligation and guilt played a huge role. Most conversations were the same, start to finish. After greetings, she'd begin with neighborhood gossip, then move on to extended family. Without fail, she gave an extended dissertation on each sibling—what they were doing wrong and how if they just listened to her, they wouldn't be in their situations.

In her opinion, Joan could do nothing right. Jude had run off to be some kind of doomsday cult leader. Anne was working too hard and didn't stop by often enough. Pete was running with a girl she actually liked. Emma, she always thought, was out of control. She never forgot to ask when I was going to settle down and marry Becky, because it wasn't right we were just living together. I should have repeated for the millionth time that Becky and I weren't an item, but I couldn't do it again. So I went along with her, agreeing with her fantasies. Since I hadn't told her otherwise, I figured I deserved the lectures.

Nothing, however, compared to the dirt she was throwing on Rob and his new girlfriend. She never liked his former one, and I wondered if anyone was ever going to be good enough for any of my siblings—or me. Living and raising a family in the same place she'd grown up did my mother no favors. She was stuck in the mud socially and mentally, and it showed more each year. With outsiders she always had a sharp tongue, so I wasn't surprised when she ripped this girl up one side and down the other as she filled me in.

She fed on rumors and conjecture, and nothing rivaled her exaggerated imagination. From the moment she learned a secret until she passed it along, it grew in leaps and bounds, never resembling the original story.

"That Sarah is jus' after yur brother fur his money. She just wants someone ta take care a her and her kids. She can't be trusted. Ya know she came here at Thanksgivin' without her kids and brought presents for all da nieces and nephews and we thought she was a really nice girl. Then it comes ta find out she has two kids and is divorced and he calls and tells us after they leave here. Not before. After. Well, we told Rob what for and he wasn't happy. Auggie tol him that if he marries her them kids will never be Izbickis—they ain't blood!" Mother ranted like an erupting volcano.

"He said that to Rob? I can't believe it. Rob loves her and is considering marrying her. He's crazy about her kids—he says they're great! Just because she's divorced doesn't make her a bad person. She probably came alone the first time because she wanted you to meet her and get to know her before you judged her. Not every divorced girl with kids is money hungry! And really, Mother? Not Izbicki blood? Are you serious? You're talking about innocent children—they're not responsible for what happened with their parents!" I said, rolling my eyes in frustration.

"Who leaves their kids at Thanksgivin' ta spend it wit a bunch a strangers? She should a bin with them, that's what I say. I seen girls like her bafore. She'll take 'im fur all he's worth and leave him penniless and heartbroke. She'll prob'ly get pregnant on purpose and trap him inta marryin' her. She is trash! Then she'll leave him and collect child support from 'im fur the rest of 'is life. I've seen this too many times, Samson, and ya need ta pay close attention or it'll happen ta you too!" she said, exasperated.

"None of us even know Sarah. You don't know what kind of person she is. You can't predict what she'll do to Rob just because the neighbor's girls did it and you watched. He doesn't have much money—or at least I don't think so—and he's not stupid!" I said. I regretted not being there for Thanksgiving; I would have loved to meet her. I felt for her now, knowing how everyone was talking behind her back. Rob and Sarah could have used someone in their corner.

"We know as much as we need ta know 'bout this girl. Ya need ta talk with Rob and git him ta see!" she added.

"Was she nasty? Did she put her feet up and expect you to wait on her? You said she came with gifts—were they junk or inappropriate? Was she embarrassing, running around half naked? Was she disrespectful? I can't see why you're so worked up over the fact that she has kids. No! I will not talk to Rob! It's his business who he loves, and it's not up to the Izbicki clan to approve! I'll see you this summer, and I'll be meeting Sarah. I hope by then everyone changes their attitudes. I'm hanging up now. Goodbye, Mother!" I said, placing the receiver on the hook.

If this was how they treated a divorced woman with kids, I knew I'd never get through the door with a man I loved.

The traffic was jammed on the back roads and I was sweating buckets. Between honking the horn and slamming the brakes, I thought about how Rob must have felt when Mother unloaded on him. He seemed so happy with Sarah—in fact, the happiest I'd ever heard him on the phone. I was heading straight to the beach to meet him and wasn't going to let thoughts of Griffin Avenue ruin it. I turned the radio up, and when traffic cleared, I hit the gas and cruised.

✶✶✶✶✶

Rob and Sarah arrived late in the night and decided to sleep in before heading to the beach. Sam was on his way to meet them, and they knew they'd be up late again that evening. After getting the kids moving, they went to a diner a few buildings down from their hotel.

It was unusually hot for the area, but the blue sky and ocean breeze made up for it. They placed their orders in the bustling diner and talked while the kids played placemat games, competing as always. Sarah sat staring at Rob. She couldn't believe she'd met such a great guy and wondered if he was really who he said he was. Trusting people wasn't easy for her. It felt almost too good to be true—and everyone knows what that usually means.

"I'm so happy we came this week. It feels great to relax and let go. I'm really looking forward to meeting Sam. After the fiasco at Thanksgiving, I'm hoping for better results," Sarah said, sipping her iced tea.

"I agree. I can't wait for the kids to see the ocean. I can't believe they've never seen it. Don't worry about Sam, Sarah; he's cool—he's going to love you," Rob said, reaching across the table to touch her hand.

"I hope so. Hard to believe you when it comes to your family, after that wonderful visit with the Waltons!" she jabbed.

"It wasn't fair to you, and I promise I'm not setting you up for more disappointment," he said.

"More like devastation. I'm still not over it, and I'm worried about stopping at your mother's on the way home. The kids deserve a chance, and I'm not convinced they'll get it. Advance warning: If either of your parents treats my kids with anything less than respect, it'll be the last time I bring them there. It makes me feel awful they feel this way. I know I'm not the ideal girl to bring home to Mother, but I deserved better than that treatment. At least Anne and Emma seemed to like me," she said. "I just want Sam to like me, too. You two are so close, and I need a brother."

She stared out the window toward rows of beach bungalows, wishing someday she could live near the ocean—preferably with Rob, the kids, and a happy ending. But she knew better than to hang her hat on daydreams. Life was full of twists and turns, and she was tired of the roller coaster. Happiness had been elusive since her divorce. It was best for all involved and amicable, but still painful for her and the kids. She wondered if Jay would ever get over it. He was close to his dad and missed him terribly. Dolly came through much easier, never having felt close to that side of the family. It had been a year full of turmoil for everyone, and it was nice to rest awhile.

*****

I checked into a room next door to Rob and Sarah's. They were out to lunch when I arrived, and the hotel clerk kindly accommodated my wish to be near them. I unpacked and wished I could see the ocean from my room. One day I'd stay only in the best hotels with the best views, but for now I made do. I put on swim trunks, grabbed a towel, and headed toward the beach, hoping to run into Rob. Just as I passed a diner, two kids came barreling out, laughing and teasing each other. It was obvious they were siblings. Seconds later, their mother appeared with Rob on her heels.

"Hey, man, fancy meeting you here!" Rob said, opening his arms for a hug.

He stepped back, about to introduce Sarah, when she stepped forward and gave me the warmest hug I'd had in years.

"So nice to finally meet you, Sam. Rob has told me so much about you and I couldn't wait—Doll and Jay, slow down! Come meet Sam!" she said to the two kids I'd just passed.

They came running, hugged me, and immediately started begging to go to the beach. We chatted as we headed back to Rob's car, and when he opened the trunk I laughed out loud.

"Man, what were you preparing for? The end of the world? Sure you didn't forget anything?" I joked.

"You never know, Sam. I'm a girl scout at heart—I pack everything including the kitchen sink! There's a method to the madness, as you'll see!" Sarah declared, grabbing the beach supplies.

She wasn't kidding. Everything had a place and she knew exactly where it was. Out came the pre-packed beach bags. The kids already had suits under their clothes. She grabbed three chairs, sand toys, a cooler of drinks, and a bag of snacks. We were off in seconds. At the beach she set up our area in minutes, and we were playing in the water in no time.

I watched the way she was with her children. It was obvious they loved each other. They were bright, well behaved, cooperative—and I fell in love with them.

I was impressed with her attention to detail. She looked me in the eye when I spoke, listened, and contributed with interest. With her humor, we were quick friends who shared much in common. We talked for hours about music, movies, psychology, and religion. We loved many of the same things—including Rob.

It was obvious Rob and Sarah were in love, and it warmed my heart to see them as a family. Once again, I wished I was like Rob—surrounded by love and my own family. But this wasn't my reality. We took photos on the beach, and after a day of fun, headed back to the hotel.

We sat on the beach each day and found fun spots to eat in the evenings. We played miniature golf, swam in the hotel pool until closing, had drinks on the patio after dinner, and stayed up half the night talking after the kids went to bed. I hadn't enjoyed myself this much in a long time and didn't want it to end. Sarah brought up family on our last evening there, and I was glad she did.

"So, did Rob fill you in on my first magical experience with your family?" she asked with a smirk. Her quick wit rivaled mine, and I loved her sharp-edged sarcasm.

"No, but Gertie did! I hear you made quite the first impression, my dear!" I responded.

"Oh, I bet you did hear that! I was so excited to meet your family. I always wished I'd been raised in a large one. It was just my mom, sister, and me. My parents divorced when I was young, and I wanted a brother to beat up Jummy after school every day for me!" she said, playfully punching my arm.

"I couldn't have beaten my way out of a paper bag! Rob and Anne were my human fortresses. First, who is Jummy?" I asked.

"He was a boy who beat me up almost every day in third grade. No lie. That was his name! Jummy Grisley. He threw a mean ice ball in winter and split my lip open—look!" she said, pointing to the scar. "And his mother had hair under her arms so long you could braid it! Seriously—it's the truth!" she added, laughing.

"Now I've heard everything! Well, if Jummy comes after you again, I'll stand behind Rob while he beats him up!" I said, hiding behind Rob.

"Oh, I have nothing to worry about at all with the two of you around!" she said, laughing.

"Anyway, I was excited. I picked out the perfect gifts for all the nieces and nephews, and after weeks of deliberation, decided it was better if my first visit was without my kids. I wanted everyone to meet me and get to know me a little before finding out I was one of those divorced women with children. You know—the ones people assume only want men for their money? I worried the whole way to your parents' house, the day before Thanksgiving, that I wouldn't fit in. How could I fit into the Waltons?" she asked, punching Rob hard in the arm.

"The Waltons? Are you kidding me? He told you we were like the Waltons? Man, what were you smoking—because I want some of it!" I rolled on the floor laughing.

"That's what he told me. But it didn't take a rocket scientist to figure out that was bologna. Within minutes of arriving, Auggie opened his mouth. That's all it took. I thought, what the heck is this? I was actually scared. Everyone sat around, silent, just staring at the television. The pièce de résistance was dinner, when your father started declaring who was responsible for providing the meal. The looks on everyone's faces were priceless. I heard your sister whisper he was on his best behavior because I was there. I was seriously concerned for him if he kept it up, because I don't mince words—and I wasn't about to start then. Several times that evening he and I almost had words, but I held back. I didn't want to embarrass Rob," she explained.

"I don't know why I said we were like the Waltons. Wishful thinking, I guess. I was afraid Auggie would scare her away and she'd think I was from a nuthouse," Rob said.

"Man, we *are* from a nuthouse! You could've warned her before she was thrown to the wolves!" I laughed hysterically.

"So the whole way home he filled me in on decades of abuse, neglect, heartbreak—and I was shocked. Heartbroken for him, for all of you. Even for your mother. I wanted everyone to like me, though that was unrealistic. After he told me the true story, I knew in my heart my kids and I would never really be accepted.

"When we got home, I asked Rob to call your parents to see what they thought. I had some trust issues with him after the trip and was afraid he wouldn't honestly tell me, so I got on one end of the phone while he was on the extension. From the minute your mother got on, she started talking about everyone else in the family—and it wasn't pretty. She showed me who she really was.

"You see, I have a theory: If someone talks about others behind their backs, they'll talk about you too. Rob interrupted and asked about me. She went on and on about how wonderful I was and how happy she was he'd found me. For a few days, it was great to feel loved. And then—he drops the bomb!

"I was so happy she liked me—and then she heard I had kids and was divorced. Then all hell broke loose! Auggie got on the phone and said Rob better not ever marry me because my children would never be Izbickis—and my blood boiled! Gertie got back on and agreed. Then she launched into a huge lecture about girls like me! I held my tongue, but when we hung up I told Rob, 'Thank God they won't be Izbickis!'" she said, talking so fast she was running out of air.

"Do they even have a clue how badly I was hurt by what they said? I can count on one hand the times in my life I just listened and didn't respond. That was Rob's mother and father, and no matter how cruel and insensitive they were, I wasn't going to disrespect them. Needless to say, this whole incident has set the stage for our relationship in the future. It's sad, because I am a formidable opponent when I need to be, and NO ONE treats my children poorly—period! Unless a miracle occurs, your parents and I will end up staunch enemies, which is really sad should Rob and I marry and have 'Izbicki' children. Nothing like starting a new life in a family of rivals!" Sarah added sadly.

"Please accept my apologies for my rude, arrogant, and ignorant parents! Consider yourself lucky—you live far away from them. Those still there deal with the madness all the time. Why do you think I live in Boston? I really am sorry, Sarah. I think you're wonderful, and it feels like we've known each other forever. And I consider the enemies of my enemies my friends!" I said, reaching over to hug her. "Good for you, Sarah! Don't let anyone in this family push you around. Don't be afraid to speak your mind. Just be yourself, and if they don't like it, too bad for them!"

"Oh, make no mistake, I will. I'd never directly disrespect your mother unless pushed beyond my limits, but your father is another story. Rob knows I have the gumption to put my Italian-Irish temper up against him any time, any day!" she declared.

We talked for hours as Rob and I filled her in on stories from our childhood. She was visibly shaken as we recalled the most horrifying events. Dolly and Jay were asleep in the adjoining room, so we cracked open a couple of beers and kept going. It was late, and we were comfortably sharing things about ourselves. Sarah shared details about her life, and I saw she hadn't had it easy either. I pulled several pillows tightly against my chest for comfort.

"You keep pulling pillows up against yourself and pretty soon I won't be able to see you at all, Sam," Sarah said, tugging at them. "Why are you trying to hide behind those pillows—or what are you trying to hide?"

"I need to tell you both something. I'm not sure how you'll react, and I'm scared," I whispered.

Rob and Sarah sat up straighter, faces full of concern.

"What is it, Sam?" they both asked at once. Sarah could see the fear and pain in my eyes.

"I'm gay," I heard myself say as the words slipped out.

"That's the big scary secret? I already knew that," Sarah said.

"I didn't," Rob added. "But man, the only thing you could've told me that would've upset me is that you were sick and dying!"

"You already knew? How? We just met this week! If Rob didn't know, then how did you, Sarah?" I asked, confused.

"I have a sense for this sort of thing. I call it *gay-dar*! Like radar. I just knew it, that's all. You have nothing to be afraid of! You're my new brother now, and there's nothing you can do to get rid of me!" Sarah said, reaching for a hug.

"I know it's not fair of me, but I was afraid to tell you because you're Christians. I've faced off with many, and they often have the harshest reaction to me coming out. Why? Why are you guys different?" I asked.

"I apologize for the reactions you've received, but it doesn't surprise us. We just see things differently than most. Our beliefs are very clear about who we are to love and accept—and that means everyone!" Sarah said with a warm smile.

"It might surprise you—and most people—how common our beliefs are. Here lies my deepest internal struggle. Usually, this is when the conversation turns to argument as I come out to folks," I said softly, waiting for the backlash.

"Well, you'll get no argument here. Even if our beliefs were uncommon, we would still love and accept you. It's not our place to be anyone's judge or jury. We don't have to share someone's belief to love them. It's not up to us to say what you—or any-one—should think or believe. Love is the most important thing," Sarah said, reaching for another hug.

We sat there, Rob, Sarah, and I, hugging and laughing as tears ran down my face. Relieved, exhausted, and a little drunk, I was so happy I thought my heart would explode.

"I can't believe you didn't know, Rob. I told him yesterday on the beach and he said I was crazy! Have you shared this with anyone else in the family?" she asked.

"Anne knows. She's known since high school. I've been struggling with telling everyone else. All my friends and colleagues know, but I can't seem to let it out to family. I'm planning on it soon. You'll know when I do—you'll hear and feel the fireworks from Griffin Avenue all the way in Pittsburgh!"

We spent the last day on the beach and waved to each other from the highway ramps. I felt so much better and couldn't wait to get to Anne's. I replayed the week's events in my mind a hundred times. It was the perfect week, with perfect weather, spent with the perfect people. I missed them already. When we stood by our cars saying goodbye, Sarah said she was holding me to our deal. I was her new brother no matter what, and she made me promise to keep in touch.

I stayed with Anne for the weekend, and she was relieved that someone else knew my secrets. I stopped to see Mother on my way out of town Sunday, and within minutes we were arguing over Rob and Sarah. After leaving the coast, they also stopped to see my parents and introduce the kids. They stayed overnight Friday but left for Pittsburgh the next morning. I knew they'd planned to stay the entire weekend, and I wondered what happened that made them change their minds.

"They pull in here Friday and Auggie is sleepin' and them kids woke him up talkin' on the porch. They were cute 'nuff, and Rob just fell all over hisself tryin' ta impress 'im and that girl! She was real quiet, like she had a secret or sumthin', and I steered clear of 'im all. Then Rob pulls out that old wagon in the garage and starts pullin' 'im round in it. The boy fell out and cried like a sissy wimp, and that girl goes runnin' over like he's a baby ur sumthin'. Auggie told him ta stop his whining and called him a wimp! Well, that girl got in Auggie's face like she was 'bout ta strangle 'im! Told him never ta speak ta her child like that! Auggie hit the roof and cussed her out, and then Rob jumped in. It was a circus, I tell ya, and it was that girl's fault. Everyone knows not ta get in Auggie's face! This is his house! He won't have it!" Mother reiterated without coming up for air.

I could believe it. These people could mess up a one-car funeral! I was embarrassed, ashamed, and furious with my parents. Mortified Sarah and her children had to endure this. Still, I smiled picturing little Sarah getting in the Marine's face—that must have been entertainment at its best. Gertie and I fought for an hour, and when I realized I was getting nowhere, I left, slamming the screen door.

A few months later, Rob proposed to Sarah, and a wedding was planned for the next spring. They were marrying closer to my parents' house because more family lived that way. I was honored to be asked to be Rob's best man and couldn't wait. Of course, I sat through endless phone calls with Mother over the details. She approved of none of their choices and was livid they didn't include her in the planning. Mother wanted a big wedding with a different bride, but they planned a small, intimate family ceremony. In lieu of a reception, they chose a private dinner at a beautiful restaurant. Instead of paying for a massive wedding, they wanted an extended honeymoon. I reminded Mother she wasn't paying for it, so it was none of her business. I thought it was a wonderful choice—the last thing I wanted was to sit through a big family-filled Polish-Italian wedding with my plus-one as Becky again.

The year flew by, and before I knew it, I was standing next to Rob and his beautiful bride, toasting them at dinner. Auggie had started drinking at the house that morning and was three sheets to the wind. His comments were getting out of hand, so after dinner and the cutting of the cake, Rob slipped away with Sarah and the rest of us went our separate ways.

Becky and I went back to Griffin Avenue, thinking our immediate family would spend the rest of the evening there. Mother invited Sarah's mother and sister too, but they begged off, saying they were tired and had a long trip back to Pittsburgh. I was sure Sarah had warned them about Auggie, and I was glad they wouldn't be exposed.

We sat at the dining room table for more than an hour before realizing everyone else was running for cover instead of joining us. Becky had a long drive to New Jersey in the morning to see her parents. Since we drove separately, she said her goodbyes and left. I was staying with Anne, who probably went home after the wedding.

I sat another half hour as Mother and Auggie went on and on about everyone who hadn't shown up. The Marine was plastered, ranting about Sarah, Rob, and everything he could think of. I realized now was as good a time as any. Time to make them even more miserable—it was only fair, since I was about to lose my mind if I stayed longer. I'd had a few drinks at the reception, and I was feeling brave.

"Well, Mother, why don't you sit down here at the table with Auggie and me?" I said, trying to sound strong.

"Okay, well, what better thing do I have ta do? Looks like no one's comin' anyway," she replied, pulling up a chair.

"I've been wanting—or should I say trying—to tell you something about myself and my life for a very long time. I guess now is as good a time as ever," I said, gulping saliva as if it were my last.

"What? Yur gettin' married too?" Mother asked. "Finally! Why didn't ya announce it when Becky was here?"

"No, Mother, I'm not marrying Becky. I told you—we're not dating. I won't be getting married, or at least I don't think so. EVER!" I said, starting to sweat.

"Sam, I'm so proud of ya. You made yur mind up—you're finally becomin' a priest like ya said ya might when you was younger?" she said, rising from her chair to hug me. "Father Bernard would a bin so proud of ya!"

Just the sound of his name spoken after years sent chills down my spine. Images of the two of us on the church floor flooded my mind. I felt myself spinning. I thought I'd faint. I thought I'd throw up.

"NO! STOP! Can you please just let me finish? I'm not going to be a priest. I actually thought becoming one would save me from this conversation. I really thought it was my answer until a very wise person told me the Catholic Church has enough issues. Mother, I—" I shouted, then was interrupted again.

"What do ya mean they have 'nuff issues? Why can't ya be a priest? You would make a—" she started.

"MOTHER, PLEASE STOP!" I yelled.

"I am not becoming a priest, and I am not marrying Becky or any other woman," I said, pain spilling from my lips.

"I am gay," I said as I stood. "I am gay."

It took three seconds flat for the Marine to respond.

"YUR A FAGGOT! I KNEW IT! KNEW IT THE DAY YA WAS BORN! YA LIKE DA BOYS, HUH? YA FUDGE-PACK-IN' QUEER! GET OUTTA THAT CHAIR AND I'LL BEAT IT OUTTA YA!" he shouted, grabbing the front of my rented tux shirt.

The color drained from Mother's face. She sat with her mouth hanging open, as if she'd forgotten what to say. I was yanked to my feet by the drunken Marine and shoved against the wall.

"GET OFF ME, YOU MISERABLE DRUNK! I AM NOT TAKING ANY MORE OF YOUR ABUSE!" I heard myself say as I shoved him off me.

Good thing he was as drunk as he was, because it didn't take much to set him off balance when I used the wall for leverage. He spun sideways, landed in his chair, and looked stunned. He struggled to his feet, but I was already at the front door, pulling it open, and he couldn't reach me fast enough. I turned and caught a glimpse of Mother coming toward me. Before I could react, she slapped me hard across the face.

"YUR GOIN' TA HELL! HOW COULD YA SAY THESE THINGS IN OUR HOUSE?" she cried, red-faced with tears streaming.

"YA GET THE HELL OUT OF DIS HOUSE AND NEVER—NEVER—DO YA HEAR ME? NEVER COME BACK, YA FAGGOT! I NEVER WANT TA SEE YUR FACE ON GRIFFIN AVENUE AGIN, AND IF I DO I'LL SHOOT YA IN THE FACE! UNGRATEFUL QUEER BASTARD! YUR NOT OUR SON! YA LEAVE THIS FAMILY ALONE! YUR NOT PART A IT AND NEVER WILL BE!" the Marine screamed.

I searched Mother's face for reassurance, for compassion, and saw only her shaking her head in agreement. I walked out the door, ran to my car fearing the Marine would go for his guns, and pulled out of the driveway, burning rubber. In my rearview mirror, I saw them standing on the porch watching me leave.

I made it almost to the stop sign before pulling to the curb. I lost all control. I sat sobbing and trembling. My nose ran, my tux shirt soaked with tears and sweat.

I knew it would be bad, out of control. But I never thought Mother would turn on me like she had. I never thought past the Marine going crazy. I never dreamt I'd be excommunicated from the family and the house on Griffin Avenue.

Then the anger rose deep within me. I hated him anyway. I despised him. I could easily stay away from them—and that God-forsaken house. I hated that house, this street, and my life there for so long. I would never be forced to come again.

It was finally done. He wanted an enemy—he got one. She wanted me to go to hell—so be it! I wasn't their son? Fine. Then Gertie and Auggie better not cross my path ever again. They wouldn't have to worry about shooting me in the face, because I could and would cut them down without thinking twice. I imagined Gertie already on the phone spreading venom through the family, and I wasn't sure I'd see any of them again except Anne, Rob, and Sarah. That was fine with me.

I was finally free. I was out now. I shared Rob and Sarah's anniversary! *How do you like me now?* I thought.

I didn't know that night as I drove out of town that it really would be the last time I entered the house on Griffin Avenue. If I had known, I might have lingered before running out the door. I might have taken in the smells, feelings, memories one last time. Not that I didn't have plenty already eating away at me.

And believe it or not, if I had known it would be the last time I saw Auggie and Gertie—except at family weddings or random events—I might have stood a moment longer, taking in their angry faces. If I had known the next time I'd reunite with Gertie as mother and son would be eleven or twelve years later, I might have held off before coming out.

If I had known the rivalry with the Marine would last until I was dying, I might have held it back a little longer, even though I believed I hated him. If I had known it would kick off rivalries throughout the family as siblings took sides, I might have held my pain and tongue a little longer.

I might have—but probably not.

We always want what we cannot have, and we never miss people and relationships until they're gone. The pain of being closeted for so many years was unbearable, and I thought nothing could rival that. But the pain of the void—of missing them, my family, and that stinking house on Griffin Avenue—did exactly that.

Because my relationship with my parents had been so bad from a young age, I believed I could be better off without them. Maybe I was. But in the quiet moments, when memories rushed my senses, I'd sit and wonder—why did it have to be this way? Many of my friends had parents who, even if they disagreed, accepted them and their spouses with love and open arms.

But it was this way, and there was nothing I could do to fix it. It would take me many years to come to terms with that. Still, every now and again, especially in those years when I was alone, I'd ask—was it worth it? Was I better off without them?

CHAPTER 34

Scorn and Fury

AUGGIE AND GERTIE STOOD on the porch watching Sam drive away. Auggie shouted and hurled his whiskey glass, which landed short of the mailbox and shattered across the drive.

"Dis ears your fault! I toll you ya coddled him like a baby! I knew he was a faggot long ago. Worthless dress-wearin' pansy!" Auggie snarled as he swung at Gertie. His fist caught her chest as she turned, knocking the air from her lungs so fast she thought she'd pass out. She clung to the railing while he stumbled down the steps, trying to see Sam's car.

Gertie staggered inside. Pain radiated from her chest down both arms. For a moment she wondered if she was having a heart attack but knew she couldn't be that lucky. After today there'd be hell to pay, and she'd need every ounce of strength. She collapsed into a chair, gasping until the pain eased enough to breathe.

She knew she needed a strategy to hold Auggie at bay, but her mind was blank. Watching him weave and spin in the street, she briefly wondered if she had time to grab a few things and run. She pictured the path behind the neighbor's house and calculated if she could make it before he turned back. But she knew from experience: Once he regained his footing, he'd be after her, and no door could withstand his force.

As she carefully made her way up the stairs to their bedroom, her eyes fell on an old portrait of the children. There, grinning ear to ear, was Samson. Such a ham—always pushing limits, always in *need of discipline. He looked frail and unhealthy in the picture, yet his dark eyes and grin tugged at her heart like never before.*

What had he done? He would burn in hell! God hated him now, and he would never see heaven. If she prayed hard enough, convinced others to join her, maybe together they could pray him into purgatory—but she wasn't sure it worked that way. Panic rising, she decided it might be best to find Father Bernard and have him talk to Sam. Surely he could change his mind.

She scrambled to the rotary dial, spinning one number at a time until at last the rectory clerk answered.

Her children had graduated parish school years ago, and she no longer knew the priests and staff well. She begged to speak with the priest in charge, insisting it was a family emergency. Father O'Brady listened to her rambling, then explained he couldn't give out personal information on priests who had served there, but offered to meet with her personally. Gertie fought the urge to scream, but before she could respond, O'Brady told her to call Monday to set up an appointment, blessed her, and hung up.

Monday? *she thought.* They could all be dead by Monday. Had things changed so much in a few years?

Exhausted, she sat on the edge of her bed, unsure what to do next. She took the picture of her children from the hallway wall. Brokenhearted, she stared at their innocent faces as warm tears streamed down her cheeks. Her finger rested on Sam. She loved him so much—maybe even more than the rest. He wasn't strong like them, and she worked tirelessly to toughen him up. She feared he'd never survive this world. He was easily broken, and she wasn't sure how to fix that.

The thought of him burning in hell was agonizing. She looked to the ceiling, wishing God would hear her, but wondered if she needed a priest to help. Couldn't God see how fragile he was? Wouldn't

He grant Samson absolution for his sins since he was so weak? She wondered why God sent him to earth without more protection.

She sobbed, begging God to spare him. Maybe the priests and her parents were wrong! They had said all homosexual people would burn in hell. Maybe they were wrong—or lying, she thought angrily. But they couldn't be. They'd never lie about something so important. The weight of what she believed to be fact shook her to her core. She fell to her knees, rosary in hand, and began to pray.

She was frightened beyond explanation—for her son, for Auggie, and for herself—as if they alone had created who Sam was. Tears poured from her eyes as she curled into a ball, rosary in hand, and howled an unnatural cry to the heavens when she realized she'd never see her son again. Never hug him, hear his voice, or see his smile. It was too much to bear.

The look on his face as she slapped him and told him to leave haunted her. He didn't know how much she loved him. How much she wanted to agree to disagree. How much she wanted to hold him one last time. He couldn't have known. And if she had responded any other way—different from what God might expect, what most of the family would demand if they knew, and especially different from Auggie who insisted on full support—they might not have survived the fallout.

Emotions hit one after another until she felt she'd suffocate under guilt, shame, and embarrassment. Maybe she had been too easy on him. Maybe she had coddled him. She felt like a failure. Was it her fault after all?

She remembered how awful everyone had been to her oldest unmarried sister, presumed to like girls. What if it came from her family? Fear overwhelmed her as she wondered if Sam had that awful "catchy" blood disease people whispered about. Would everyone she loved now be infected? Was it on her hand—the one that slapped his face?

She ran to the bathroom and scrubbed her hands until they were red and swollen.

She had once again done what was expected of her—by faith, family who would be ashamed of her and their nephew, and most of all by Auggie, who demanded nothing less. Yet she knew even that wouldn't satisfy him.

Hours passed, and when she heard the rusty screech of the old screen door she scrambled to put on as many layers of clothing as she could. Maybe it would exhaust Auggie's need to vent his rage with as little pain as possible. She knew too well that hell had no fury like the Marine scorned.

✶✶✶✶✶

As Gertie retreated inside, Auggie took two steps at a time, stumbling down the stairs and across the yard.

"That freak stopped up der by the stop sign! Prob'ly crying like the sissy wimp he is! He better keep on truckin' or I'll put a bullet through his thick skull! He comes back ear, I'll beat the life right outta 'im!" he screamed, staggering into the street.

Drunk as he was, his eyes darted left and right, searching for curious neighbors. What if this got out? He'd be ruined, ridiculed. Everyone feared the hard-shelled Marine—except his one close friend down the street—but now they'd have ammunition to destroy his reputation.

Embarrassment burned hotter than the liquor. Anger reddened his face; sweat poured down his forehead. Who was that laughing? He could hear them, loud in his ears. He clutched his head and spun, but saw only blurred houses. They were all talking, all gossiping behind his back.

Paranoia and confusion fueled more garbled threats as he stumbled into his driveway. He tried to run toward the garage, but the more he pushed, the further it seemed. With a final burst of brute force, he collapsed face-down on a pile of burlap bags by the garage, motionless, as mocking faces haunted him.

Hours later he crawled into the garage, found his paper bag of relief, and gulped until it was empty. Propped in a sitting position, sobering, he battled the urge to go inside for more whiskey and replayed the day's events.

Not twenty-four hours earlier, everything was the same as al-ways. Now hell had broken loose like a dam giving way. How did this happen? *he thought.* I lost two sons in the same day—one to a money-hungry hussy, the other to the queer I always knew he was.

Embarrassment crushed him. Good thing he wasn't still in the military—those guys would've made mincemeat of him. They doled out horrific punishment to faggots, real or imagined. We put the hurt on those guys so bad they had trouble walking for a week. That turned them around, made them think twice, *he thought.* That queer didn't come from me. Maybe Gertie had an affair.

He closed his eyes and pictured his never-married aunt, ru-mored to like women. His bachelor uncle too—"pretty boy" who never wanted a woman slowing him down. Panic rushed his sys-tem. Maybe this did come from me.

He pulled himself upright, stumbled inside, and poured a fresh glass of whiskey. All he could picture was Sam with some faceless man, laughing, making a fool of him—then both burning in hell.

The flames reminded him of being ten, when his father caught him half clothed in the barn with a neighbor boy. He could still hear him screaming they'd burn in hell. He and the boy ran as fast as they could.

Draining the glass, Auggie staggered upstairs and punished Gertie for everyone's transgressions until he had nothing left to vent.

CHAPTER 35

House in Order

IT WAS FOURTEEN MONTHS after Rob's wedding and my confrontation with my parents, and I had no idea where the time had gone. I was spinning out of control on so many levels I was reaching critical mass. I had no restraint. I'd become a supercilious manager of salespeople I once respected but now wondered why they breathed. I had nothing good to say about anything or anyone. My arrogance drove some of my best team members to seek work elsewhere. I had little respect for authority, challenging every rule as if meant only to slow me down.

I smoked and drank excessively while flaunting success in every gay bar I could find. Puffy eyes and a bulging waistline did little to deter advances, especially when I bought rounds for the room. Hundred-dollar bills provided the companionship I craved. Friends dropped, and one-night stands defined relationships. My spending was out of control. I replaced wardrobes as if they were outdated the minute I bought them. I frequented the best restaurants but never felt full. I binged on junk food; the freezer brimmed with ice cream. The cupboards, desk, and car console overflowed with snacks. I shoved handfuls into my mouth as if famine loomed, chasing flavors but never satisfaction. I ate, shopped, smoked, drank, danced, and worked from dawn to dusk until I finally pushed myself over the edge.

One morning I woke hungover, unable to stand after several tries. Pain in my abdomen was excruciating. I couldn't move or take a deep breath. It had been building for days, and with bloody stools and weight dropping off me despite constant eating, I knew I was in trouble. Exhausted, I sat on my bed. I'd had similar episodes as a teen, but nothing like this. After watching me for days, Becky had enough of my excuses and strong-armed me into a doctor's office, threatening me all the way.

I hadn't been to a medical doctor in years. If I had an issue, I went to my chiropractor. There didn't seem to be anything he couldn't fix, but when I called for advice, he reminded me medical doctors had their place, too.

Waiting over an hour was exasperating. I belittled and complained to everyone in sight. I spent the first minutes berating the doctor for wasting my time, then sat open-mouthed as he described what he thought I was facing. After defending his tardiness, he wrote a referral to a gastroenterologist.

I had never heard of Crohn's disease. The word *disease* alone rattled me—other people had diseases, not me. Little did I know, Crohn's wouldn't be the worst thing I'd face. I told myself I was strong; I'd already lived through hell. I refused to accept it. I reasoned the doctor was mad at my admonishment and was trying to scare me. I grew angry. I had too much to do to be sick—places to go, people to see, food to eat. *Sick* wasn't in my vocabulary.

Until it was. The gastroenterologist appointment went much the same, minus the anger and apologies. He prescribed rest, diet changes, no smoking or drinking, steroids, antibiotics, and ordered every test ending in "-oscopy." Colonoscopy, endoscopy, X-rays—I didn't see the need, but I followed through like a sheep to slaughter.

When the diagnosis came, I felt like a kid walking into the middle of a dodgeball game without knowing the rules. I left the office stunned, and for the first time in years, time seemed to grind to a halt.

I had big meetings, a lunch date, and a dinner date at two of the swankiest places in town that day. I didn't have time for illness—until I found myself on a park bench, sniveling like an abandoned four-year-old. A chill crept across me as raindrops pounded down.

I glanced around, searching for something, though I wasn't sure what. People looked, then quickly looked away, avoiding my pathetic expression. Wetter and colder by the minute, I sat trapped in a trance that held me still. Hours passed. The rain stopped, the sun returned. A cardinal landed beside me, chirped as if scolding, then flew to a tree branch. A car horn and children's laughter behind me pulled me back.

I checked my watch—I'd missed the meeting and lunch, was close to missing dinner—but I didn't care. The wind had gone out of my sails. I was a ship dead in the water, more tired than ever before.

I forced myself up and walked toward the lot where my car sat illegally parked. A yellow citation flapped under the wiper. Once this would have infuriated me; now it stirred nothing. I tore it free, got in, and merged cautiously into traffic. That evening, I drifted in and out of sleep in the bathtub, draining and refilling the water as it cooled.

I used sick and personal days to get a grip. I sat for hours researching Crohn's, reading how stress contributed to symptoms along with everything else I'd been doing to my body. More than anything, I lived in the moment—something I'd rarely allowed. Alone, I functioned minute to minute. But as soon as life, business, and people crept back in, I lost track of what was real.

Back at work, I still felt like a powder keg. I couldn't focus or multitask as before. When pushed—or when I needed to push— anger surged out of control. I found myself unable to perform and worked hard to hide my new inadequacies.

I started a strict macrobiotic diet, but the benefits never outweighed the side effects of my medicines. I kept a detailed food diary, tracking triggers. I searched for natural treatments—herbs, homeopathy, chiropractor, acupuncture—but realized I couldn't keep bouncing between medicine and alternatives. I quit smoking and drinking, which helped control my spending somewhat.

Even when something worked physically, my bipolar moods and outbursts created stress and chaos, undoing any progress. I was losing respect from colleagues and friends and knew it wouldn't be long before I lost them completely.

Three months after my diagnosis, it all came to a head. Our largest client threatened to fire us. We worked day and night to prepare a revitalized ad campaign, desperate to win them back. Every team member gave everything, nerves fraying as tempers flared.

The morning of the presentation, we met for one last roleplay. I was obsessed with every detail, determined to win. Playing the client, I hurled every obstruction, every tough question I could think of. The team responded with solutions and value points even I hadn't considered. But it wasn't enough. I wanted the close.

I pushed myself—and them—relentlessly until thirty minutes before showtime. We were red-faced, sweaty, and starving, but I still felt we hadn't nailed it. We broke to get ready, set to meet in the conference room.

In my office I chugged water, brushed my hair, and hurried to the men's room, straightening my tie. No one heard me enter. I had become the subject of conversation.

The ridicule was staggering. I hadn't heard things like that about me in years.

"Does he really have to be such a worthless prick? What a jerk! That wimp couldn't sell his way out of a paper bag, yet he expects gold from us!"

"The queer has lost his edge, man. No—he's jumped over it. I don't even know him anymore," two of the top salesmen said at the urinals.

I hadn't been called a queer since Griffin Avenue—at least not where I could hear it. Rage filled me, erupting volcanically without warning. Both men jumped at the volume of my response. I don't remember everything I said. I came dangerously close to getting physical, but it was their answer to my final words that hung in the air.

"You're not the man who hired us. You're nothing like the person we remember. We don't know what happened to you, but whatever it is needs to leave and crawl into a cave with you. We shouldn't have called you names, but what do you expect? You need to get your own house in order, Sam, before you judge us for blowing off steam! I don't know about him, but I quit!" my top salesman said, reaching for the door.

I stood alone in the men's room, speechless. Five minutes before the most important presentation of our careers, my best salesperson had just quit. I washed my hands, looked in the mirror, and saw the same hurt, ashamed, lost expression I'd worn as a kid.

I hurried down the hall to the sales office and begged him not to leave. Luck was on my side—he picked up the proposal, smiled, and walked into the conference room with more confidence than I'd seen in weeks. We closed the deal, but with that close came an opening.

After a long afternoon of contracts and congratulations, I pressed the elevator button for the top floor. When the doors opened to the penthouse offices of the CEO, president, and vice president, I paused, admiring the views stretching across the city. My boss's secretary congratulated me and ushered me inside.

He barely spoke before I tendered my resignation. He looked shocked, but not surprised. He knew I'd been spiraling for a while and that sooner or later it would affect my job. Instead of accepting it, he offered me a leave of absence.

"Take as long as you need—so long as it's not more than six months," he said with a laugh.

"You're the best sales manager I've ever had. I don't want to lose you, but we can do without you for a while. Go on, Sam—get your house in order like you said. Then come back and help us do the same. We'll be needing you by then, I'm sure," he said, shaking my hand.

For a minute I hesitated, frozen in place. *What in the world was I doing?* Yet it felt good to be understood, needed, affirmed by a man I respected. I put one foot in front of the other, cleaned out my desk, and walked calmly to my car, unsure where to go next.

CHAPTER 36

Adventures

MAX AND I SPRAWLED in the grass by the lake, both panting after an aggressive tennis ball game. It had to be the hottest day in July. After giving him a drink from my bottle, I guzzled what was left. I sat up just as Max mistook the little energy I had left as an invitation to play again. A family of ducks splashed in front of us, diverting his attention, and he ran to the water's edge. Struggling to my feet, I caught up as he barked and jumped in and out of the water, hoping to snatch a duckling. I snapped his leash on just in time as the mother duck rose, wings flapping, quacking a loud reprimand. She and Max argued until I dragged him away. Thankfully, his short attention span saved me from joining in.

Walking Max was always a distraction for me, though an adventure for him. Other than television, it was the only one I had. For six months I'd been in survival mode, fighting an intense desire to end it all. Every day since my diagnosis and leaving my job had started and ended the same. Each morning, after walking Max, I searched for new options. If there was a special diet, I tried it. If there was a therapy, I enrolled. I was desperate for the golden ticket, the cure, the explanation, the next best thing that would magically give me a portion of my life back. I left no stone unturned.

Physically, I seemed to be doing well. I was literally half the man I'd been six months ago. Most people thought I was too thin. When I looked in the mirror, my gaunt reflection shocked me—I looked nothing like the man I remembered. Early on I read that eating for survival would bring physical healing and promote other kinds too. But after devouring everything written on the subject, I realized I'd been using a cocktail of food, alcohol, cigarettes, and work to live in a hazy fog. It spared me from reality. It was far more fun than real life.

I missed it—the mesmerizing effects, the euphoric trance. I craved the highs but not the lows. Without it, I felt flat, lifeless, and close to relapse—until I remembered the physical pain it caused. The healthier I felt, the more I wanted to go out and have fun. But my definition of fun would eventually drag me right back to where I started.

I realized quickly that the funk I was experiencing had little to do with my physical health, so the search for remedies began—and I was running out of options. I started with general counseling, trying several different counselors, male and female, searching for a fit, but soon realized it would take more than one-on-one chit chat for any breakthrough. I was a rookie, foolishly expecting counselors to tell me what was wrong so I could follow their advice and get back to life.

My doctor recommended a psychiatrist. I worked with one for weeks but made no headway. Prescriptions offered no relief—only nausea and a new mental fog. I joined multiple support groups: children of alcoholics, Crohn's sufferers, gay and lesbian issues. But so much information from so many sources left me disoriented and, ironically, more alone in a room full of people.

I was lucky to still have some friends I knew would be there if I asked, but I couldn't open up. When they asked how I was doing, I'd say, "*I'm out on another adventure.*" To family, I described it the same way, making it sound like an exciting journey—but never using the word *therapy*. I was embarrassed, ashamed, and felt like a complete failure for needing it. I thought it made me look weak and crazy, and I feared losing even more respect than I already had.

Art and music therapy, yoga, transcendental meditation, biofeedback, hypnotherapy, and visualization were among the things I tried—and failed. I moved on to acupuncture, tai chi, massage, and energy work. They offered some relief but not enough to keep me motivated. I was game for any technique that promised healing or peace. I even tried aromatherapy, but the scents only brought back memories of childhood labor in the fields and nursery.

I became fascinated with energy and spatial theories, sorting myself into smaller pieces—almost like a pie chart—in hopes of understanding. If we are all made of energy, how could I refresh mine when it was filled a hundred percent of the time with past and present burdens? Then I made what I thought was a minor breakthrough.

Weeks earlier, I'd received an invitation from a bohemian friend to attend a poetry reading. I hadn't been to one since college and didn't know people still held them. After an hour of listening, I was searching for excuses to leave, but none seemed acceptable. Just as I resolved to stay, an eighteen-year-old boy stepped onto the makeshift stage. Relaxed, he began to speak, his voice calming the restless crowd of thirty or more.

Reading from a wrinkled yellow memo pad, he spoke about personal space. His words struck me when he said we must own both what we let in and what we allow to leave—internally in our hearts and minds and externally in the world around us. The melodic quality of his voice and the depth of his writing mesmerized the audience. I didn't want him to stop.

When he whispered his final line, I thought it was for effect, but then a tear slid down his cheek. He apologized and turned to leave. As he descended, the crowd rose in applause, louder and louder, until he smiled and waved on the next reader. While attention returned to the stage, I slipped out in pursuit of him.

He was leaning against a tree just outside the door when I began firing off questions, leaving no room for his reply.

"Man, we are consumers of our own space. When we run out of room for junk, we consume others. Sorry, but I don't have space for your junk. You need to let go of some. The answers you need are inside you. I don't know your story, and you don't know me well enough to share it. Understand?" he said, holding me at a distance.

I was stunned. At first I felt rejected, then angry at this young punk—but weeks later I realized he was right. I envied his freedom, and he wasn't about to let anyone take it from him. That was exactly what was wrong with me, and I knew it. I needed to find a way to let go, but I didn't know how.

After walking Max that day, I called my friend Petyr, whom I'd met through mutual acquaintances at a West Coast conference. He was in an intensive therapy program. I was encouraged when he explained how it had changed his perspective, so I immediately wrote a letter to the foundation offering it, asking how to enroll as soon as possible. I described my situation as clearly as I could.

I waited eagerly for a reply, only to learn it would take months before there was a place for me in the program. Panicked, I wrote them a sob story, hoping they'd see my urgency. Thankfully, they did, and accelerated my entrance. I was headed for what I hoped would be healing.

All that was left was convincing my boss to grant more personal leave, which I feared he couldn't. In the end, he agreed. I also needed to tell Rob and Anne about this latest adventure.

"How long will you be there, Sam?" Rob asked with concern.

"As long as it takes—or as long as I can afford. I'll be staying with others in the program. I have to eat, drink, and sleep this stuff, so I'll probably be unavailable most of the time," I shared.

"Okay, well, whatever you need. I hope it works for you. Sarah wants to ask you something—hold on," he said, handing her the phone.

Sarah was recovering from a cesarean. I was an uncle again, this time to the tiniest preemie I'd ever seen. They'd sent pictures from the neonatal unit—six weeks early, lungs not fully developed, but a fighter. She'd been released two weeks earlier.

"Sam, hi, I love you. Would you have time to stop here before you head west?" she asked.

"I love you too. Why? I'd love to meet Lily, but I thought a visit so soon might be too much for you."

"Too much? You're never too much. We aren't Catholic, but we're using their tradition—we were wondering if you'd be Lily's godfather?"

I was floored, honored, and in tears.

"Are you kidding? Yes! I'd love that. Thank you so much!" I said, choking back emotion.

When I finally looked at the clock, two hours had passed. We hadn't spoken much in weeks, and it felt good to catch up. Having them in my life made me feel lighter, more connected.

"I miss you guys and can't wait to see you. I'll let you know my flight arrangements. I'm so excited—and I'm coming hungry. I want some homecooked food before I start this program," I said to Sarah.

"I may not be able to fix anything else, but I can remedy your hunger. Will spaghetti and meatballs followed by homemade chocolate cake work?" she asked with excitement.

"My mouth is watering already! Thank you, Sarah, and thank Rob too. I don't know where I'd be without you both and Anne.

Call you in a couple of days!" I said, hanging up. I knew I'd regret eating everything she promised, but it would be worth it.

Two weeks later, I sat eating cake at their table. The scene was chaotic but wonderful as I watched them as a family. Later, holding Lily on my chest, my heart felt so full. This was what I always wished for—a family of my own. Why did I have to be who I was? I was weary of traversing between what I saw, what I dreamed of, and who I was.

There was no remedy for it, but I hoped the adventure out west would help me accept my life. My biggest wish was to clear out the garbage I carried and make room for new memories. Maybe learn to accept my life for what it was. It was a lot to expect, but I couldn't hope for less. At this stage, it felt like my only hope.

CHAPTER 37

Said and Done

THE FLIGHT TO CALIFORNIA threatened to be an event in itself. I was scheduled for coach, but when I reached the gate, I couldn't imagine hours surrounded by what felt like a million crying babies. I loved babies—just not on planes. With serious work ahead, I upgraded to business class.

Once settled and cruising, I put in my earphones, arranged snacks that the program would soon forbid, and pulled out my yellow tablet. I felt compelled to capture everything in my mind before the program began and my perspective shifted. Later, I wanted to revisit these notes—pure, unaltered, undiluted.

After landing, I picked up my rental car and drove to Foundations. Intake was running two hours behind, so I drove around to get my bearings. Spotting a toy store, I pulled in. I was always hunting for the newest toys to send my nieces and nephews.

Kneeling to inspect the Star Wars section, I felt a small hand on my shoulder. A boy, maybe four, spoke in a sweet voice. "Hi, my name is Will. Do you like Star Wars?"

"Yes, I do, Will. My name is Sam. Do you like them too?" I asked, sitting cross-legged on the floor.

"Well, yes, I do. What is your favorite *carrotter*?" he asked, struggling with the word.

As I answered, Will crawled between my knees and perched on my thigh. He wrapped an arm around my neck and nestled into my shoulder. His openness melted my heart, and I fought back the rush of emotions. We sat nearly half an hour talking and laughing while his dad shopped nearby.

I became overwhelmed by the thought that—if life were different—Will could have been my son. Choking back tears, I stood, lifted my broken heart, and told him goodbye. I left the store with tears streaming and wandered the parking lot trying to collect myself.

When I regained composure, I found myself again in front of the toy store. Certain he and his dad were gone, I ventured back inside. Turning into the last aisle, there was Will again. His eyes lit up. He ran, grabbed my hand, and eagerly pulled me through the aisle, pointing out toys and firing off questions.

"Daddy, this is my special friend, Sam, and he likes toys too!" Will said, beaming.

"Nice to meet you, Sam. I appreciate you keeping him entertained—I feel like I should pay you for babysitting," his dad said, lifting Will into his arms.

"I am not a baby, Daddy!" Will declared, snuggling close.

"It was my pleasure," I replied. "He's an amazing, inquisitive young man—and definitely not a baby." I winked.

"Thank you, I think so too. Tell Sam goodbye, Will. He probably has more shopping to do."

"Bye, my special friend Sam. Have a nice day!" Will said, waving.

I stood mesmerized, watching through the store window as the father kissed his son's forehead and helped him into the car. I could feel their love from where I stood. It shattered me. I realized how much I missed a close relationship with my father—how I wished he had loved me as Will's dad did. I longed for a son who would love me unconditionally. The truth that I would never have my father's love, never call anyone Daddy, engulfed me. I sobbed until I could barely breathe. Forcing short breaths,

I swallowed my pain, drove to Foundations, and began what would become a long, belabored journey toward healing.

Four months into the program, I looked out at the azure skies above Los Angeles. I was finally in my own room on the penthouse floor of an apartment complex used by Foundations. Until then, I'd shared with my friend Petyr, who first told me about the program. When a slot opened, we were separated.

That night, all participants were scheduled to gather in the lobby to watch the new year arrive together. I wasn't attending. Depression had a stranglehold on me. I felt homesick, frustrated, and abandoned—even though I was the one who had left.

Before leaving, I'd sent Christmas cards to everyone I loved, with generous checks tucked inside. I shopped frantically for my nieces and nephews, wanting them to have something special. At the time, I told myself I expected nothing in return, but when no one called to thank me, I questioned my motives. On Christmas Day, I waited all day for a call. None came.

That evening I gave in and called Rob. Love and excitement filled the conversation, and I envied them. The kids were thankful, and Dolly and Jay said they missed me and wanted another visit. I was touched. Yet when the call ended, the ache returned—I still felt hurt, forgotten, and overlooked. They had sent gifts, but deliveries weren't permitted while enrolled, so they were being held until graduation back into the outside world.

I spoke to Anne and enjoyed talking to her kids, but when I called Emma, Joan, and Peter, the conversations felt more like chatting with acquaintances than with family. I had seen Anne before I left, but it had been over a year since I'd spent time with the others. Emma had just given birth to her first baby girl, and while I was excited to hear the details, I felt so far removed from it all. Differing schedules had kept us apart, but my relationship with her usually never missed a beat. Even when she moved back to Griffin Avenue during financial struggles, she'd call or send messages through Rob, and once she had her own place again, we made up for lost time. I always enjoyed being with her, even if it was just listening to her albums. Our shared love of music, sports, and TV bridged the age gap and kept us close at heart.

The rest of the family kept me at arm's length, careful not to appear disloyal to anyone else. We avoided real conversations, and their actions made clear where they stood. I reasoned that if I wanted acceptance for who I was, I also had to accept their disapproval—but I wanted more. Joan and Peter disapproved but stayed somewhat caring, as long as I didn't involve them in my "gay life." Jude, however, took the hardest stand, aligning with Auggie and Gertie, condemning me outright.

My heart felt heavy as I stared out the window. Nothing could have pacified me except a plane ticket home and Rob or Anne waiting at the gate. But I had made this commitment and was following through, wherever it took me. Leaning my head against the warm glass, I watched people below. I wondered where they were going, who they loved, and if they were happy. They looked it, but I knew appearances deceived. I strained to see two young men walking hand in hand—something I'd never witness back home. I longed for that kind of open affection, a hand to hold before everyone and God.

Anxiety surged at the thought of God. The gap between us had grown so wide my beliefs felt blurred. Still, fear itself proved I hadn't let go completely. I blocked thoughts of Him as much as possible, until moments like these forced them in. Exhausted, I fell onto the bed, staring at the ceiling until sleep overtook me.

I woke disoriented, the remnants of a dream clinging to me. It was Thanksgiving, though the kitchen looked like a cafeteria. I stood in a food line, always ending up last. Each time I tried to reach family and friends at a table, I was swallowed by the crowd again. A bright light shone from one chair. God sat there with Father Bernard at His side, inviting me to sit on His lap.

Shaken, I tried to shake it off but couldn't. I grabbed a pen and recorded the details. There was no hidden meaning—it was exactly how I felt: left out, chasing closeness but never arriving. Still, it unnerved me. Relief came when I saw the clock. I'd slept through the midnight gathering downstairs and wouldn't have to lie about missing it.

The nap, though, left me wide awake. I wandered the room until my eyes met the reflection in the huge mirror above the desk. I couldn't escape it. Since moving in, I'd fought the repeated temptation to render it useless.

It was the first day of the new year—time to sit down and evaluate how I was doing. At Foundations we had no outside contact except two phone calls a month, more only on holidays. A strict diet stripped away the usual comforts, leaving us exposed to raw emotion minute by minute. At first I doubted I could handle such crushing isolation, but eventually decided I should repeat the practice once a year after graduation to check in on myself and my goals.

Early on I endured days in a quiet padded room, pounding anger into the walls. I spent hours talking to empty chairs, imagining my parents, God, Father Bernard, and others sitting before me listening.

My first breakthrough came in a soundproof room. Alone and defenseless, I curled into a ball in the corner, hugging my legs. Suddenly a pivotal memory from Auggie's school of hard knocks flooded back, so vivid it felt present rather than past. The Marine's words echoed in my ears. If I had ever felt worthless, this moment sealed it.

He had lifted me by the front of my shirt, feet dangling in the air, shouting in my face: "Da biggest mistake I ever made was gettin' married and havin' kids! But havin' you—lettin' ya live, you little piss ant—was my worst mistake!"

The crushing pain of those words broke me. I was my father's greatest mistake. I don't remember everything that followed, only that hours later I was soaked in sweat and tears. At least now I knew where it had begun.

The next major breakthrough came after hours of screaming that I hated them. At first I thought the rage was toward my parents, but soon I found myself shouting, "*I hate you, Sam.*" In the depths of my soul I despised myself for not being the son they could love. I was fighting a civil war inside. Nations in civil war are divided and paralyzed, and so was I. Each day I won and lost at the same time. If I could let go of the battle, maybe I could finally pull the parts of me together and be whole. Realizing what I was doing to myself gave me hope that one day I could declare a ceasefire.

Another dramatic discovery came in an evening group session. That's when I met Marcus—a man with the bluest eyes I had ever seen, long dark hair resting perfectly on his shoulders, and a British accent that melted my heart. His smile lit up the room. We had instant chemistry, and he became my partner during sessions. He drew things out of me no one else ever had. We became close friends, and I knew I was in trouble. Marcus was straight. That truth should have stopped me, but I was falling fast, and he could see it.

One evening, as we sat with chairs facing each other, he lowered the boom. "Sam, it's likely you're falling in love with me. I'm not distressed or threatened by this. May I share what I'm observing?" he asked, reaching for my hands.

"Um … I'm not sure what to say. Sure, go ahead," I replied, dry-mouthed and nervous.

"Okay. Do you often fall in love with people you can't obtain?"

I swallowed hard as anger rose and fell in waves. He was right. I had fallen in love with him—and, truth be told, I always seemed to fall for men I couldn't have. I was rarely attracted to gay men at all, and though I'd loved a few women, those relationships went nowhere.

"And so," Marcus continued, "is this reminiscent of the love you couldn't, or didn't, acquire from your father or mother—or both—as they were your original examples of love?"

Oh, how I melted when he spoke.

"Yes, Marcus. Yes, it is. I'm searching for love I cannot obtain."

A single tear slipped from the corner of my eye, unleashing a flood. I was inconsolable for most of a day. I knew the truth deep in my heart and mind, but in that moment, it arrived with such clarity that I shattered into a million pieces—only to watch those fragments pull back together again for another battle, another time.

I wrote hundreds of letters to my parents, to God, to Father Bernard—letters that would never be sent. I realized I had never actually liked my parents. I loved and hated them, but I would never have chosen them as friends. This realization felt disloyal and required endless therapy, both personal and group, as I wrestled with the guilt of it.

In those months, I shed more tears than I thought possible, until I was drained to the point of drought. Still, the digging continued. Just when I thought I had reached the bottom, I struck something deeper. The program's mission was to help each participant uncover core trigger points. I felt primed, blistered from digging through the debris of my past, and sensed I was on the cusp of something monumental.

Petyr and I had only brief encounters in the corridors, elevators, and group sessions after we were assigned different rooms. He had been in the program longer than I had, so he was part of events I wasn't privy to. Foundations scheduled an evening of entertainment—usually a meal with some sort of musical presentation—to break up the monotony of weekly routines. Everyone, no matter which level they were in, was required to attend. It grieved me to shower and dress for the event; I was emotionally exhausted and wanted nothing more than to pull the covers over my head and disappear. On the way down, I ran into Petyr, who looked just as reluctant.

"I am clearly in no shape to mingle," he mumbled.

"That makes two of us. Let's sit as far in the back as we can," I said, stepping out of the elevator.

The transformed dining hall resembled an upscale restaurant, complete with tablecloths and china. The menu still followed the strict dietary guidelines, but serving it that way made it seem more palatable. A piano player and violinist played softly in one corner. Petyr and I slipped into seats close to the exit.

Thankfully, we were the only two at our table.

"So, how's it going, man?" I asked between bites.

"It's going, and that's about all I can say. I've hit a roadblock and I'm not progressing. How about you?"

"I'm exhausted from the momentum."

"That's good. I'm glad someone is progressing," he said just as a woman approached.

"Hi, Sheila, this is my gay friend, Sam," Petyr introduced with a mouth full of food.

We exchanged pleasantries, and after she left the room, I shoved my plate aside and turned to Petyr.

"Seriously? Why did you introduce me that way? 'This is Sam, my *gay* friend'? What business is it of hers? That's what aggravates me about being homosexual. People are introduced as friends, family, colleagues, or neighbors—but not as their sexual preference. No one says, 'This is my straight friend, Polish friend, or married friend.' Why am I always introduced as the gay friend? It doesn't give anyone a chance to know me before they know my orientation, which should be of no concern to anyone. It hangs in the space between me and everyone in my life.

"If you're born Black or into another nationality, people accept that there's nothing you can do about it. You're not raised with dreams of becoming something else since you can't become something else. Society doesn't brand you a pervert who can be reformed. I have no control over being homosexual, yet I face constant rejection because of it. It's not fair—and it hurts deeply!" I ranted.

"I know others face different forms of persecution, but this feels worse. Add to that the pain of not being able to marry and have a family. Real men don't deal with that. They also don't have to sit their families down and say, 'Here—I have a pile of crap for you to handle from now on.' From then on everyone is just uncomfortable."

"Sam, I apologize," Petyr said. "I've never stopped to think about this. But what I hear is that one of your core issues is accepting your difference. Do you truly accept yourself for being gay? Do you feel the need to be forgiven for it? And ... do you not feel like a 'real' man?"

"No, I don't think I'm a pile of crap. I have a high opinion of myself," I answered quickly. "I think I'm as real a man as any other, and I believe I've accepted my homosexuality. Forgiven myself? Hmm ..."

"I didn't ask what you *think,* Sam. I asked what you *feel.*"

He had me. Clarity can be a brutal beast.

In the days that followed, my private sessions focused on my opinion of myself. I went through all the stages of grief as I laid to rest the dream of ever being straight. I had lived in denial, bargaining and hoping for some miraculous intervention.

Depression had shadowed me since childhood. I now stood at the door of acceptance but couldn't quite cross the precipice.

After a particularly vicious private session, I craved companionship—even if only in a group. I slipped into the last available seat, staring stoically at three women and three men who seemed more entertained with each other than working on issues. The guide arrived late and quickly noticed my silence.

"Sam, if you would, pull your chair back from the group for a few minutes. When you're ready to participate, rejoin," the guide instructed.

Like a child sent to the corner, I sulked and moved as directed. Now outside the circle, I watched three women and three men face each other. The setup triggered childhood memories of being different and alone, even surrounded by my six siblings.

I observed closely. By now I knew most of the participants, especially Sheila—the woman Petyr had introduced me to—who sat nearest me. All eyes were on her. She was a natural comedian, quick with humor and sarcasm. I always thought she could have been a late-night talk show host. But beneath her wit I sensed pain. Still, she always managed to lift the mood. Over the last weeks we'd grown close in a balanced way: My very existence supplied her with material, and she supplied the laughter I so badly needed.

At that moment she was joking with one of the men, who was again elaborating on a story we'd all heard countless times. He was exceptionally wealthy, married to a beautiful woman, father of three wonderful children, loved his career, and had never known abuse or bullying. Yet happiness had always eluded him. He was here to explore why, though he clearly wasn't satisfied with his progress. Today, though, he seemed in a lighter mood.

"So, I feel for your lack of happiness, man," Sheila said, grinning. "But if all that money can't buy you some, I'd be glad to help. How about you 'man up' and buy me some happiness? I'll happily accept any donations you want to throw my way!"

He laughed and offered Sheila the change in his pocket, but she waved it off, saying it would take far more to buy the kind of happiness she wanted. Her words ricocheted in my head like ping pong balls. *Man up. MAN up. MAN UP!* My heart raced, blood pressure spiked, and heat flushed my cheeks.

"Sam? Sam?"

The guide's voice broke through, but I couldn't answer. She crouched beside me and touched my hand—and I exploded.

"MAN UP! BUCK UP! GROW SOME! TOUGHEN UP! BE COOL! STOP BEING A BABY! BOYS DON'T CRY! STAND TALL! BE STRONG! MEN DON'T CRY! DON'T BE A SISSY WIMP! BE A MAN!" I shouted, pacing in circles, arms wrapped around myself. Out of control, I couldn't stop.

The group scrambled aside, pressing against the walls as they watched my meltdown. I cried, screamed, ranted, and collapsed into a corner, weeping.

When I opened my eyes, the room was empty except for Mike, who sat on the floor next to me. His eyes were red and swollen—he had been crying too.

"Sam, you okay? Want me to help you to a chair, or up to your room? Or do you want to talk about what just happened?"

"I guess it's pretty clear to everyone that I found my core trigger," I said in a raspy voice. Everything—time, energy, emotions, environment—had boiled together and aligned like planets to ensure I hit my crucible.

"Yes, Sam, I believe you have. Take comfort in knowing your core is a common one for men. In fact, it was mine—and probably most men who come through these doors. We can't share that ahead of time though. Each man has to reach it in his own way."

"But it seems so shallow. So universal. It's just life, right? How could it cut so deep? How could it damage me like this?" I asked, swallowing hard.

"How could it *not* affect us?" Mike replied. "Think about it, Sam. From the youngest age, society—and those we love—lay out the rules. We're handed a definition of manhood that's supposed to prepare us for life's realities, but it robs us of being babies, boys, teens, and, later, men. That definition bullies our spirits. We're told to never show feelings. To be strong, knights in shining armor, protectors, saviors. Weakness is hunted. So we hide behind masks, terrified of being seen, and we carry the weight of the world in silence. We shame and humiliate each other every time vulnerability shows. And for you—as a homosexual man— the pressure is even more brutal." His voice was soft, but edged with anger and disappointment.

This was it—my core trigger. Something I had no control over. I couldn't change it or fix it. I would have to live with it, like the rest of the male population. The only way it could truly be healed was if society itself changed. Maybe one day others would turn it around. But for me, being homosexual only amplified it. I would never meet society's definition of a man, no matter what I did. Born a failure in those terms, I would always fall short, no matter my strength, hard work, or successes.

It wasn't that I hadn't known this before, but now I felt it with clarity, and I understood its weight. I had to accept it, even if I didn't like it. That would take time. I needed compassion for myself. I needed to forgive myself for failing to meet the impossible demands of society. Strange stirrings rose in me, and I knew true change was on the horizon.

From that day on, group therapy conflicted me. I compared suffering, ranking my pain against others, and felt shame when I shared, as if my story wasn't valid. I had been silenced since childhood, and now I was baring everything—and felt naked and unsafe. Yet I also grew more compassionate toward my male counterparts, finding a kind of camaraderie in the struggles we all carried.

In private sessions, I let myself be vulnerable, but without the group's support, I often felt hollow afterward. I was evolving, but I couldn't see where it was leading. Would I wake up healed one day? Or wake up too tired to keep reliving this pain? I was exhausted from it all.

Walking away from the window, I sat thinking about the week ahead. I dreaded going back into sessions and resented how understaffed—and expensive—the program seemed. I was getting less time with Mike, my main therapist, and I felt abandoned. After mulling it over for hours, I decided to ask for a private consultation the next morning to evaluate my progress.

I was in for a rude awakening. As soon as the director, Mike, and my guide sat down with me, I began spilling out my concerns. The director interrupted after only a few minutes.

"Sam, excuse me, but I had to push several meetings back to accommodate you. It appears this could have been handled between you and Mike. Is there anything you need from me that he can't handle?" he asked abruptly.

"I am paying a fortune to be here, and I want to know why I'm not progressing further. I'd also like to know why expenses keep escalating. I'm getting less and less time with Mike when he seems to have plenty for others. He refuses to answer my questions and doesn't seem to understand why I'm asking them," I said, avoiding eye contact with Mike.

"Sam, the cost of the program hasn't changed since its inception. Everything was laid out in black and white before you entered, and you signed off on it. Any extra fees are the result of your own choices in therapies and the frequency with which you schedule them. You continue to choose private sessions. You are allotted no less time than anyone else, and Mike has logged his time accurately. I don't think he'd start falsifying records now.

"You seem to have grown possessive of him and his time. Shifting from possessive to aggressive is generally a sign that you've reached the end of the road. I'm sorry, but I need to go. I'm confident Mike can take it from here," the director said, walking out the door.

I was stunned and deflated. I looked at Mike. I had indeed become obsessive and possessive of him and his time. I was identifying too closely with him and projecting my feelings onto him, expecting feedback that wasn't his to give.

"Sam, I've been waiting patiently for you to realize you no longer need to be here. You've done well working through your feelings. I was waiting for you to reach the point where you no longer saw value in the program. I think you're there but afraid to ask, 'Is this it? Is this all there is? Because if it is, then I have a life to get back to,'" Mike said softly, with confidence.

He was right, and I was disappointed. I came here for help, wanting to walk away fully healed, but I had moved on without realizing it. I was frightened and unsure, yet too exhausted to keep digging everything up again. I had to let it go, return to the world, and face life as it was. Mike couldn't heal me. The pain I carried could only be undone by those who caused it—and that wasn't realistic. The words spoken to me, etched painfully in my heart and mind, could never be taken back. No apology was coming from people who thought they had done nothing wrong. I had to release it all and deal with the pain as it surfaced in the future.

Strangely, I did feel freer, able to meet life without the same heavy constraints of old needs and wounds. In that moment, I decided to pack up and go back. I knew I had further to go, but I finally had tools to face what remained.

Suitcase in hand, I willed myself through the long corridor that led to the front door. Gleaming shards of LA sunlight spilled through the cracks at the threshold, pulsing and beckoning me forward. Fear and uncertainty engulfed me. It was the light at the end of the tunnel, a rebirth into a strange new world. I could feel Billy and Aaron pushing and pulling from inside as the three of us became one—an integrated, stronger version of Sam the Man.

For the first time since I was a boy, I walked alone. With all my strength, I pushed the doors open, stood in the warmth of the sun, closed my eyes, and let it soak my tear-stained cheeks.

In retrospect, I see that healing came through experiencing, acknowledging, and validating my pain. Those few months narrowed my world into a tiny box of hurt, people, and circumstances. It consumed me, easier to face away from life and everything in it. What I didn't realize was how valuable time itself was. I spent precious months wrestling with the past, striving to make my life and the world more beautiful instead of enjoying what was right at my fingertips. I was trying to gild the lily—or was I? In the end, it didn't matter. After all was said and done, hindsight is twenty-twenty.

CHAPTER 38

In the Beginning Part II

MY REEMERGENCE INTO LIFE was mind-blowing. I suffered culture shock on every level. The sun seemed too bright, sounds amplified, food strangely bland—except anything with sugar, which tasted better than ever. My senses were overstimulated, and I found myself distracted by the tiniest things. I marveled like a newborn at raindrops sliding down rose stems, ants dragging crumbs, or butterfly wings in the breeze. Sunsets filled my eyes with tears, colors bursting through a fresh prism. Life without the cloud of depression and anxiety was intoxicating. I stood taller, walked farther, and breathed deeper, absorbing it all.

I didn't want to leave LA. My hotel overlooked the ocean, and at night the surf lulled me into the deepest rest I had ever known. Each morning I woke rejuvenated, walking the shore and watching nature's drama unfold. Days slipped by as I craved more time to explore.

I became enchanted with one eclectic beach community. In the northeast, no matter how hard I tried, I always stood out. Here I blended in. Diversity wasn't just tolerated—it was celebrated. Guitar-playing skaters, chainsaw jugglers, half-dressed dancers, and gay and lesbian couples strolling hand in hand all added to its charm. Its nonconformity warmed my heart and opened my mind. For the first time, I felt "normally abnormal."

I wandered the streets, browsed bohemian shops, and discovered a small homestyle restaurant with no name on the door.

The waiter explained, "Everyone knows we're here and the food is exceptional—why would we need a name? Does your kitchen have one?" I loved the owner's ingenuity. It broke every rule of advertising, yet the place was packed, with a line fifteen deep.

I searched for a word to describe how I felt about the area, but nothing quite fit. I hiked the beach, sat beneath palm trees, and left LAX exhilarated by newfound freedom.

As I boarded the plane, the sensation of leaving something behind lingered until I realized—it was my heart, left with my footprints in the sand. I missed Max, my family, friends, and even my job, but now I knew where I belonged. So much had shifted within me. I was anxious to see how the "new me" would interact with life back east.

The first weeks home were filled with family and friends. Wonderful, yes—but something was missing. I couldn't settle. The sights that once thrilled me felt dull. I had always loved Boston's historic row homes and cultural blend, the charm of its waterfront—but now the contrast with LA was overwhelming. My dreams replayed the West Coast, and all I wanted was to pack everything and move before the feeling faded.

Obstacles loomed, the biggest being employment. The thought of living again under gray skies and squeezing through narrow streets made me edgy and combative. My return to work loomed that Monday, and I oscillated between relief at financial stability and melancholy at the thought of staying.

It was a foggy morning as I raced the clock, planning to arrive early for a quick sit-down with my boss to catch up on what I'd missed. I had half expected a welcoming committee but quickly reminded myself of the circumstances under which I had left. A few familiar faces greeted me warmly, but many were new. My desk was buried in files and correspondence, the cherry wood barely visible beneath the glass. The air was musty, and dust flew as I opened the blinds. Staring at the chaos, I fought the urge to run. This office—once a dream—now felt like a cage.

I grabbed a yellow tablet, coffee, and went in search of my boss, finding him in the break room.

"Sam, welcome back! We missed you. You look incredible—must be the West Coast breeze! Sorry your office is such a mess, but with the reorg I wasn't sure you'd want to stay there anyway," he said as we boarded the elevator to his office.

"Reorganization? Fill me in," I asked, settling into a chair.

"Well, Sam, we're expanding to the West Coast. We've finalized a deal on a beautiful office complex in an LA suburb and are assembling a team to launch it."

I couldn't believe what I was hearing.

"I'm interested in a position in LA, if one's available," I blurted.

"I was about to offer you my job, but this is even better! My family is settled here, and moving would have been difficult. If you're serious, I'd like to offer you vice president of sales at our new West Coast branch, effective immediately."

"Compensation?" I asked.

"Your pay will double, with a strong bonus package, full health coverage, and relocation expenses. You'll also build your own team once you're settled."

"Sounds great. We can finalize details as we go," I said, shaking his hand before heading to HR to start the paperwork.

Ecstatic, I told Becky over dinner. She was supportive, with one condition—full custody of Max. It stung, but I knew she was right. I'd be working around the clock to launch the office, and he deserved stability. I spent the week arranging the move and then called Rob and Anne. They were thrilled and promised to visit once I was settled.

Three weeks later, I was unpacking boxes in my West Coast office. The view from my penthouse corner window left me breathless. At last, the world felt within reach. My voice would matter here. This branch would run like a well-oiled machine—once I had a team in place.

I searched for an apartment with an easy commute and signed a short-term lease near my favorite beach. At only eight hundred square feet, it still felt like a mansion—my first place entirely my own. Just seven months earlier I had arrived here a broken mess, but now I was stepping into a new job, a new home, and a new life. I left nearly everyone I loved 2,600 miles behind, determined to start fresh.

At first, I was lonely. I missed familiar comforts, but I also felt bold and energized. Each morning I buttoned a crisp three-piece suit and remembered the Salvation Army wardrobe and school uniforms of my youth. Sliding into the leather seats of my new red sports car, I felt Billy's boyhood dreams finally realized. This time I wouldn't compromise who I was. I felt no pressure to pretend. From this new vantage point, I had found refuge. I was still different, but here everyone was, and blending in meant simply being myself.

Sitting in my favorite nameless restaurant, I watched a chainsaw juggler perform on the street. For a moment my mind flickered back to the starving kids in China my mother used to mention, and I smiled at the contrast. Then I heard the rumble of an old truck shifting gears as it turned down the street. For a split second, the sound triggered the same fear I once felt on Griffin Avenue. But this time I laughed at myself. The only warning system I needed to pay attention to here was for earthquakes.

CHAPTER 39

Day of All Days
Part II

THE SUNSET'S RADIANT ORANGE rays blanketed the beach as far as the eye could see. I sank into the warm sand, closing my eyes and letting the glow linger on the inside of my eyelids. I hadn't felt this relaxed in years, if ever.

A deep, wonderful laugh stole the moment. I peeked through squinted eyes to find its source, smiling before I even knew why. The sun distorted my view, but I caught the silhouette of two people hugging goodbye. When one walked in my direction, my heart raced and butterflies filled my stomach. By the time the sun disappeared and the full moon rose, I knew I had met the most meaningful person of my life.

Within days, this sandy-haired, light-eyed beauty filled my heart and life like no one before. We fit together like puzzle pieces I'd long given up on. Within months we were inseparable, convinced we were invincible. Within a year we pledged vows of commitment before family and friends, sure nothing could ever part us.

A few years later, Billy's dream home stood proudly in an up-scale neighborhood. But at the same time, the life we were building began to collapse. At the first sign of adversity, we shattered like glass on marble floors, pulling painful fragments from our hearts for years. Days were spent smiling at dinner parties, nights dodging pottery hurled in exasperation.

During that time Sarah had her own struggles with Rob. I seemed to have all the right answers, and she often thanked me for saving their marriage. Perhaps that was why she devoted hours to consoling me. She recognized all too well the marks of a failing relationship. Her words became a treasure trove of wisdom—something we both needed. I hoped I might one day put it to use with someone new, though I doubted I would.

"You know, Sam, we meet someone along the way in life and fall head over heels in love with them, and we want them to love us as much as we do them, and we start on this mystical, starry-eyed journey. In the beginning we do whatever it takes, be whomever we need to be, no matter what the toll is on us. We bring old, worn-out expectations and unrealistic dreams and try to use them again and again even though they didn't work in former relationships. We fear being rejected as we are, so we transform ourselves into what we think this new partner wants and needs.

"We start with a beautiful empty piece of monogrammed luggage on wheels that can turn any direction with ease. But it has two people trying to navigate it, each pulling in directions dictated by past experiences and future expectations. We begin with a burning desire to please and cooperate. The fire ignites, the wheels gain traction, momentum builds. The luggage grows clumsy as we work for connection. Old baggage from the past pushes against the seams.

"We don't stop and think it through—everyone has their own definition of what a relationship should be, and they can be very different. If we don't get what we need based on our preconceived ideas, things grow turbulent. Instead of allowing the other person to be themselves, we conjure up ideas of what we think will make them happy, filling the luggage with things that have nothing to do with reality. Then we're disappointed when the wheels won't turn where we want them to. Or the opposite happens if we are self-centered and see only what we want.

"Before long the fire wanes and we can't see through the smoke of confusion and anger. In the end, instead of a beautiful piece of luggage turning smoothly in any direction, we're left with a torn, singed, ugly bag full of garbage with wheels spinning everywhere but where we want to go.

"Sam, we don't do the work in relationships. We need to put in the time. Give what our partners say they need, and be careful not to take more than we need. We should ask questions, leave out assumptions, respect and encourage each other's dreams. And we need to know early if we truly share desires so we're heading in a unified direction. More than anything we need to listen.

"But we don't. We pack our gear, head away from the firestorm, and the cycle repeats. The good thing is that if we catch it soon enough, we can find beauty in the ashes and start again with new luggage, new growth, a new journey. This, as you know, is what happened with Rob and me, and I'm so happy we're on a new journey together this time," Sarah shared during one of our long phone conversations.

I wished I had come to her as she had to me, before everything went up in flames. There would be no beauty from these ashes. Our flame wasn't extinguished—we became arsonists and destroyed, with words and actions, any chance at new growth. I sat thinking about the disaster of a relationship falling apart right before my eyes and realized that most of the time we were together we took more than we gave. Within weeks of our fourth year, we were finished, and neither of us wanted to be the one to say goodbye. We opted for time apart, which stretched into months, and then our journey was over.

It's frightening now to look back at such beauty, such confidence, such certainty—and wonder how I ever trusted my decision-making abilities again. The reemergence of Crohn's was the beginning of the end. Surgeries, painful recoveries, and the dehumanizing ordeal of an ostomy bag pushed us closer to the edge.

But the final straw—the true day of all days—came when my blood work returned with questionable results. We agreed to be tested together, and when the results came back, we each responded differently to our six-foot-under diagnosis. We were HIV positive, and we knew all too well what that meant for our futures. We didn't have one.

The AIDS epidemic was out of control across the globe. Advancements had been made through monumental efforts. Rock Hudson's AIDS-related death, the Ryan White story, and the passage of the Comprehensive AIDS Resources Emergency Act after White's death raised public awareness. But there was still no cure. Bottom line: It still felt like a death sentence. AIDS had ravaged the gay community, and we had attended so many funerals over the last few years that we had lost count. But we never once stopped to think it could be us. If we did, we never discussed it—probably because we were too afraid to face it.

In the millisecond it took the doctor to speak our results, time came to a complete stop. We sat motionless. I had been near the edge of a precipice before, but nothing about Crohn's felt as final as this. At first, neither of us could respond until a constellation of desperate questions flew from my lips.

"Is there a chance the results could be wrong?" I asked, fighting for hope.

"No, Sam. We sent them out twice. You have more urgent issues than your partner, whose T-cells look close to normal. Yours are low—likely from Crohn's, since your immune system is already compromised. Not low enough to be classified as AIDS, but concerning," he said.

I went numb as a black veil lowered across my mind, heart, and soul. I don't remember our ride home. When we arrived, we went our separate ways, each seeking solace. One chose to party in denial; the other hid under the covers in fear and desolation.

I drifted in and out of sleep, waking only long enough to sink back into oblivion. After exhausting all my sick, vacation, and personal days, I worked from my home office. I paced the empty rooms and halls of our beautiful home alone. I sat staring at sunsets from one of our five viewing decks. At night, I cried for comfort; each morning, I watched the clouds roll across the mountains, filling the living room—and my life—with fog-like beauty.

Weeks after our "let's do some time apart" split, I sat, ate, drank, and slept in rooms haunted by ghosts of us, our friends, and past visits. I lost hours at the dining room table, replaying laughter from dinner parties with Anne, Emma, Sarah, and Rob, who had flown out to help me through surgeries and to celebrate successes. Alone on the deck, rocking in my favorite chair, I remembered sitting there half the night with Sarah after we saw *Phantom of the Opera*, drinking wine and crying. Later, I sat in the same spot consoling Lily after she sobbed through the show. So many memories, so little time left to make new ones.

Thankfully, neighbors were scarce as I blasted Chicago's "Hard to Say I'm Sorry," Journey's "Who's Cryin' Now," Quarterflash's "Harden My Heart," and every other song that mirrored my feelings. The only companionship was a lone hawk that often perched on the deck railing. Over time he allowed me to feed him seeds from my palm. It felt as if he waited for me to join him soaring above the clouds, visiting everyone I loved—though most likely he was just interested in the seeds.

Calls and messages from friends and family increased, their patience gone. Sarah and Rob insisted I visit, refusing to accept my excuses. I hesitated. I knew what being HIV positive meant—but would they? Only a few close friends battling the same nemesis knew. I had informed as many others as I felt obligated to, but there were few left. I believed I knew where I'd contracted HIV, but telling him was impossible—he'd already died, and I'd attended his funeral back east.

The thought of telling my family terrified me. I feared the same rejection I'd faced when I came out, but worse now. I knew it would scare them, and most weren't educated with the facts. Many still believed HIV could be passed through touch, shared toilets, doctors or dentists, playgrounds, or public pools. Friends told me their families had barred them from homes, afraid of "breathing the same air." That kind of isolation horrified me—until I realized I was already subjecting myself to it.

I decided I was done mourning my life before I was dead. I wouldn't give in to depression another minute. I would mount up and fight the good fight, whatever it took. That day in my doctor's office, I asked for every treatment available. I called friends in the same position and asked about their regimens. It saddened me to hear that many resorted to desperate measures, some even traveling abroad for treatments not yet approved in the States. I gathered information on buyers' clubs to secure medications I might need. The endless frustration only fueled my determination. After investigating every option, I settled on what I felt was best. I was already doing many of the recommended things, so I felt slightly ahead of the curve. Facing the diagnosis head-on helped me come to terms with my fears.

I booked flights back east that week. My plan was to stop at Anne's first, then Sarah and Rob's, and finally Emma's. Anxiety consumed me, but I had no choice. I was piecing together a plan for the rest of my life, and their reactions were crucial. Anne was a nurse, so I hoped she would understand more than most—but I still feared her response.

Anne was alone when she pulled up at the curb. We weren't even off airport property before I asked her to stop at the nearest restaurant. I wanted a public place to talk, thinking it might control her reactions. She protested that she had cooked my favorite meal and my niece and nephew were waiting, but when I insisted it was important, she pulled into a lot and demanded I tell her before we went inside.

She was shocked, frightened, yet reassuring as the words tumbled out with my tears. She admitted concern but was glad I told her so she could take precautions. Even the medical community didn't fully understand AIDS, she explained. I wasn't sure what precautions she meant, but as we hugged and cried, I knew she wouldn't desert me as I'd feared. Our time together felt almost normal, and when she dropped me back at the airport, I asked her to wait a day or two before telling anyone so I could speak to Rob and Sarah first.

At the arrival gate, Rob, Sarah, and all the kids were waiting, jumping up and down when they spotted me. Within minutes small arms wrapped around my legs begging to be lifted. They now had four children. Andrew, the youngest, was dark-eyed and dark-haired like Rob and me. At two years old he wanted to ride on my shoulders, but I was too weak, so he perched on my luggage and rode to the car.

There was no private moment as I had hoped, but once the kids were tucked into bed, I sat with Rob and Sarah and poured out my heart.

"I was so afraid you were ill when we couldn't reach you. What does this mean, Sam? And what can we do to help?" Rob asked.

"It means that I am going to put up the biggest fight I can muster," I said confidently.

"I've been researching everything I can on HIV, because I worried this conversation might come one day. Any of us could've ended up in the same position from a transfusion or something else. I had one myself in the hospital and later received a letter saying they weren't sure about the integrity of the blood, recommending regular tests. I was scared, too, and felt education was my only defense. But they are making breakthroughs in the research. You need to look on the bright side and stay as positive as you can," Sarah said.

"How are you feeling now, Sam? Is it your HIV or your Crohn's acting up?" Rob asked.

"Right now I'm not feeling too shabby, just a little weak from the last bout of Crohn's."

"We don't know how you do it, man. It's been one thing after another for you and I'm sorry," Rob added. "You okay? I didn't mean to upset you."

"Some days are harder than others, but I'm looking at Crohn's as the precursor to what I'll probably deal with in the future. You didn't upset me at all. Sorry if I seem preoccupied, but what you said hit me between the eyes. You know, the thing about *my* Crohn's or *my* HIV illnesses? I know it's just a figure of speech but I'm making an effort not to speak of these illnesses in a possessive way. I want to see them as enemies, not part of who I am. It's not your fault. I've been evaluating how people and close friends with diseases refer to illness and symptoms, and I'm choosing to handle this differently. Like Sarah said, I need to be as positive as I can. There is nothing positive about either illness, and you were the first person to say it that way—it's making me really think.

"If everyone wouldn't mind, I'd rather not call it *my* HIV or AIDS or *my* Crohn's disease. They may have claimed me but I'm not claiming them. They're only challenges I'm facing; I don't own either. I just don't want them to become part of my identity. I am Sam—not Sam who has Crohn's or is HIV positive. I'm sorry. I'm not mad—I'm just adjusting."

"I guess we all have some adjusting to do, Sam. If it makes you feel better, we'll refer to it any way you'd like. It really is just an old figure of speech, but I see where you're going with this and why," Sarah said as concern grew on her face when I sneezed. "You sure you're feeling okay, Sam?"

"Yes! Please, Sarah, you don't need to worry so much. Calm down, girl!" I said with a big smile. "I have a headache, probably from sleeping on a different pillow, and I need my neck adjusted. Guys, listen, this could be a short road or a very long journey. You have to choose your times for concern. Save it for when I really need it. I promise when it's bad I'll let you know. Think about it—we all get sick. I was sick before I was diagnosed with any of those things. More often than not it's going to be a normal illness, just amplified due to my immune system. I'm sorry if I sound ungrateful for your concern, but I feel the more I talk about *them* the more power they have over me and my life. I'm ready to face issues that arise from them, but they are not me and I am not them," I said, laughing.

"I am amazed that you see it that way. I envy your ability to think things through and come up with new angles! I can tell you right now with all you are dealing with I'd be too scared to think!" Rob shared as he sat closer.

"Rob, so many of my friends succumbed to the fear of AIDS. Their every moment while still alive was wrapped into it. I don't want to live frightened half out of my skin by what could happen next. I don't want to run from pillar to post trying to fight the good fight for the cause. I want to be educated and strategize how to beat this enemy. I'll eventually hook up with groups promoting awareness and education, and I probably will volunteer some time, too, but I don't want that to be the highlight of life. I want to be known and remembered for the positive things I am, did, and do."

"The problem is that we don't know what to say or do when someone we love is ill. We don't want to seem insensitive and not ask how you are, but we also know bringing it up keeps it top of mind for you. It's an awkward bind we're in. How would you prefer we show our concern—but not? If that makes sense to you?" Sarah asked.

"Look, I understand the conundrum I place everyone in, but each of us has the right to deal with things as we deem appropriate. If everyone were like me there would probably be no changes, no breakthroughs in research, no cure. I'm not an activist and wish I had it in me. I just want to deal with this in a way that doesn't remind me daily what I'm battling. I want you and me to spend our time enjoying more pleasant things. I'm sorry. I'm raw right now, still establishing my own rules of engagement. Of course I want understanding, companionship, and compassion, but I am not interested in sympathy. I want to live my life, talk about the same things I did before the diagnosis as much as possible; I want to be seen as the same person I was—I am.

"I know this may sound like I'm judging others who handle it differently, but I'm not. I'm only saying if I own this thing, it will own me. I intend to live my best life first and deal with whatever comes after. Please don't live in fear because of me. For God's sake, I could get hit by a bus tomorrow, but I don't want to remind myself of that fact—nor let it stop me from crossing streets," I explained.

"Sarah, you said it earlier. The more I dwell on the negative, the worse off I am. I know it's there and it's hard not to see and feel what it's doing to my mind and body, but I'm not going to give up, let it stop me, or let it control my life. I promise you that. In fact, in the future you'll hear me refer to it as my health issue. I'd rather give power to words like *health issues,* because that can infer good issues, than to words like *HIV, AIDS,* and *Crohns,*" I added, choking back tears.

"We understand, Sam. If you promise to tell us how you're progressing and when you need help, we'll go back to just saying hi and what's new. You're going to beat this, and we'll be there every step of the way. You're welcome to come stay with us anytime. We're here for you and just a phone call away," Rob added as he and Sarah wrapped their arms around me. We laughed and cried together. It was truly a day above all days knowing they loved me no matter what I faced.

The rest of my visit was wonderfully normal until I opened the bathroom door with blood dripping from my nose and fingers as I tried to control the flow. Sarah jumped to her feet, pulled on plastic gloves, and for a moment froze—but only for a moment. She warned the kids away, handed me tissues, and rolled up the blood-stained shower mat under my feet. She asked me to sit on the tub and let the rest drip into the toilet. I followed orders as if she were my mother. She sealed the tissues, carpet, and gloves in a plastic bag, tossed it outside, and sat back down as if nothing had happened.

"Why are you looking at me like that, Sam? Yes, I was scared. Yes, I wanted to protect myself and the kids—but I won't let it stop me. Fear will not run my life. I'm educated enough on the facts and will take precautions as needed. But this is our life. You're our family and we won't let it separate you from us. That's all there is to it! I'm sorry for my blunt honesty, but I've never been anything but straight up with you and I'm not starting now," she said, scolding me like one of her children.

I fought the strangest feelings. Was I insulted? Embarrassed? Horrified that people were afraid of me? I stood, mouth open, until she spoke again.

"Oh, come on! If this was the other way around you would've jumped faster than I just did and you know it. And you probably would've ripped me a new one for not being more responsible and cleaning up before I opened that door. You would've never let me get away with that. After all, you make it your mission to force me to be my best self on a consistent basis, don't you?" she added, almost begging for a fight.

She was right. I burst out laughing—so hard my stomach hurt. She sat for a minute watching me. Obviously my health issues weren't the only infectious things in the room, because before long she was laughing so hard tears ran down her face. I walked over, saluted her as if she were my superior, clicked my heels together, and marched out of the room.

Several months later, I flew back east for Dolly's wedding. Several of my siblings attended, and though it was wonderful to see them, I was hurt and saddened by their hesitation to have personal contact with me. I heard that some didn't want me in their homes or around their children in the future. I knew it was a standard fear reaction, but it still hurt in ways I couldn't describe. I caught them eyeing me up and down, glaring at the ruined parts of me, or sneaking looks when they thought I wasn't watching—their sad, sympathetic, pathetic expressions cut deeper than any illness ever could. I despised their casual reactions as I spoke, as if I were a stranger. I knew I was the subject of their conversations, because silence often fell just as I entered. I wanted to yell and scream and play into their theatrics, but I knew I'd be giving them exactly what they wanted, and I refused. Part of me was angry, but I decided it wasn't worth the effort to confront them. I was simply grateful it was over before I knew it.

I decided to visit a few friends I hadn't seen since moving west, and after traveling from state to state for several weeks, I stopped back at Rob and Sarah's before returning home. I was feeling well enough to go back to work and anxious to resume life. I called Sarah with my travel plans, and she promptly shared that Gertie was hitching a ride with a friend and would arrive the next day.

I hadn't spent time with my parents in thirteen years. We had crossed paths at weddings, but our exchanges were brief and cordial, more like acquaintances than family. I wasn't sure how I felt about being under the same roof as my mother again. Rob called her to ask if she wanted to see me on my way back to California. To everyone's surprise, especially mine, she said yes.

I was perplexed. Was she curious what I looked like with health issues? Did she want one last chance to call me out? Emma had told me she was terrified I might infect people. So what was behind this sudden interest? Still, I had to admit I missed her—and even Auggie. How could that be possible? Had I been away long enough to dull the pain?

I arrived to find her standing in Sarah's kitchen. She smiled, gave me a light hug, then pulled away. Over the next two days we spoke about the weather, my job, old neighbors, Auggie, and the ever-growing list of grandchildren. She was polite and courteous, but it was clear the years apart had carved a space neither of us knew how to fill.

Before Rob drove me to the airport, I hugged her and told her I loved her. She didn't reciprocate. She didn't seem to care whether I came or went. It felt as if we were strangers, and it was hard to understand how I could have come from her womb yet be met with such distance.

Her plan was to stay a day longer and hitch a ride back with the same friend who had brought her. From Sarah's nervous replies and hyper-vigilance toward my needs, I could tell she expected Gertie to misbehave once I left. She stripped my bed and gathered towels as she usually did when guests departed.

As Rob and I pulled out of the driveway, Gertie waited until the car was gone. Just as Sarah entered the laundry room, she unleashed what she had apparently held back for days.

"Don't ya know yur husband worries 'bout yu takin' care a Sam? He's scared yur gonna catch the AIDS from 'im! Ya need ta worry 'bout yur kids and my Rob bafore ya worry 'bout that queer!" Gertie ranted.

Sarah stood dumbfounded, debating whether to respond or wait for Rob. But then she realized Rob would never confront Gertie. In fact, none of the Izbickis ever did—whether with Gertie, Auggie, me, Emma, or anyone else. They swept things under the rug, whispering behind each other's backs to anyone who'd listen, but never addressing issues directly. Sarah decided she was done with that.

"I seriously cannot believe you just said that. That is your son. Your sick son. Your blood. He is a precious human being. I should say you should be ashamed of yourself in so many ways, but you and Auggie have doled out enough shame to cover the globe ten times over. If you had cared for him from day one, he wouldn't need anyone else to do it. Why do you persist in stirring up trouble where there is none? Why do you fabricate stories and reject anyone who doesn't live up to your nonexistent ideals or anyone who doesn't have your blood flowing through their veins? Wait, now you are rejecting ones who *do* have your blood flowing through their veins. I was about to applaud your efforts with Sam. I thought you were brave and willing to change and accept things with him. Just when I think I have you figured out, you surprise me with a whole new scope of ignorance.

"Why did you say you wanted to see him? Curiosity? Maybe so you could say you saw him now that he is ill—because you didn't want anyone accusing you of abandoning him when he was in need? Or maybe you are just nebby? Maybe you wanted more material for your stories? Well, now you have all the material you need to go home and spread around lies and distortions about how things went here. At least if you are talking about me you are giving someone else a break.

"I have held my tongue for years out of respect for you and the fact that you are Rob's mother, but I will no longer sit by and listen to your cowardly comments. If you had something to say about any of this, why not say it honestly in the light of day in front of everyone involved? I know why—because you want no witnesses to your venomous comments so you can deny them later.

"This is my home, my husband, my children, my life—and Sam is my brother whom we love and cherish and will be there for come hell or high water. You don't deserve him, and in fact, you don't deserve any of us. Period. You know, Gertie, all any of us ever wanted was for you to love and accept us as family, but I guess that is too much to ask."

Sarah spoke without raising her voice as she loaded the washer. Relief washed over her. Holding so much inside for years had been exhausting, but now it was out in the open. This was a day she would not forget anytime soon. Unfortunately, neither would Gertie.

Gertie stood silent for a moment, then fled to her room and packed. Sarah watched as she set her suitcases by the front door and sat on the couch. The kids were playing outside when Rob arrived home. The minute he opened the door, Gertie started.

"Um not stayin' where um not welcome. Ya need ta drive me back now!" she said, shaking from head to toe.

"What happened here, Mother?" he asked softly.

"I'll tell you what happened," Sarah said firmly as she entered. "Gertie claims you worry about me taking care of Sam—that I'm putting myself and the kids in danger. She even called Sam a queer. So I set her straight." Sarah then repeated everything she had said earlier.

Rob stood glaring at both women, then picked up his mother's suitcases and drove her six hours back to Griffin Ave. On the turnpike, Gertie rattled on without pausing for breath. Rob said nothing. He knew better; it wasn't worth another battle. He dropped her at the front of the house and began the long drive home.

At the stop sign at the end of the street, Auggie rolled past in his truck, a paper-bag bottle in hand. He swerved and nearly hit Rob's car, missing by inches. Too drunk to notice, he never even realized it was his own son.

Rob turned onto the turnpike, cranked the radio, lowered the window, and sighed. It had been one heck of a day—of all days, weeks, months, years, and a lifetime.

CHAPTER 40

Faith and Control
Part II

IT WAS THE EARLY '90s, and battles raged abroad and at home. The Gulf War ended, riots against discrimination erupted in LA, and I was engaged in my own private war against the cruel invasion ravaging my body. Few knew what I was enduring. Back at work in my LA office, I quietly fought the side effects of treatments. As soon as one symptom subsided, another appeared. I joked that if I could charge rent to the army occupying my body, I'd never need to work again. Humor helped me cope.

Business was booming and my workload doubled. "Idle hands are the devil's workshop," I'd mutter, hearing the Catholic nuns in my head.

I was down fifty pounds. The prescribed diet was healthy but low in calories, and I longed for milkshakes and cookies-and-cream ice cream to maintain weight. I knew I couldn't tolerate them, but sometimes indulged and paid the price. My clothes hung off me, so I bought new suits hoping to appear stylish—or at least as though my weight loss was intentional. Instead of compliments, I received strange, questioning looks. Self-consciousness grew, along with paranoia that everyone from the mailman to checkout clerks somehow knew my diagnosis.

Occasionally I'd pass someone who looked as I did, and our eyes would meet with wordless compassion. I began shopping at odd hours to avoid crowds. Social anxiety tightened its grip, and there was nowhere to hide. Each day my illness became more physically obvious. I often sent proxies to client meetings and hesitated to greet unexpected visitors. Yet I wasn't completely alone—many of my friends were carrying the same social stigma, whether real or imagined.

Rob visited for a few days, and we spent most of the time enjoying restaurants or watching golf. I always felt stronger, braver, and safer when he was around. He had been my constant from birth, and I loved our time together—especially now that I suspected we'd have far less of it than I once imagined.

Sarah came soon after and I eagerly prepared for her arrival. I ordered fresh flowers for the vases, had the yard and decks cleaned, and planned a small dinner party. I hired a personal chef and decorator, ordered our favorite wines, and invited a few friends. It was my first party since the diagnosis and my first as a single man again. The excitement energized me, and I had to admit I did a fine job pulling off the details.

Lately, I had newfound faith in my talents and business acumen. If I could thrive while enduring so much, what might I accomplish when I won this war? I trusted my judgment and felt fate was on my side. As long as I held my position at the company, I believed I could face any financial issue. Whatever I couldn't see in the future was fate's concern; I would handle the rest.

I had just finished a book that spoke to me in ways I had never experienced. It described how all beings are made of energy, how our physical bodies simply encapsulate us, and how each vibrates on unique frequencies. Experiences, people, and opportunities that shared our frequency would be drawn to us. Like when you meet someone and instantly feel like you're on the same wavelength—it finally made sense.

I worked diligently to follow the book's recommendations, convinced I could tune myself to a better frequency. Confidence surged. Despite health issues, I trusted myself, my doctors, and my treatments. Nothing, I believed, could pull me down or knock me off my pedestal. I needed no more than what I had already set into action.

I waited at the curb at LAX as Sarah wrestled with her luggage. I popped the trunk, stowed her bag, and for a split second, thought of my old baggage—but the new me wasn't having it. We hugged and drove off, chattering like schoolgirls. At a light I watched her rummage through her purse for photos to share. She radiated comfort and ease, and I marveled at how she could after all she had endured.

"We'll stop for lunch, then head up the canyon. I have to work this afternoon, but I'll be home for dinner. The chef should be there already working on the menu. If you'd like, I can call my therapist and arrange a massage for you."

"You're kidding, right? A massage? Never had one in my life! If I relaxed I might fall to pieces and you don't want to put that back together. Lunch sounds good though. You're hiring chefs now? Amazing! I thought I'd be cooking for you, but I'll happily hand over the spatula. I've never had a personal chef cook for me," she said with a furrowed brow.

I had reserved a table at one of my favorite restaurants, requesting a view. Instead, we were seated in a corner beside the kitchen—no view, just noise and constant traffic.

"I specifically asked for a table with a view. Do you know who I am? I am a regular customer here. You call this customer service? I'm in advertising and this rates as customer no service! I expect a transfer to the table I requested and I wish to speak to your manager immediately!" I ranted at the maitre d'.

"Please accept my apologies, sir. We do our best to accommodate requests, but we are busier than expected this afternoon. Let me see what I can do," he said, red-faced and whispering as I sat down reveling in my authority.

Sarah was clearly uncomfortable, looking as if she was about to blow a gasket. I was furious they had upset me and now Sarah, too—what a way to start her vacation. The maitre d' returned and led us to a new table. We were presented menus, and after reviewing them, I chose a wine and entrée I knew she'd love. She cleared her throat and fidgeted uncomfortably. Sipping wine, I began filling her in on everything that had occurred since we last spoke. Before she got a word in, our food arrived cold and undercooked—this was the final straw.

"You over there!" I shouted, raising my voice at our waiter. "Remove these dishes immediately. Not only are they cold, they are undercooked!" As he approached, I waved my hands toward the plates, demanding their removal. "Get this garbage out of my face! I demand to speak to the manager!"

After arguing with the manager and causing a scene, our food finally arrived hot and done to perfection. I sat savoring the flavors as Sarah sat silently pushing her food around her plate.

"What's wrong, Sarah? I can't believe this has happened here of all places. The price of lunch alone should guarantee quality service and food to die for! Is your food still undercooked? Heads will roll," I said, raising my hands again to get the waiter's attention. Sarah cleared her throat, shifted in her seat, and her eyes met mine—I knew hell didn't have the fury I saw in them.

"Are you kidding me? Who are you and what have you done to my wonderful brother, Sam? I have never been more embarrassed in my life! Who do you think you are? I have been married for a very long time and not once in all those years did Rob even attempt to order for me! I am fully capable of ordering my own food. Even though it was nice of you to bring me here for a treat, I can afford my own if it means you won't be the one deciding for me. There are few things in my life that I get to control, and one of them is my food. The other is how I treat those around me despite my frustrations. I was a waitress for many years. It's a hard job and it pays nothing. Do you think these people were put on earth to please you today? I'm thinking not! They are humans and they make mistakes, and if that had been me you just shouted at and ordered about, I would have dumped soup in your lap and put you in your place! I wouldn't have waited to be fired; I would have quit. There were ways to discuss your issues and disappointment when you arrived here. You are acting obnoxious and entitled. I don't care if their prices make you feel a sense of entitlement—you still did not have to belittle and humiliate them in front of all these people. You have no clue what their lives are like and what this job means to them. Your arrogance trumps your rudeness. Sorry, but I never mince words. You owe them all an apology and a very nice tip. By the way, I hate fish and you should know that after all these years. And I drink white wine, not red! You will be lucky if they didn't spit in your food back in the kitchen!" she said sternly in a lowered voice as she rose and headed to the lady's room.

Well, this wasn't a meal I could finish. I gagged at the thought of sputum in my food. I waved the waiter over, asked for the check, and paid promptly, adding a generous tip as Sarah suggested—though I wouldn't let her know it. Pulling to the curb, I saw her exit the restaurant searching for me. We rode through the canyons in silence, but I was furious. She had some nerve speaking to me that way after all I had done to make her stay special. I wasn't giving her an inch. She owed me the apology, and if I didn't get it soon, I had no problem dropping her at the airport. The ticket goes both ways! I wanted to put her in her place but instead dropped her off in the driveway and drove away. I sneered as she stood there, mouth hanging open.

The rest of the day went as I had planned. When I arrived home late that afternoon, I found Sarah in the kitchen working side by side with Jon, the chef I had hired. It infuriated me further. I poured a drink, went outside, and sat fuming in my new teak rocker. I could hear Sarah laughing as Jon coached her while she chopped vegetables. I was paying this man so she wouldn't have to cook, and there she was working in the kitchen as if to defy me.

"Sarah, come here, please. Don't you think it's redundant to have two chefs in the kitchen? Let the man do his job that I am paying him very well to do!" I yelled from the deck.

"Seriously, Sam? I was asking him to teach me how to use the different knives in the block. Tell me who died and made this a Sam-tatorship?! What's wrong with you that you need to boss everyone around and constantly remind everyone how much money you have and how important you are?" she replied, taking the rocker next to mine.

"Clearly, there seems to be some kind of mistake here. I went to great lengths to make this event special for you and you are cutting me down at every turn!" I spewed.

"Cutting you down? You are a one-man wrecking ball! I am honored you went out of your way, but I don't feel like I know you right now. You know me, Sam—I'm a cheap date. I don't need fancy things or expensive frilly events. I live a simple life with four kids and Rob. You seem to forget where you came from."

"I don't dwell on where I came from. This is my life now and I am king of my castle and if you have a problem with that ..." I stopped before saying something I couldn't take back.

"Why are you being so argumentative? This is not the Sam I know!"

"You are the one being argumentative! This is the new me. This is my home and my life and I control what goes on here.

Things were out of control for too long—no longer! I won't allow interference. Period. You have no idea how things are done at this level. If I don't act, I'll be taken advantage of. My status affords me some luxuries and entitlements. You don't know what you are talking about!"

"Oh, patronize me one more minute and you're gonna be wearing that drink, Mr. High and Mighty!" she snapped, stomping back into the house.

Well, that was telling her! She needs to think about what I said. An hour later, guests began to arrive. The chef served drinks as I turned up the stereo. Sarah hadn't come down yet, and I was anxious to introduce her to my friends and colleagues. After cocktails, dinner was ready—still no sign of Sarah. I grumbled under my breath and went searching. It was rude of her not to appear at a dinner party arranged for her. I knocked on the guest suite door—no response. Cracking it open, I found her sitting at the window watching the sunset.

"Sarah, we are all waiting for you. Dinner is served," I said, tone angry but controlled.

"Oh, really, Sam? I was waiting until you told me I could come out of my room since you are in control here. I did, however, take the liberty to shower and get ready for dinner. I hope that was alright with you?" she said sarcastically.

She followed me downstairs and the evening went smoothly, as if nothing had happened. I remembered evenings like this all too well from my recent past and wondered if these walls would one day hold pain as Griffin Avenue's had. After the last guest left, Sarah sipped wine on the deck, moving to the music in the night air. She was amazing and such a mystery. Because of my struggles, our conversations often centered on me. I realized I had no idea how she was really doing or if she needed me. Too late to talk, I went upstairs and, through the glass, watched her dance.

I woke later to an eerie silence. The lights and music were off, the kitchen spotless, china back in the cabinet. The only trace of the dinner party was the floral centerpiece on the dining table. With cold water in hand, I looked outside and saw Sarah huddled under a blanket on the deck recliner. I had barely stepped through the door when she spoke.

"Sorry, Sam, I hope I didn't worry you. I was out here enjoying the starlit night and I couldn't bring myself to walk away from it. It's gorgeous and it makes me feel so close that I can almost touch them," she explained, gazing at the sky.

"I wasn't worried. I thought you were in the guest room. I was thirsty and my stomach was bothering me so I came for a drink and there you were."

"It's so beautiful and peaceful out here. I hear coyotes howling and wonder where they are. I'm glad this deck doesn't have ground access or I'd be a midnight snack. I was lying here thanking God for those beautiful stars! I like to think one isn't a star but my grandma peeking through to say goodnight," she shared softly. "When I was a little girl, she and I would stand in her yard looking up …" *She stopped as she realized he wasn't listening. Who was this man? As he walked away, she brushed at the tears forming in her eyes and whispered a prayer to the one who placed the stars in the night sky.*

"People sneaking a peek from heaven? I'll pass on any response. Good night," I said, heading back to bed while Sarah continued star gazing.

There was a strange distance in the first days of her visit. For the first time, we were disappointed in each other. We didn't click like usual, and our conversations felt forced. She was definitely the problem, I thought. It all came to a head four days before her departure. I was having work done on the driveway and hired day workers to plant shrubs in the new flower beds. Their work was substandard and not meeting my approval.

"I cannot believe the horrendously dreadful job these lowlifes are doing at my expense! It's so hard to find good help nowadays. That's what I get for hiring them. They loiter outside that employment place every morning waiting for work. I feel sorry for them, hire them, and this is what I get. I did better work as a child in Auggie's nursery than these fat, ignorant adults do. You'd think they'd appreciate someone giving them a job. What a bunch of losers! I am so tired of explaining what I want done! It's exasperating!" I shouted, tripping over lawn equipment and nearly falling on the porch while Sarah followed me inside. She stood with hands on her hips, glaring.

"What? Give it a break, Sarah! Are you really going to defend those idiots?"

"Dang, Sam, this new life of yours has gone to your head! Be careful up there on that pedestal—it's going to hurt when you fall!" she shouted, pacing. "It wasn't long ago you were them. Do you forget so easily? Do you know anything about their lives that you call them idiots and drunks? The 'fat' guy you insulted has a sick wife and two kids. He can't afford the kind of food you buy or the personal chefs you hire. You don't know if there's a medical reason he's overweight. You overcame food addictions, but others may not have, so for you to criticize them is hypocritical! The others have families, too, and desperately need work. Some travel hours at night just to line up for a chance. They aren't trained in this field; most barely speak English. If you took the time to explain and give examples instead of ranting and scaring them, you'd get what you want. You demand nothing but understanding, love, and acceptance—yet give none? What in heaven's name has gotten into you? If I were Catholic, I'd call for a priest and some holy water! Man, you are killing me here!" she added.

I wasn't sure what to say. Her words stung, but I knew she was right. Disappointed, I slipped into my home office and shut the door. Through the blinds I watched Sarah step outside to apologize to the workers. She brought them water, joked with them, and within half an hour they volunteered to get back to work. She stayed nearby, describing what I wanted, and before long the flower beds looked exactly as I had envisioned.

I realized I had acted just like Auggie did when I was young, and I couldn't believe my audacity. At dinner I apologized to Sarah. She was right—it had all gone to my head. And it wasn't the only thing there. In the night, a fever spiked to 103 degrees. Sarah sat beside me, cooling my forehead with wet towels. I heard her whispering prayers and humming softly, and I wondered if God still knew I existed. But I could tell He knew she did. My newfound faith in myself was slipping as I closed my eyes and hoped her prayers would be answered.

CHAPTER 41

Crossing Lines
Part II

SARAH EXTENDED HER STAY to care for me. She was up day and night answering every moan and groan, and I appreciated it immensely. She had me eating, drinking, and back on my feet in no time. I showered, poured a glass of juice, and began leafing through the mail piled on my desk. As I tossed junk into the trash, an envelope slipped out. The return address was Jude's.

I hadn't heard from him in years, except for the occasional plea for money to further his mission—letters that always ended up in the trash. Sometimes I missed him, then quickly remembered who he was. The family grapevine kept me informed. Recently I heard he was a self-proclaimed leader of a cult in Kentucky, living off the surrendered holdings of his followers. Rob said Jude's doctrine had scammed many over the years, just a revised version that denied Christ. Sadly, people in pain will cling to anything that promises to make them feel whole—perfect prey for someone who knows how to exploit weakness. Rob and I knew all too well what it felt like to be Jude's prey. Our brother, if nothing else, was a gifted manipulator.

Jude's mandate was simple: People attend his gatherings, he offers hope and redemption, then indoctrinates and converts the lost. Souls desperate for someone to think for them soak up his doctrine like sponges and become his sheep.

They must surrender everything—family, fortune, possessions—in order to join. Lives unravel as mothers, fathers, and children pull apart, quit jobs, sell belongings, and donate it all to Jude, who then dictates how it's spent. He severs them from their past, abolishes holidays, and forces them to work in the fields to sustain the cult. Members are also obligated to recruit and raise more money. Jude's hierarchy of trusted men impose rules and consequences, including one that demands all converts drop to the ground to pray in unison whenever a horn sounds, regardless of season or circumstance. They are detained and enslaved in the name of God—and Jude. Leave it to him to wield the cross as bait for unsuspecting prey. He wasn't the first to use such tactics, and sadly, wouldn't be the last. Of all the men I'd known, he was uniquely suited for this kind of heist, showing no remorse, just like the Marine.

I sank into my chair, holding the envelope as though it carried a contagion. I debated throwing it away, but a small voice urged me to at least read the first line. I tore it open to find a long letter in Jude's handwriting. Most could say what they needed in a page or two, but not my brother. He was long-winded and loved the sound of his own voice, something that carried into his writing. Flipping through six or seven pages, I caught a few words—it wasn't going to be pretty. "God says" appeared everywhere, with Scripture citations sprinkled throughout. I dropped my head onto the desk. I wasn't strong enough for more.

Sarah entered the room, concerned with my weakness, and asked if I needed help. "Sam, please. You do realize who wrote this?"

"Yes, my brother—my blood—wrote this. That is all I need to know right now," I answered as I headed back to bed.

Sarah followed, and once I was situated, she returned to the letter and began analyzing its contents.

I woke to the aroma of chicken soup drifting from the kitchen. Weak and slightly disoriented, I made my way downstairs and found Sarah stirring onions.

"What are you up to?"

"I am making wedding soup, your favorite! There's also a chocolate cake in the oven! Comfort food for ailing spirits. Otherwise, my depression will meet your apathy lately and we can't let that happen. Do you hear me?" she replied sternly.

"Yes, I hear you. Do as you please; I'm heading back to bed," I muttered, sipping water. It sounded good, but I couldn't have cared less. I felt like I was drifting through fog, unable to see a light at the end of the tunnel. My heart felt torn in two, and it would take more than soup and cake to glue the pieces back together.

"Sam, stop! Come back in here pronto, mister!"

"I am not one of your children, Sarah! I'm exhausted. I don't want to talk about this right now!" I whined.

"Well, want to or not, we *are* going to talk! You NEED to," she said, pulling me back and pushing me into a chair.

"That letter was garbage, written by a man clearly suffering from narcissistic personality disorder. I counted twenty-eight—I repeat, TWENTY-EIGHT—'I's' throughout. If that isn't proof of how sick he is, I don't know what is!" she ranted.

"Sick or not, the pain is relative," I replied as tears flowed again.

"Sam, let me apologize for him. It's horrendously sad to see how ego destroys. Think about it—he came from the same broken childhood you, Rob, and Anne did. Each of the seven of you was shaped by that fight-or-flight environment. This letter reflects that damage," she whispered, then sat beside me.

"So I am somehow to feel less hurt because he is damaged like me? I am supposed to look past the insult and injury from this narcissist?"

"No, not at all. From the looks of that letter, he, of all of the seven of you, appears to be the most damaged. He looks as if he was determined to find a father, a protector, a God of some sort and couldn't find one, so he designed one to fit his needs. I shudder when I think of how many in his wake will suffer from his damaged spirit? I wonder how much he needs to take from others to fill the gaping void inside himself. It's sad how damaged we all are, but Jude takes it to a new level."

"Poor, pathetic Jude! My heart breaks for the king of manipulators! He has fooled even you!"

"He hasn't fooled me at all. I am just trying to give him the benefit of the doubt. Otherwise, I am left with the obvious and it sends chills down my spine."

"Dare to think the unthinkable, Sarah. It's there you will find the truth. He was born this way!" I said.

"So the environment with which you were all exposed only fed his unquenchable needs? So you are saying he is a delusional psychopath or worse, if there is anything worse?" she replied, remembering all the information she had gathered over the years from his siblings as they recounted Jude's actions and reactions toward them throughout their years together.

"BINGO!! What do we have for her??? You get the prize!"

"Sam, I am trying to help here. I am not the enemy. It kills me to see you in this much pain. I want to find him and hurt him. I am not trying to justify what he has done. I am trying to understand it."

"I know. I'm sorry for lashing out at you. You give people way too much credit, Sarah, and you forgive far too easily!"

"I'm sorry you see it that way, Sam. I look back over my own life and see some of the things I've done that have caused irreparable damage, and I consider myself blessed that anyone could or would forgive me. The way I see it is if I can be forgiven, then I can forgive. In the long run it's only me that suffers if I don't. People go on with their lives not thinking twice while I sit and brew over things. It only hurts me, and by forgiving them, I can move on."

"So I just forgive and forget and that makes everything okay again!? Really?"

"No! That's entirely up to you and way too early in this game. Forgiving doesn't mean I forget. Far from it. Nor does it make what others do to me right. It just means that I let it go, because I have enough to carry around without their added garbage. It's hard in the beginning, but it gets easier every time I feel the freedom that comes with it. I'm not even suggesting you forgive Jude right now. I'm just explaining myself and struggling to understand. That's all."

"Let me help fill in the blanks for you. Jude was born with an innate ability to win people over. We all fell victim to him as children, but he had it out for me in particular. He would start by giving me the attention I desperately needed, and then tell me I was his favorite brother. He could be so loving and supportive that I was putty in his hands. I would do anything for him, and his wish was my command. Then, just when he had me where he wanted, he'd throw me under the first bus he could find and walk away without remorse. We all fell for it, and it gave him power to control and use us. His callousness rivaled Auggie's. He doesn't need to search for victims—they're drawn to him like a magnet. He feeds off weakness, lives parasitically off others' sacrifices, and has no morals or conscience. There's no limit to how far he will go to get what he wants. This cult thing must be feeding him well, because it's the longest he's ever stayed in anything—other than college, where we joked he'd get a lifer award."

Sarah sighed. "That explains why he demands isolation from his followers. He can control them and live off of them longer. How sad is that?"

"Everything is all about him in the end. Jude's sense of entitlement tips the scales. If one of us was sick, he claimed our symptoms to steal attention. He'd bump into others, become them, then boast he was better at their lives than they were. And I won't even go into his obsession with his Polish looks. He's always been captivated by his own image in the mirror," I said as Sarah removed the cake from the oven. The aroma filled the room, distracting me.

"That's pretty much how Rob has described him in the past. It would seem that knowing all this firsthand would help you to deal with this letter, Sam, but I know despite all you're saying, you really love your brother. The whole thing is so sad. I'm going to let this cake cool and then ice it, and the soup ought to be finished in about three hours, give or take a few. You should be good and hungry by then," she added grinning. "I understand that you are hurt and I know there isn't much I can say or do, but I really feel like we need to talk not just about Jude here, but we also need to address this letter's content. I know this isn't a subject you like to talk about given your history with people using religious condemnation as a weapon of choice in regards to your life."

"I knew I wasn't going to get away easy with you, Sarah. I sincerely don't know where to start. He rambles on and on. I need a team to dissect it, along with that cake, there," I replied, pointing at the cooling chocolate.

Sarah could feel the old judge in her react and spring into action. It angered her that not only did she have to help Sam through the remnants of Jude's proclamations, but now she felt tasked with the religious aspects too. She had grown tired long ago of mopping up after zealots who left trails of destruction. This hit a raw nerve, and Jude had gone too far.

"I am not sure where to start, either. I know you well. I know your heart. I know you have probably had a closer relationship with God than most of the people I've been exposed to. You just hide behind the painful dilemma you find yourself in. I'm not wrong even if you tell me I am," Sarah said with a wink. "We have discussed this issue on multiple occasions, so don't get all philosophical with me, man!"

I smiled, if only at the sight of her confidence. "I know this is a subject very near and dear to your heart. I won't pretend that I'm looking forward to discussing this issue, as I am filled with doubts as to whether or not you should be having this conversation with an obviously possessed man," I replied.

"Well, before we order in the holy water and priests I think we should pour a glass of wine and celebrate the fact that I made you smile," she added, reaching for a corkscrew.

"I know how you feel. I have been accused of the same thing many times in my life, so we have something more in common than our love for chocolate and good wine," she said, pouring us each a glass.

"Sarah, I appreciate all you do and have done for me, but it's okay if you want to bow out of this one. Truly, I understand. I get it. God loves me. We have been here and done this," I said, sniffing and sipping my wine.

"Bow out? Then I would be guilty of not performing my religious duty, and we would all end up in hell in a handbasket! I don't know about you, but I'm not keen on that idea, and I have far too much experience with all of this to waste it. I hope you don't feel like I am crossing the line discussing it with you.

Anyway, if Jude is right, we wouldn't be able to get a priest on short enough notice, because they must be busy out here!" she replied, nearly spitting out her wine as she laughed.

"It's sad that there is even a need to try to convince you that God loves you. He loves me, you, and Jude. He doesn't play favorites. I also know that it is people like Jude and so many others that have caused your reaction. I used to react the same way. I can't explain what Jude did or why anyone else does what they do. It's no wonder that people have problems believing the whole thing. Maybe Jude was destined to be in your way or path in order for you to find the energy and strength to reach up and past him and still believe, or maybe he was ordained to be in your life to try to dissuade you from being all God wants you to be. I can't explain why God allows it all to happen, but I believe by allowing it and him in your life that it can all be used for good, not necessarily for bad. Only He knows and the space between you and God is a direct path from your heart to His, Sam. So ask Him. I'm not foolish enough to try to explain things that defy explanation. I can't impart to you in a way that you would understand why I feel differently now, but I do. It has taken a lot of years, and I am judged on a regular basis for what I believe, and it may not be as painful as what you have experienced, but it comes from the same judgment. I just know it isn't important what I've done. It's only important what's been done for me, for all of us, and how I finally understand the freedom that it has given me," Sarah shared as she lined up the ingredients necessary to ice the cake.

"I think most people's knowledge of the Bible, God, and Christianity is limited to others' renditions of it and the level of their exposure. I believe it has been so over-analyzed that we miss what is simple. My kids get the message easily, but then adults get involved, and it's lost in translation," she added stirring as my mouth watered. She brought the beaters over to me for her traditional taste-testing.

"I agree. It was easy for me as a young boy. Despite the chaos in my life, I found hope and refuge in my faith and in my tree," I agreed, licking the frosting as if it were my final meal on earth.

"For me it was the constant guilt from hell-and-damnation sermons and the rejection from Christians—who I knew all too well were worse off than I was—that pushed me to the edge. The use of Scriptures as guided missiles caused mass destruction in my spirit and I considered many things I now regret, now that I'm beginning to understand grace."

"I hear you and understand completely. What's different now?" I replied as she continued spoon-feeding me icing.

"Grace is harder to sell than swampland in Florida. It's a free, no-strings-attached gift from God and it means I don't need to work for it at all, but I sure thought I did. I worked so hard for it. I thought I could somehow earn it—that I'd be good enough to die for—until I realized it was free. Before that, I worked to look good to everyone else, because surely I had to appear perfect, or people wouldn't believe I was a Christian. I was exhausted and gave up when I couldn't pull it off.

"I know your experience is different than mine as far as where you found God when you were young, so I won't bore you with those facts. My experience bred distrust and anger that grew into an out-of-control monster. For years I believed the distorted stories told by fools who left their heads instead of their hearts on the altar. Those stories gave birth to new ones, and they became *my* story: I will never measure up, never try hard enough, never be good enough, and God forbid, I will never be clean enough to enter heaven's gates.

"It translated into my vision of myself and my future, and its stranglehold tanked my self-esteem. They were the stories I told myself every chance I had—my excuse for failure. I blamed everything and everyone, including God, for my inability to make my dreams come true. I told myself something long enough that it became my reality. The only person I could trust was me—and I couldn't even do that. Then who could I trust?

"I remember lying in bed saying, 'God hates me. He wants to punish me because I am such a horrible human being and an even worse Christian.' Fortunately it never stole my faith in God. It made me doubt and question—but I think those are healthy responses. If we follow without questioning, we might as well be Jude's sheep."

"I agree we share some of the same feelings and experiences. I ask myself often how do I survive all of this and still believe in God. Most often I don't know what to believe anymore. It's not popular among my friends or in this society to have faith in God. It's fine to have faith in the unseen—energy, spirits, both dark and light, or even in a higher power that created the universe— but it frowns on belief in God, and even more on belief in Jesus," I responded. "I know why and often find myself between a rock and a hard place when I try to dissuade that thinking."

"I understand that, and it's not just within your circle of friends—it pervades society and feeds off every insecurity we have. Most of us just want love and acceptance— camaraderie, mostly in our misery. Some act like they have nothing to deal with, especially pastors. When I hear a sermon from a pastor who is transparent about his struggles, my faith grows in leaps and bounds. But I'm sure they suffer from fear of exposure and judgment, too.

"Most churches I know teach forgiveness and love, but they fall terribly short when it comes to acceptance and letting God work with and through whomever He chooses. I believe many gay people feel insulted when they're called sinners. Am I right?

We are all referred to that way, and it turns them away from God. Why would anyone let man's words do that? We don't know exactly what it was originally supposed to mean, but I believe the intent was that we *all* fall short of perfection—and if we were perfect, we would be God, and we're not. Could you imagine millions of little gods running around?

"I was taught that some kind of instantaneous change would come over a new believer if they made a serious commitment to God. If that's true, then there must be a whole lot of people who weren't serious at all. I don't doubt God can work within a person to bring about healing and growth, but I now see it's more often the effort of people working extremely hard to make those changes—and that's why the recidivism rate of going back to their old lives is so high.

"I believe if there is a need for change within me, God will show me and work with me to do the changing. I can work night and day and get nowhere on my own. He doesn't make mistakes, and His timing isn't ours. That kind of teaching creates damage, filling people with failure when they aren't instantly able to change into what they or others think they should be. As humans we want instant results, and when we don't see something tangible we begin to doubt," she added, smoothing the final layer of icing. "Sad thing is, we work hard toward something already taken care of two thousand years ago—and so many don't realize He welcomes us, arms open wide, just as we are."

"Yes, to answer your questions. That's an interesting perception. We want our cake and to eat it too," I replied, winking and moving toward the cake. Sarah smacked my hands and pushed me back into the chair.

"Don't mock me, you heathen. I'll give this cake to someone more deserving," she said laughing.

"Forgive me, but you are tempting me! I'm drooling. Just a slice?"

"No! You'll ruin your dinner!"

"I never understood how it could ruin my dinner. If I eat the cake, the soup will be ruined?"

"I wonder if my kids sit around trying to figure that one out. I'll tell you what I tell them—it will because I said so! You, my dear, are changing the subject. If you want, I'll shut it up!"

"No! Please proceed. You've piqued my curiosity," I answered, licking icing from my finger after a stolen swipe.

"Where was I going? I think what I'm trying to get you to see is that this also applies to you, me, and even Jude. We all judge by what's drilled into our heads. Jude is wrong in so many ways, but he believes he's right. I want to judge him, but I can't. Neither can you, not unless we desire the same judgment."

"And the seventy times seven, turn the cheek, and so on. I'm not sure you want to go here," I said, growing annoyed. "Then we move onto the ones that tell me I must search elsewhere when seeking God, because I am not welcome in my present form. It's apparent I cannot have a relationship with God as a homosexual abomination! Period and the end!"

"Now you are annoying me. Alright, Mr. Know-It-All! Following *your* train of thought as you compare it to sin—can a person have a relationship with God and be a liar? Even though lying isn't smiled upon? Does He love us any less? He is all- knowing, and He knows all humans lie, so we are in the same boat. Does He still love us even when He knows we'll continue to tell even white lies, and our chances of overcoming it are probably futile? Now apply this to judging.

"How about cheating on taxes? Gluttony—as you'll exemplify in about an hour when I serve dinner? Betrayal? Divorce, adultery—back to back depending on where you find them? Gossip?

Anger—it's mentioned more than two hundred times in the Bible. Hate over eighty times. Lying and greed fifty times each. So, basically, you're saying you cannot have a relationship with God if you are gay, and it's only mentioned seven or eight times? Yet everyone else can, when their issues are emphasized more?

"Have you considered that God is at the beginning and end of your story? He already knows all the details, good and bad, and understands. Couldn't you agree to disagree with Him until, if and when, He shows you differently? So what you're saying is He took everything else in the world on the cross—except your issues? It's crazy this is even an issue. I wonder where it will all lead one day."

"You sound like Zach. I'm always impressed with his eagerness to share his view. He is my voice of reason when I'm confused, and there's rarely a time I hang up without being changed for the better. His sense of humor and timing are uncanny. Where will it lead? Nowhere—it'll be an argument forever. I just want to live a normal life; most gay people do. A job, home, marriage, family, then retire in Arizona or Florida. I can't imagine we'll ever marry legally, let alone in a church. And children? Many friends had others carry babies for them, and there are countless children who need homes, but people think it's better they rot in the system than be adopted by a stable gay couple. They think no parents is better than two of the same sex. To answer your question, yes, that's what it feels like. Look under *abomination* in the Bible and you'll see a picture of me!"

"Well, then maybe we should call Zach now. Or maybe you should try to hear what I am saying. You missed the point. We all share the space with you under *abomination,* dear—including me. Why? Because in Proverbs it says that liars, murdering innocent people, being prideful, devising wicked plans, mischief makers, false witnesses, and sowing discord are abominations.

Who is left out from that? No one. And the *abomination* translation isn't even in all Bibles.

"My point is we let people who misuse the Word convince us we can't have a relationship with God. We all do it to some extent. It's rejecting God because of man's words. And it's all in the delivery and the messenger. That's where I was tripped up. As a four-year-old child in the front pew of a tiny cult-like church during adult services, I was fed stories of hell and damnation and ceremonial protocols instead of love, peace, acceptance, and freedom.

"Maybe because fear and damnation are powerful motivators in a child's mind. My mind absorbed the preacher's words, and those became how I perceived God. No child comes into this world thinking they are bad or God hates them, that one race is better than another, that being gay or straight is an issue, or that it's their job to judge others. There's no biological predisposition for hate—it is taught," she replied.

"And on your other point, I can't understand why people struggle with gay or lesbian people being parents. You need a license to drive a car but nothing to be a parent, and there are plenty of heterosexual parents who should never have had children, let alone adopt. Many children suffer at the hands of straight people, yet they still let them foster and adopt.

"I am even more confused as to why it isn't legal for gay people or those with gender issues to marry when monogamy is promoted everywhere. If partners in life are committed, they should have access to the same protections the law provides for spouses. And don't get me started on churches! They married my parents, your parents, me—more than once—and we weren't perfect when we married! They marry liars, gluttons, adulterers every day!

"If they believe in Jesus and are taking their issues to God like everyone else, how is it different? God is big enough for it all. The excuse is always: 'It's a blatant display of sin, and marrying a same-sex partner shows they won't stop the behavior.' Yet it's fine to marry those hiding what they are? That contradiction makes their argument invalid. It's unfair, unjust, and discriminatory—and it turns people away from God!

"Mark my words, change will come out of nowhere and everywhere all at once. Walls will crumble, dams will burst, and Christians will have to decide whether to throw anchors or life rafts. It is unacceptable to bully in Christ's name, to hold signs hurling hate, or to harm anyone in the name of God. One day, discrimination laws will be enforced, and same-sex marriage will be legal. Then what? Cruelty does not equal righteous anger. And honestly, who needs an enemy when Christians themselves are sometimes the most hateful and judgmental? I fear they won't see it until it's too late," she added.

"Oh, it might be coming, but sadly there will always be discrimination. I can see it now—when laws are enforced, some will claim *they* are the ones discriminated against. Not that it makes them right. Freedom allows personal belief, but when it spills into public discrimination, that's where the problem lies. What goes around comes around, and tides will turn against them if they don't stop," I chimed in.

"I pray people figure this out sooner rather than later, remember where we came from, and fill their mouths with heartfelt apologies—remembering we are all 'the least of these.' What would be great is if scientists proved you were born gay, Sam. That would be the icing on the cake! I love asking people who claim being gay is a choice who in their right mind would choose all of this? And what about children who know at a very young age? Did they choose that? We Christians are to be a light in the world, not a traffic light. It's sad, Sam—when we aren't busy fighting the world, we fight amongst ourselves. We aren't perfect or the most loved. We should be asking God to forgive us, for we know not what we do. Who died and left us judge and jury? It certainly wasn't Jesus. I pray one day we realize we can share our stories and vulnerabilities to show the world we are free. What a message that would be. We are the ones who need to come out to the world, Sam, not you. You are setting the example for us," Sarah added.

"I couldn't agree more. I'm not as optimistic, though. I can only hope someday it changes. It depresses me, so I'm moving us on. You're right about children—I loved church masses and never walked away condemned. It was the nuns' rules that got me. Auggie and God looked the same to me—and now the fear-mongering conservatives," I shared.

"Sorry, you know me. I can get carried away with this whole issue. Good point. It's hard to see a heavenly Father who is filled with love and freedom when our only examples are our earthly fathers," Sarah said as she gave the soup a stir. "In both of our cases they may not have shown love in a conventional way, but I think they loved us the only way they knew how at the time."

"I have always since I was very young thought God and Auggie were interchangeable when it came to discipline and anger. I had it beat into my head. Interesting concept, Sarah. Very interesting."

"Think about it, will you? Because it makes sense. He isn't a mean drunk lying in wait for an opportunity to beat you with a belt. I can promise you that much!"

"Thanks for the visual," I laughed until it hurt.

"My pleasure. If you get nothing more from this conversation than a good laugh then I haven't failed completely!"

"You haven't failed at all. I see what you are saying, and I will take it all under consideration. Like I said, I struggle with the whole issue. Sometimes I want to yell 'UNCLE' and give up!"

"Well, I am glad you haven't yet. If you didn't care at all, that would be one thing, but I've been there over the years and know you have taken this whole situation, yelling, kicking, and screaming to God for years. You didn't give up believing; you just gave up trying to be someone you're not, that's all. Never stop going back to ask Him the hard questions and ignore all the outside voices telling you can't. Don't give up on Him. He hasn't given up on you. Don't let people's words stand in that gap. It's unfair of them to rob you of that, especially if that person is Jude."

"Your intentions are good and I appreciate you trying to make me feel better. Jude's letter keeps rolling through my mind like a ticker tape."

"Sam, he is full of it! There is no mention in any Bible of the *spirit of homosexuality*—at least not in the ones I've searched. You are not possessed by this so-called demon and have no need for holy water. I've searched thoroughly. I've heard all kinds of phrases thrown around, and this one just isn't there. It's *Christianese*—language pulled together through assumption and speculation. I can only imagine the fear and pain this accusation can cause, but I need to believe it's not intentional when they use it. They can't add to or take away from the Bible, though translations can be confusing, depending on which one a person favors. Aside from that, it's ludicrous that Jude can just appear in the form of a letter, spewing his vitriol and get away with it! I wouldn't want to be him. The New Testament says what we do to the least of these (those in need), we do to Jesus. Jude has crossed the line! If your spiritual health meant so much to him, why not show up and discuss it face to face? A letter is cowardly. He rambles; you can't rebut. That wasn't about you or concern for you; it was about him, his control, and his need to hear himself. Period! Sorry, I'm just so tired of people pulling things from an empty tomb to justify their actions," Sarah said as she set the table.

"Ah-ha! So the gay community isn't the only one with a secret agenda!" I teased, sneaking another swipe of icing.

"Sam, you are incorrigible! Of course not! Sit a minute, and I'll join you in the practice of gluttony. Remember—it's all about love, which is mentioned three hundred-plus times in the Bible. It even says we are nothing without it. Maybe someday you can dig deep and find the love you still have for your brother and forgive him. Or maybe not. I love you, Sam. Now, let's eat!" Sarah proclaimed, scooping wedding soup into my bowl.

Interesting. Intriguing. Hope. Famished.

As I sipped the warm soup, I realized how hungry I truly was—physically and spiritually. Sarah's words and the soup seemed to fill the void. I was on the mend, heart and soul—or at least it felt that way, and that was enough for the moment.

CHAPTER 42

Accommodations and Asylum Part II

THE WEEKS AFTER SARAH left were quiet. The rooms felt hollow, and so did I. I returned to work but struggled to keep up, knowing my time at the office was nearing its end. Another round of Crohn's robbed me of strength, and I pushed until I landed in the hospital facing another surgery. The doctor's prognosis wasn't good; they needed to remove a large section of my intestine, and this time, an ostomy bag would be permanent. Defeat hung heavy, and as much as I resisted, I had to face reality.

Anne flew out when I was released, and she was exactly what the doctor ordered.

"Sam, I have all of your things organized beside your bed. Dinner's in the oven and the laundry's done. I was thinking of running to the store for a few things. Is there anything you want me to pick up?"

"Yes, I'll make a list. But don't you think your trip would be more productive if you waited until the store actually opens? It's barely 8 a.m.! Someone needs to bottle what's in you and sell it! They'd be a millionaire!" I said, astonished at her energy and how she got more done before daylight than others did all week.

"Oh, this is nothing, I can assure you! By now my whole floor in the ICU would be taken care of and I'd be going back around a second time!" she said, smiling.

"I believe it! If I could just find about four of you to use in my office, things would be humming again."

"Sam, about that. I know I'm hitting a nerve, but have you considered slowing down?"

"Considered it? I have no other options. The doctor says this is it for me—I need to retire now. Who retires at thirty-seven? The idea depresses me so much I can't wrap my mind around it."

"I'm so sorry. I know this isn't what you dreamed of. The doctor is right, Sam. It's time," she said sadly, running her hand through what little hair I had left, like when we were children.

I closed my eyes, feeling young and protected again. Reality lived on the other side of my eyelids, and I didn't want to face it. Why couldn't I just lay here and be that younger version of myself again? Then the old reality intruded, and I opened my eyes.

"I know. I've seen it coming. I've been searching for a place in Arizona, flying out on weekends to look. The climate works wonders for me, and I have a house in mind. I just need to commit. A real estate agent will list this place once I move. He believes, and I agree, that buyers will be more receptive if they aren't confronted with a dying man. I can't leave every time there's a showing—it would be too much. I just need help packing and organizing my personal items. I'll hire movers for the rest. Most of the furniture will stay here to stage the house."

"Wow, you've done a lot of planning. I had no idea. How about I help while I'm here? I'll have you ready to roll in no time!"

"What did I ever do to deserve such a wonderful sister? Yes! I'll take you up on that, but it's a lot of work!"

"Pfft! Work? This is nothing! You'll see!" she said, leaving far too early for her trip to the store. She was exactly who I needed.

Before she came, I felt crushed by the prospect of doing it all alone.

I informed the agent in Scottsdale that I was ready to put in an offer that afternoon. Just before dinner, I owned a smaller one-level home with a pool on a scenic lot in Arizona. Anne spent her two weeks packing, organizing, and hiring movers. I ordered temporary furniture until mine arrived after the sale, and arranged to ship my car ahead so I could fly in. Becky would help me settle on the other end, and when the furniture came, Rob and Zach volunteered to be there. When the car came to pick up Anne, I held her in the driveway as if I'd never see her again, then stood engulfed in silence as it pulled away.

The drive to the office two weeks later was difficult; tears blurred my vision. I brushed at them and scolded myself, but they refused to stop. It felt like a sniper's shot when I pulled into the lot and saw my name replaced by my successor's on the sign. I felt small, insignificant, cast aside. My chest tightened as I sat stunned. Clearly, I had defined myself by my status more than I'd realized. I had only submitted my resignation a week ago—how could they be so insensitive? Couldn't they have waited until I cleared out my office before handing it over?

Furious, I slammed the car door and marched toward the building. *I'll fire them all!* I thought, until slowing at the door, disoriented. I was on the wrong side of the complex. Mortified, I returned to my car, staring at the sign. This wasn't my spot—it wasn't even my company. How had I made such a stupid mistake? Slowly, tears ran down my cheeks.

I had wrestled for weeks with the possibility that my faculties were slipping, but this confirmed my fear. It also validated my decision to resign and move on. I couldn't live under sympathetic glances and whispered reminders from colleagues when they discovered my decline. I wouldn't.

Finally, I drove around to the correct side of the building. There, slightly faded by the California sun, was my name still in place. Relief softened me as I walked inside.

My office was exactly as I had left it weeks ago. Someone had dusted, opened the blinds, and placed fresh flowers on the sill. This space had been my home away from home for what seemed like forever. The file boxes I carried inside looked foreign against the chair by my desk. Slowly, I filled them with personal items, saving one for the awards that had hung with pride above the credenza. I held each one, remembering the events where I'd received them. Once, they were symbols of accomplishment. Now they reminded me only of what I could no longer achieve. I stacked them carefully until they filled a box and part of another.

I searched the room one last time, then stood at the penthouse windows for a final glance. The custodian came and began loading my boxes onto a cart. I told him to leave the two boxes of awards and discard everything else. He wheeled what remained of my career down the hall, and I watched as the elevator doors closed. I felt hollow.

Taking the last boxes, I walked the corridor, saying goodbye to anyone I passed. A few poked their heads out to wave, but mostly business continued as usual. No cake, no farewell party, no watch for years of service—just me and my boxes.

At the dumpster beside the building, I set the boxes down. One by one, I lifted the awards and tossed them in. They no longer meant anything; they held no real value and would mean even less to those sorting through my things after I was gone. At least that's what I told myself. I dropped the empty boxes on top and walked away.

One down, one to go, I thought as I headed back up the canyon to finish the job there.

I spent those last weeks in the canyons with memories as my only companions. Each day their voices echoed through my dream home, following me from room to room as I carried out my routines. I knew every memory personally, and they weren't about to let me leave quietly.

I met regret in one room and defeat in another. Joy lingered in the chair by the fireplace, reflecting on Christmas trees of the past. Pain stood in the doorway where goodbyes were said. Loneliness pressed from the corners, while love shone brightly in the kitchen. Happiness giggled like a child at the dining room table, and anger pointed toward the spot where shattered pottery once lay. Sadness rested on the cushion-filled couch in the family-less family room as tears filled my eyes again and again.

Surprise waited on the deck reminding me of the hawk. "Remember me?" love whispered, fidgeting next to fear, desperation, and pain as they sprawled across my king-sized bed. And while grief lingered by the front door, courage stood just outside it.

As I stepped out with courage, I realized this home now sheltered memories more than me. It had become their asylum, holding the remnants of what was left until future owners created new ones. I could almost hear sadness crying from the walls, and like the house on Griffin Avenue, I suspected some memories had rooted themselves so deeply they would never leave. Some, like me, might never find peace.

CHAPTER 43

Rivals and Archrivals Part II

AFTER TWO MORE YEARS of fighting the good fight, the enemy within was winning, and battle fatigue consumed me. I had hardly settled in Arizona when the troops invaded with fury. I spent more time down than up, and though Anne, Rob, and Sarah rotated visits to care for me, I was desperately alone in my battle. AIDS, my archrival, was consuming me. If asked how I was doing, I lied. To voice the truth felt like raising a white flag, and I wasn't ready to surrender. There was no retreat, no regrouping—only casualties. My immune system lay in waste, and I wasn't sure it had one more round in it. I hoped for a truce but got none, so most days I reflected on unfinished business.

When I first moved into my new home, I battled uncertainty and disorientation. I joined a local HIV/AIDS support group that met weekly. Sad as it was to sit among men who seemed mere caricatures of who we once were, I felt, for the first time since my diagnosis, that I had something to contribute. I also volunteered to talk with young people just coming out about safety, giving them hope while finding purpose again for myself. Their struggles—physical, emotional, spiritual, and legal—moved me deeply. For a moment I even considered law school, but knew I'd never reach the finish line.

I toyed with piano lessons, took up yoga again, but in the end, goals are for those who have time. I had little. So I set smaller

ones: Surviving a hard day or just living in the hours. I rewarded myself for the victories and showed grace for the failures. I
became comfortable with life's snail pace because it sharpened
my awareness of the beauty and complexity around me. Slowly
I shifted toward resolve. Instead of disciplining myself for it, I
welcomed it.

You learn to pick your battles, and I was saving my reserve for
one last goal. As lofty as it seemed, I wanted to gather my family—especially my rivals—one more time. If we could open our
hearts, maybe things could be better than they had ever been.
I hoped that after I was freed from this frail shell, my siblings
would find each other again. We had always been stronger as
one.

It took two years of reflection to reach this point. I needed
closure. I needed to forgive and be forgiven. I longed for freedom
from the past and all it carried, yet struggled with how to find it.
Anne, Sarah, Rob, and I had discussed my options many times,
agreeing that a phone call or letter left too much to assumption.
I needed to face them. I wanted to look into their eyes and show
them how much they meant to me despite our differences.

I longed to pull together that tight-knit special ops unit under
one roof again and confess how wrong we were to believe growing up and apart was natural or good. I wanted to shout back
through time that the greatest lie of childhood is the illusion of
endless time—that we can always do, be, or say what we want
when we're older. The truth is, we are never free; time enslaves us
all. It dictates our years, and none are exempt.

We all know life's ending. No one survives, but only those living through death's process grasp the full weight of those words.
We never realize what we are missing until it is gone. We wasted
years on disagreements and misunderstandings.

I might not be able to impart wisdom to them, but I could still reconcile. To do that, I needed to forgive. Easier said than done.

I worked through each issue individually, battling myself, giving up ground, then regaining it until I knew I could face my siblings honestly with a new outlook. The hardest to forgive were the easiest to recall. Why do our minds hold tight to loathsome memories and strain to remember happy ones? It saddened me to know I might never convey how much I loved and cherished them all, but at least I could try. Just when I felt I had reached that goal, I realized further progress required including Gertie and Auggie. Extending forgiveness to them promised to be painful and tedious.

To forgive them, I had to put myself in their shoes—an almost impossible fit. When we meet someone new, we want to know their stories, their details, and we analyze them to understand who they are. With parents, the opposite occurs. Our idea of them is skewed by their role in our lives, often filtered through discipline. We only want them to understand us. Envisioning them as ordinary people was difficult, but I forced myself to remember their own stories—their childhoods, education, and experiences. I had to see them not as parents, but as the man and woman, the young adults, and the children they once were. Slowly the walls began to crumble, and light seeped into the places where judgment had stood.

Over the years, my siblings occasionally shared that my parents missed me. Joan said Mother was distraught over the distance. Rob noted Father had shown concern. Emma claimed both were devastated after the night I came out. Anne recalled finding Mother sitting silently, holding my picture. But I never gave their pain much thought. Mine was too expansive to make room for theirs. It had been devastating for both sides to accept that we would never meet each other's expectations, and so the line in the sand remained.

I sat for hours imagining I was Auggie—first the abandoned child, then the Marine facing death, then the husband and father. From birth to abandonment, enlistment, combat, and finally the crushing weight of providing for a wife and so many children, I walked his walk in my mind. How desperate and confused was he? A simple man with minimal education or exposure, he only knew what life had shown him. I stretched beyond the pain and destruction he caused me, but still saw uneven scales. This process didn't spare me pain, but I knew I had to look past it to proceed.

Gertie was easier to face. Her life spoke for itself, and despite her actions, I knew she loved me. The agony we both lived through was enough to give her a pass. I had to release it all now. Hard as it was, I admitted they didn't fully understand what they'd done to me—and on those terms, I could forgive.

At last I bundled the issues with my family into one package and decided to put my plan into action. Anxious but hopeful, I addressed seven elegant invitations and sent them off, then waited impatiently for responses.

Four days later, as I rested on a chaise by the pool, the phone rang.

"Sam, you really outdid yourself this time. These invitations are beautiful!" Sarah said before I could even say hello. "You really are flying everyone out to Scottsdale for your fortieth birthday weekend? I'm so excited! I will start the search for a babysitter today. You really do not have to pay for the hotel and car on top of it all! I am so, so, so, so excited!" she added.

"Hello, Sarah!" I slipped in before I lost another chance. "I do what I want, remember? Do you think I overdid it? I don't want to offend anyone."

"You sent these to everyone? Even Gertie?" she asked.

"Yes, I'm really anxious. Yours was the first response I've received!"

"Good for you, Sam. Hang in there. There will be one for sure. I just hope it's the one you want it to be."

"I just hope they have the courtesy to respond. I need to make reservations for the birthday dinner within the next couple of days."

"If you don't hear just let us know and Rob will call around and get the scoop. You really don't have to use a restaurant. We can cook!" she added.

"No. That is not an option. I am taking care of everything. It's my treat! You know how long I've grappled with this, and I'm ready to face what comes with it. I think I am."

"I know, Sam. It should be them coming to you, not you to them at this point, but I am so proud of you for stepping up and following through with what is in your heart."

"Thanks, Sarah! Hug the kids and I'll get off in case anyone else is trying to call."

That was the first of six calls I received that afternoon. For some it had been years since we spoke. My efforts brought total support and I was touched beyond words. Every sibling committed to come, so I arranged flights and hotel rooms for everyone that day. I reserved the restaurant and chose a menu.

The only thing left was waiting for my parents' response. Days turned into a week and then two, and just when I had given up, the phone rang—it was my mother. She was loving and sympathetic but declined, saying she couldn't handle the flight at her age. We spoke briefly and ended with the standard "take cares" and goodbyes. I set the phone down and sighed. It was fine. I was fine. No dramatic reaction. No expectations. Just acceptance.

The next several weeks were packed with details, all managed with lists. I wanted everything perfect. I included several friends in the celebration, and they arrived before my family.

"My family is coming," I said to my reflection in the mirror. I had grown accustomed to my image, but some hadn't seen me for years. I couldn't let insecurities, however overwhelming, interfere with my plan. I shoved them down and held my head high.

I had arranged for all of my siblings to be on the same connecting flight, and I mused at the thought of them sharing stories and drinks across twelve seats in a row. I arranged individual cars for each couple and one for Anne and Emma to share, in case they didn't want to attend everything. I wanted them free to roam if they chose.

The celebration began at 6 p.m. Friday with a catered BBQ in my backyard. I fussed with details and waited at the front door. One by one, cars filled my driveway. Sarah, then Rob, Anne, and Emma came through the door with everyone else at their heels. I barely recognized some after so many years, and I looked past their awkward glances at what was left of me, moving everyone to the patio.

The evening was filled with music, food, laughter, and childhood recollections. By midnight I sat by the pool marveling at what once felt impossible. Minus a few stiff moments between Jude and my gay friends, the evening was a success.

The next day brought an afternoon pool party before everyone retreated to the hotel to prepare for my birthday dinner. We met at a beautiful restaurant that hosted private dinners under the stars.

As I rose from my seat at the head of the decorated table, I looked into each sibling's face and held my gaze for a second or two. Our lives had gone in seven directions with seven outcomes, yet here we were, together. I wanted to remember this moment. Gone were the slammed hands, harsh words, and remnants of flipped tables and food in flight. Only love sat at this table, and I wanted to soak it in.

I had rehearsed all week for this moment, but the words caught in my throat as I fought back tears of joy. I lifted my glass and began my toast.

"Here's to the Izbicki clan. Rob and Sarah, you are the wind beneath my wings! Rob, you were and are my humble gatekeeper and I cannot impart to you how much it has meant throughout my life. I cannot express my love for you both in mere words," I said as tears welled in their eyes. Sarah moved her lips whispering, "I love you."

"Anne. Where do I begin? You have been my harbor for as long as I can remember. Your arms were always there for me to huddle beneath each time I needed warmth, comfort, and protection. I cannot tell you in words how very much I love you," I added as she rose to hug me.

"Emma, my sweet baby sister. You have filled my life with love and laughter. You kept me young and curious and never fail to ground me. I love you more than words could ever express," I shared as she ran and threw her arms around me.

"Joan, Jude, and Peter, and your amazing partners, you will never know how much I have loved and missed you and how honored I am that you accepted this invitation."

"Alongside those I call family, the greatest gift I have ever received has been the friendships I've been lucky enough to have. More importantly, the caliber, intensity, trust, and commitment of these friendships is nothing short of amazing. Becky, Zach, my newest friend, Lexie, and all of you here today, thank you for loving me, caring for me, and taking care of my heart and mind through all these years. I love you all! Let's eat!" I said as we raised our glasses.

Several of my loved ones rose and toasted me, but I was lost in the fog of a perfect birthday dream, basking in the wonder of it all. A huge birthday cake with forty candles lit up the night along with the stars shining above our heads. I was reminded of the night when Sarah and I were on the deck in the canyons. Were they stars or lost loved ones keeping an eye out for me? If they were loved ones, they were welcome to attend.

Finally, an end to the battles of yesterday. No day could rival this one. I felt contentment and resolve. I could go forward knowing I had made my peace.

*****

Sarah watched through the airplane window as Arizona grew smaller and the sun set on the horizon. She and Rob were exhausted from all the fanfare, as was everyone else. Everyone dozed during the flight, but Sarah couldn't sleep. It had begun with such excitement and anticipation, but the ending felt bittersweet. Based on what she knew, this would be the last time all seven were together under one roof, and it was heartbreaking. Next time there would be six as they mourned their loss.

She was relieved Sam finally had his moment, and that was what mattered most. Forgiveness goes a long way, and if he could forgive those who had caused him pain in the family, then she needed to find it in her heart to forgive also.

As she drifted in and out, she leaned her head on Rob's shoulder and pictured Sam alone again after the festivities. She wondered how long he could hold on. How long could he keep up the fight? Sadly, she would receive the answer to that question sooner than expected.

CHAPTER 44

Exit Strategy

AFTER GETTING SOME MUCH-NEEDED rest from the planning, preparations, and fanfare of my birthday, it was time to plan the next and final event of my life—an exit strategy. If nothing else, I was organized and always worked better with a plan of action. More than once in my career I had to conduct exit interviews with employees I was forced to let go. They were never easy, usually ending with hard feelings on both sides. They often began on a positive note, supposedly to soften the blow, but that only added to the confusion. I'd seen every reaction— surprise, confusion, sadness, bargaining, anger. Over the last several years, I had cycled through them myself. They weren't pleasant, but they were necessary. Resolve was the precursor to acceptance, and I was finally ready to stop fighting futile battles and face the inevitable.

I wasn't living anymore. I was only existing. What purpose could be served by prolonging suffering? My life had no quality or quantity. It was messy and out of control, and I refused to go out in flames. I would leave in an orderly fashion. Mine would be a graceful exit if it killed me. At first, the process seemed simple—though time-consuming—but I had underestimated it. I made lists and more lists, then revised them. The devil was in the details. Soon I was overwhelmed, and a friend suggested hiring an organization specialist. I hesitated at letting someone into my private dilemma, but it made sense.

I answered an ad in a weekly journal and scheduled an appointment. I was anxious, but from the moment Lexie entered my home and took on the project, I was impressed. She was young, beautiful, full of energy and promise, and she had serious organizational skills. She managed me and my issues with ease, often coming early and staying late just to spend time with me. She started as an employee but quickly became a friend, and before long, family. I was blessed with a companion who seemed to know my needs even before I did.

Together we went through everything I owned, down to the tiniest object, and found a home for it. We purged as we surveyed the mountain of belongings I had hoarded over the years. It was a grave undertaking. Everything had to go to one of three places: garbage, donation, or endowment. Most things were easy to sort; few held meaning for me now, and I couldn't take any of it with me. I didn't make haphazard choices, though. I considered what each item represented and who might appreciate it most. I wanted my gifts to mean something to their recipients. At times I felt frustrated that I didn't have more to give.

After all the tangible items had a designated number and place on my yellow tablet, we moved on to my personal correspondence. I had always been a saver—of time, energy, money, and things—and it pained me to throw away anything that might serve a future need. But now my home contained only what I needed and what would soon belong to others.

We saved the hardest task for last: reading through twenty-five years of correspondence. I had refused to part with a single note, card, invitation, photograph, or letter. I sifted through boxes of journals, evaluating their contents word for word, shredding anything I thought might cause pain or judgment beyond the grave. I wept, laughed, and marveled as I read sentiments from the past, wishing I could turn back time and relive some of those moments. In the end, I kept only a few things from each person as reminders of my gratitude for their love and care.

I also held on to a few painful letters from those I had forgiven but not forgotten—perhaps because discarding them felt like discarding my own pain. Maybe I wanted them left behind as reminders to their authors, though I doubted I still carried venom. More than anything, I wanted to leave a testament that words spoken in anger cannot be taken back, no matter how well-intentioned.

My final task was to ensure a financial legacy for my nieces and nephews.

Satisfied with my progress, I rested knowing my home and affairs were in order. Those left behind would not face a nightmare when I passed. Every detail but one had been addressed, and soon it would be. It was time. I picked up the phone to call Sarah.

"Hi, Sarah! How are you hanging?" I asked, trying to sound positive.

"Sam, I was just going to call you! How weird! Great minds, huh?"

"Yes, think alike! How many times has this happened since we met?"

"I know! Only about a million! I wanted to see how it's going there and how you're doing. I just had this feeling today you needed to hear from me."

"Well, I guess I can confirm your feelings. I am ready. Are you?" I asked. An uncomfortable silence followed.

"Don't you do that! You hear me? We had a deal—no tears and no fears!" Sarah said. "Of course, I'm ready. But are you? Really?" she asked, knowing too well I was. *She fought back tears and fended off fears but was losing the battle. She longed to just say no and hang up.*

"Yes, and we've had this conversation once too often."

"Alright, when? How long do I have to make arrangements?" she asked through sniffles.

"Two weeks. That's long enough. By then the hard part will be under control. I'll make your plane reservations this afternoon and the process begins tomorrow. Okay?"

"That will be fine, Sam. I'll let Rob know as soon as he gets home. And please call anytime over the next two weeks if you need us. We love you," she answered sadly.

Sarah hung up the phone and fell to the floor sobbing. What was she doing? How could she do this? She had to and there was nothing she could do to change it. She promised Sam and wouldn't abandon him. She attended counseling for months after they made this deal and she still didn't feel like she had the answers she needed. It unearthed emotional, mental, and moral dilemmas within her. She had hoped and prayed something would change, a cure would be found, a miracle would happen. But here she was, it was time, and she had to find it in her heart and mind to be ready.

After we hung up, I sat in silence. This was it.

Several months earlier I had flown Sarah in for a visit. I needed help and companionship, but I also had an ulterior motive. I knew I would need someone to care for me at the end, and she was the obvious choice. Anne and I had already planned for her to handle medical and hospice needs, but I needed someone more flexible. Sarah, working in real estate, could set her own schedule, take time off, and travel at a moment's notice. She required a babysitter, but had several reliable ones. The process might take a month or more, and I didn't want others upending their lives because of mine.

I considered Emma. She was strong and independent and wise beyond her years, often understanding what baffled others. But I refused to let her see me at the end. I wanted her memories of me filled with laughter, not sorrow. So it had to be Anne and Sarah—or so I believed.

During Sarah's visit, I asked if she would be willing to stay with me when the time came. A friend had lent me a video showing a man's journey from diagnosis to death, leaving nothing to the imagination. When I asked if she would be with me, she anxiously volunteered as I knew she would. Still, I felt she needed to be prepared for anything she might face.

We pulled the blinds in the family room and, as she watched the video, I monitored her reactions. In the end, we were both in tears.

"Sam, my God! I cannot even fathom you having to experience those things. I knew it was bad—but this bad? Of course I will be here! You will not face this alone!"

"I am terrified, but I'm banking on being so far gone by then that I won't care. Thank you, Sarah. Anne will come for the last week until I'm placed in hospice. I toured several and chose the one that fits my needs—even the room, if you can believe that! So this is how it will work," I said, explaining what I had in place.

"So, you'll call me, give me a time frame, and I'll fly out and …"

"Yes, Sarah. I'll just call and ask if you're ready, and you'll know. Remember, no tears and no fears!" I added, sealing the deal.

My decision to end the battle wasn't made lightly. My body rejected food constantly. The smallest bite could bring hours of dry heaves. I sipped water but couldn't keep down even a tablespoon. I was wasting away with no strength left to fight. A feeding tube posed its own problems, and my options were few. More often than not I was hooked to an IV to replenish electrolytes, the only way I could take medications. I went over, through, and around every obstacle without success.

I would not be kept alive by machines. I wanted to remain in my own home and bed as long as possible. I consulted with doctors and put into action the only thing that brought relief. Over the next two weeks, while waiting for Sarah's arrival, I was weaned from medications and all sustenance. No food. No water. Nothing.

It wasn't hard or sad, because forcing these things into my body was killing me anyway. To keep doing the same thing over and over expecting a different result was insanity.

One friend told me I was committing suicide, and I laughed. Suicide implies choice. Nothing I've described was a choice—it was inevitable. I had no strength to go on.

My life was over, and I intended to exit gracefully—with humility, dignity, and control. We come into this world painfully, and we go out the same. In the space between, we fight to live all we can before finishing the course. I had a plan, or thought I did, and if it was up to me, it would be carried out with perfection. I worked feverishly to raise my arm above my head, but I had no strength. At last, I gave myself permission to raise the white flag of surrender and implement my exit strategy of all exit strategies. Nothing in my short life brought greater relief.

CHAPTER 45

Pipe Dreams/ It's All in Your Head Part II

I JERKED AWAKE. THE alarm blared louder than normal on my bedside stand. I squinted at the display but couldn't see straight. Vertigo overwhelmed me, forcing me back onto the bed. I had no time for this. I shook my head, trying to gather my thoughts. What day was it? It had to be a workday, otherwise I wouldn't have set the alarm.

Empty-headed, I hoped today's schedule would appear in my mind's eye, but nothing came. Slowly I pulled myself upright. Why was I so weak? Why wouldn't my muscles cooperate? At the edge of the bed I groaned and rubbed my eyes. Fear ran through me. Was I sick? Why couldn't I think straight? I was forgetting something—something important, I was sure. I needed to pull myself together.

My surroundings blurred. Where was I? I recognized my furniture but couldn't comprehend why it was in this room. Silence enveloped me. A line of light slipped beneath the blinds. Night or day? The alarm had gone off, so I must have needed to get up early. As I searched for clues, I felt lost.

Slowly, like a cat stalking prey, memory returned. I was in my bedroom, in my own home. Where? Scottsdale. That's right. I had moved here. My dream retirement community, though

I wasn't near retirement age. I'd planned to retire and die here years later.

I switched on the light. My stomach twisted, and I fought the urge to vomit. Then I remembered: I didn't need to get ready for work. I was no longer employed.

In the bathroom, the light flicked on, and my reflection explained why. I stared at what was left of me—this hollow image of who I once was. Barely recognizable. How could I be? I was an inmate in AIDS' concentration camp, with no hope of rescue or release.

Concentration. My mind worked on such a bizarre level now I couldn't focus on any one issue for more than minutes without looping back or drifting off. Fragments of images surfaced—pieces of a larger canvas, often blurred. Verses from poems, notes from operas, lyrics from old songs appeared and vanished without reason. I worked feverishly to weave any of them into a complete thought. Of all the symptoms I feared, memory loss and the inability to think topped the list. Merging thoughts into sentences grew frustrating, and anger and fear only made it worse. I couldn't bear being reduced to a senseless, rambling idiot. I would never allow that.

Feverish, yes. I plucked the thermometer from the counter and placed it under my tongue: 103 degrees. I forced down a couple of pain pills without water—the one luxury I allowed myself. Had I already taken some? Too late now. I wasn't lucky enough to die from an overdose.

I walked slowly back to bed, yanked the blanket over my head. Balding rapidly, chilled by fever, I still refused to turn off the ceiling fan. I needed air circulation. I rolled over and glimpsed dawn approaching. I had nowhere to go, no one needing me. I closed my eyes, willing myself to sleep, but landed in that zone between asleep and awake.

The alarm hadn't gone off at all—it was another fever-induced pipe dream producing its sound. I relived this so often now it no longer stirred emotion. As I drifted into oblivion, I rationalized that my thirty-year habit of rising early for work or school was dying harder than I was.

Dawn. Most days droned on this way, dawn to dusk, since I had implemented my exit strategy. Some days were better. On those, I forced myself out of the house, even if only to sit by the pool. I'd stay as long as I could hold my head up, drinking in the sounds—a single bird singing, vehicles beyond the backyard wall, neighbors arguing. I isolated each noise, guessing its source: truck, car, bird, the buzz of a hummingbird at my feeders. The sounds were beautiful, and tears often welled in my eyes.

Television distracted me, but I craved connection with life—sounds, feelings, sights I had taken for granted. Hours slipped by as I listened to music, each note and word flowing through me, penetrating deep.

Words. I spoke them aloud, savoring each syllable as it rolled off my tongue. Oh, how I loved words. I grieved the times I wasted them in arguments, wondering if I had spoken in ways that mattered. When I still had my faculties, I read everything I could get my hands on. So many subjects fascinated me. I was hungry for knowledge I had no use for and no one to share it with. I yearned to learn, to understand.

Now, even dust motes floating through shafts of sunlight amused me. I listened to seconds tick by, willing them to stop. I was desperately alone—loving and hating it, depending on the day. I often felt reclaimed by nature, as foliage overtakes abandoned cabins, erasing any trace of the dwellings they once were. The isolation was daunting.

Hungry. I was no longer hungry. A hollow emptiness sat where sustenance once resided. Friends dropped by when they could, bringing meals or forbidden treats they knew I loved. Food had taken on new meaning over the last several months as I bucked the rigid diets meant to prolong my life. I binged on whatever I wanted, though most times I managed only a tablespoon.

When I could eat, I'd hold food in my mouth, savoring the sensation as it awakened my taste buds. Each morsel reminded me how quickly I once devoured meals. Now my digestive system rejected everything. While I starved, my unwelcome squatters—Crohn's and AIDS—were never hungry. They despised nutrition. Still, I savored every bite, even knowing it would soon end up in the bucket always within reach. The experience left me exhausted and wracked with pain. Why was I prolonging the inevitable? Eventually, I stopped even this minimal life-sustaining process.

Starve. I was starving for stimulation. I became preoccupied with the life of my housekeeper, also HIV positive but doing incredibly well. When interviewing applicants, most prospects dwindled after seeing me or hearing the tasks required. Some were frightened by AIDS; others by the labor involved.

Admittedly, I was a slave driver when it came to cleanliness. It was all I had left to control in my otherwise chaotic existence, and I confess I sometimes overreacted when things weren't done to my standards.

I lived vicariously through my housekeeper's young, active life. His adventures captivated me. I would sit, eyes closed, listening to every detail, wishing with all I had that we could switch places, if only for a day.

Work. I passionately missed my job, especially the health coverage. I used to despise commuting and swore stoplights were invented to torment me, yet I would give a limb to be healthy and stuck in rush-hour traffic now. I even missed "death by meetings," especially the problem-solving. I missed the sound of my own voice carrying sales principles like musical notes.

Sometimes I pulled out my empty briefcase and reminisce over past clients and deals. I thought of former coworkers, the times we laughed, fought, and cried over details that mean nothing now. Every so often I would wake and, before moving, begin to plan my day—only to remember it was already planned by the terrorist running through my veins, day and night without constraint.

Management. I had been in risk management for years. The shift from managing hundreds of employees and projects to managing HIV/AIDS and its opportunistic sidekicks was grueling, with endless overtime and unexpected "bonuses."

My new charges had names like Diazepam, Filgrastim, Sargramostim, and Epoetin Alpha—supposedly life-sustaining, yet unruly and unpredictable, each with side effects. The cost of compensation boggled the mind.

My extended staff included doctors and nurses, along with the hired hands of infusions, injections, and transfusions. Lawyers and insurance agents settled endless claims. All claimed to work on my behalf, yet they kept me busier than ever.

In my former position, I had an assistant manager to mop up details. Now, without anyone to help interpret the flood of information doctors spewed—assuming I still had the capacity to grasp it—I was lost. I often sat dumbstruck as they rattled on, nodding instead of asking questions. I feared they would detect the dementia I was ashamed to reveal. If added to my list of symptoms, it would strip away what little freedom I had left.

At home I'd try to recall their advice but usually came up empty. Thankfully, now the only folks waiting for my direction were those at the hospice clinic that I had painstakingly chosen.

Partner. I desperately missed having a partner in what little remained of my life. I suffered from touch deprivation, craving someone to hold me, someone who made me feel safe and loved. Hugs from friends and family were wonderful, but I longed for passion and intimacy. I missed having a spouse.

I used to automatically extend my hand when meeting someone new—until it became clear no one wanted to touch me once AIDS became visible on me. Most kept a safe distance, both physically and emotionally. Isolation was the cruelest side effect of AIDS; my social life had died long before I would. Even fellow victims pulled away. Those without symptoms resisted the burden of caring for someone so close to death. Who could blame them? Many of my gay friends had already lost partners and dreaded new commitments at a time when we needed them most.

In the past, I concealed my diagnosis as long as possible. When I finally revealed it, I knew what it meant. I had seen the movie, read the book, and knew the ending by heart.

Fear. I lived with terminal fear. I knew none of us could stay in this lifetime, but I felt unprepared for death. Society doesn't teach us about dying. We avoid the subject unless it happens to someone distant. We're short-sighted, grasping for words, offering empty gestures. We can't care for the dying without facing our own mortality. We detach, patronize, act as if death itself is contagious.

We fear what comes next. We dread accountability, the black hole, regression, or even progression. Depending on our beliefs, we fear returning—or not returning at all. We fear venturing where no one survives. We marvel at those claiming glimpses beyond the grave, but they never return with souvenirs: *I've been to heaven and all I got was this T-shirt.*

We fear proof, or the lack of it. We fear that our faith is wrong, even when evidence in our lives confirms it. We fear it won't be enough. We fear leaving as we arrived: alone. And still, as a society, we isolate others, when no one is exempt from death.

Unable to articulate fears, we stay silent—except when someone claims certainty about the afterlife, filling the air with words no silence can contain. Intentions may be good, but results can devastate.

I marveled at hospice workers. They seemed to have conquered what the rest of us could not. They faced daily what we all fear most. They stared death in the face until it no longer scared them.

"Silence is golden," I used to say, but lately it has grown so deep I swear I can hear the disease coursing through my body, veins, and mind. I often talk to myself just to break it, yet my voice sounds different. Without the ebb and flow of an audience, I grew less impressed with it. We gain strength in who we are from the reactions of others. With no one to react, to impress, or to move, my voice felt like nothing but sound.

Ebb and flow. I missed the forward motion of life. Now I existed within the strict confines of the ebb. The only thing I was flowing toward was death.

I positioned myself at the window at an angle where I couldn't see my reflection. I used to study people's faces, watching them move quickly through life, unaware of me behind the glass. I wondered what it was like to be them—if they were happy, loved, and dreaming. Now I just sat and wondered.

Before beginning this final process, I occasionally had "good" weeks when I could venture out. Most often, though, my trips were limited to labs, doctors' offices, and hospitals. In waiting rooms I studied faces that mirrored what I would soon look like, while others stared blankly at mine. They were the face of my future, just as I was the face of their past. I looked at them and wept inside. I missed me.

Weep. I cry more than any man should ever have to. An endless fount of tears, I'm moved by what once seemed insignificant. I weep with joy, with sorrow, and sometimes for no reason at all. Rarely do I feel drained of the emotion. At the least opportune moments, a tear escapes, racing down my cheek as if chased. I've grown accustomed to them and seldom stop their progress. They prove I'm alive. They are evidence not everything has been stolen from me. They reveal my strength and weakness, and I am not ashamed.

I weep for how often we are swayed by tears and the emotions behind them. Then I weep at how often we ignore them in others, unaware of the pain our disregard causes. I cry trying to measure how many times I did so, hoping I never quelled someone else's passion. I weep at how easily we believe such pain doesn't matter. I cry for our ignorance, our blind eyes, our selfishness and pride.

I weep because we move too fast—and not fast enough. Because we give in before reaching our goals. Tears once flowed at children's laughter, and now as I grieve my inability to be a father. I used to cry at the homeless, and again when passing multimillion-dollar homes. I am a bundle of contradictions.

I weep for the tenderness shown to me on my hardest days. Because without each other, we have nothing. I want to shout that we are a human tapestry, each thread vital, yet I cry for the times we don't accept, offer, or ask for it.

Tears flowed during movies, at couples holding hands, at sunrise and sunset. Now I weep remembering the taste of chocolate. The scent of a flower, a spider weaving a web, can bring them on. I cry for the loss of friends and family. I cry at how much we avoid crying. We're told to "suck it up," shamed into controlling what should be released.

I weep at the evening news, at what we are doing to our world—air, oceans, land, trees. I cry all day for trees, because I miss *my* tree. I sob over what we do to ourselves and others—and what we fail to do. I cry tears of joy and sadness over nearly everything.

But mostly, here and now, I grieve the loss of life, identity, dreams, and faith. I grieve the faith of my childhood. Nothing makes me weep more than speaking to God—or questioning His existence. Soon I will weep without tears, mourning their loss. I will miss them.

Identity. What or who was I now? I hadn't the foggiest idea. My labels had always threatened to define me—by society or by how others perceived me—and I'd worn plenty.

First came baby, boy, child, son, grandson, brother, and friend. Then student, young man. The church and God's Word labeled me Catholic, Christian, child of God, light of the world—and sinner. These rooted deepest in my soul.

There were egregious labels from the Marine and society, too numerous to rehash. In my career I became assistant, then Mr., boss, manager, vice president, president. Politically I was a Republican gay man, along with whatever else society placed on me. From my personal life: uncle, godfather, partner, lover, gay. None of them ever truly defined me. Now I couldn't reconcile myself with any of them.

I was also labeled by class—first low, then middle, later upper income—as well as race, heritage, and orientation. To be fair, I don't know that I was ever content with any identity. I always searched for a "new and improved" me. Stopping felt like surrender, though I now see that was a cop-out. I often criticized others I thought were settling, wanting to appear innovative, striving for life's best. But that was a farce.

I was constantly under construction, erecting new images to cover my inability to accept myself. I was never certain who I was. The more discontent, the more miserable I became. That misery fueled further reconstruction, and the more reconstruction I displayed, the more attention I received. I loved and hated myself for it.

With so much labeling, it's a wonder we aren't all diagnosed with multiple personality disorder, trading hats and faces in relay style without missing a beat. Yes, I was still many of those labels in word—but not in deed. Unable to fulfill their definitions, who was I now, other than Sam, nearly dead, trapped in this mangled shell?

Inside I still felt like that fragile, confused baby boy who slipped into this world alone.

Child. I was ever aware of how I failed to bring about Billy's childhood dreams. We shared this hollow shell, and I often felt his pain and disappointment. He never asked for much. I accomplished most of his dreams—jobs, suits, cars, homes—but the one that slipped from my grasp was the happy family we both wanted.

We wanted marriage, like any other couple. We wanted sons, daughters, grandchildren. Labels, laws, and judgments stole that chance. In reality there are plenty of deviant people—straight and gay—but I wasn't one of them. I knew I would have been a better father than my own, and it amazed me that society deemed him fit to procreate while denying me. In my heart, I knew I'd have been an exceptional daddy, treasuring every moment.

Instead, I treasured music and art. I had gadgets, china, crystal, wealth—all of which would outlive me, though meaningless now. I'll leave them, along with what remains of my fortune, to those I love. Yet it feels like leaving nothing. No child, no legacy, no mark on this world.

I was always a little dramatic, but passion now consumes me. Did I pass on one good thing? Help someone? Give love? Exhibit character, integrity, strength, courage? Will anyone emulate my choices? I think yes.

Even if only measurable in faded memories and yellowed photographs, someone will remember me and smile. Someone will recall when I helped, loved, or showed compassion. Someone will sigh at what I taught by example. Someone will laugh remembering something I said or did. That will be my legacy of sorts, and I have no choice but to be satisfied with it.

Prepared or not, my time here was ending. Reviewing my accomplishments as if cramming for finals, I'd say I earned enough for a passing grade in this lifetime.

End. I was relieved I had formed an exit strategy before losing my faculties. I was forced to face facts. My life would be summed up in that narrow forty-year space engraved on my newly purchased urn. However short that distance, it was all I was given.

Even if a cure had been found yesterday, it wouldn't turn back the clock. More years wouldn't mean quality. It was too late. Only a miracle from God could change things. My support system and bank account were dwindling. I was well off, but not wealthy enough to buy top-notch care that promised nothing while stripping me of everything. I had worked too hard to end as a pauper.

I had exhausted every effort and no longer had the strength to persevere. I had proven resilient in the past, but now I had no hope of survival. AIDS and Crohn's were killing me, and despair drained what little I had left. I was finished. I can't recall the moment this revelation came, but I believed it to my core—or what remained of it. Still, ridding myself of the nagging feeling that I had left something undone, some purpose unfulfilled, was near impossible.

God. The concept of God had been effortless as a child. My acceptance was uninhibited, carefree. I floated six inches off the ground in church—except when conviction of a million wrong thoughts and deeds weighed me down. But when guilt and condemnation were stripped away, and I was drawn into the mystical drama of reverence and love, I could not deny His existence.

I lived for those moments of freedom, feeling accepted, protected, cleansed from the inside out. Rolling onto my side, I drifted back to that time before the world intruded. I instantly felt the warmth, comfort, and tranquility I had craved for what seemed an eternity. Transformed into my six-year-old self, I felt my head resting on the chest of my protector, my God, His arms enfolding me.

Peace engulfed me and I sobbed as warm tears dampened His chest. Never in my life had I felt such release, such compassion. No pain, no sorrow—just love. Within minutes, my adult mind intruded with questions, anger, confusion. I opened my eyes and returned to reality.

I. I rummaged through memories of conversations with close friends and advisors over the years, dissecting religion and philosophy. Fragments surfaced: Vibrate at higher frequencies to move on; live a life of love and goodness to be transformed; sacrifice now, be rewarded later; when life ends, we simply stop existing; die for this God or that one and receive sexual rewards; follow these rules or those to be redeemed; God sent His Son to die in our stead so we might have second chances.

One belief followed another like a spinning top, swirling through my mind like a dust devil as I tried to block them out. So many concepts, so many details—yet all circling common themes and outcomes.

Belief. "What do I believe?" I asked aloud, startled by the courage it took to voice what I often avoided. I had asked others that question often enough, but when had I last asked myself? Was I ready for the answer? I was never ready for the next stage in life—or death.

No one else was here. *What do you believe, Sam?* I could not answer. Flashes of my life passed before me, reminders of the things and people I had lost. Was I headed toward the precipice between life and death by choice, or by man's words? Was there ever a choice?

You have my undivided attention, God, I thought, half expecting the ceiling to collapse under the weight of it. I closed my eyes waiting for lightning—but silence prevailed.

I rolled to my side, wincing, and sought rest. My life replayed before me like a ghost of Christmas past. Darkness slammed doors while windows of light poured open, portraits of people and connections glowing through the cracks.

Behind the armor I'd built from anger, fear, and disappointment lay beauty, love, and support. The gates of my fortress cracked open, letting in light that shone like sun on new snow. For a moment I felt it—until old pain rushed in to smother it. Had I thrown the baby out with the bathwater?

Had I missed what mattered while nursing pain and protecting my heart? There was much to be thankful for, warmth hidden in the cold. It wasn't all bad. Not all painful. There had been light where once I saw only darkness.

Had my confusion created a kind of dementia, clouding my perception and blocking memories of joy? Both failures and triumphs lay before me, but now the triumphs shone brighter. Had I spent my life so intent on blocking pain that I also blocked love and peace?

Had I based my conclusions only on man's words, in anger and distrust?

And then it was silent again. Nothing light or dark. Nothing real or imagined. Just me, curled in a ball in the cellar of my emotions. I had bottomed out. There was nothing left, and I couldn't even reach the stairs to the first floor, where the remnants of my life waited.

Bay. The only image my mind held was of a calm ocean with a rust-colored walker, half in and half out of the water, abandoned. Waves brushed against it, whispering my name.

I walked through the sand and reached for its dark, seaweed-covered handles. As I touched them, the walker disappeared. I understood. No props this time.

Weak, I knew I had to take a step. As I did, the water held the weight of my remains. I took another step and whispered through parched lips, "God, can You hear me?"

A still, small voice answered inside me: I had been heard.

Before I knew it, I was halfway across the bay.

Wait—was that a mustard seed of faith I felt for a moment? Or was it all in my head?

CHAPTER 46

Said and Done
Part II

SARAH'S ARRIVAL BROUGHT COMPANIONSHIP to otherwise lonely days—and an endless stream of mourners coming to say farewell. Oddly, I felt I was attending my own funeral as each came crying, hugging, and holding me for the last time. Zach and his new wife, Jordan, were the last to visit, comforting me with their embrace and prayer.

Finally alone, Sarah moved me daily from bed to couch and back again. We spent days flicking through TV channels, searching for distraction as we waited for the grim reaper. We laughed, cried, even fought one afternoon when I thought I heard her using the microwave. I knew she needed to eat, but I was jealous of her ability. I wondered how she managed to conceal her meals when I knew all she wanted was to feed me.

She asked several times if I'd reconsider food and water, and I lashed out like a spoiled schoolgirl. She began spending more time on the patio reading while I watched, waited, and withered. It angered me, and by the time Anne arrived three weeks later, I had nothing left but emotions. My inability to think straight made me lash out in frustration.

"She does nothing but sit out there and read!" I snapped.

"She's been out there half an hour. We're splitting our time with you. She can't eat or drink around you and needs fresh air," Anne replied. "She's been here with you three weeks, Sam."

"I'm right here, Sam," Sarah said as she entered from the patio. "I go out there a little while each day. I need fresh air. I'm never out long—it just seems that way to you," she added, smiling as she rearranged my pillows.

"No! You're out there for hours! Sometimes I have to go looking for you!" I shouted.

"Sam, you can't go looking for me. You can't walk alone anymore. It's okay, though. I'll stay inside more if it makes you feel better," Sarah said, winking at Anne.

Anne's arrival was a godsend. She had come just in time for my final stages, when medical care would soon be needed. The past several weeks felt like a year, in sharp contrast to earlier visits when her time seemed to end too soon.

I was sure I was right. Or was I? Days and hours blurred. Was I still leaving my bed, or had I been there all along? It was all confusing.

Anne and Sarah exchanged looks of understanding. Dementia was taking hold along with other symptoms that I had not noticed. Within days I was confined to bed. By week's end I couldn't roll from side to side without help. My body no longer produced fluids, and I slept more than I was awake. By midweek I barely recognized my surroundings, struggling even with their names.

They grew accustomed to my sudden cries and outbursts, taking turns sleeping on the couch outside my room to respond quickly. Baby monitors were placed around the house in case they were out of earshot.

Meals were sparse—licorice, peanut butter and jelly, crackers, whatever came from a bag—eaten on the far side of the house. Any use of the kitchen upset me.

The phone rang often with people asking for updates, but Anne and Sarah struggled to explain what they were witnessing. They feared adding to the confusion. Gertie called daily, lamenting the imminent loss of her son, and it broke their hearts to know her suffering.

"Mommy! Owwww! Mommy!" I cried out in despair. Once, Anne held the phone to my ear so Gertie and Auggie could speak their love and say goodbye.

I felt restless and tried to move. Gone again. The light was brighter than anything I had seen—or was it felt, touched? My senses were confused, unreliable. Again it appeared, beckoning me to investigate, pulling with a million hands. No, guiding me. I feared it and revered it. Warm and welcoming, yet cold and aloof.

I inhaled sharply and the rush of oxygen pulled me away. Back to here, or there, or wherever this place had become. I struggled to open my eyes, but a thousand-pound weight held them shut. Light poured through the crack and I was here again.

I knew this place, knew the objects in view, but their names escaped me. Squinting hard, I focused on the moving figure at my side. Sounds of comfort came from it. Girl? It seemed right, so I repeated it until the word formed audibly.

"Girl? GIRL?" I blurted.

"Sam, I am here," Sarah said, leaning close so I could see her eyes. She wanted me to know my effort to communicate wasn't in vain. "Are you in pain?" she asked, longing for one of my sarcastic answers, but knowing I no longer understood where I was or what I said.

"Girl with the shawl. You will keep me alive. Do I still have my red urinal? The insurance one?" I asked.

Sarah and Anne exchanged glances, resisting laughter at the bizarre request. Exhaustion left them raw; humor was the only shield against tears. Sarah lifted the urinal for me to see. I hadn't used it in days and never would again—my body was long depleted of fluids.

"It's not red, Sam, but here it is. Is this what you're asking about?"

"OOOH!" I snapped. "The one in the out room."

"You mean your red sports car?" she asked. "Yes! Yes, you still have it. Why are you worried about it now?"

"It's beautiful!" I muttered as I slipped back into dreams.

Sarah wasn't sure if I meant the car or something only I could see in the distance of my mind.

"Hey! Hey!" I mumbled.

My mumblings were frequent, mostly inaudible. Sarah and Anne knew I was talking to someone, somewhere out there. Delusions and dementia had worsened; I was deteriorating fast. I often cried out in pain, heartbreaking to witness.

Karen, a hospice aide, had helped Anne place a port in my chest days earlier so she could administer morphine. Anne pressed the button, and my breathing became almost undetectable. Then, suddenly, I opened my eyes wide and spoke clearly, as if nothing were wrong.

"Do you see them? Do you see them out there?" I said, staring toward the backyard window.

Anne moved closer, pulling the blinds wider.

"Yes, Sam, we see them. Who are they?" she asked. But beyond the glass was only blue sky and four Alberta spruce trees lined neatly in a row.

"The four men—standing there," I mumbled, smiling. "I'm having my own meeting with them."

My smile revealed blackened teeth. Anne glanced at Sarah, then back at my pillow-framed face. It tore at her heart. Once I weighed nearly one hundred ninety pounds; now she doubted I was seventy. My six-foot frame resembled wartime images of concentration camp prisoners. I was skin and bones, looking twice my age.

Tears flooded her eyes as I lay exposed, unable to bear even a cotton sheet. I showed every final stage sign. They shifted me side to side to ward off bedsores, revealing purple Kaposi sarcoma lesions climbing my back.

Symptoms piled from countless opportunistic infections. Mold grew beneath the tape on my port within minutes of a change. She had stopped trying to brush darkness from my teeth.

Sarah called Rob. "It's time," she told him, and they discussed his flight for the next day.

"Shirt changes colors at the intake valve. Can I read it before you wash it?" I blurted, eyes closed. "Did the four women buy the four cars on the lot? The four guys who make T-shirts are here for me," I added, trying to explain.

"You're very talkative today, Sam," Anne replied, knowing I wasn't listening.

"I see you speaking English today, Hersee. Your colors are beautiful," I said, opening my eyes—if that was the right word.

"Why, thank you, and yes, I am!" Sarah said, smiling as she shifted my pillows.

"I need a banana. I've been eating crap all day," I said, pointing to the other girl. "What company are you with? No outfits? Lily is in this movie! That water's the wrong color for that urinal. It's sweet tea!"

Anne and Sarah grinned. I had begun calling Sarah "Hersee" the last several days. Anne climbed onto the bed, running her hands down both sides of my face, comforting me like a child. She whispered, "I love you, Sam. I love you," as I drifted into deeper sleep.

The following night was awful. I woke every ten minutes crying out in pain. Anne pressed the morphine pump, but nothing eased me. By morning they had to rely on nonverbal cues to guess my needs, often fruitlessly. Midmorning I quieted, seeming to rest, so they took turns napping. But in late afternoon my desperate cries woke them.

"Do you see it? It's so beautiful!" I exclaimed. "The colors are brilliant—it's rainbows! Such a beautiful light. I can't reach it! I want to join the line of those not dying, but it's too long. The dying line is short." Beauty stretched across the horizon, and I wondered why they couldn't see it.

The skin on my arms hung slack as I raised them, reaching for something not of this world. Tears filled their eyes.

"Go to it, Sam. It's okay. Everyone's waiting for you. Go to God, Sam. Grab onto a rainbow," they urged together.

"It's time to call hospice," Anne said sadly as Sarah nodded.

The team arrived within minutes, wrapping me gently in a sheet. Garrett, the ambulance driver, helped place me on a gurney. My morphine was increased for comfort. Tears streamed down Sarah and Anne's cheeks as they hugged me, promising to follow close behind.

Sarah walked beside the gurney to the ambulance at the front door, clutching my hand, unwilling to let go. She feared I might pass en route and longed to ride with me. As they pushed the bed inside, I sat up for the first time in weeks.

"I made a big mistake this time, didn't I?" I asked.

"No, Sam. You didn't. You had no choice. I love you so much. Just rest," she whispered through tears.

At the local airport, notice was left with the airline counter to inform Rob upon landing. He was told to pick up his car and drive directly to hospice.

Sarah and Anne waited outside as I was cleaned and made comfortable. Minutes felt like hours. When they entered, I was so quiet they feared they had missed my final moment. I looked peaceful, almost serene. Standing on either side, they held my hands, willing me to stay.

I struggled to speak through labored breaths. Sarah sensed I was asking for Rob.

"Hang on, Sam. He's on his way. He'll be here soon. I promise," she said.

With tear-stained cheeks, they hugged me and whispered goodbyes. My vitals wavered, my breathing ragged. A few minutes later Rob arrived, tears streaming, with Lily and Andrew in tow.

Dolly, now married with a son, and Jay, away at college, couldn't come on short notice. With no sitters available, Rob had brought the younger children, knowing my affairs might take a week to settle after my passing.

The two stood quietly by my bed, tears in their eyes. They worshiped their Uncle Sam—their superhero—and struggled to express their grief.

I struggled to speak as Rob leaned close.

"I'm here now, Sam. Right here beside you. Everything will be alright. I'll stay by your side. It's okay to go. I love you."

I inhaled deeply, exhaled with relief, and fell silent.

*****

I was aware of my surroundings but free from pain and fear. It was finally over, and a new beginning lay ahead. Like a monarch emerging from its chrysalis, I shed my broken shell and was free to fly.

"Sarah! Sarah! Look at me! I'm floating! I'm free!" I shouted, though she couldn't hear me. "Well, we'll see about that," I thought, heading toward a big red bow hanging on an iron bar above her head. "Can you see me now?"

*****

At the sight of Rob holding his brother's hand and her children's tears, Sarah became overcome and stepped outside to compose herself. She looked up, searching for words, when she noticed a huge red bow hanging from an iron bar overhead.

It began to spin round and round, though no wind stirred it. Something in the air had shifted. Peace flooded her, and she knew in her heart all was said and done. He was on his way.

"Godspeed, my brother. I love you," she whispered as the ribbon spun once more and came to rest.

It Was Finished

HERE, FREE OF TIME, I watched as my ashes were laid to rest beneath the tree that once sheltered me. I felt the sorrow of those gathered as if it were my own. A lone hawk flew low, and my loved ones watched in awe. I had promised to send a sign if I could, and I smiled knowing I wasn't the one who sent it. It was simply another way to give those left behind faith that they were being heard. I wished I could share that truth, but wishing holds little value here.

If I had one wish … How often I said those words in life—often enough that my beneficiaries would be rich if nickels were given. Now, for the first time, I can share them post-earthly existence.

If I had one wish, it would be for health—and the time it would have given me. But if that was impossible, then my wish would be to realize I didn't need one. I only needed to believe and do whatever I wished for. The energy I spent coveting wishes could have been directed at pursuing them.

It had worked in most areas of my life, at least when there was a direct path to the goal. Why wouldn't it have worked otherwise? When paths were carved, results were expected. One plus one is two. Twelve years of school plus four more of college and hard work should equal a career. Wrong choices brought regret. Yet even on those paths, outcomes were predictable, and I always wished they could have been different.

It was the gray areas that perplexed me—the times I was forced to dig deep and have faith. Not because they were uncertain, but because the best solution was rarely the easiest, most fun, or most acceptable.

I wish I had more faith. I wish I hadn't cowered in fear or worried what others thought. I wish I had the courage to stand, untrapped by another's judgment, fears, or obligations. I wish I hadn't let men's words rob me of what I knew in my heart.

If I had many wishes, the greatest would be that I'd known faith exists outside the confines of others' rules and restraints. I wish I could impart how much impact words both do and don't have. I wish I had understood I was never alone in my struggles and pain. And beyond all wishes, I wish I had realized it really was all about love—from beginning to end.

Regrettably, lacking faith was what I shared most with some of my friends. They would likely be disappointed in my change of view now. I spent most of my adult life verbally questioning the unseen. Yet in my heart I knew of life beyond earth.

I gave it countless names, called it all the things professed by history's great thinkers and writers. I jumped on nearly every bandwagon in search of answers to validate my theories. But in the end—and we all reach the end—there is only one explanation.

We come into life pushed through a long dark tunnel, alone. It's not hard to think leaving life would be much the same. I don't mean the birthing process mirrors dying, but both carry the unknown. Babies feel anxiety in birth; we likely feel it in death. And believe me—I was anxious.

In the end, I didn't vibrate on a higher level, phase in and out, or get taken by aliens. I didn't change bodies. I simply vacated the awkward shell that never fit me. Until now I haven't moved on—not because I had more to do, teach, or learn, but because none of us control those things.

I believed I was prepared, content with my decisions. I planned every detail, just as I once planned social and business events. I hadn't controlled my entrance into the world, but I was determined to control my exit. Divine intervention had seemed absent in my life, so I assumed it would be absent in death. I thought I was in control.

Thankfully, I was wrong.

I spoke those words, then was given a glimpse of beauty beyond comprehension. My last words fell short of what I wanted to express. Countless reasons for my life and suffering flooded my senses like air filling lungs. Instantly, I knew why and what my existence meant, and whether I had fulfilled it. In those final moments, it was that mustard seed of childlike faith that led the way. And when it was finished, I couldn't have been more surprised at how little control I ever had—how little we all have.

Not a soul—men, women, or children—rose above this place without astonishment. And like them, I found grace, peace, and an abundance of love waiting for me.

A Note from the Author
to the Story's Inspiration

(found among the author's papers after her death)

Dear Stan,   2/2/2013

I thought of a million things I wanted to say to you today. It seems so small just to say thank you and I miss you. I wanted to thank you for all the times you were there. For being my friend, my brother. For helping me to save the most valuable thing to me. For being so hard on me sometimes because you could see my potential when I couldn't. For asking me to spend your last month with you and for preparing me so thoroughly for the harsh realities that I was going to experience by doing so. I never knew why— you wanted so many others to remember you on better days, at better times, in better ways. I have fought for seventeen years to understand why you didn't want me to remember you in better times. I have finally figured out the answer why. The answer to your final question is no, Stan, you struggled so hard with that question. I can finally say I am almost finished doing what you had asked me to do. Rick loves and misses you beyond words and is so honored by your trust, but you knew that from the beginning. Also, yes, you were right. I am so sorry things didn't go as you hoped they would but you knew that too. And lastly, the answer to your other question is yes, they all knew how very much you loved them and how very much you cherished their love for you. They all miss you, especially your mom, sisters, brothers, nieces, and nephews…. You left an awesome legacy in the hearts of all whose lives you touched…. Save a place for me….

Love, Shari

Resources for Your Journey

The story you've just read is about forgiveness, healing, and rediscovering God's love that never excludes. If you're walking your own path toward wholeness, the following books, ministries, and communities can help you take your next steps.

Faith & Healing

- **Evolving Faith** — An online community and annual conference founded by Sarah Bessey and the late Rachel Held Evans, creating space for those who are reimagining faith and belonging. evolvingfaith.com
- **The Bible for Normal People Podcast** — Peter Enns and Jared Byas offer thoughtful, grace-filled discussions about Scripture and spiritual growth. thebiblefornormalpeople.com
- **The Liturgists** — Conversations on faith, science, and meaning for people who feel spiritually homeless. theliturgists.com

Books

- *Wholehearted Faith* by Rachel Held Evans and Jeff Chu
- *Approaching God: Accepting the Invitation to Stand in the Presence of God* by Steve Brown
- *Torn: Rescuing the Gospel from the Gays-vs.-Christians Debate* by Justin Lee
- *A Bigger Table* by John Pavlovitz

Healing from Trauma & Emotional Pain

- *Try Softer* by Aundi Kolber — A Christ-centered approach to emotional healing through self-compassion.
- *The Body Keeps the Score* by Dr. Bessel van der Kolk — Understanding how trauma lives in the body and how to heal.
- *What Happened to You?* by Dr. Bruce Perry and Oprah Winfrey — A compassionate look at the roots of trauma and resilience.

Organizations

- **RAINN** (Rape, Abuse & Incest National Network) — Support and resources for survivors of abuse. rainn.org
- **NAMI** (National Alliance on Mental Illness) — Free mental health education and support. nami.org
- **Faithful Counseling** — Online therapy that integrates mental health and Christian faith. faithfulcounseling. com

Affirming Faith Communities

- **The Reformation Project** — A Bible-based nonprofit promoting LGBTQ inclusion in the church. reformation-project.org
- **Q Christian Fellowship** — A vibrant, Christ-centered network of LGBTQ+ people and allies. qchristian.org
- **Beloved Arise** — Supporting and celebrating LGBTQ+ youth of faith. belovedarise.org
- **The Christian Closet** — Counseling and spiritual direction for LGBTQ+ Christians and allies. thechristian-closet.com

- **FreedHearts** — Founded by Susan Cottrell, offering grace-filled support for LGBTQ+ individuals and families. freedhearts.org

Forgiveness, Reconciliation & Spiritual Growth

- *Forgive: Why Should I and How Can I?* by Timothy Keller
- *The Return of the Prodigal Son* by Henri Nouwen
- *Untamed* by Glennon Doyle — A powerful call to live in truth and freedom.
- *Grace Can Lead Us Home* by Kevin Nye — A compassionate reflection on mercy, justice, and community.

Scripture & Reflection Tools

- **YouVersion Bible App** — Free Bible access, reading plans, and affirming devotionals.
- **BibleProject** — Short, beautifully animated videos explaining the Bible's big story. bibleproject.com
- **Lectio 365 App** — Guided daily prayer and meditation. 24-7prayer.com/lectio365

If you enjoyed this book, will you help me spread the word?

There are several ways you can help me get the word out about the message of this book . . .

- Post a 5-Star review on Amazon.
- Write about the book on your Facebook, X, Instagram, LinkedIn—any social media you regularly use!
- If you blog, consider referencing the book, or publishing an excerpt from the book with a link back to my website. You have my permission to do this as long as you provide proper credit and backlinks.
- Recommend the book—word-of-mouth is still the most effective form of advertising.
- Purchase additional copies to give away as gifts.

The best way to connect is by visiting

ShariPacanowski.com

www.ingramcontent.com/pod-product-compliance
Lightning Source LLC
Chambersburg PA
CBHW070555300726
48975CB00006B/1595